A NIGHT TOO DARK

In 1991, Dana Stabenow, born in Alaska and raised on a 75-foot fishing trawler, was offered a three-book deal for the first of her Kate Shugak mysteries. In 1992, the first in the series, *A Cold Day for Murder*, received an Edgar Award from the Crime Writers of America.

DANA
STABENOW

"Kate Shugak is the answer if you are looking for something
unique in the crowded field of crime fiction."
Michael Connelly

"For those who like series, mysteries, rich, idiosyncratic
settings, engaging characters, strong women and hot sex
on occasion, let me recommend Dana Stabenow."
Diana Gabaldon

"A darkly compelling view of life in the Alaskan bush, well
laced with lots of gallows humor. Her characters are very
believable, the story lines are always suspenseful, and every
now and then she lets a truly vile villain be eaten by a
grizzly. Who could ask for more?" **Sharon Penman**

"One of the strongest voices in crime fiction." *Seattle Times*

"Cleverly conceived and crisply written thrillers that provide
a provocative glimpse of life as it is lived, and justice as it is
served, on America's last frontier." *San Diego Union-Tribune*

THE KATE SHUGAK SERIES

DANA STABENOW

A NIGHT TOO DARK

First published in paperback the UK in 2014 by Head of Zeus, Ltd.

Copyright © Dana Stabenow, 2010

9 7 5 3 1 2 4 6 8

A CIP catalogue record for this book is available from
the British Library.

Paperback ISBN: 9781908800787
eBook ISBN: 9781781850466

Printed and bound by CPI Group (UK) Ltd,
Croydon, CR0 4YY.

Head of Zeus, Ltd.
Clerkenwell House
45-47 Clerkenwell Green
London EC1R 0HT

www.headofzeus.com

For Pati Crofut

about time,
considering how many of her experiences
I've stolen for my books

GOLD.

Number 79 on the periodic table. "Au," from the Latin *aurum*.

The most precious and prized of metals, used for currency beginning with the Egyptian pharaohs in 2700 B.C. and down through the ages by all nations as the metal of choice in the manufacture of those coins of highest value, the aureus, the solidus, the ducat, the guilder, the sovereign, the double eagle, the Krugerrand.

A malleable and forgiving metal, an ounce of pure gold can be beaten into a sheet large enough to gild the roof of a small home, although it is more dense than lead. It doesn't corrode, which makes it perfect for jewelry, although in its pure state it is too soft to stand up to repeated use and so is alloyed with other metals—copper, silver, nickel, or palladium—so that a wedding ring will last through a golden anniversary.

Gold is tasteless, although in the 1500s a Dutchman invented a liqueur called Goldwasser in which he sprinkled gold flakes. Medieval chefs used gold to garnish sweets before sending them up to the high tables.

Gold is an excellent conductor of heat and electricity, and resistant to oxidation and corrosion, making it useful in electronics and dentistry. It was used to plate the copper disk of recorded greetings on board *Voyager 1*, a hundred astronomical units out and counting. It is included in speculative designs for solar sails for spaceships and solar collectors for space habitats. Scientists have built gold nanospheres to work with lasers on a cure for cancer.

Gold is rare. Of all the noble metals, only mercury is more infrequently found in the earth's crust.

Mythological gold is as seductive as gold manifest. Midas asked Dionysus for the gift of turning everything to gold with his touch, only to discover a mixed blessing when gold food and drink proved to be indigestible. Jason's fleece, Kidd's treasure, Pizarro's El Dorado, Sutter's Mill, Siwash George's Rabbit Creek, Yamashita's Buddha—in any reality, in any century gold enthralls, enchants, intoxicates, and is the downfall of many an otherwise sensible man or woman who succumbs to its siren song.

Gold.

At last report, $940.48 per troy ounce on the world market....

ONE

MEMORIAL DAY

FATHER SMITH WAS THE PROUD proprietor of a forty-acre homestead in the Park, along with a wife and seventeen children, all of whom still lived at home.

Not that he would ever have admitted it, even to himself, this registered as nothing compared to the fact that he was the sole owner of the subsurface mineral rights to his forty acres, and that said forty acres abutted Beaver Creek.

Beaver Creek hosted a very nice run of king salmon in the summer, its many small feeder creeks offering narrow, shallow gravel beds for the salmon to lay and fertilize their eggs. It also supported a healthy population of beaver. It was one of the Park's larger creeks, a fifteen-mile tributary of the Kanuyaq River that rose in the northern-most foothills of the Quilaks, drained south-southwest, and in high water was navigable to just above the Smith homestead. The creek formed the homestead's eastern lot line.

The homestead had been previously owned by an Alaskan old fart who had staked a gold claim on Beaver Creek and had proved up on the homestead by building a cabin there and living in it. Thirty years later, on the other side of a bad divorce, he'd been in a hurry to vacate the premises before his ex-wife, also known as Rebecca the Raptor, nudged her lawyer into investigating the property title with a view toward adding it to her rapidly accumulating pile of marital assets.

Father Smith had furnished the capital and Park rat Louis Deem the insider knowledge, and together they had gone equal partners on the purchase. Things became complicated when Louis was murdered, but now, at long last, Judge Singh in Ahtna had ruled on his petition and granted Father Smith clear title and sole ownership. "Joint rights of survivorship" was a fine, statutory phrase. Father Smith had Ahtna attorney Pete Wheeler draw up his own will immediately afterward. Seventeen heirs, eighteen if you counted Mother Smith, could prove troublesome to each other and to the courts, but that, Lord willing, was a long time off and not to be worried over at present. Man proposes, God disposes.

Judge Singh had arrived at her verdict despite a feeble and barely legal protest from Louis Deem's roommate, sycophant and de facto coheir Howie Katelnikof, and a more ably argued but equally futile complaint by the Parks Service. Father Smith did not consider Howie as a future problem. The Parks Service was another matter, their proprietrary regard for all lands within their boundaries well known to Park rats, whether the property had been grandfathered in or not. Father Smith had no doubt there were legal challenges from the Parks Service in the future. God tested the faithful in many ways.

But now it was time to revel in the present. Time now to draw up plans to extract the gold he knew was there, never mind the old fart's assertion that he'd never pulled out more than an ounce of dust at a time. A sluice box, perhaps, creekside. Or, dare he think it, a dredge? A small one, to begin with, and then he'd see. God helps those who help themselves.

A smile spread beneath the thick white beard that flowed from chin to waist. His Carhartt bibs were frayed and stained, the black-and-red plaid Pendleton shirt beneath it patched and faded, and the Xtra Tuffs on his feet looked like they'd been gnawed on by ferrets, but there was a spring in his step and a sparkle in the bright blue eyes beneath the brim of his hat. He wore the creased and grimy leather fedora at a sober angle, as befit a man of substance and property.

He'd hitched a ride from the courthouse in Ahtna to Niniltna with Martin Shugak, who had a crush on Abigail, the eldest of Father Smith's daughters. In a place where men outnumbered women seven to one, that crush was shared by every other male Park rat between the ages of sixteen and forty. Abigail, erstwhile fiancée of the late Louis Deem and the seal on the land deal between the two men, remained uninterested. On the whole Father Smith was pleased. He wanted a suitor for Abigail who would bring something more to the Smith table than raging testosterone. A strong back, a willingness to work, and his own Caterpillar backhoe loader, say. By all accounts, Martin Shugak was not that man, but a ride from Ahtna to Niniltna over fifty miles of lumpy, bumpy, unmaintained gravel road, offered for whatever reason, was not to be refused.

Martin let him off at the edge of town after trying and failing to secure an invitation to dinner at some future date. Niniltna was in the throes of its Memorial Day celebration, which featured a parade, to be followed shortly thereafter by a potluck barbecue at the gym. The parade began with the white Blazer with the gold shield of the Alaska State Troopers on the door moving in slow and stately fashion up Riverside Drive, followed by a dozen veterans in clean but tattered uniforms, marching proudly out of step, with Demetri Totemoff and George Perry carrying the flags and Bobby Clark driving Jeff Talbot's camo Jeep with Miss Niniltna sitting in the backseat. Someone had coached her in the beauty queen wave, elbow-elbow, wrist-wrist.

An anonymous flatbed had been commandeered by the Niniltna Native Association and was manned by the four aunties, sitting in a half circle on upright wooden chairs, a quilt checkered with the colors of all fifty state flags spread over their laps.

Spaces between the floats were filled with every kid in Niniltna who had a trike, a bike, or a four-wheeler, dressed in their interpretation—or their parent's—of wounded Revolutionary War militia men bearing flag, fife, and drum. They clustered close behind the dump truck, and some of their imitation leather jerkins were so full they were leaking lines of candies, the instantly recognizable spoor of the eight-year-old Niniltnan during a parade.

Because Global Harvest had rolled out a gigantic dump truck, with a dozen employees of the Suulutaq Mine in the back clinging to the sides so they wouldn't slide out. The bed was half raised, inside which could be seen the employees standing calf-deep in candy. They were literally shoveling it over the side, a rain of—Father Smith stooped to scoop up a handful—Jolly Ranchers mixed with Dove Promises.

Everyone who wasn't in the parade was watching it, and next to him Iris Meganack unwrapped one of the chocolates and gasped. "Look!" she said, holding out the foil wrapper so people could see.

On the inside of the bright gold wrapper was the Suulutaq Mine logo, the golden sunburst with the line of mountains behind it. You had only to raise your eyes to the horizon to see that same line of mountains repeated against the eastern sky.

"That must have cost them a fortune," Harvey Meganack said, respect warring with envy in his voice.

"Not as much as it cost them to bring that dump truck in from the mine," someone else said. "How the hell'd they do that, anyway?"

"Helicopter."

"Herc."

"Drove it in from Ahtna, hasn't even been out to the mine yet."

"I wonder if they'd rent it out? I got a hundred yards of Bloody Creek gravel needs moving. That puppy'd get it done in a day."

The kids swooping down on the thrown candies paid no heed. They were too busy stripping foil and stuffing chocolate into their mouths.

Father Smith pocketed his handful and went for more, filling both pockets and the pouch on his bibs. He was only thinking of his kids back on the homestead.

He cheered the parade and appreciated the barbecue to the tune of three heaping plates' worth, indifferent to or outright ignoring the baleful glance of the four aunties who had descended from the flatbed to work the serving line. Afterward he hitched a ride up the Step road with Oscar Jimenez, partner with Keith Gette in a greenhouse that marketed fresh greens to gourmet restaurants and wholesale food stores as far away as New York City, and cut peonies in bulk to florists worldwide. Rumor had it that they were partners in the carnal sense as well, which made them unnatural, godless freaks of nature and unclean to boot, not to mention no prospect as sons-in-law.

However, he did notice that Oscar was driving a brand-new Ford Super Duty Super Cab F350 V8 Turbo Diesel long-bed pickup. Their business must be doing well. He wondered if perhaps it wasn't his duty to try to help Oscar and Keith through the difficult task of accepting their true identities, to lead them from the homosexual wilderness into the hetero-sexual Promised Land. God wanted to heal them. Marriage was a part of that healing process. He himself was God's humble servant.

These musings were interrupted by the sudden realization that the leather seat felt very warm beneath his hindquarters. He grabbed the dash, half rising, panicking at the thought that he'd wet himself.

"Sorry," Jimenez said. "Should have warned you. Heated seats." He flicked a switch, and Father Smith subsided, trying to hide his embarrassment. He kept his hand on the door handle as a precaution against any assault on his virtue, as who knew what else could be expected from someone so self-indulgent as to own a vehicle with heated seats, and he debarked the truck with dispatch at the turnoff to his homestead. He raised his hat and gave polite thanks for the lift, because there was no excuse for bad manners, and lost no time in hoofing it down the trail before Jimenez could offer to take him to his very doorstep.

The trail had been blazed out of the wilderness around bogs and rises with a D-6 Caterpillar tractor. Today, around the second rise, Father Smith came upon a pickup truck parked in the middle of the trail.

This was odd, as "trail" was something of a misnomer. The route into the Smiths' homestead wasn't two years old, it had been maintained even less often than the main road, and the surface was not an invitation to regular traffic. Parts of it were constantly under water, other parts had been retaken by belligerent alders determined not to be dispossessed. To find a strange vehicle on the trail argued one of two possibilities, that the driver was either very lost or poaching game on the Park lands that abutted the Smith homestead.

It was an elderly Ford Ranger three-quarter ton, the bed empty, dark blue paint rusting beneath a solid layer of grime that appeared to have been accumulated during the life of the vehicle. It had Washington State plates. Father Smith approached with caution, pushing himself between the encroaching thicket of diamond willow just beginning to bud and the driver's side of the truck. "Hello?" he said.

The cab was empty. He looked around. Sparrows and chickadees were singing, crows and ravens were cawing, in the distance he heard the incongruously cheery chirrup of an eagle. Not far enough away, brush crunched beneath the feet of some larger animal.

He suppressed the unworthy desire for something heavier in the way of defense than the aged hunting knife in the worn leather sheath strapped to his belt. He reminded himself that God was on his side. "Hello?" he said, raising his voice. "Anybody around who belongs to this truck?"

No answer.

He put a tentative hand on the door handle. It wasn't locked.

"Hello?"

Still no answer. He opened the door and peered inside.

There was a handwritten note taped to the steering wheel.

He contemplated this in silence. The truck, parked on the trail to his homestead, was in itself an anomaly. A note taped to the steering wheel was bizarre.

He would have been less than human had he not yielded to curiosity and read it.

The note had been written in black ink with a broad nib, printed on a blank eight-and-a-half-by-eleven-inch sheet of paper in large block letters, neat, upright, legible. The content was direct and to the point.

I am returning my body to nature.
I do this of my own free will.
Please do not look for me.

"Oh my god," Father Smith said, with a dismaying lack of reverence. "Hello? Hello! Hello, out there!" He cupped his hands and shouted. "Come back! Come on, nothing's so bad that you have to do something like this! God loves you! You can come home with me, have a meal, be with my family! Hello? Hello!"

He called and shouted for a good quarter of an hour, but only the birds replied.

TWO

"HE HAD TO GO up to the mine," Maggie said.

Kate went on alert. "Why, what's going on out there?"

Maggie shook her head. "Not the Suulutaq, the Kanuyaq."

The Kanuyaq was a dilapidated collection of buildings clustered together on the end of a mountainous pile of gravel tailings four miles up the road from Niniltna, the remains of a copper mine whose owners had closed up shop back in 1936. It had long since been stripped of anything salvageable, right down to the railroad ties under the tracks pulled up after the last train out. As any Park rat could tell you, railroad ties were useful items for house foundations, raised-bed gardens, and wooden bridges in need of resurfacing.

The Suulutaq Mine, on the other hand, was a gold mine, fifty miles south-southwest of town, inaccessible by road—so far—and a going concern. Two years before, Global Harvest Resources Inc. had discovered forty-two million ounces of gold, as well as commercial quantities of copper and molybdenum, on state leases in the middle of the Iqaluk Wildlife Refuge. They had, last time Kate checked, a hundred people on site, primarily engaged in drilling core samples in a continuing attempt to define the boundaries of a deposit that had thus far refused all limitation. They were also assembling the studies and documentation for their environmental impact statement. When the EIS was completed, accepted by the powers that be, and ratified by all the relevant state and federal agencies, as Kate had no doubt it would be, Global would go into production and their on-site population would rise to an estimated two thousand.

"Abandon hope, all ye who enter the Park," some wag had written on the Roadhouse wall in big black Marks-A-Lot letters. "Global cometh."

Not without effort, Kate put the thought aside. It would be years before a producing mine came to pass, years of attorneys representing Global and the Sierra Club and fishermen's associations and miners' guilds and the state government arguing their clients' causes in one court after another. Sufficient unto the day would be the evil thereof. In the meantime, she was in search of her errant trooper. "Okay," she said, "what's going on up at the Kanuyaq, then?"

"Wasillie Kvasnikof called in a report that some of the off-shift Suulutaq guys were partying up there and wrecking stuff." Maggie was pulling off her dress jacket as she spoke. "It's still private property, you know."

"I never said it wasn't," Kate said. "What's with the fancy dress?"

Maggie's mouth turned down at the corners, and she tossed the blue jacket with the Alaska State Trooper insignia on a chair. Hurled it, more like. Mutt, standing on Kate's right, cocked an apprehensive ear. "Since Jim is on call, I had to drive the Blazer in the parade."

Translated, this meant Sergeant Jim Chopin had taken the first opportunity that came his way to dump leading the parade off on Maggie Montgomery, his clerk, dispatcher, and warden. "If you were in the Blazer, what's he driving?"

"He went up with whoever it was that came whining into the office," Maggie said. She wasn't in a good mood. "You

12

should see the call sheet since they went into full gear out there, Kate. Nothing but trouble. We don't even get goddamn holidays off anymore."

Maggie didn't often use profanity, and "out there" was understood by Kate to be the Suulutaq Mine, not the Kanuyaq. "I know. Jim hasn't made it home for the last three nights." That came out a little more forlorn than she had meant it to, and she said, "Bobby says you can't hardly get in the door of the Roadhouse these days."

For a moment it looked like Maggie was going to burst into tears.

"It's jobs, Maggie."

"I know," Maggie said, with an emphasis that brought Mutt's ears up. "I know," she repeated in a more subdued tone. "It's just that—"

All anyone ever wanted to talk about anymore was the goddamn Suulutaq Mine and what the mine was going to do to the Park. It was especially all anyone ever wanted to talk about to Kate, who, as the reigning chair of the board of directors of the Niniltna Native Association, the largest governing body in twenty million acres of Park lands, might be imagined to have some say in the matter.

My life used to be so simple, she thought now, and she interrupted Maggie without compunction. "Anybody in back?"

Maggie was hurt, and let it show by the curtness of her reply. "Petey Jeppsen. Oh, and Willard, of course."

"Willard" was Willard Shugak, Kate's second or third cousin, or maybe her first cousin once removed—she could never remember which. There were a lot of Shugaks in the Park. There were a lot of Shugaks in Alaska, come to that. One thing she couldn't and didn't ever forget was that Willard was Auntie Balasha's grandson, that her daughter and his mother had been an alcoholic, which made Willard a victim of fetal alcohol syndrome. He was a simple, uncomplicated soul with a gift for the inner workings of the internal combustion engine. He couldn't read a Chilton manual to save his life but he could fix anything on four wheels blindfolded. Kate walked back to the cells.

Willard, tall for an Alaska Native and carrying an increasing amount of weight, greeted her with his trademark beaming smile. "Hey, Kate! You come to get me out?"

"What are you in for this time, Willard?"

Willard's beam failed and his brow creased. "I don't know, Kate." Short-term memory was not Willard's strong suit. His long-term memory was even worse.

"Were you bothering Cindy again?"

He hung his head and mumbled something at his shoes. "I don't remember." He peeped at her and looked away again. "Hey, Mutt!" He reached through the bars to give Mutt a rough pat. Mutt's tail gave a halfhearted wag.

The thing about Willard was he really didn't remember, or he didn't remember much. Jim had probably locked Willard up more for Willard's own safety than because Cindy had caught him stealing Reese's Peanut Butter Cups from her store again. Cindy had threatened to shoot him last time. "That Chopper Jim," Kate said, shaking her head. "He sure can be tough on a guy."

"He sure can, Kate," Willard said mournfully. "He sure can. But he's a nice guy anyway, you know?"

Kate had extensive, detailed personal experience as to just how nice Sergeant Jim Chopin, pride of the Alaska State Troopers, could be. With an effort she kept her face solemn as she nodded back. "Where's Howie, Willard?"

Howie Katelnikof, amateur blackmailer, professional thief, and practicing weasel, was Willard's roommate. His one redeeming feature was that he took care of Willard. He took *good* care of him, as even Kate, unwilling to grant Howie the slightest virtue, had to admit. Howie saw to it that Willard was dressed in clean clothes appropriate to the season, had at least one hot meal a day, even if it was nuked out of the freezer, made sure his sheets and towels were clean once a week, and, when Howie wasn't off stripping a carelessly parked snow machine for parts, Howie was Willard's constant companion. Given the low life expectancy of most FAS/FAE victims, Howie was the main reason Willard, now in his early forties, was still around. Since no one wanted to see Auntie Balasha burdened with Willard's care, Howie had a free get-out-of-jail card with most Park rats.

Of course, should he cease caring for Willard in the style to which the Park had become accustomed, said get-out-of-jail-free card was liable to be revoked, immediately and without notice. "Where's Howie?" Kate said again.

"I dunno," Willard said. "Around somewhere." He brightened again. "Say, Kate, you know Maggie, up front?"

"I do know Maggie, Willard."

"She's got some of those Girl Scout cookies, you know, the ones with the chocolate in 'em?"

Willard was always hungry and he had a fatal predilection for anything sweet. "You want some?" Kate said.

Willard nodded, his head bobbing so hard he knocked Anakin Skywalker out of his shirt pocket. His eyes went wide with dismay and he caught the little action figure in clumsy hands just before it crashed on the floor. "Wow," he said, patting Anakin on the head and tucking him back into his pocket with reverential care. "That was close." He looked at

Kate. "So will you ask her, Kate?" Cookies he could remember.

"I'll ask her," Kate said.

Willard beamed again.

Turning, she caught sight of Petey Jeppsen in the opposite cell. "Hey, Petey."

Petey, lying flat on his back and staring at the ceiling, said, "Hey, Kate."

"What for this time?"

Petey was tall and thin, with deep-set dark blue eyes, hollow cheeks, and stiff dishwater-blond hair cut short in no perceptible style. He wore worn jeans and a dark blue fleece over a plaid shirt. His voice was deep and low and would have been pleasant on the ear but for its suggestion of a whine. It was only a suggestion, though, a distinct improvement from the last time she'd had any serious contact with him, when the whine was threatening to take over his entire world view.

He had closed his eyes at her question, willing her away. She stood where she was. He sighed and opened his eyes to stare at the ceiling again. "Howie Katelnikof knew a guy who—"

"Yeah, you can stop right there," Kate said. "Come on, Petey, you know better than to hook up with Howie for any reason whatever. What the hell were you thinking?" Not to mention that Petey was here and Howie wasn't. She was proud of the mercy she showed by not pointing that out.

He took a deep breath and let it out, slowly. He sat up, slowly. He leaned forward, slowly, to rest his elbows on his knees. He raised his head to look at her, slowly. "What the hell else am I supposed to do, Kate?"

"Get a job?" Kate said.

He snorted, but there wasn't much life in it. "Nobody wants to hire a felon." He was gathering steam and in spite of

16

the subject matter she was glad to see there was some life left in the kid. He was only—what? Twenty-two? Twenty-three? "Nobody wants to hire a felon, or rent them an apartment, or make a car loan to one, either."

Have you ever been convicted of a felony? The question was on every job application, every loan application, every rental agreement. "There are programs," she said. "Your probation officer—"

He laughed. There was no amusement in the sound. "My PO. I check in with him once a week just so he can tell me how worthless I am. Yeah, he'll get me set up with a program, all right. He probably gave my name to Howie when Howie went looking for someone to help him clean out that garage. And his first call right after that was probably to Chopper Jim."

"Your folks—"

"No," he said, his voice rising. "They told me never to come back. I don't want to, anyway. I've had about all I can stand of preaching."

The Jeppsens were born-again Christian fundamentalists who had moved to the Park twenty-some years before. Except for a dispute with the Kreugers over a common property line that had escalated into a shoot-out at the Roadhouse four years before, and a Jeppsen sister named Bonnie who had aced a Krueger out of the postmistress's job, the Jeppsens generally tended to stay down on the homestead. Kate knew them by sight, and because of Bernie's bitter comments about being deprived of a potential starting forward for the Kanuyaq Kings she knew that Petey had been homeschooled, but that was about it. "You should have—"

"I know that, Kate," he said, angry now. "You don't have to say it, I know what I should have done. I said so, in court.

17

I testified against the other guys. I thanked Judge Singh for the short sentence and I promised her I'd walk the straight and narrow when I got out. But I can't get a job, which doesn't matter because I don't have any way to get to it, and I don't have anywhere to go after the job's done for the day anyway. What the hell, I might as well go back to jail. At least I'll have a bed and three squares."

He flopped back on the cot and put his arm over his eyes.

"You won't forget about those cookies, will you, Kate?" Willard said, anxious.

She turned and walked to the outer office. "Maggie, could Willard have some of those—" She was interrupted by the door opening.

Auntie Vi walked in—with something less than her usual bounce, Kate noticed—followed by another woman, a stranger to Kate. She was tall, at least five ten, and slender with a smooth fall of dark blond hair that cupped her chin in a controlled wave. Her forehead was high and narrow, her eyes were an indeterminate blue, her nose long and thin, and her mouth straight and firm. She wore a black Windbreaker with the Suulutaq sunburst embroidered on the breast.

Her eyes considered Kate, passed on to Maggie and took in the uniform shirt. "Are you the trooper dispatcher?"

"Yes. Maggie Montgomery."

"Holly Haynes. I work for Vern Truax out at the Suulutaq Mine."

Kate and Maggie exchanged glances. "Superintendent Vernon Truax?"

Haynes smiled. "That's my boss. I'm the staff geologist, and Vern's number two. I understand you're also a notary public?"

Maggie nodded. "Yes, I am."

"Great," Haynes said. "Ms. Moonin and I have a bill of sale we'd like to have notarized." She looked at Kate. "Wouldn't hurt to have a witness, Ms.—"

"Shugak," Maggie said. "Kate Shugak."

Haynes's hand in Kate's was cool and smooth, her nails clean and clipped, her cuticles neat and under control. "Kate Shugak," she said. "The same Kate Shugak who is chair of the board of directors of the Niniltna Native Association?"

"There's only one," Maggie said, and maybe only Kate heard the "thank god" that was implicit at the end of her sentence.

"Good to meet you," Haynes said. "I've heard a lot about you, I've been looking forward to it."

Kate released Haynes's hand and looked at Auntie Vi. "What are you selling, Auntie?"

Auntie Vi's face was a sight to behold, the expression on her round, wrinkled face registering such a complex mix of emotions that Kate was hard put to identify them all. Fear, triumph, relief, defiance, and that was just for starters. Was it actually, physically possible for Auntie Vi to feel embarrassment? Kate would have bet large against it, and she would have lost.

"I sell mine my boarding house," she said.

AUNTIE, WHAT THE HELL are you doing?"

Kate had pulled Auntie Vi into Jim's office and closed the door behind them.

"I sell mine my boarding house." The diminutive eighty-something stood straight as a board, looking rather as if she were facing a firing squad of one.

"Okay," Kate said, "I got it the first three times you said that. Why?"

19

Auntie Vi tried for an insouciant shrug and almost pulled it off. "They pay my price. No haggle, I ask, they write check." She pulled a piece of paper from her pocket and brandished it.

The number of zeroes on the end of the amount made Kate blink. "Didn't they want an appraisal, or an engineer's report?"

Auntie Vi shook her head. "They need beds for mine workers going in going out. Get stuck because of weather maybe, got business in Niniltna maybe, only house in town with enough beds for sure." Head jerk toward the outer office. "She say save them money to buy instead of rent. She ask price. I tell her. She write check."

Kate's mouth opened and closed a few times with nothing coming out, which pretty much expressed her immediate reaction. Viola Moonin, lifetime Park rat, one of the original founders of the NNA, one of the grand dames of her mixed tribe of Aleuts, Athabascans, Tlingits, Haidas, and one lone Tsimshian. Not to mention the stray infusions from Scandinavia, Eastern Europe, Africa, Asia, and South America. Subsistence fisher, hunter, trapper, net mender, world-class quilter, and all-around entrepreneur, owner and proprietor of the village of Niniltna's first and only bed-and-breakfast establishment.

Viola Moonin, one of the four aunties, the de facto moral center of the Park, the court of its first and last appeal, and for a brief moment mercifully past, its Star Chamber.

Viola Moonin, the first to speak out against the Suulutaq Mine and the danger it represented to the environment and the lifestyle of the Park.

Viola Moonin, the first to sell out.

Outside the door Kate heard Mutt give a whine with the hint of a growl on the end of it, audible enough that she must have her nose jammed into the crack. Mutt didn't like being shut on the other side of any door between her and Kate. "What are you going to do?" she said.

Another jerk of the head. "Run it for them. They pay me." Auntie Vi smiled, and the resultant baring of teeth engendered a remarkable resemblance to the half husky half wolf on the other side of the door. "They pay good."

HAYNES AND MAGGIE TURNED their heads when the door to Jim's office opened again. Mutt thrust her nose beneath Kate's hand and the feel of that thick gray pelt against her skin steadied her. She took a deep breath and looked at Maggie. "She's made up her mind. It's a fair offer. Let's get this done."

Maggie notarized the bill of sale, Kate witnessed it, and Maggie made copies for everyone.

Kate folded hers into quarters and was tucking it into a hip pocket when the front door opened again. All four women looked around and beheld Father Smith, who removed his stained leather hat with undeniable grace. "Ladies."

"Mr. Smith," Maggie said, accent on the honorific. Kate nodded, Auntie Vi stared right through him, and when no introduction was forthcoming Haynes said, "Holly Haynes, Suulutaq Mine."

"Father Smith of Beaver Creek."

In spite of his attention to his manners Father Smith looked less affable than usual. In fact, Kate thought, he looked downright worried.

"How can I help you, Mr. Smith?" Maggie said.

"I found an abandoned truck on the road into my homestead," he said.

They listened to his story in silence. Maggie looked at Kate. "I don't know when Jim'll be back."

"You go find that one now or him dead," Auntie Vi said.

21

"Maybe dead already anyway."

Haynes's eyes widened, but as usual Auntie Vi had summed it up in a manner that would have pleased Strunk and White. "When was the last time you were down that road, Mr. Smith?" Kate said.

He thought. "Ten days ago."

"Your family been into town since you been gone?"

He shook his head. "I doubt it. Nothing to come into town for."

He met her eyes with a bland expression, and whatever opinions Kate might have had about his family's need to leave their remote homestead she had learned the hard way last year to keep to herself. "So, the pickup might have been abandoned there an hour after you left," she said.

He nodded.

"Or an hour before you got there." Kate looked at Maggie. "I'll go get a Grosdidier, and then we'll go up and get Dan O'Brian." The four Grosdidier brothers were the Park's EMT team, and Dan O'Brian was the Park's chief ranger.

Maggie nodded. "I'll tell Jim what's up when he gets back."

THE GROSDIDIER DRIVEWAY WAS full so Kate had to park on the road. Smith waited in the pickup. Mutt followed Kate.

It was a two-story, two-bathroom, four-bedroom house, typical of the post-log cabin construction boom in the Park in the mid-seventies. It was always cheaper to go up, requiring a smaller foundation in construction and less in the way of heat in operation. A detached garage the size of a small hangar stood to the left. Both buildings fronted the river. An aging but sturdy dock was built on the bank, to which was moored a thirty-six-foot drifter named *Audra Sue*, resplendent in a brand-new coat of white paint. Kate paused with her hand on the door for a closer look. Yes, the brand-new red trim line began at the bow with a square cross. She had to smile.

She pushed open the door and stepped into a small room crowded with mismatched chairs that had all seen better days. A large empty wooden spool sat in the middle of the room, laden with magazines ranging from *Guns & Ammo* to *Cosmopolitan*. The *Redbook* issue facing Kate's direction had a picture of the original Charlie's Angels on it.

Kate had barely enough time to see that several of the chairs were occupied before a small form impacted her legs with such force she almost went over backward. "Kate! Kate! Kate!"

"Katya!" She scooped up the four-year-old and tossed her in the air.

Katya laughed her delightful chuckling laugh. "Do it again!"

Kate did it again and then set her down with a grunt. "You're getting too big for shot put, girlfriend."

Katya was promptly attacked by Mutt, who used her nose to roll Katya around the room. Katya giggled some more, and squealed when her *South Park* T-shirt rode up and Mutt's wet nose pressed against her bare back.

Kate smiled at Dinah. "Hey. The brat okay?"

Dinah, a wispy, blue-eyed blonde, Bobby Clark's wife, Katya's mother, and a practicing videographer, looked up from *Time* magazine's special report edition on the death of Diana, Princess of Wales, to smile and shake her head. "She needed her polio booster."

"Where's Bobby?"

"On the air."

"Oh yeah? What frequency?"

Dinah shrugged. "You know it changes every day."

"I know."

Eknaty Kvasnikof was there, elbow resting on the arm of his chair, holding a hand wrapped in a bloody piece of cloth straight up. He nodded. "Kate."

"Natty." She nodded at his hand and raised her eyebrows.

He grimaced. "Working on the engine. Trying to work a bolt loose." He shook his head.

He looked tired, and there was an anxious crease in his forehead. A recent graduate of Niniltna High, Eknaty was skippering the family drifter for the first time this summer. He was the oldest, there were five younger sisters and brothers back home, and a father with lung cancer.

Kate thought for a moment, while Mutt stepped up and pushed her nose beneath Natty's hand. He rubbed her ears, a faint smile lightening his features.

"Would Willard be any use to you, Natty?" Kate said.

Natty looked up. "Jesus, Kate." It was all he said, but it was heartfelt.

She nodded. "He's up the post. Tell Maggie I said to release him into your custody. You have to keep him working, you understand? You can't let him stray off on his own, you've got to keep tabs on him."

Natty looked uncertain. "What about when the job's done?"

"We'll worry about that then. Shouldn't be a problem so long as you keep him in cookies and candy bars. Keep him busy and out of trouble, and he'll keep your engine purring like a cat on overtime." Her hand rested on his shoulder for a brief moment. She turned to the woman sitting a few chairs down. "Ulanie."

Ulanie Anahonak was a thin, tense woman with scant dark hair, a sallow complexion, and a gaze so intense Kate had often wondered if she were myopic. "Kate," she said, and turned back to leafing through an issue of *Ladies' Home Journal* with Nancy Reagan on the cover.

The door to the clinic opened and Matt Grosdidier's voice was heard. "If you'd come here right away, Phyllis, right when you knew—"

"I told you, I didn't—" The woman's tearful voice came to an abrupt halt when Phyllis Lestinkof turned her head and met Ulanie Anahonak's eyes.

There was a brief silence that felt somehow uncomfortable, although Kate did not know why. "Hey, Phyllis," Kate said.

Phyllis looked away from Ulanie, it seemed with something of an effort. Her smile was strained. "Hey, Kate." A plump young woman with a round, brown face and hair in a pixie cut that made her look like a post-Frank Sinatra Mia Farrow, if Mia had been Aleut, Phyllis was, for a miracle, sober. She didn't look happy, although Kate hoped it wasn't because of lack of alcohol.

Phyllis glanced at Matt and flushed. She took a deep, albeit shaky breath and summoned up a smile, looking straight at Kate and only at Kate. "Nice to see you," she said, "gotta go, Auntie's waiting on me."

The door closed softly behind her on its hydraulic hinge.

"Kate," Matt said. "What's up?"

He met her eyes with apparent frankness, but she noticed he was showing a little color, too. She refrained from casting a meaningful look at the door that had closed behind Phyllis Lestinkof and said instead, "Got somebody lost in the woods up near the Smith place. I want a Grosdidier to go with when we go looking for him, in case he's hurt when we find him."

Matt blinked at her, tilted his head back, and raised his voice, already a fine, stentorian baritone. "Mark, Luke, Pete!

Get the lead out, let's clear the waiting room."

Thirty minutes later Eknaty had stitches and a bandage and Katya a red spot on her upper arm and a cherry lollipop. Ulanie had departed on Phyllis's heels without treatment or explanation. The four Grosdidier brothers, Matthew, Mark, Luke, and Peter, took no notice, they were too busy hoping out loud that they'd find the driver of the truck alive. Barely alive, preferably, with multiple open wounds. Broken bones would be a bonus, an open fracture best of all, multiple open fractures nirvana. They checked the massive aluminum tool chest bolted in the back of their fire-engine-yellow (custom painted) Chevy Silverado, in which was stowed a vast array of medical paraphernalia that for all anyone in the Park knew included a cure for cancer. For sure no Grosdidier had ever dived inside it and come up at a loss for what was needed at the scene. The Niniltna Native Association had paid for most of it. Kate had a sneaking suspicion that the NNA had paid for the Silverado, too, but she'd never had the heart to go back and look at the records to be sure.

"All present and accounted for!" Mark said.

"Lock and load!" Luke said.

"Let's roll!" Peter said.

Matt said, "Okay, boys, let's saddle up." The four of them piled into the two bench seats of the extended cab, Matt as usual at the wheel, and if they could have peeled out they would have. As it was, gravel sprayed the wall of the garage and everything hanging on it received yet another layer of chips and dings. They stayed on Kate's bumper all the way up to the Step, where the two-car convoy parked in front of the group of prefabricated buildings that made up Park head-quarters. Tucked against a Quilak foothill, the Canadian border at their back and the Park rolling out before them in all its glory, the view was superb out of any window. The Step, a wide, level ridge running north-south, had enough room for a dirt strip big enough for a Cessna 180 to get out with a full load of confiscated bear bladders, moose racks, walrus tusks, and fur pelts illegally harvested from wolves, wolverines, beaver, mink, and marten.

Dan was in his office.

He was not alone. Standing, or rather slumping across the desk from him, was a sad sack of a guy, midforties, brown hair and eyes, medium height, medium build, with a chin and a waist that both showed distinct signs of regular meals. His chin also bore trace evidence of having tried to grow a beard but it just wasn't in the cards. His Carhartt overalls were worn at the elbows and knees and looked as if they had begun life on a far smaller man. His boots were used, the toe of the right boot having been punctured with what might have been the claw of a hammer, or maybe a hatchet. He carried threadbare musher gloves leaking down feathers that when donned would reach to his elbows and a flapped cap with the right earflap missing.

He was arguing with the chief ranger. Any Park rat could have told him that was a lost cause. "You want to hike up to Bright Lake?" Dan said. "At this time of year? With the snow still twelve feet deep in some places? Why?"

"I like the name," the guy said.

Dan was rendered momentarily speechless.

"It doesn't matter where I want to go," the guy said. "You told me to come back when I got geared up. Well, here I am, all geared up."

Dan surveyed said gear, which looked like it had been excavated from the nearest trash pile, and didn't bother to hide his contempt. "Mr. Davis, you said you wanted to spend a month covering a hundred miles in the Park. I'm telling you that, uh, gear you've managed to scare up from god knows where won't last you fifty feet."

"You saw my tent," the guy said, "it's a good one."

"It was a good one," Dan said.

"And I've got an emergency locator transmitter." This last was said with a good deal of pride.

"Yeah," Dan said, "well, I'm not signing any permit for you just so I can come haul your ass out when you stumble into trouble, which sure as shit you will, and set off your ELT, which also sure as shit you will. Now get out of my goddamn office, and don't come back until you've got a fucking clue as to what you're doing!"

Kate thought of Maggie. Happy Memorial Day, everybody.

Davis, red-faced and sullen, clumped past Kate and the Grosdidiers without speaking. His boots weren't laced and they must have been too big because one of them almost slipped off his foot. He tripped on the threshold and the Grosdidiers might have had their first Kate-related case of the day then and there if Pete and Matt hadn't caught him and set him upright again. He yanked his arms free of their grasp and clumped off without a word of thanks.

Dan looked around and acquired Kate as a target. "And what the hell do you want?"

A little over medium height, thickset without being fat, red hair cut in a buzz, and bright blue eyes glowering from beneath a shelf of a brow, the chief ranger of the Park was not to be trifled with in this mood. She told him what the hell she wanted without excess verbiage. The Grosdidier boys kept their mouths shut. It seemed safest.

"Fuck me," Dan said, his mouth a tight line. "Not another one."

"Another one?" Kate said. She didn't want to set him off again but this sounded interesting. And possibly relevant.

"Happens all over the national parks, people thinking they can walk in and just disappear. They're right, mostly, but what they don't figure is that we have to go look for them anyway. Clueless assholes." The last two words were almost a shout and appeared to be directed at the now empty door. He got to his feet. "Show me on the map."

A map of the Park covered most of one wall of Dan's office, color-coded for ownership—federal, state, Native corporation, urban, private. The yellow dots signifying land privately owned were barely visible in the sea of green that represented federal parks and wildlife refuges. Smith found the Step road, traced it down to the turn-off, and stopped about half an inch in.

Dan's sigh was heartfelt. "Great," he said, "just dandy." He tapped a red pin. "Eddie saw a grizzly male thereabouts a couple of days ago. Big one, he said, he figures record size, gorgeous golden brown hide."

"Thought Park rangers weren't supposed to think about Park bears in terms like 'record size' and 'gorgeous hide,'" Kate said.

Dan snorted. "Yeah. Like monks don't think about sex." He strapped a .357 to his waist and reached for the .30-06 in the gun rack next to the door. "Let's go."

The convoy of trucks rumbled down the hill and pulled up in back of the abandoned pickup an hour and a half later, good time due to the still semifrozen state of the road.

Kate found the registration in the glove compartment. "Dewayne A. Gammons," she said.

" 'Dewayne'?" Mark said.

" 'Gammons'?" Luke said.

"What's the A stand for?" Peter said. "Aloysius?"

The Grosdidiers snickered en masse.

The glove compartment yielded further the vehicle handbook, a square of foil that proved to be a Trojan condom with a three-year-old sell-by date, and a box of cinnamon Tic Tacs with two left. A more extensive search beneath and behind the bucket seats turned up an empty pint of Windsor Canadian, a lug wrench, an oil filter still in its box, an air filter ditto, a book of matches from the Ahtna Lodge, a Suulutaq Mine flyer extolling Global Harvest's environmentally friendly policy that looked as if it had been used to swab oil from a dipstick, and a single round of ammunition.

The cartridge was maybe an inch long. Kate wasn't a gun nut, with two weapons to her name, the 12-gauge shotgun in the rack next to the door back home and the .30-06 in the gun rack in the cab of her truck. This was a much smaller cartridge for a much smaller weapon. She handed it to Matt, who flattened his hand and cradled it in his palm. The Grosdidiers crowded around.

"CCI," Mark said.

"Twenty-two," Luke said.

"CB Long," Peter said.

They looked up at Kate and said in a chorus, "Girly gun."

"Or a kid's," Matt said, handing back the round. "Rifle or revolver, not designed for auto or semiauto. Range maybe a mile with a tail wind. Not a lot of oomph, not very loud, used mostly for plinking and taking out your local feral squirrel. Six, six-fifty a box, a hundred rounds per."

"And, you'll notice, not fired," Dan said. "Probably dropped it when he was trying to load the gun so he could shoot himself. Really sucks how that didn't work out. Can we go find this jackoff now or what?"

He looked at Kate. She wasn't listening to him, her head cocked, concentrating. "Did you hear that?" she said.

His head whipped around and he looked hard at the dense wall of brush lining the side of the trail. One hand unsnapped his holster, the other half-raised his rifle. "What?"

They all listened then. An eagle called in the distance, a full, piercing cry, answered by a raven's malicious croak nearer by.

"Nope," Matt said, "didn't hear anything." He didn't make fun of Dan's nervousness. None of them did. No Park rat with the most minimal sense of self-preservation would dream of making fun of anyone on the alert for hungry bears in the spring.

"I don't know," Kate said, "I thought I heard a shot." She looked at Mutt, who had those parabolic antennas that passed for her ears up and scanning for intelligent life in the universe. Alert but not alarmed. Of course a gunshot in the Park was like the smell of dope at a Jimmy Buffett concert, familiar and expected. "Probably my imagination."

She bagged and tagged the bullet, more because she knew what Jim would say if she didn't than from any real conviction that the unspent round was evidence of anything other than a strong tendency toward melodrama. Odds were that somewhere between the truck and wherever he was now, Mr. Gammons had rediscovered the will to live. There was a story she remembered reading about people jumping off the Golden Gate Bridge who had survived, every one of whom reported having changed their minds on the way down.

On the other hand, it was spring, the moose were in calf and the bears were up and hungry. There were plenty of ways to die in the Park without shooting yourself. "Okay," she said, "which way, do you think?"

They surveyed the thick, impenetrable brush with less than

31

enthusiasm, even the Grosdidiers. Bushwhacking was not a fun way to spend an afternoon. "Let's spread up and down the road," Kate said, "look for where he went in."

Luke found crushed fireweed and a bent alder branch about ten feet from the pickup's front bumper. Mutt took point, nose sensing something the rest of them would never be able to smell. Kate, holding her .30-06 at the ready in front of her, went in next, followed by Dan and the brothers. Smith, with the smug air of one who had done his duty by God and country, had left them to finish his interrupted walk home.

It was a still day, and clear, the sun well into its daily twenty-hour journey around the summer horizon. The spruce were thick here, but they were dying from the spruce bark beetle infestation, too, which meant a lot of them had fallen over, or tried to. It didn't make the going any easier, and the third time they'd had to get down on their hands and knees to crawl beneath a horizontal trunk there was increasing skepticism displayed concerning Mutt's trailing abilities.

"Just don't let her hear you say that," Kate said.

"Yeah, but who works this hard to off themselves?" Luke said.

"Yeah, what's wrong with a nice little bullet to the head?" Mark said.

"Yeah, and you realize we're going to have to pack this fucker out when we find him," Peter said.

"Maybe he'll be able to walk," Matt said, without much conviction.

"Could be worse," Kate said. "At least it's too early for mosquitoes."

But they were all thinking about that gunshot Kate thought she'd heard.

The going was rough and got rougher. They stumbled

through patches of ice and snow that the shade from the forest had hidden from the sun. The rest of the time the surface beneath their feet ranged from bare, frozen ground to wet moss. Everyone's jeans were soaked to the knees, and Matt, who had a particularly fine head of hair, had lost some of it to clawing spruce limbs. More comments were made, most of them profane.

Kate, the smallest of them and therefore the quickest through the underbrush, said, "Jeez, what a bunch of whiners. You'd think you guys had never been hunting in your lives."

Mutt, who had been appearing and disappearing in front of Kate for the last hour, rematerialized to nip at the cuff of Kate's jeans. She turned, looked over her shoulder, gave a peremptory bark, leaped over a fallen tree, and vanished again. Kate clambered over the same trunk and was suddenly and blessedly in a large clearing on the south-facing slope of a small hill. She stood there blinking in the bright sunshine, breathing in deep gulps of cool, clean air. She felt as if she had just emerged from a long, underwater swim.

She looked around for Mutt, spotting her at the top of the clearing, fifty feet away. Mutt was dancing impatiently in place, giving out an occasional imperative yip. At her feet was a haphazard pile of dead brush and leaves lumped together over something else, at which Kate was instantly certain no one was going to want to take a closer look.

The five men thrashed their way out of the brush and came to a stop behind her. "Oh man," Matt said, spotting Mutt immediately. "I was really hoping…"

"Yeah, me, too," Mark said.

Something caught the edge of Kate's vision and she looked around, scanning the edge of the clearing. At almost the same moment something large started thrashing through the bush about halfway between them and Mutt.

"Oh fuck," Dan said, followed by the sound of safeties coming off all around.

Kate was still holding her rifle in front of her but she didn't raise it to her shoulder or sight down the barrel. Mutt hadn't charged or put herself between Kate and the noise.

The crashing came nearer, and the bear whose food cache they'd just stumbled on came growling and stumbling into the clearing, bringing the better part of a dense clump of alders with him.

Only it wasn't a bear. It was Old Sam, and he wasn't growling, he was swearing, loudly enough to be heard all the way back to the road. He stumbled to a halt, spit out an alder leaf, and glared at them.

"Something chasing you, Old Sam?" Dan said.

"No, there is nothing fucking chasing me!" Old Sam Dementieff, a lean and leathery old fart, near as anyone could figure ninety-five going on forty and cranky with the wisdom of accumulated years, drew himself up and bent a fulminating eye on the ranger. "I was looking for you. Heard you had a search party going. Figured I'd lend a hand."

Kate looked at the toes of her wet boots with an intensity they did not merit. Matt was inspecting the straps on his pack, Mark was whistling a happy tune, Luke was scratching at a nonexistent mark on the immaculate barrel of his .30-30, and Peter was squinting at the cloudless sky in search of the next incoming front.

Dan eyed the well-worn, well-kept Model 70 Winchester over Old Sam's shoulder. From years of long and usually alcohol-involved conversations over the bar at Bernie's Roadhouse, Dan knew that Old Sam believed absolutely in the hunter's maxim "Use enough gun." The Model 70 was known to the cognoscenti as the rifleman's rifle, and Old Sam's had a serial number well below 600,000, making it a drool-worthy object of desire to any hunter worthy of the name. His preferred cartridge was the .458 Winchester Magnum, which could put down half a ton of bear and an incoming ICBM with equal efficiency.

It was the half-ton bear, however, that more nearly concerned the chief ranger, steward of everything on two wings and four legs within the twenty-million-acre Park.

Dan looked at Kate. She had her back to him, now absorbed in examining the inside of one of Mutt's ears. The Grosdidiers had double-checked all the equipment they carried, and had fallen back and regrouped at a safe distance.

Absent a carcass—an ursine one—there wasn't a thing Dan could say, but he gave Old Sam a hard look anyway, just to keep in practice. Unintimidated, his usual attitude, Old Sam gave him a hard look right back. Kate said, "Let's see what we got here," and walked to the pile at the top of the clearing.

They came to a halt in a loose half circle. It wasn't pretty, but no one humiliated themselves by averting their eyes. "Oh, great," Dan said, sounding more irritated than horrified.

The Grosdidiers said nothing. It was obvious that no heroic efforts at saving life and limb would be necessary today.

The brilliant spring sun shone down without mercy, illuminating a scattering of moose droppings, an eagle feather, and a jumble of human remains.

The body proved to be in several, well, actually, many pieces. There seemed to be no head. Nothing was left of the torso but a gaping hole, at the back of which the vertebrae, amazingly still attached to one another, could be individually counted. Both femurs were visible through scraps of torn flesh upon which the blood had dried hard and brown. All of the bones had bite marks, and one of the femurs had been cracked open and the marrow sucked out.

What remained had been scraped together and covered with a loose layer of dead spruce boughs, dry grass and brown leaves, and dirt. There were claw marks all around the pile, as well as bits of clothing, a dark blue flannel cuff, the waistband of what had been a pair of Levi's.

Kate picked up a pair of white men's Jockey briefs, an elastic waistband barely attached to a ripped-out crotch.

The men cringed and squeezed their knees together in a single involuntary action.

Kate let her hand drop and bent a thoughtful gaze on one particular, very large set of claw marks that had ripped through a clump of moss campion, leaving four very clear parallel scars in the earth beneath.

"He'll be napping close by," Old Sam said. "When he wakes up, he's going to want seconds."

"I don't know," Dan said, "looks like he pretty much licked the plate clean on the first serving. He's probably long gone."

If Old Sam didn't look at the ranger with outright contempt, he did give a comprehensive snort. The Grosdidier brothers began to cast nervous glances around the clearing.

"Why take the chance?" Kate said. "Let's move like we got a purpose. Get out the bags while I take some pictures." She pulled a digital camera from one pocket and took shots of the remains from every direction and several establishing shots to show them in relation to the rest of the clearing. "Okay," she said, stepping back.

The Grosdidier brothers produced heavy black plastic bags right out of the air, one each, and there was a concerted rush as everyone leaped to pick up the body part nearest to him and stuff it in the bag. There was no reverence displayed

36

toward the remains and no horror or disgust, either, just a single-minded haste to finish the job and be away from the clearing as soon as humanly possible.

"Okay," Matt said, scooping up an arm whose hand flopped horrifically from its wrist, "that's it." The words were barely out of his mouth before the four brothers had vanished one and all into the undergrowth, black plastic bags slung anyhow over their shoulders.

"Right behind you, buddies," Dan said to the air, and followed them.

Kate looked at Old Sam.

If it had been anyone else, any other Park rat, he might have looked conscious, ashamed, possibly even repentant, but this was Old Sam. "I would have reported it."

"You used somebody's dead body for bear bait?"

"I would have reported it," he said again.

"Yeah, sure, Uncle," Kate said, "after you got your bear, and after you'd skinned him out, and after you'd packed out the bladder and the meat and the hide."

"Come on, girl."

She looked at him in amazement. It could not possibly be that Old Sam of all Park rats was going to try to justify his behavior, and to someone fifty years his junior at that.

And then he broke out the uncle grin, one part Gabriel to nine parts Beelzebub. "You know I don't like bear meat."

Kate's search for words adequate to the purpose was futile and brief. "Oh, the hell with it," she said. There was never any getting one up on the old man. "Let's just get out of here."

Old Sam raised a critical eyebrow. "You're crankier than usual, girl. What's going on?"

Kate, exasperated, said, "We're like two seconds away from vivi-section and you want to have a conversation?"

She turned and got one foot out before he grabbed her arm and spun her around like a top. "I taught you better than that, girl," he said, Old Sam at his sternest. "You speak respectful to your elders."

"There isn't a bay handy you can toss me into today, Uncle," she said. "Let's move."

"We'll move when I say we move and not before, girl." Again with the stare that seemed to see all the way through to her bones. "That boy okay?"

"Johnny's fine," Kate said. "Johnny's great." The truth of that statement made her voice soften, and they both relaxed some. Neither noticed when Mutt's head whipped around. "Johnny's a gift. Jack left me the best part of him. There's no trouble there."

Old Sam grew more forbidding. "Jim giving you a hard time?"

"No! No," Kate said. "There's nothing wrong, Uncle, or there won't be, so long as we get moving."

Mutt's eyes, fixed on the edge of the woods, narrowed, and the hair on her back began to rise. Again, nobody noticed.

"It's the job then," Old Sam said.

"It's not the damn job, Uncle," Kate said. "I can handle the job, and even if I couldn't it's only another year."

He squinted down at her, steady dark eyes on either side of a hawk nose, that and his height handed down through four generations from a Norwegian whaler on his mother's side, brown skin already darker from a day in the spring sun inherited from a series of Native ancestors starting with Park rats—and if you went back far enough there was probably some Inupiat and Yupik in there somewhere, too. Old Sam was a mongrel, like Kate. And like Kate, he knew bullshit when he heard it.

He wasn't hearing it now. He cocked his head and said with unaccustomed gentleness, "What is it, girl?"

He was the only one who had noticed. Or the only one who asked. "I'm just feeling, I don't know." She hesitated.

"What?"

"Crowded," Kate said.

Her answer surprised them both, Old Sam because it wasn't the one he was expecting, and Kate because she hadn't known it was there. She tried to make a joke of it. "The world is too much with us nowadays. It didn't used to be."

"Crowded," he said. "Huh." Old Sam looked thoughtful. "Mine getting to you, girl?"

"No!" He cocked an eyebrow at the explosive emphasis of the word. "No," she said again. "It'll be a good thing, Uncle. There will be industry, and a tax base, and jobs to keep the kids home. Villages are dying up and down the river because the kids are leaving. Chulyin, Potlatch, Red Run. There's no one left in Tikani except for Vidar Johansen, and he's older than you." She paused. "Auntie Vi sold her B and B to the Suulutaq Mine people this morning. She's going to run it for them."

"No shit?" He shook his head, it looked as if in admiration. "How 'bout that old broad. I hope she held them up for all the traffic could bear."

Kate told him about the zeroes on the check.

He whistled, long and low. "All right, Vi." He looked down at Kate's woebegone expression. "'All change is of itself an evil, which ought not to be hazarded but for evident advantage.'" That grin broke out again at her look of astonishment. "Sam'l Johnson. What, you thought you were the only one in the family who ever read a book? Girl, I got—" He broke off, looking over her shoulder.

Kate turned to follow his gaze and beheld a Mutt who had retreated all the way back down her genome to the Jurassic era. Her ears were erect, her hackles were standing straight up, her back was arched, and her lips were drawn back to expose all of her teeth all the way up to her gums. Her head was sunk down between her shoulders, her front legs were spread and planted, and she was en pointe. As if she had only been waiting for their complete and undivided attention, she let forth with something between a snarl and a sonic boom.

Which was about when the noise registered on Kate's consciousness, a not-distant-enough sound of brush crunching underfoot from beyond the edge of the lower side of the clearing. It seemed to all three of them to be coming nearer, fast.

Kate looked around. The guys were long gone.

Mutt took a step forward. "No, Mutt," Kate said as forcefully as she could. "No."

Mutt snarled, yes, snarled at her, and Kate cuffed her once, hard on the side of her head. "Mutt! No!" Mutt whined once but she didn't drop and roll, and Kate knew she had to get them out of there pronto or there would be blood spilled. She didn't want it to be Mutt's. She jerked her head at Old Sam. "Come on, Uncle, time to go."

They retreated backward, away from the increasing crashing and thrashing in the bushes, the tops of which were now moving violently, as if in a strong wind. Whatever it was was moving pretty fast, and to move that fast through that primeval old-growth forest it had to be pretty big.

Old Sam carried his Model 70 at the ready, the business end pointed at the noise, backing up, mouth spread in a rictus of a grin, a demonic light in his eyes the twin of the one in Mutt's eyes. His legs were twice as long as Kate's but he was

40

moving half as fast. "Uncle, come on," Kate said through her teeth.

Old Sam spoke without looking around. "What's the matter, don't you trust me?"

"Not one inch," she said.

He threw back his head and laughed, a resonant sound that rolled across the clearing and did not go unnoticed by whatever it was that was coming down on them like a freight train. There was an immediate protest from the violently moving brush, a cross between a pig's squeal, chalk on the blackboard, and screaming tires on pavement. Kate had heard that sound before.

"Sounds cranky, don't he," Old Sam said. He was very calm. "Don't know how comfortable I'm going to feel with that breathing down my neck on the way back out to the road." He looked at the shaking brush, calculated the trajectory of the force behind it, and then made the mistake of looking at Kate. She stood there, all five-foot-nothing and 120 pounds of her, a scowl on her face that would have put the fear into Hannibal Lecter. "Mutt," she said, the name cracking like a lightning-struck tree, but he knew she meant it for both of them.

Old Sam sighed, lowered his rifle, and turned to slide past Kate, moving with a swiftness and a silence remarkable for the same man who had come crashing out of the brush an hour before. He was noticeably lacking any of the unseemly haste displayed by the Grosdidier brothers and Dan O'Brian in their retreat, of course. It was a matter of pride.

Well, pride goeth before a fall, because Old Sam tripped over something and went sprawling flat on his face. He flung out his hands to catch himself and lost his grip on his rifle, too, an unpardonable sin, a Park rat would rather lose his life than his firearm. It disappeared into the edge of the forest.

"Uncle!"

"Shit," he said, more in disbelief than in anger.

Mutt went from malevolent to hysterical, barking and growling and snapping at the air, straining forward as if against a leash. "Mutt! No!" In a moment, Kate knew, there would be no restraining her. There was nothing else left to do, so she planted herself in front of Old Sam's prone form and raised her rifle, pulling the stock into her shoulder and sighting down the barrel on the tiny bead at the end of it. Her heart was beating so fast and so hard it felt like it was going to explode out of her chest. She ignored it as best she could and concentrated, taking in a long, deep breath, blowing it out again slowly through pursed lips, then another.

There was a long, lingering moment where everything seemed to slooooow down, to decelerate, where the world stepped on the brakes with a firm, insistent foot. It was a moment, too, where someone seemed to have turned the volume button all the way down to one. On Kate's peripheral vision she could see Mutt barking savagely, spittle flying from between her teeth in an almost graceful arc. Behind her she could sense Old Sam scrabbling to his feet. She knew he must be cursing, knew that the brush was rustling as he searched for the Winchester, but she couldn't hear it.

Her attention never wavered from the opposite side of the little clearing. She was ready when she caught just the merest glimpse of sunlight on a rich shining hide before the grizzly exploded into the clearing. He was running flat out, straight at them, squealing and growling a challenge, turf kicked up behind him by those long, sharp, deadly claws. Distantly, as if it were happening to someone else, Kate could feel his weight hitting the ground, a steady, rhythmic vibration up through the soles of her feet. His thick, gleaming hide rolled in loose, flapping folds around flesh diminished by a winter's hibernation.

He couldn't possibly have been moving that fast before, the thickness of the brush would have impeded him as surely as it would have stopped Kate and Old Sam's escape. Once he was in the clearing he moved at a flat-out four-gaited gallop, the hind legs following the forelegs in a dedicated integration of muscle and bone and attitude that she would have recognized as sheer beauty if she hadn't been the prize at the finish line. He was the size of a Humvee, coming at her with the hammer down and armored with teeth and claws, and she concentrated all her awareness on the tiny bead at the end of the barrel of her rifle. She blew out another breath, and held it.

The bead wavered a little before steadying. Bead and bear's head sprang into acute and equal focus. His head came up in mid-stride, some instinct as primeval as the forest behind him alerting him to the danger. For a fleeting moment their eyes met, and it flashed through her mind that she had seen that expression or something very like it before. The eyes, dark, near together, nearsighted, and bent on the annihilation of his target.

Looked just like Harvey Meganack when he was intent on scoring against Kate at an NNA board meeting.

She pulled the trigger without volition, an act of instinct and self-defense. As if it came from a great distance, she heard the report of a rifle shot. After what seemed like forever felt the rifle's butt kick into her shoulder.

The bullet penetrated eye and occipital bone and ricocheted around the inside of the skull. The bear's head flung back with such force that it broke his neck. His front legs went out from beneath him, but the forward motion backed by his mass was so great that he slid the remainder of the twenty feet between them.

When his body slid to a halt, his head flopped forward. The tip of his short, blunt nose was just touching Kate's boot.

THREE

"MOST OF THE TIME I just love being a ranger," Dan said. "But I admit there are days that do test that love."

Jim saved the document and hit the Print button.

Kate had given her statement first. Then, because she was still seeing the world through a transparent veil dotted with large dull black spots that kept fading in and out, she walked down the hill on shaky legs to the Niniltna Native Association headquarters. Annie Mike kept a cache of Stouffer's frozen mac and cheese in the break room freezer. Kate felt like she hadn't eaten in a week.

She was a little closer to human again when she and Mutt walked back into Jim's office, just in time to hear Dan say, "Do you believe that George Perry? Saying you'd have to wait to ship the body to the crime lab in Anchorage until a later flight?"

"He got it on the plane," Kate said.

"Sure, after you leaned on him," Dan said, looking around at her.

"He's a busy man these days."

"He sure as hell is," Dan said. "Suulutaq has him on contract, did you hear? Freight flights and crew changes every day of the week. And did you hear about the grader?"

"No, what?"

"They've brought in a grader dedicated to keeping the air-

45

strip out there level. A John Deere motor grader, six-wheel drive. And they bought it new. Brand-new. Just like that, walked in, plunked down a check, and drove it off the lot."

Kate looked at Jim. "Grader envy," she said.

"Ever been on that moose trail to the Step?" Jim said.

Kate had just that morning. She desisted.

"Demetri was telling me that he wanted to go to Anchorage on Monday and George told him he didn't have a seat open until Thursday," Dan said. "And Bobby said George told him he was in the market for a couple more airplanes and to spread the word. Plus, he wanted to hire Bobby to fly for him."

Jim pulled Dan's statement from the printer. "Sign here."

Dan signed.

"What was going on up at the Kanuyaq Mine?" Kate said.

Jim rolled his eyes. "Some of the guys from the Suulutaq camping out in the mess hall."

"Doesn't sound so awful."

"Wouldna been, if they hadn't brought a dozen cases of Oly with them, along with four of the local girls."

"Which girls?" Dan said.

Kate gave him a halfhearted glare. "I thought everything up there was boarded up."

"Yeah, well, you know how that goes. Anyway, I ran them off."

"No arrest for trespassing?" Kate said.

Jim snorted. "What's the point? There isn't anyone from here to Anchorage who hasn't been up there, sifting the ruins for souvenirs."

"How many people are working out at Suulutaq now?" Dan said.

"A hundred as of May first."

"A hundred and ten, if you count the admin crew that got here in March," Kate said.

"Bernie's thinking of hiring a bouncer," Jim said.

"Not a bad idea. You can barely wedge yourself into the Roadhouse these days. It has increased the fight-or-flight reflex." Dan reflected. "Not to mention the competition for women."

"How many women out at the mine?" Kate said.

"Eleven," Dan said.

Kate looked at him, an eyebrow raised.

"Yeah, okay, I'm paying attention, so sue me. I'm single and of age." He leered.

"Sounds like Prudhoe Bay," Kate said. She had worked undercover in the Alaskan oil fields some years back. She remembered only too well what being the only woman in a room full of a hundred men felt like.

"I'm getting run ragged by Park rats who aren't used to having this many people around, and who want me to lock up every second person they meet just on general principle," Jim said. "I'm worried about what's going to happen when the road to Ahtna opens this year. Going to be one hell of a summer."

"What kind of trouble are the new mine guys getting up to? Other than trashing the old mine, that is."

"Nothing big, at least not yet. Chickenshit stuff, drunk in public, reckless driving, trespassing, coming on too strong to the local girls, who aren't used to it. And whose parents definitely aren't used to it."

"Drugs?"

"Some, but picayune so far, retail, not wholesale." He grinned at Kate. "We got the only aspiring wholesaler last year." The grin faded. "That'll change, though. Young men and money. Recipe for recreational drug use."

"Kate, when are we getting cell phone service in the Park?" Dan said.

Kate was taken aback by this abrupt change of subject. "How the hell should I know?"

"Since you're the Lady High Everything around these parts these days, is how. I hear thirty-six villages in the Y-K Delta have cell phone service now and they're expecting to add another fifty-nine villages between Dillingham and Barrow before the end of next year. What the hell's the holdup with the Park?"

"Do you really want to be that much in touch with the rest of the world, Dan?"

"It's either that or the rest of the world passes us right on by, Kate."

"Let them pass," Kate said.

Dan looked at Jim and spread his hands. "What're ya gonna do?"

Jim, who had already had this conversation with Kate, more than once, kept his mouth shut.

"Did you hear Global gave the school a grant for a satellite link and a computer for every kid?"

"I heard," Kate said.

"Starting this fall, every kid in Niniltna Public School is going to be online." They could hear the envy in Dan's voice. He would have a lot easier time holding on to employees if he could offer them Internet access on the Step.

"I heard," Kate said.

Dan grumbled. "You heard, you heard. Probably get cell phones in the Park just about the time the rest of the world is upgrading to communicators with a universal translator."

"Geek," Kate said.

"Luddite," Dan said.

"Children," Jim said, keeping it mild. "Play nice."

Dan looked at Kate's mulish expression and decided he'd pushed things far enough for one day. The seed had been planted. Now time for some fertilizer. "How about a cup of coffee and a doughnut on the Parks Service?"

"I don't know," Kate said, although she recognized it for the peace offering it was. She'd been charged by bears before and suffered the same adrenaline rush followed by the subsequent enervation and the same onset of ravenous hunger. The only remedy was massive caloric intake. "Laurel's packing them in these days. You think we can get a seat?"

They opted to walk down the hill, and had to jump out of the way of a four-wheeler being driven too fast by a young man clearly inexperienced in its operation, with three whooping friends hanging precariously off the back.

"I didn't see that," Jim said, "and neither did you."

A booth emptied out in the Riverside Café as they walked in. They scooted into it just ahead of a couple of young men Kate had never seen before. Mutt's unblinking yellow gaze might have had something to do with the perceptible pause in their rivals' step. She waited for her humans to take their seats, and then trotted past them. Kate turned to see Auntie Balasha, who was sitting alone at a corner table with bright fabric draped over the other three chairs. She was making change out of a gray metal cash box for a young man holding a recycled grocery bag. Through the thin plastic of the bag Kate could see more bright fabric.

"Excuse me," she said, and got up to follow Mutt. Auntie Balasha's color heightened at their approach, but she smiled at the young man as she put his change in his hand. "There, authentic Native dress perfect present for girlfriend. You come back for present for your mother and your auntie sometime, too, okay?"

The young man mumbled his thanks and took himself off.

"Ha, Mutt," Auntie Balasha said, and looked up to meet Kate's eyes. "Katya."

"Hi, Auntie," Kate said. On closer examination the drapes of fabric resolved themselves into kuspuks, essentially a Yupik hoodie in various lengths worn by both sexes and more often of late by Alaska Natives of all tribes. To the educated eye they bore distinct signs of having been mass-produced. There were only three different fabric patterns and the rickrack had evidently been a bulk purchase because it was the same on every sleeve edge and hem. Each one conformed to the same minimalist design with no skirts and no pouch pockets. "You're making and selling kuspuks?"

Auntie Balasha, her color still high, gave a defiant nod, and Kate realized with something of a shock that she was embarrassed to have been caught out in mid-enterprise. "Young mens want Alaska presents for their womens," Auntie Balasha said. "So I make kuspuks."

"How much you charging?" Kate said.

"Hundred dollars each."

Kate was impressed. "All right, Auntie," she said, in a tone she tried to make admiring rather than condemnatory. First Auntie Vi, now Auntie Balasha.

"Handmade," Auntie Balasha said.

"So I see."

"Authentic Alaska Native souvenir."

"It sure is."

"Made in Alaska by Alaska Native."

"No question about that."

Auntie Balasha, relieved, relaxed into a confidential mood.

"I give Laurel ten dollar each sale for table rent." She leaned forward and said in a lowered voice, "I talk to Thor. Maybe we open gift shop in town." She beamed past Kate. "Ha, young man, you like?"

Kate allowed herself to be elbowed aside and returned to the booth, sliding in next to Jim. "What's going on?" he said.

"Bloody Mary over there is taking the sailors for all they've got."

Dan craned his neck to look. "What's she selling, quilts? Oh, I see, kuspuks." He sat back. "I should pick up a couple of those for my mom and my sister."

"You absolutely should," Kate said. He was looking over her shoulder, and she looked around and saw Holly Haynes sitting at the counter in front of a half-eaten patty melt and a mug of coffee, the mug featuring the current NNA logo, which at this distance looked like a kindergartner's finger painting. Kate tried not to wince at the sight, instead exchanging a nod with Haynes, who nodded back. There was a man she didn't know sitting next to Haynes in conversation with Demetri Totemoff sitting next to him, but the rest of the café's clientele were young men in their twenties, scruffy and none too clean, loud of voice and rough of manner. They had money and they were determined to spend it, even if the only places in Niniltna to spend it were the Riverside Café, which didn't serve alcohol, Bingley's one-room store, which did not sell alcohol, and the gift shop located mostly on a corner shelf in the post office, which didn't ship alcohol. There was no road from the mine to Niniltna and Suulutaq picked up an employee's airfare only when they were changing shifts, every two weeks. Since the snow had melted and the ground dried out, four-wheelers had been sprouting like weeds from Niniltna to the Roadhouse. Kate had dark suspicions as to where the vehicles had sprouted from, most of them involving Howie Katelnikof.

All of the miners and Park rats present were there for the only espresso drinks served between Niniltna and Ahtna. They also lusted after the lovely and nubile Laurel Meganack, too, almost as much as they lusted after her green chile cheeseburgers.

Today Laurel wasn't working alone. "You've got new talent," Dan said, craning to see around Laurel when she brought them menus.

"Hands off," Laurel said. "Heather's working out, and I'd like to keep her a little longer than the last three girls I hired. Hey, Mutt."

They nodded at each other, woman to woman.

"Kate," Laurel said.

"Laurel," Kate said. Laurel was still a trifle peeved with Kate for the verbal roughhousing Kate had given her father last year during a murder investigation, but since then they had conspired together with Auntie Vi and Matt Grosdidier for the greater good, and as it happened for Laurel's greater good in particular. Both Jim and Dan were aware, in their dim male way, that constraint had existed, and that it was now gone. Good, they got to eat.

Laurel took their orders and swiveled off, a pocket Venus with thick dark hair sleeked back into a severe ponytail, a thin white T-shirt that displayed to advantage every detail of the low-cut, lacy bra beneath, and jeans that looked as if they'd been sewn to her body. Laurel was a good fry cook and a world-class barista but she knew what brought them in the door.

"Truth in advertising," Dan said, mesmerized.

"No misleading of the consumer there," Jim said, rapt.

Both men recalled themselves at the same moment and

gave Kate identical guilty looks.

She laughed at them.

It was an incongruous and yet somehow outrageously sexy rasping rumble of amusement. Laurel and Heather weren't the only women in the room worth a second look, and Kate was worth a third.

She wasn't a classic beauty, five feet, 120 pounds, and, compared to Laurel, modest curves. Her black hair was cut very short and gleamed beneath the fluorescent lights with an almost iridescent sheen. Her olive skin was clear and looked velvety to the touch. Her Aleut cheekbones were flat and high and her eyes were a changeable hazel she had inherited from multiple multiethnic forebears, beneath the eyelids she had inherited from the Asian ancestors who had crossed the Bering Sea land bridge into Alaska twenty-five thousand years before.

Her mouth was wide and full and when she bothered it was capable of curling into a sensual smile that revealed a set of white, even teeth that had everything to do with heredity and nothing at all to do with the dentist. On closer inspection, beneath a rounded but very firm chin, there was a white, roped scar that bisected her throat halfway between chin and clavicle, almost from ear to ear. The more alert might have figured out it was the cause of the husky voice and the rasping laugh. She didn't dress to attract, clad in jeans that fit comfortably and a cream-colored mock turtleneck beneath a navy blue sweatshirt with UAF NANOOKS on the front. Her feet were shod in worn boots with steel toes.

An ordinary getup on an ordinary Alaskan woman. Still, that laugh sent out a siren call that appealed viscerally to the testosterone in every male within earshot. Once heard, it was never forgotten, and men wanted to hear it again, preferably from a horizontal position. Heads turned, eyes narrowed, butts shifted in chairs, and Jim closed his eyes and shook his head.

Conversation at the round table in the center of the room was rising in volume and the laughter was becoming raucous. Kate watched as a pint bottle was produced from the pocket of a pair of grimy overalls and passed around the table in a stealthy manner. She nudged Jim with her elbow.

"I'm begging you," he said. He was seated on an inside seat with his back to the revelers, both deliberate and determined choices. Laurel arrived at tableside, bearing their orders, appearing to him as an angel from upon high. All he wanted to do was eat and drink his meal in peace, if not quiet.

The green chile cheeseburgers were thick and juicy and loaded, and Laurel had remembered to bring them malt vinegar for the homemade fries. Kate, whose post-ursine enhanced metabolism had forgotten the frozen mac and cheese faster than a six-course Chinese dinner, was seduced into devoting all of her attention to the plate in front of her. When she emerged from gustatory heaven, the noise at the round table had risen another decibel level.

And then, as if someone had turned a switch, the noise shut off. Kate looked around to see what was going on.

Jim did not.

Phyllis Lestinkof was standing at the round table, a hand on the shoulder of one of the young mine workers. He was red-haired, blue eyes bright in a freckled face, with an awkward ranginess of build that made him look tall even sitting down.

He shook off Phyllis's hand and said something to his friends that made Phyllis redden. "It is, too!" she said, and reached for his shoulder again. This time she laid hold and shook it.

This time he slapped her hand away.

The scene at the clinic that morning replayed itself in Kate's mind, and many things were clearer now than they had been then. She pushed her plate back.

"I'm begging you," Jim said, without much hope.

"You're repeating yourself," Dan said, watching events unfold with the judicious eye of a drama critic. Did those idiots not see an Alaska State Trooper in full regalia sitting ten feet away?

"Oh, hey, man," one of the redhead's friends said. "No call for that."

"Fuck off," the redhead said, or spat, more like. He looked embarrassed, and angry.

Several of the more prudent young men around the table pushed back their chairs and gathered their legs beneath them, ready to leap out of the line of fire when the shooting commenced.

"No call for that, either," the friend said, his own face reddening. He looked at Phyllis. "You okay, honey?"

Phyllis burst into tears. "It's his, it really is, and now what am I going to do? My mother—"

"This is such bullshit!" the redhead said, leaping to his feet and in the process knocking Phyllis off hers. She fell backward with a cry that Kate judged to be more startled than angry.

Her champion leaped to his feet to go to her aid. Mistaking this for aggression, the redhead pulled a knife.

Kate was on her feet and in between the two combatants before he was able to use it.

"Always been quick as a snake," Dan said.

"Is there blood yet?" Jim said.

Kate blocked the knife wielder's right hand with her left one, reached up under his right arm with her right hand, grabbed his right wrist, stepped in closer to him, turning left and stepping to the side as she did so, and brought the hand holding the knife down smartly. The redhead let out a startled squawk and dropped the knife before he stabbed himself in the thigh.

"Aren't you going to do something?" Dan said.

"Not feeling the need to," Jim said, sloshing more vinegar on his remaining fries.

Just for the hell of it, just because she could, Kate grabbed the redhead's wrist and kept going, bending her knees and using his own momentum to roll him forward. She was so much shorter than he was that he was forced to bend forward, over her back, to remain attached to his arm, which he had discovered was now in an iron grip. In the split second between the moment when he lost his balance and the moment when he fell on her she straightened her legs with a jerk, shoving her back into his torso. He performed a half gainer with a midair twist, to land flat on his back on the table in front of Dan and Jim.

The table held but the impact jarred the entire room. Dan was pretty sure he saw some dust shake out of the join where the wall met the ceiling.

Jim, who had moved his glass and plate out of the way in the very nick of time, said in a stern voice, "Son, you brought that on yourself."

Dan assisted the redhead back to his feet with a vigorous shove, but he fell forward on both knees with a double crack that made everyone in earshot wince. Meantime, Kate heard a rustle of feet and turned to see that Phyllis's champion had switched sides, and in addition was making a gross error in judgment by charging in her direction with vengeance written all over his face. This was a mistake often made by non-Park rats. When you didn't know her, Kate Shugak seemed on first

56

sight like such a tiny little thing, and she was a woman at that. It was easy to underestimate her, and that, as his redheaded friend had already discovered, was one of her biggest assets.

However, in this instance it was another woman who confounded his intent. From the counter, Haynes stuck out her foot. He tripped and went sprawling on the floor, pancaking on his face and skidding almost to the door across Laurel's well-waxed linoleum. In three quick steps Kate was on him, one hand on his collar, the other on the seat of his pants.

"Allow me," Haynes said, and opened the door. Phyllis's erstwhile champion was hurled through it to the street outside, where he was narrowly avoided by Galen Heideman on his four-wheeler. Galen's sharp and succinct comments on this surprise impediment to lawful traffic were clearly audible through the open door.

"You were saying?" Jim said.

Dan was laughing too hard to speak.

"By the way, Ned," Haynes said to the young man sprawled in the dirt, "you're fired. And so are you, Jason," she said as Kate assisted the redhead out the door, too. Haynes turned to run a considering eye over Ned and Jason's remaining friends, who divested themselves of their chairs and the café in short order.

Kate looked at Phyllis, who was now sobbing. Kate took a step toward her.

"Leave me alone!" Phyllis said, and fled, the door slamming behind her.

"Well, then," Laurel, who had come charging out of the kitchen with a sauté pan in one hand and a spatula in the other, said. "And who picks up their checks?"

"I do," Haynes said.

"Appreciate the help," Kate said.

Haynes shrugged. "You didn't need much. We don't tolerate any bad behavior by our employees anywhere in the Park. Not if we can help it." She smiled again, with more mischief in it this time. "Besides, it was fun. Felt like I was Dean Martin backing up John Wayne."

Kate couldn't help it, she had to return the smile. "Buy you a refill?"

"Sure."

Haynes paused to hand her mug to Laurel. She collected the two plastic bags full of groceries reposing at the foot of her stool and followed Kate to the booth.

Kate looked at the bags. "I heard they fed you pretty well out at the mine."

Haynes smiled and shrugged. "No matter how good it is, camp food gets old after a while. Sometimes you just don't want to go to the mess hall. Everybody has food in their rooms."

Kate made introductions, and Haynes sat across from Kate, next to Dan. He was clearly thrilled.

"And you'll have the kitchen at Auntie Vi's when you come to town." At Jim and Dan's puzzled looks, Kate said, "The Suulutaq Mine just bought Auntie Vi's B and B for a flophouse when their employees have to overnight in town."

Haynes grimaced. "'Flophouse.' Ouch." She waited a fraction of a second too long for Kate to retract the term, and looked at Jim to help her out of the awkwardness. "Sergeant Chopin? We've met."

He nodded, mopping up salt with the last fry. "Your boss introduced us last time I was over to the mine."

Haynes looked at Dan. "And you are?"

"Chief Ranger Dan O'Brian, National Parks Service," Dan said, "and after that little rodeo, yours to command."

Haynes laughed. "I appreciate that. Holly Haynes. I work for Vern Truax over at the Suulutaq. Listen, all joking aside," Haynes said to Kate, "I'm sorry about that. We tell our employees at orientation that it's one strike you're out when it comes to roughhousing the neighbors." She smiled her thanks when Laurel brought over Haynes's mug, which she announced as a skinny latte double tall with a shot of hazelnut syrup. She waved away Kate's money with a "Thanks for the bouncer work."

Haynes looked back at Kate. "Most of them listen. Some of them don't."

"Young men and large amounts of money," Kate said, quoting Jim without attribution. "It's a combustible combination. What I'd like to know is where they're getting the four-wheelers to come into town."

"So would we," Haynes said with feeling. She hesitated. "We could restrict all employees to the mine."

Dan snorted, Jim smiled, and Kate sighed. "Yeah, you could, but since everyone in town with anything to sell"—she hooked a thumb over her shoulder in Auntie Balasha's direction—"would kill us both if we did, probably a bad idea. Besides. They'd come in anyway. They'd find a way."

Haynes nodded. "They're a long way from anywhere."

"You could go to week and week," Kate said. "If they were only going to be on shift for seven days, they might not be so antsy to go anywhere in their off time."

Haynes shook her head. "Not gonna happen. In fact, when we go into operation we'll be going to month and month."

Kate closed her eyes for a moment, and next to her she felt Jim let out a long sigh. She opened her eyes again to see Haynes regarding her with sympathy. "Comes down to money," she said. "Flying people in and out every week gets expensive. Changing shifts once a month makes more fiscal sense. Could have been worse."

"How much worse?" Kate said.

"Head office was making noises about eight-week shifts. Vern managed to talk them down from that." She shuddered.

"Speaking of flying," Dan said, "you've pretty much taken over George Air."

Haynes looked confused. "Chugach Air Taxi Service," Kate said.

Haynes's brow cleared. "Oh. Well. You won't let us build a road." She shrugged. "Anyway. Our guys get desperate enough for a drink or new faces, they'll hike in if they have to."

Dan groaned. "No, please, I don't need any more of that in my Park." He told her, naturally with advantage, the story of the hiker on his way to Bright Lake.

"You just let him go?" Haynes said.

"He's a grown man. It's public land. If he shoots something he shouldn't, or fishes something he shouldn't, or builds a cabin where he shouldn't, then I can do something. But just walking out on it? No law against that. Unfortunately."

Jim finished his Coke and shifted into trooper mode. "Ms. Haynes—"

Haynes smiled at Jim. "Holly, please."

"Okay, Holly, we've got another problem."

"What's that?"

"A resident found a pickup abandoned on the road in to his house. Subsequent investigation revealed that the truck was registered to someone we have reason to believe may have been employed at the Suulutaq Mine."

Haynes stiffened. "Name?"

"Dewayne Gammons."

She frowned, thinking. "The name is familiar."

"Someone will be out to the mine tomorrow to ask around. That okay with you?"

Haynes inclined her head. "Of course."

"I appreciate your help."

Haynes took Jim's nod quite correctly, a clear dismissal, and stood up to make her farewells. Both men watched her all the way out the door, Dan with speculation, Jim with a pucker between his eyebrows.

When the door closed behind her Dan said, "Auntie Vi sold out to the mine?"

"She didn't sell out," Kate said, annoyed, and forgetting for the moment that she'd thought the same thing in so many words that morning.

"They made her an offer she couldn't refuse?"

Kate sighed. "Pretty much."

"She headed for a condo in Maui now?"

"No, she says she's going to run it for them."

Dan snorted. "Yeah, that'll happen, Vi Moonin taking anybody's orders."

"Ms. Haynes's bad memory notwithstanding," Jim said, "Mr. Gammons is, or was, in fact, an employee of the Suulutaq Mine." He had called the mine on their sat phone from his office sat phone when Kate was down the hill gorging on mac and cheese. "He was hired last year, according to mine superintendent Vernon Truax. He and, Truax says, about four thousand other people responded to an ad that Global Harvest ran in newspapers in Alaska and on the West Coast. Gammons was one of forty-eight hired. That is, of those employees who weren't hired from the Park."

Global Harvest Resources Inc. was losing no opportunity to curry local favor. They'd hired fifty-two Park rats from Ahtna to Cordova to Niniltna last January, keeping most of them on at reduced pay over the remainder of the winter so as to retain their services for when the snow melted in the spring and operation commenced. Not to mention giving them a taste of regular paychecks, something quite out of the ordinary in the Park.

As Kate kept reminding them and everyone else, they could afford it. She was going to see about Global Harvest affording week-on, week-off shifts, too. Wasn't much point in being chair of the board of the Niniltna Native Association if she couldn't throw a little weight around for the common good. "What did Gammons do at the mine?"

"According to Superintendent Truax, he was a roustabout on Gold Shift."

"What's a roustabout?" Dan said. "I got visions of Elvis here."

"Again, according to the good superintendent, a roustabout is someone with a strong back who is capable of doing what he's told." Jim shrugged. "A little bit of everything, it sounds like, loading and unloading freight, getting it from the airstrip to the correct delivery point, warehouse, administration building, mess hall, dormitories, drilling rigs. They police the site—Superintendent Truax made sure I understood that they're very big on a clean worksite."

"Good for them," Dan said, "or I'll be all over their ass."

This was blowing smoke with a vengeance. Dan didn't really have any say about it, since the Suulutaq discovery was located on a series of state leases on property the state of Alaska had retained when the Iqaluk Wildlife Refuge was created around them. As chief ranger of the Park Dan O'Brian was very much a federal employee. Neither Jim nor Kate commented on this logical disconnect, however. Logic wouldn't stop Ranger Dan if he perceived Global Harvest to be shitting anywhere near his nest.

"His fellow workers say he was suicidal?"

"According to Truax, none of them noticed. I don't think most of them knew he was missing, to tell the truth." Jim turned to look at Kate. "Tell me something. How many employees do they really need out there right now? To do the job they're doing at present?"

"Can't say for sure, never having started a gold mine up from scratch myself. But, yeah, be my guess there is a lot of make-work going on. They want to keep the Park rats happy."

"And the Niniltna Native Association, and their shareholders," Dan said, "of which, allow me to point out one more time, you happen to be chair of the board of directors."

"Yeah, yeah, yeah," Kate said. Eight months into the job that had been wished on her by four determined aunties, she wasn't even going to be comfortable with the title.

"You haven't come out for or against the mine yet," Dan said, prodding her. "When's that gonna happen?"

"Never, if I have my way," Kate said under her breath. To Jim she said, "From what I saw there isn't enough left of Gammons for his best friend to identify."

"It is his truck."

"That's not enough."

"There's a personnel file, according to Truax, and everyone hired had to take a physical. There's a blood type. There's at least enough left of the body to make a match. It doesn't take much these days." He leaned back. "Want to take it on for me?"

"I beg your pardon?"

"Come on, Kate, don't tell me you didn't see this coming. All I need is a positive ID on the body and case closed. Easy money for you."

63

"Yeah, but I'd have to go out to the mine."

He gave her a look. "You know you're dying to see what's happened out there since they started up work again this spring."

"You gonna make me notify the next of kin?"

He winced. "No. That's the trooper's job. I'll make the call. It's just—"

"What?"

The lines at the corners of his mouth deepened. "When I was in Ahtna last week, testifying at that rape case? During those same two days Maggie fielded calls for a child sexual assault in Chistona, a domestic violence incident in Red Run, a gang rape in Slana, three break-ins of homesteads along the river, and a murder-suicide on a homestead somewhere between here and Ahtna that I never heard of before and neither one of us can find on a map." He shook his head. "On top of all that I got fifty wannabe Park rats running around after their shifts thinking up new ways to get into trouble. Where the hell they get all that energy after twelve hours of hard labor is beyond me. I'm up to my ears just trying to keep the peace in the Park. This Gammons is pretty rote, a by-the-book suicide by Alaska, and I'd sure appreciate it, Kate, if you'd dot the i's and cross the t's on this one."

"Jesus, man," Dan said, only half kidding, "don't grovel."

"I'm not groveling," Jim said, patiently for him. "I'm just tired."

There was a wealth of weary in his voice. Kate's heart melted. "Sure. I'll do it."

Jim pulled the folder out of a capacious inner pocket and handed it over. "Thanks. I owe you."

"You'll pay me," Kate said.

She was rewarded by what she felt was only a pale simulacrum of his trademark shark's grin. "In legal tender, or you want to take it out in trade?"

She shook back feathered wisps of hair from her forehead and gave him a speculative glance from eyes that were momentarily more seductive green than innocent hazel.

What the hell, a tired shark still had teeth that could later be put to creative use. "How about both?"

Dan labored to produce an appropriately gagging sound, but what came out was only a long, drawn-out sigh of pure envy.

They stepped out the door and again had to leap out of the way of another four-wheeler, driven this time by a completely different young man, also a stranger to them, and this one with six friends hanging off the back.

Dan stared after them. "Either of you guys ever see a movie called *Local Hero*?"

FOUR

KATE PICKED UP JOHNNY at the school potluck, and was persuaded without difficulty to give Van a lift as well. As girlfriends went, in respect to the now sixteen-year-old male Kate had taken in tow three years before, Vanessa Cox ranked right up there. A slender, self-possessed brunette, she seemed far older than her years, which might have had something to do with her early orphaning and her later adoption by Park rat relatives who had turned out to be less than satisfactory guardians.

Absent any other living relatives, Kate and Jim had pulled all available state strings and custody of Vanessa had been granted to Billy and Annie Mike, who had raised six of their own and recently adopted a half Korean, half African-American baby from Seoul. There was always room for one more at the Mikes' house. Vanessa, once she was sure she was wanted, had blossomed in Annie's care from a tomboy in bib overalls and a ponytail to a very attractive young woman dressed in a Realitee cardigan over !iT jeans tucked into a pair of Ugg boots that laced up the front. She was even wearing makeup, although Annie's fine hand could be detected in how much, amounting to a touch of mascara to emphasize already ridiculously long eyelashes and a gloss of lipstick on a firm mouth notable for its placement over a decidedly square if delicate chin.

Johnny had noticed. That they were now a couple was taken for granted. Kate had had The Talk with Johnny, and again with him and Vanessa together, both times to his excruciating embarrassment. She'd repeated it a third time when he bought his pickup, this time to his exasperation. "Jeez, Kate, you think I didn't hear you the first hundred times?"

"I'll never be a candidate for World's Greatest Mom," Kate said without apology. "How bad a grandmother do you think I'd be?"

He rolled his eyes. "Dad had The Talk with me when I was ten."

"He did?" Kate thought of Jack Morgan, dead almost four years now. First her boss at the Anchorage DA's office as she became a legend as a sex crimes investigator with a conviction rate record that stood to this day, and then, inevitably, her lover. Jimmy Buffett had cemented the deal, she remembered with a faint smile. They'd first made love after they'd fought over Jimmy moving from acoustic to electric. She was still right, "African Friend" was still Jimmy's best song to date.

She waited for the pain to strike at the memory of the tall, ugly man who had known her better than anyone else in the world. Instead, she felt only the sweet sorrow of his absence, and gratitude that she had had him in her life for so many years. He had forgiven her everything, not so much as a look of recrimination over her short-lived affair with Ken Dahl when she returned home to the Park after burning out on the job in Anchorage. That their affair had helped get Ken killed was something for which she still felt a lingering guilt, but Jack had never said a word. Later he had given his life to save her own, a sacrifice he had made willingly, and he had died in her arms with a laugh on his lips.

67

And he had given her Johnny. She looked at his son, boding to be as tall, and if not quite as ugly then as memorable in feature and as independent in personality. "I'm not a mommy," she'd told Jack a long time ago, and he'd saddled her with a twelve-year-old son in response.

Well, she still wasn't a mommy. They were friends, her and the kid. She was older and tougher so she could make what she said stick, for now. Just because she had resorted to blackmail to keep his mother from taking him away didn't mean anything. Except that she loved him, first for his father's sake and now for his own. *Johnny's a gift*, she'd told Old Sam, and it was the simple truth. He was a smart, funny kid who had grown into a young man of such promise it almost hurt her eyes to look at him. After a lifetime spent in a determined search for independence, she now had a hostage to fortune.

Jack had to be laughing his ass off somewhere. Of course he'd had The Talk with Johnny at age ten. He would probably have had it with him at age six if he hadn't recoiled from the need to use pictures to make himself understood.

Today, Van and Johnny slid into the cab of the four-wheel-drive Ford Ranger XL long-bed Super Cab Kate had received as a fee for babysitting Mandy Baker's Beacon Hill parents during their one and only visit to the Park. Mutt already took up a large portion of the bench seat but they managed to pull the door shut on the mashup.

Four years ago, the truck had been bright red and brand-new, but there had been a series of unfortunate encounters with a Super Cub, a grizzly, and a Park rat with a .30-06, so the bloom was rather off the pickup rose. The previous owner of the truck was crossing the parking lot outside the school, and Kate rolled down her window. "Hey, Mandy."

"Hey, Kate. Hey, Mutt." This as Mutt peered around Kate,

ears pricked forward. "Hey, kids." Mandy gave the pickup the once-over, followed by a mournful shake of her head and the rote comment. "My poor baby."

Kate gave the rote response. "Takes a licking, keeps on ticking. How's your folks?"

"Good. They might come up again this year." Mandy smiled. "Seems they know some of the members of the board of GHRI."

Mandy Baker, known to the dog mushing world as the Brahmin Bullet, the fourth woman to win the Iditarod and the third to win the Yukon Quest, was now working as the dedicated Alaskan spokesperson for the Suulutaq Mine, at a hefty salary and with generous stock options that earned an even more generous amount of shares in Global Harvest Resources Inc.

"Be good to see them again," Kate said, and it wasn't a polite lie. Mandy's Boston Brahmin parents had turned out to be something of a surprise to everyone concerned, including themselves. She nodded at the school. "You signing up to get your GED?"

"Very funny," Mandy said.

"I met your staff geologist today."

"Holly Haynes?"

"Yeah, first she bought Auntie Vi's B and B for the mine."

Mandy looked unsurprised. "They've been talking about the need for a place. I told them Auntie Vi's B and B was the only suitable house in Niniltna for what they needed."

"And then she helped me break up a knife fight in the Riverside Café between a couple of your other employees."

Mandy swore under her breath.

"Be careful what you wish for," Kate said.

Mandy heard the bite in Kate's voice and gave her a sharp look.

On a gruesome day the previous winter, Global Harvest's former representative to the Park had met an end that was still discussed over the bar at Bernie's with fascination, revulsion, and not a little awe. Up until that day, Mandy Baker had been a musher and a damn good one, but Iditarod and Yukon Quest purses went only so far, and besides she wasn't placing in the money as regularly as she once had. Previously a trust fund had made up the difference, but in the current depression, with a hundred dogs to feed and vet bills and a live-in boyfriend who needed the occasional bail money, it didn't go as far as it once had, either. She could have asked her parents for a loan on her inheritance, which would be considerable, but Mandy was a proud soul who didn't like to ask anybody for anything. The only solution to the bills piling up on her kitchen table was to get a job.

She was probably Kate's oldest friend in the Park, after Bobby Clark. And she was Global Harvest's new representative to the Park.

"So, what were you doing at the school?" Kate said.

Mandy nodded at Johnny and Van. "I'll let them tell you about it. See you later."

She slopped through the mud to a Ford Explorer with the now familiar sunrise-over-the-Quilaks logo on the side and drove off.

Kate put the Ranger in gear. "What's she talking about?"

Van was tucked beneath Johnny's arm. They exchanged glances. "Mandy made a speech at the potluck. The mine's offering summer jobs to kids sixteen and older."

"Really," Kate said. "What kind of jobs?"

"Roustabout."

Kate thought back to Jim's definition of roustabout. "What would you be doing, exactly?"

"Picking up trash," Johnny said.

"Washing dishes or making beds," Van said.

"Scrubbing pots."

"Janitor work."

"Typing and filing."

"Oh." They bumped over a section of washboard without anyone being ejected out of the pickup, a minor triumph in the days between breakup and summer. "So the job's just for the summer?"

"Yeah."

"Hourly?"

"Yeah."

"Minimum wage?"

"Yeah, but anything over eight hours is time and a half, and holidays are double time."

Federal minimum wage was currently $6.55 an hour. Time and a half would be $9.83. They were both sixteen. Kate didn't know if state law required them to be eighteen to work overtime. She wasn't sure if the state was geared up yet to send a labor inspector out to the Suulutaq, though, and it wasn't like Johnny and Van didn't know what a long day was like. "What's the shift?"

"Twelve hours a day, seven days a week, two weeks on, two weeks off. But Mandy says depending on how good we are and what needs to be done, there's the possibility we could work back-to-back shifts straight through the summer."

Kate ran a rapid mental calculation. Twelve hours times seven days equaled eighty-four. Forty hours times $6.55 was only $262, but forty-four hours times $9.83 was $432.52. "Almost seven hundred dollars a week total," she said out loud. Twenty-eight hundred a month. Even if you figured a third for taxes, it was still a fortune to a teenager. Especially one who lived in the Park, and with the economy in the toilet it looked like a king's ransom. Kate had been squirreling away a quarter of every paycheck into Johnny's college fund but this would at the very least pay for textbooks.

"What about crewing on the *Freya*?" she said.

Johnny looked uncomfortable. "Do you think Old Sam will mind much?"

"He hates breaking in new help," she said. It was true. It was also true that Old Sam had hired Johnny in the first place so he could keep Kate on as a deckhand. At least at first. However, Johnny had proved himself, both as a quick learner and as remarkably reliable for one of whom Old Sam referred to as the hormonally challenged.

"It's a lot of money, Kate."

Given the dismal predictions for this year's salmon run, it was probably more than he'd make on the *Freya*.

But money wasn't his only consideration, and maybe not even his first consideration. Kate watched Johnny and Van exchange another glance, and the unspoken thought was mutual and obvious. If they both got jobs at the mine, they could be together over the summer. Kate wondered how good an idea that was.

Well, at some point, you had to trust that you'd raised them right, and if she had little confidence in her own embryonic parenting skills she had a great deal of faith in Annie Mike's. Nevertheless, she saw no harm in letting them sell her on the idea. Kate also had great faith in the child-rearing instincts of Lazarus Long, who had famously said, "Do not handicap your children by making their lives easy."

"They're going to hire the Grosdidier brothers to teach an EMT class so we can respond to emergencies," Van said.

"And the culinary union is going to send in chefs from

Anchorage to teach institutional cooking," Johnny said.

"And we get paid to take the classes," Van said. "It'd be part of our job."

GHRI going after the next generation with a vengeance. Still, Kate couldn't detect a flaw in the offer of free education. She pulled into Annie Mike's driveway and they trooped inside. Annie had coffee and lemon sugar cookies waiting.

Annie already knew about Auntie Vi selling the B and B, so Kate favored her with a description of her heroic disruption of the knife fight in the Riverside Café, and Annie retaliated with an eyewitness account of Bonnie Jeppsen and Suzy Moonin bitch-slapping each other around the post office, as near as anyone could make out just for the fun of it.

"Well, at least that won't be Suulutaq related," Kate said. "Annie, you hear about these summer jobs the mine's offering the kids?"

Annie nodded, her face placid and calm as ever. A short, plump woman with straight brown hair that fell in ordered strands from a side part to a pudgy chin and brown eyes that remained bland in expression no matter what the provocation, Annie dressed in Jelly Belly-colored polyester pantsuits that Dinah Clark freely speculated she had bought a gross of straight off the rack at JCPenney in 1963. No one disagreed, and besides, Annie's rainbow figure was a welcome sight in the middle of a dark Alaskan winter. Her style, however retro, most decidedly did not make her a figure of fun.

Kate thought of Annie Mike as an auntie-in-waiting, although given recent history she wasn't altogether sure Annie would be flattered at the comparison. Annie Mike was half Athabascan and half Aleut, with some Swedish thrown in from a Cordova connection and a rumor of African-American on her mother's side. This was attributed to Hell Roaring Mike

Healy, who had scattered enough seed up and down the Alaskan coast in his time to have been the progenitor of all the residents of Ahtna, with maybe Fairbanks thrown in for good measure. It was indisputable that Annie was the granddaughter of one tribal chief and the widow of another, and she had served as secretary-treasurer of the Niniltna Native Association since its creation. Kate, less than nine months in office after succeeding Billy Mike as the chairman of the board of directors, had come to regard Annie as her lodestone. She relied on her for Annie's institutional knowledge, which was second to the knowledge of no other shareholder. That bland expression and that blinding rainbow attire were misdirection, camouflage to distract attention from the sharp intelligence, the acute perception, and the unshakeable integrity that was the woman beneath. If Annie said something was okay, Kate had learned that it indisputably was.

Kate licked sugar from her fingers and waited for judgment to be rendered. Johnny and Van, well aware of the esteem in which Annie Mike was held by her tribe, in the Park and not least by Kate Shugak, waited, too, with some anxiety.

Annie frowned and the kids looked at first dismayed and then ready to argue, but Kate knew from experience that the frown was more an expression of deep thought than of disapproval. "I wish they'd proposed it to the board before they'd announced it to the kids," she said.

"That was my first thought as well," Kate said. She meditated on her coffee. "However, I see their point in taking it directly to the kids themselves. For one thing, not everyone enrolled in Niniltna High School is a Niniltna Native Association shareholder."

Annie nodded. "They want to make the offer to everyone, not just Natives."

"Yes." Kate looked at Johnny and Van and the corners of her mouth quirked up in a smile. "And they knew perfectly well that it'd be hard to say no to paying jobs for the kids, once the kids heard about them." She looked back at Annie, smile fading. "Let's face it, Annie. Fish and Game projections aren't good for the Kanuyaq runs this year. The economy's tanked. Sure, Global Harvest is trying to buy their way into our good graces. But it's a pretty good paycheck for someone their age, and it's not like our kids have that many options. I can't think of any Park rats whose lawns need mowing."

Annie nodded again.

Johnny and Van held their breath.

Kate reached for another cookie, and paused for an appreciative moment to admire its golden brown perfection. Stevenson was right, sometimes it was better to travel hopefully than to arrive. "They're going to pay that money to somebody, Annie."

Annie reached for a second cookie herself. "True," she said. "It might as well be our kids."

Johnny and Van, recognizing victory, beamed.

Kate took a bite of cookie and let the lemon and sugar dissolve blissfully on her tongue. Although arriving had its own rewards.

It was at least a counterpoint to the uneasy feeling that she'd just consented to the thin end of the wedge.

KATE AND JOHNNY PULLED into the clearing at the homestead as Jim was getting out of his Blazer. As usual Mutt leaped from the cab of the pickup to lavish an ecstatic greeting, her tail wagging hard enough to start a Force 5 gale.

Although Kate couldn't keep the smile from spreading across her own face, so who was she to talk. "I figured you'd be late. If you made it home at all."

"I told Maggie the hell with it and sent her home."

"Anybody left in the cells?"

"Well, since Maggie told me she sprung Willard to the custody of Eknaty Kvasnikof on your say-so, only Petey Jeppsen's left. Especially since I refused to arrest the bigamist."

Kate and Johnny exchanged a glance. "And thereby hangs a juicy tale," Kate said.

"Yeah, but first I need a beer."

They went inside, Johnny detouring through the shop, where his truck was in for maintenance. Kate hadn't touched anything while he was at school. The deal was they'd do any necessary work on his pickup together, that was how he'd learn, but you had to watch her. She stole books you were reading, too.

Jim went straight to the refrigerator and pulled out a bottle of Alaskan Amber. Uncapping it, he tilted his head back and took a long swallow. He felt better immediately.

Kate was peeling Saran wrap off the top of a deep brown mixing bowl. She bent down and sniffed.

"What's the latest yeasty masterpiece?"

She looked up and smiled at him. He didn't see stars, he told himself, it was only his imagination. "Same as the last, only I halved the amount of yeast, and I'm going to knead the salt in between risings."

"You might as well be speaking in tongues," he said.

She laughed, the same low husky rasp that she'd rolled out at the Riverside earlier in the day. Mine, he thought, and even he couldn't have said if he was referring to the laugh or to the woman. Both, probably. He wanted the whole package. Still. Amazing.

Constancy wasn't exactly Jim Chopin's middle name.

He went into the living room to consult the theater system with surround sound without which he had insisted no house was truly a home, and saw Johnny's iPod in the sound dock. He hit Play and moments later Mos Def's "Caldonia" from the soundtrack of *Lackawanna Blues* filled the air.

"Oh yeah," Kate said, and he grinned at her through the pass-through.

"What's for dinner?" he said.

"Fried Spam and eggs."

"Excellent," Johnny said, emerging from the bathroom to do a quick knee-drop to the beat.

Jim looked at Kate. "Hey, what can I tell you?" she said. "It's my Native culture calling to me. You know Alaskans are second only to Hawaiians in consumption of Spam."

"And I hear second only to Utah in downloading porn," Johnny said, jumping into a hip slide across the floor to the door of his room, through which he slung his daypack.

"How we can hold our heads up in public ever again," Jim said.

"I don't want to know how you know that," Kate said, looking at Johnny.

Johnny's grin was cheeky. "Just wait till the Park gets online. Then we'll be number one."

She thought of the computers targeted for the school and shuddered. She'd floured the counter, sprinkled two teaspoons of salt over the flour, and turned out the dough. Before they had begun construction, the Park rat house-raising committee had measured her from sole to waist and made the countertops Kate high, which coincidentally made it very convenient for Jim to stand behind her, slide his arms around her waist, and snug her head beneath his chin.

She stilled. "I'm covered in flour."

"I don't care."

"Not to mention which," Johnny said in pretend indignation, closing his bedroom door behind him with a distinct thud, "the kid's standing right here."

"True," Jim said. He felt Kate relax against him, a warm, firm presence. God, she felt good.

"And waiting for the story about the bigamist." Johnny looked at him, face eager. Troopers told the best stories, and he sensed this one would be a doozy.

He felt Kate stir. "Unhand me, sir."

Reluctantly Jim let her go. He took his beer to the couch and stretched out so that he could watch Kate over the open counter that separated the kitchen from the living room. He took another swallow, and draped an arm around a furry neck conveniently offered. His women had him surrounded. He sighed. Mutt sighed. Eric Clapton started in on "Layla." In the kitchen, Kate rolled her eyes and kneaded coarse salt into bread dough that she worried might be a tad bit too wet.

"So who is it?" Johnny said.

"The bigamist? Well, since both wives found out today and I'm guessing it's going around the Park by Bush telegraph right now—" He paused. "You know, we should tune into Park Air to night, see what Bobby's got to say about it."

"Who is it?"

"Because you know he'll have something to say about it."

"Jim!"

The chorus was loud enough to make one of Mutt's ears twitch. It tickled his cheek, but that wasn't why he laughed. "Actually, you don't know him."

"Oh." Johnny was disappointed.

Kate looked at Jim. "But we know the wives." It was a statement, not a question.

"Oh, yeah."

"Oh, yeah?" Johnny said, perking up again.

Jim looked at Kate, knowing this was where the story would lose some of its humor for her. "Suzy Moonin."

"Crap," she said. "Poor Suzy."

"How many kids has she got now?"

"Three, I think. Or maybe it's four. Anymore she sees me coming, she heads the other way. Plus I think she must be getting her booze somewhere else, because I haven't seen her at the Roadhouse lately." Kate's eyes darkened. "You haven't heard any rumors of a new bootlegger in town, have you?"

Jim shook his head. "No. But you know it's just a matter of time, Kate. With Suulutaq bringing all these new people into the Park, all these young men making real money, some of them for the first time in their lives, drug and alcohol abuse is going to skyrocket." He sighed. "Along with drug-related crime."

Kate gave Johnny a severe look.

"What?" he said. "What'd I do?"

"It's not what you haven't done, it's what you will do that worries me," she said.

"Kate! I haven't done anything!"

"You say that now."

"Jeez. I'm not even old enough to drink." He turned his back on her and said to Jim, "Who was the other wife?" He was only sixteen, he couldn't even see twenty-one from there, and he was much more interested in the now.

Jim gave the ceiling a pensive stare. "You'd think the guy would be smart enough to know that all the mail for the Park funnels through the Niniltna post office."

Kate and Johnny's eyes met. "Bonnie Jeppsen?" they said together. "Yep."

"You're kidding!"

"Nope."

"But she just got divorced!"

"Evidently, she just got remarried."

"No!" Kate and Johnny said together, savoring the horror of it all with unconcealed delight. Petey's older sister wasn't a Park favorite. This was partly because she had one of the few steady jobs around, and partly because you never knew when you walked into the post office if she was going to try to convert you to the ways of the Lord when all you wanted to do was pick up your mail. "Annie Mike said she saw them fighting in the post office. Was that why?"

Lynyrd Skynyrd started begging for three steps more. "Yes, it was. And while she wasn't smart enough to know she was his second wife that month, she was smart enough to intercept his check when Global mailed it to him. Probably in violation of seven or eight federal laws, but I'm choosing to ignore that for the moment. Or until a U.S. postal inspector shows up on my doorstep."

"Which," Kate said, thinking out loud, "of course sent Suzy hot-foot to the post office to put a trace on the check. Bonnie kind of laying herself open to that by opening the post office for two hours on holidays because she knows everyone will be in town for the parade."

"Exactly," Jim said, a gracious nod going to this most apt pupil. This most apt pupil stuck out her tongue. "And between the two of them they had just enough brain to figure out that they were both married to the guy the check belonged to. So when they got done slapping each other around, Bonnie closed up the post office and they came down to the post." He sought comfort in his beer.

"Were they loud?" Kate said, looking sympathetic.

"They were loud," Jim said, with a shudder. "They were foul-mouthed and abusive, too, to Maggie. And even to me." He was wounded all over again at the memory. Women were never mean to Chopper Jim Chopin.

"How could they," Kate said, and even Lenny Kravitz wanted to know who's that lady. The aptness of the iPod's musical commentary made her laugh.

"Yeah, yuck it up, Shugak," he said, "but I've a mind to pitch this right in your lap."

"I've got a job," she said, and batted her eyelashes at him. "Got it just this afternoon."

"True. Damn it." He brooded in silence, and Johnny decided the fun part was over and departed for his room and the joys of Maroon 5 on his iPod. Up till now he accessed his iTunes account on Bobby Clark's computer. But next fall, his own computer with his own Internet connection. iTunes, Facebook, World of Warcraft, he could hardly wait.

Jim put on a CD he had mixed under Johnny's supervision.

"Jim," Kate said in the kitchen, "about Petey. Did you catch him in the act of something?"

He made a disgusted sound. "Ah, Harvey reported seeing him and Howie cleaning out Feodor Williamson's garage. You know Feodor's been conspicuous by his absence lately, but that doesn't mean it's open season on his homestead, he's probably just catting around Anchorage like usual. I couldn't find Howie but I found Petey at the Roadhouse, and he wouldn't give me a straight answer to anything I asked him. Pissed me off, so I locked him up on general principle."

Kate nodded. About what she'd figured. "If I can find Petey a job, will you spring him?"

He looked at her in surprise. "Since when did you start saving Jeppsens, Kate? So far as I know you haven't spoken to Petey since he helped Cheryl shoot up the Roadhouse."

She shrugged. "I went back to say hi to Willard and saw Petey there. It's not easy for him, trying to come home after prison and make some kind of life for himself."

"It shouldn't be," Jim said with an edge to his voice. "Good boys aren't convicted of felonies." Elvis weighed in on "Jailhouse Rock."

Kate couldn't disagree with him, but she said again, "If I could find him a job, would you spring him?"

Jim growled. In sympathy, Mutt growled, too. It forced a chuckle out of him. He scratched behind her ears, an effective therapy for irritation caused by idiots. "I suppose so. Maybe. If the job was in another state." He looked at her. "You know, Kate, a smart judge once told me I could either be a cop or a social worker, but I couldn't be both."

"I'm not a cop," she said. It sounded pretty lame even to her own ears so she changed the subject. "So, who is the bigamist? Somebody from the mine, I take it?"

"After Mandy fired Howie, she needed someone pronto to mind the site, so she flew to Anchorage and hit Job Service."

"Oh god."

"Yeah, I know. She did check with me to see if the two guys she hired had records. They were clean, so far as I could tell without fingerprints. She put 'em to work caretaking the site, and kept them on after breakup when the drill rigs and the building modules and the crews and the rest of the outfit showed up. It's one of them. Baker by trade, so they put him to work in the kitchen when they went into operation. Name's Randy Randolph."

Kate laughed.

"Yeah, I know, kind of, what's the word? When something sounds like it means? Onomatopoeic?"

Kate cast her mind back to those ghastly days in seventh-grade English. "Homophonic, I think you mean."

"Yeah, whatever. Randy is Randy." Jim shook his head and drank more beer.

"What's he look like?" Kate said, curious. "Is he some kind of Greek god, or what?"

"I don't know. I haven't talked to him yet. I haven't even seen him yet. Listen, Kate."

"No," she said.

"All I want is for you to talk to him, get his statement."

"No," she said.

"Both Suzy and Bonnie had marriage certificates. Suzy's was in February and Bonnie's was in March. Randolph's name and signature on both. Didn't even change it. Guy's either gutsy or dumb, won't know which until somebody talks to him."

Kate reflected, covering the two loaf pans with Saran wrap and setting them in a warm corner to rise. "Mandy couldn't have hired him before December. He didn't waste any time."

"Nope. Come on, Kate, you have to go out to the mine anyway." He added craftily, "You can bill it as a separate investigation."

She heaved a martyr's sigh. "All right," she said, as they had both known she would. "I'll find him and talk to him for you. I'd like to see this Lothario for myself, anyway."

She came around the counter and sauntered toward him. He admired her while she did so. Yeah, maybe she didn't have the figure Laurel had, but when she wanted to, Kate could telegraph her intentions in a way that was little less than incitement to riot. Jim had watched plenty of women walk in his lifetime, both toward him and away, and he had never appreciated the amalgamation of brain and bone, muscle and flesh the way he did when it came wrapped in this particular package.

"Beat it," she said to Mutt.

Mutt flounced over to the fireplace, scratched the aunties' quilt into a pile, turned around three times, and curled up with her back most pointedly toward them.

Kate smiled down at Jim. Just like that, Jim got hard. And she knew it, he could tell by the deepening indentations at the corners of that wide, full-lipped mouth. "Jesus, woman," he said. If he wasn't flustered, it was as close as he ever got.

"What can I say," she said, "I have special powers." He was pulled to a sitting position with a fistful of shirt and she climbed aboard. She settled into the saddle and looped her arms around his neck, her eyes laughing down at him.

He could feel the heat of her through her clothes, through his, and he fairly wallowed in her scent, a combination of wood smoke, a faint tang of verbena from the soap she used, and today the yeasty smell of bread. "Jesus, woman," he said again, or mumbled it into her neck. The line of her scar brushed his cheek and he pulled back to trace it with his lips.

She shivered against him, her head falling back. "Possibly we should take this upstairs."

"Possibly we should." He was pulling her T-shirt free of her jeans.

"I mean before the kid comes out and catches us going at it on the couch."

"Yeah." Her breasts were firm and warm, the nipples hard against his palms.

"Might give him ideas."

"That'd be bad." He slid his hands down to her hips and pulled her tight against him. God, even through two pairs of jeans he could feel how ready she was for him.

She pulled back to look at him through her lashes. "And you know how much I hate being interrupted in my work."

"Me, too." He hooked an arm beneath her butt and got to his feet, and Mos Def serenaded them with "Destination Love" all the way up the stairs.

FIVE

JIM WENT WHISTLING OFF to work the following morning, the spring back in his step and the sparkle back in his eye. Kate tried not to sigh as she watched him go, escorted to his ride by his other love slave. Mutt stood and watched, abandoned in the clearing, tail slowing in sorrow as the Blazer drove into the trees and out of sight.

He was such a cliché, tall, blond, blue-eyed, broad of shoulder, narrow of hip, a real California boy. You expected him to get out the surfboard any minute, if not for the blue-and-gold uniform and the ball cap with the seal of the Alaska Department of Public Safety on it. And the gun on one side, the bear spray on the other, and the handcuffs tucked into the back of his belt. Not to mention the indefinable air of authority, the confident, easy stride, the quick reflexes at need, the sudden, unexpected strength of body and mind.

The seductive smile that was a weapon all on its own.

No, her own sense of well-being could not be denied, now could it. She laughed a little at herself. Was that all it took, a little "How was your day, dear?" and some great sex? They hadn't even bothered to come back downstairs for dinner. Jim had made them an enormous breakfast, eggs, chicken-fried caribou steak, gravy, and most of one of her loaves of bread, which had risen to alarming heights by morning, baked quickly in a hot oven, sliced too soon, toasted and slathered with butter. Nectar and ambrosia, he'd said. Manna from heaven, she'd said. Oho, so I'm heaven, am I? he'd said, and the food cooled on its plates while he demonstrated.

"So, did the earth move?" Johnny said next to her, making her jump.

She laughed but she blushed a little, too. "None of your business."

He mock grumbled around the kitchen. "Didn't even get any dinner last night. I'm a growing boy, I'm starving, do I have to stay starved?"

She opened the oven and pulled out a full plate that had been keeping warm against this moment. "I'll make you some toast while you get started on this."

"That's more like it." He carried the plate to the table and dug in.

They cleaned up, got dressed, and headed for town. Kate dropped Johnny at the school, one week to go before summer vacation. He hesitated with his hand on the open door. "So, we can apply for the job?"

She nodded.

"And you'll tell Old Sam?"

"No. You'll do that yourself."

"Dang," he said. "Worth a try."

"Would have thought less of you if you hadn't," she said. "Later."

THE CHUGACH AIR TAXI hangar itself hadn't changed at all. It was the activity in and around it that made the scene look like a stop-motion video by Dinah Clark.

The hangar, a square box two stories high, had a much smaller box attached to its front right corner. A black, hand-lettered sign on a white background read OFFICE over the door of the small box, and on the wall of the big box overhead a larger, fading sign, CHUGACH AIR TAXI SERVICE, INC.

The hangar doors were open, revealing not the familiar Cessna 206 nor the equally familiar Piper Super Cub but instead a de Havilland Single Otter. Kate looked closer. No, her eyes did not deceive her, it was in fact a turbo.

Nearby, a de Havilland Beaver on wheels was warming up, with a pilot she'd never met giving her the once-over through the wind-shield. From where she stood, it looked like every seat was full.

She went into the hangar and found George, tall, skinny, shovel-shaped unshaven jaw, lank dark hair thinning out on top. He still looked like George in oil-stained striped overalls and a greasy pair of Sorels. What didn't look like George was the rectangular piece of electronic equipment sprouting from his right ear. It bristled with knobs and dials and extruded an antenna from one end.

"Yeah," he said into it, "yeah, I know, but I need you now. Whatever they're paying you, I'll double it, just get here tomorrow." Mutt trotted forward and shoved her head beneath his free hand. He looked down, saw her, and then looked around for Kate. "Okay? Good. I'll see you on Thursday. Gotta go." He pressed a button. "Hey, Mutt." A rough scratch behind the ears had Mutt's tail wagging. "Hey, Kate."

"Hey, George." She nodded at the device. "Is that a satellite phone?"

He looked at it, too. "Yeah." His expression was somewhere between proud and sheepish.

She raised her eyebrows. "Just like downtown."

"Listen, Kate," he said, "I'm glad you're here. I need to talk to you about something."

"What?"

"We need cell phone service in the Park."

"You been talking to Dan O'Brian?"

"Who? No, I been talking to everyone, and we're all saying the same thing."

Kate had a cell phone. She'd bought one in Anchorage a couple of years before. It worked in Anchorage. It didn't work in the Park. She tried to remember when she'd seen it last, and came up blank. "I'm sure that as soon as AT&T figures out how to make a cell phone system pay for itself in the Park, they'll be knocking at the door."

"They are knocking," he said. "Didn't Demetri tell you?"

"No." Other than the quick glimpse she'd caught at the café the day before, she hadn't seen much of Demetri lately, and never long enough for serious talk. This time of year he was usually up at his lodge in the Quilak foothills, getting ready for the summer influx of fly-in trophy fishermen. She wondered, not for the first time, what the lodge was pulling down every year. Demetri had had some big names up there, names even Kate, lacking satellite television and Internet access, recognized, including movie stars, rock bands, business moguls, European royalty, Silicon Valley entrepreneurs, and those among the rich and famous whose main purpose in life seemed to be getting on the covers of *Us* and *People*. Clients in those zip codes didn't go anywhere on the cheap.

George flapped his hand in front of her face. "Hello? Anybody in there? ACS Alaska told Demetri that they're working on a plan to put a cell tower in every village along the river from Ahtna down to Chulyin, and from there hopscotch them overland to the mine." He held up his sat phone. "I can't keep up with the business on this thing, Kate, everybody I need to keep in touch with has a cell phone."

Behind them the Beaver roared down the runway and lifted ponderously into the air, on a heading south-southeast.

A four-wheeler with a tow hitch was pulling the Otter out of the hangar. She had seen neither four-wheeler nor driver before. "Impressive."

"You have no idea," he said. "Can't hardly find Otters anymore, single or twin. Everybody's got them working, there just ain't any for sale. I had to fly to fucking Finland in February to find this one."

"Finland?" Kate said.

"Well, actually, Cameroon."

"Cameroon?" Kate said.

"Well, by way of Paris," George said, and spoiled his deprecating tone with a wide grin.

"George," Kate said, "what the hell have you been up to?"

"No," he said, in a manner that could only be described as coy, "that should be, 'George, where the hell have you been?' And the answer is almost all the way around the world." He grinned again. "And in a hell of a lot less than eighty days."

"I didn't even know you'd been gone."

"I was only gone a week, in February, just long enough to track this puppy down and arrange for it to be brought back."

"Is it a turbo?"

"Yup." He didn't bother hiding his pride. "Came home by way of the shop in Vancouver."

"Going turbo, isn't that kind of expensive?"

"It sure as hell is," he said. "It's run me a million and a quarter so far."

"I didn't know you had that kind of cash."

"I don't. I got a loan."

"Global Harvest?" she said, not really guessing.

He looked a little furtive, and then decided to confess

straight up. "Yeah. Mandy said they want to buy and hire local as much as they can, so I went into Anchorage to talk to Bruce."

"Bruce O'Malley?"

He nodded, looking almost happy, something of a triumph for a guy whose natural gloom rivaled Abraham Lincoln's.

Bruce O'Malley was the chief executive officer of Global Harvest Resources Inc. In January, with much fanfare, he'd bought a building in downtown Anchorage and opened what would, he claimed, be the headquarters of the Suulutaq Mine. "The buck doesn't go to Houston," he said, beaming at the television cameras, which clip Kate had viewed on YouTube on Bobby's computer. "It stops right here in Anchorage, Alaska." He'd moved his family to Anchorage, too, enrolled the kids in local public schools, and it was rumored that he was about to declare his intention of becoming an Alaskan citizen, to the extent that he was even going to turn in his Texas driver's license in exchange for an Alaskan one.

"At least GHRI is putting their money where their mouth is," Kate said. She was aware even as she spoke that she was damning with faint praise.

"It's been a godsend, Kate," George said, and he was dead serious now. "As you well know, the population in the Park has dropped every year for the past five years. For a while there I was scared I was going to lose the mail contract, because the volume of mail was dropping like a rock right along with the population."

Alaska, because of the remote location of so many of its communities, lived and died by air mail. The U.S. mail contracts were all too often what kept the wolf from the Alaska air taxi door.

"You know how the Postal Service likes to contract for

larger aircraft because they get a lower rate for bypass mail. I was really sweating out the last negotiations, I thought for sure they'd award the contract to Bill Taggart at Ahtna Aviation because he runs Caravans. And then they discovered the gold."

"And O'Malley rode in like a white knight."

He met her eyes without flinching. "Pretty much. I'm self-employed, Kate, just like you. I don't have health insurance and I'm not Native, so if I get sick I lay down and die. I don't have a retirement plan, so about all I have to count on is Social Security, which is a joke."

This was inarguable and they both knew it. "We should have gotten jobs with the state," she said.

He snorted out a laugh. "Yeah, right, like anyone in Juneau in their right mind would hire us to put out the trash."

" 'Anyone in Juneau in their right mind' is an oxymoron anyway."

"Or just a moron," they both said together, and laughed. A safe moment to change the subject. "Got something going out to Suulutaq?"

He looked at the Beaver on the horizon. "You just missed it. Gold shift crew change." He nodded at the Otter. "Blue shift is headed for town."

Indeed, the young men waiting to board the Otter looked thirsty and horny. She saw a Kvasnikof and a couple of Moonins in the bunch who until now had been able to afford the trip into town only when they settled up with the fish processors at the end of the salmon season. She didn't even want to think about the kind of trouble they could get into going into town twice a month year round with money in their pockets.

A man in a flight jacket, someone else Kate had never met,

came up to George with a clipboard. George scanned, nodded and signed, and handed it back. They both watched him trot out to the Otter and climb into the pilot's seat, and the engine begin to whine.

"Well, hell," Kate said. "I need a ride out to Suulutaq. Jim needs me to talk to some people out there."

"Well, hell," George said with another grin—it seemed to be his expression of choice nowadays—"if it's on the state's dime I'll fire up the Cessna and take you out myself. They got good Danish in the mess hall."

"Where's the Super Cub?"

"I sold it."

George disappeared into the office, leaving Kate gawping after him.

George Perry was a Bush pilot. Bush pilots didn't sell Super Cubs. They just didn't.

"You sold your Cub?" she said when he came outside again.

"Yeah, there's a guy in Ahtna who's been after it for years." He looked at Kate and registered her shock. "It didn't fit into what the business is becoming, Kate. What I'm looking for now is another Single Otter. Maybe two, with one of them dedicated full time to freight runs running direct between Anchorage and the mine."

"Jesus, George," she said, caught between respect and dismay. "Coming on pretty strong, aren't you?"

"The mine needs a lot of air support," he said, "and it's going to need a lot more, especially since you won't let them build a road. Okay by me," he said, waving off her inarticulate protest, "but if I can't supply said air support, they'll go looking for someone who can. I can't serve both the mine and the Park on the equipment I have. I got a chance for the big time here, Kate, and I'm going for it."

She digested this while he preflighted the 206, parked in the weeds on the other side of the hangar from the office. Sitting there in the shadow of the building, the Cessna looked a little forlorn, if not downright unloved, and seemed to perk up at being called back into service. George waved Kate over and they climbed in, Mutt jumping into the back, which had been stripped of its other four seats. She sat with her head between the two humans, ears pricked forward in anticipation. The Cessna started at once and without further ado George rolled out onto the runway and lifted into the air. Half an hour later they were touching down at the Suulutaq Mine.

Kate had been to Suulutaq the previous winter, when it was the scene of a homicide involving a couple of Park rats. At that time, it had been covered by twenty feet of snow, which had almost buried the white ATCO trailer with the gold stripe around the edge of the roof. There had been a couple of other outbuildings that only just qualified as sheds, and an orange wind sock on a pole sitting at the end of which, if you looked hard, you could see the faintest simulacrum of an airstrip outlined on the surface of the snow.

This insignificant little outpost had been dwarfed first by the high, wide valley in which it squatted, and second by the Quilak Mountains, two rocky, out-flung arms of which embraced the valley and which permitted only the narrowest possible opening in a pass to the west that tumbled down a precipitous slope leading to the eastern edge of the Kanuyaq River. This remote location was accessible in winter by snow machine and in summer by four-wheeler and year-round by airplane, so long as said airplane was equipped with tundra tires. There was no road.

And there wouldn't be, Kate thought now, looking down

as George made a slow right bank over the now almost unrecognizable location. Not if she, as chair (interim) of the Niniltna Native Association, had anything to say about it. Dan and George were both right about that, even if she'd never say so out loud.

Last winter the camp had been virtually deserted, the lone employee on site a caretaker, whose isolation was alleviated only when his week was up and the alternate caretaker arrived for his shift. Or when someone was poaching game at the head of the valley, where the Gruening River caribou herd wintered.

Now the snow had retreated to the tops of the mountains, and the mine site was a sea of mud surrounding seven prefab modular buildings and an assortment of heavy equipment ranging from what Kate supposed was the infamous John Deere grader to Caterpillar tractors in two sizes, a backhoe loader, a crane truck, and a couple of forklifts. Some were digging holes in the newly thawed ground. Others were smoothing rudimentary tracks to connect the buildings, airstrip, and drilling rigs. Some were shifting cargo stacked on pallets at the end of the runway to one of the buildings below. All were in operation.

Kate looked for a fuel dump and found it, a heap of 150,000-gallon fuel bladders that must have been brought in by sling via helicopter. The bladders were surrounded by a Ready Berm, and a drive-through berm was inflated nearby, where a dump truck was being fueled with a collapsible hose connected to a fuel pump connected to one of the bladders.

"Where they getting their electricity?" Kate said into her mike.

"Oil-powered generators for now," George said, the static making his voice sound as raspy as hers, "but they're looking into wind and solar and hydro. One of the engineers told me it'll probably be a combination of all three. And they found a low-sulphur coal deposit up the valley, they'll probably rope that in, too."

"Gravel?" They'd need a lot of gravel for roads and pads for building sites. The production life of the Suulutaq Mine was projected at twenty years. Twenty-year-old buildings in Alaska were regarded as permanent, if not downright historic.

He pointed at a notch in one wall of the valley. "They found all they need in a creek bed thataway."

"They keeping to leased property? Not encroaching on Iqaluk?"

He looked at her, one eyebrow raised. "Do you really think they'd screw around this early in the game?"

"I think nobody's watching them very close yet," Kate said, "and I think they'll try to get away with as much as they can before anybody is."

Scattered around the valley at various distances from the camp were five drill rigs. All five were active, the crown and traveling blocks and drill lines visible and in motion through the network of the derricks.

George made another circle. The Beaver was just lifting off the end of the runway for the return trip back to Niniltna. "Seen enough?"

Kate nodded, and George brought them into a neat three-point landing on the rudimentary gravel airstrip that had been bladed when the snowpack melted, which, along with everything else, had cost GHRI a whale of a lot of money.

But at eight hundred dollars, no, Kate corrected herself, now more than nine hundred an ounce, they could afford it. Recessions always drove people toward gold and stocks in gold mining companies. It was the commodity that never failed.

And Alaska had more of it than almost anyone else in the world, and the Suulutaq Mine had more of it than any other mine in Alaska.

They got out of the Cessna, Mutt trotting ahead to baptize a compactor, which appeared to be the single piece of heavy equipment within ten miles that wasn't at present in motion. Kate and George walked toward the edge of the small rise that supported the airstrip, where they paused for a moment to look down at the camp. There were five small modulars and two large, arranged in two rows. Doors were connected by rudimentary wooden boardwalks, Kate would bet at the insistence of the people who had to mop the floors.

They followed the road down the side of the rise. The mud was beginning to dry out under the influence of the increasing strength of the sun, but it still sucked at their feet as they dodged heavy equipment to the entrance of the office building. There was a bull rail with electrical plug-ins out front with a pickup and a van nosed up to it. Placed conspicuously over a generously sized set of double doors was a large and colorful rendition of the Global Harvest sunrise-over-the-Quilaks logo. It was, Kate had to admit, very attractive.

George pointed at the doors. "That's the admin offices. I'll be in the mess hall." He pointed again. "The big building in the back. Come get me when you're ready to go."

He vanished around a corner. Kate pushed one of the doors open and she and Mutt walked into a large room that took up most of the first floor of the building. There were desks interspersed with long flat gray folding tables. The walls were lined with four-drawer beige-enameled metal filing cabinets. A 1:10,000-scale map of Suulutaq dominated one wall, with a much smaller map of the Park tacked onto a corner, and a map of Alaska the size of a hardback book pinned as an afterthought to one side.

A young woman, dark and plump and of Yupik descent if Kate was going to make a guess, was typing something into a computer. She looked up, exchanged glances with Mutt, and said with superb unconcern, "May I help you?"

"Yes," Kate said. "My name is Kate Shugak. I—"

"Yes, Ms. Shugak, just one moment, please." The young woman abdicated her desk with no undue haste and made a beeline for one of the tables, where a man and a woman Kate saw was Holly Haynes were hunched over a long strip of paper marked with a continuous, spiking graph. The young woman murmured into the man's ear, and all three looked across at Kate. He evidently found her attire—the usual blue jeans, sweatshirt, jacket, and sneakers—and perhaps her lack of entourage less than convincing. He looked back at the young woman for confirmation. She nodded.

Holly Haynes said something. He straightened with a nearly audible snap of his spine and made brisk work of the office maze to arrive in front of Kate, where he could beam down at her with what she could not help but read as tremendous insincerity. "Ms. Shugak! I've heard a lot about you, it's so nice to meet you in person!"

Kate repressed the urge to step back from both the volubility and the slight spray of his greeting and recovered her hand before he broke any more bones in it. "Thank you. And you are?"

He gave out with a laugh that seemed to her even less sincere than his demeanor. "Of course, of course, what was I thinking. I'm Vernon Truax, Suulutaq superintendent. Come on, let's head on up to my office. Whoa," he said, noticing Mutt for the first time. "That your wolf?"

"Only half," Kate said.

Truax, regarding Mutt with a healthy mixture of alarm and respect, said, "Only half? Well, that's okay, then." It sounded more like a question than an assertion. Either way, Kate didn't answer. "Uh, Holly, join us? Thanks, Lyda."

The plump young woman resumed her station at the desk near the door. Haynes abandoned the strip of graph paper they'd been poring over to follow Truax, Kate, and Mutt upstairs to a corner room that, however prebuilt it looked, still had two large windows facing south and west. Executive offices were the same whether they were in Suulutaq or on Ninth Avenue in Anchorage.

"Kate Shugak, Holly Haynes."

"We met in town yesterday," Haynes said, amused. "I told you about it at dinner last night."

Truax didn't like the reminder. "Of course, of course. Well, Kate Shugak." He said it like he was referring to one of the faces on Mount Rushmore. Kate was afraid for a moment he might bow, or maybe even genuflect.

"She's the chairwoman of the board of the Niniltna Native Association," Truax said, like nobody in the room knew that, "and I don't have to tell you how important it is that we give them every access to our work here." Like nobody in the room knew that, either.

This instant recognition and the subsequent bootlicking were not going to be an asset in her day job. It had been foolish of Kate not to have expected it, and she realized now that it was something to which she would have to give some serious thought.

An entire way of life seemed to be vanishing right before her eyes, and she had to put a sharp brake on the rising melancholy that recognition cost her.

"Sit, sit," Truax said, and instead of taking the seat at his desk pulled up a third straight chair to form a circle in front of it. She had to admire his instincts for currying favor. He was certainly better at it than she was. "Can we get you anything? Coffee, tea, water, soft drink? No?"

Vernon Truax was a thickset man in his late forties, with a broad, ruddy face and large, scarred hands. He was balding and while eschewing the ever popular comb-over he did wear his remaining hair in a thick fringe, probably in an attempt to hide the batwing ears that stuck out from his head at almost ninety-degree angles. He wore Carhartts that had seen honest sweat and hard labor. Kate had done her homework, as Jim's agent and as Association chair, and she was familiar with Truax's background. Degree from the Colorado School of Mines. Mining engineer twenty years in the field, the first six for Rio Tinto and the last fourteen for Global Harvest. No nonsense, bit of a temper, thought well of by his bosses, respected but not feared by his employees. The Suulutaq wasn't his first mine. For that alone Kate was inclined to forgive much.

Truax was waxing fulsome on the storied partnership between the mine and the Niniltna Native Association and when he got to the hands-across-the-Park refrain Mutt, perhaps sensing that Kate's patience was beginning to fray, gave a vigorous sneeze that had just enough snarl in it to put a momentary stop to the apparently inexhaustible flow. Kate used the opportunity to interrupt Truax with a charming smile that begged forgiveness for her rudeness, partnered with the indefinable but nonetheless distinct impression that told him she didn't give a damn if he was offended or not. "Mr. Truax—"

"Vern, please. And I hope I may call you Kate?"

"Of course," Kate said. "Vern, I have to apologize for not making this clear from the get-go." Not that he'd given her the opportunity. "In fact I am not here in my capacity as board chair of NNA. I'm here to make inquiries after one of your employees. Well, two, actually, but I'd like to start with a Dewayne Gammons."

Truax exchanged a glance with Haynes, who raised her brows and shrugged. "Oh. I see. May I ask why?"

"Sergeant Chopin, the Alaska State Trooper stationed in Niniltna, hired me to."

"I see." But clearly Truax did not see. "I spoke to Sergeant Chopin yesterday on the sat phone as regards this matter, and Holly here told me that he'd said he would be sending someone out. I naturally assumed it would be another trooper."

"There isn't another trooper assigned to Niniltna," Kate said. "I am a licensed private investigator. The state frequently hires me to assist the troopers in those cases that might not be, shall we say, front burner."

"Oh," Truax said after a beat. "I see." He exchanged another glance with Haynes, and then rose to his feet and went around to sit at his desk.

Kate appreciated the signal. She even got up and moved the chair in which he had been sitting to one side and readjusted her own chair so that they could see eye to eye across his desk. Mutt reacquired her spot at Kate's right hand, maintaining her Muttly sang-froid. Haynes was wearing a poker face, she might have been alarmed, aghast, amused, or all three at Kate's effrontery. She exchanged a glance with Truax, and there was a quality of intimacy there that made Kate wonder at the closeness of their association. It could be merely that they were longtime coworkers. Which would not necessarily preclude a romantic relationship. She looked from one to the other from beneath lowered lids. Truax was wearing a wedding ring. Haynes was not.

"About Mr. Gammons," Kate said. "He does work here?"

"He does," Truax said. "Or he did."

"Did?"

"He hasn't shown up for work in, hell, a month?" Truax buzzed his intercom. "Lyda?"

"Yes, Vern?"

"Bring up Dewayne Gammons's personnel file, would you?"

A brief pause.

"Lyda? Did you get that? Root out Dewayne Gammons's personnel file and bring it up to my office pronto."

"Right away, Vern," Lyda said.

Her voice over the speaker sounded different this time, hesitant, maybe even a little fearful? A few moments later the dark, plump young woman appeared in Truax's doorway, manila file folder in hand. Kate watched her as she walked across the room and wondered if she was always that pale.

"Kate, this is Lyda Blue, everybody's right hand around here. She and I have worked a couple of Global digs together. Lyda, this is Kate Shugak, the chair of the board of the Niniltna Native Association and someone to whom we want to give every facility, you understand?"

Lyda gave Kate a long, unsmiling glance. "Yes, Vern."

"Lyda is from Bering," Vern said, like he was expecting Kate to pin a medal on him for hiring local. He took the folder from Lyda and gave it to Kate without looking at it.

She accepted it without opening it. "You say Mr. Gammons hasn't shown up for work in how long?"

Vern looked at Lyda. Lyda said, "Almost a month." She nodded at the file. "It's all in there. Date hired, last day on the clock, date terminated."

"Did you know him, Ms. Blue?" Kate said.

"I know all the employees at Suulutaq, Ms. Shugak."

"Did you know Mr. Gammons well?"

"No better than any of the other employees."

Kate wasn't so sure. She'd caught a glimpse of an almost imperceptible falter in the bland smile, but she wasn't going to pursue it here, in front of Lyda's employers. "Thank you, Ms. Blue."

"Thanks, Lyda," Truax said. He waited until the door closed behind her, and looked at Kate.

"Sergeant Chopin will have told you that Gammons's truck has been found about halfway between Niniltna and Park headquarters," Kate said. "And that a search party found a body not far from there."

Truax tried to look concerned. "Is it Gammons?"

"Sergeant Chopin has sent the body to the medical examiner in Anchorage for identification."

"How did he die?" Haynes said, speaking for the first time.

"Again, details will have to wait on the findings of the medical examiner." Kate opened the file and gave the contents a brief glance. She looked up and said, "I see he worked in Stores. Would it be possible for me to talk to his coworkers?"

"Certainly," Truax said. "But didn't you say you had questions about two of our employees, Kate?"

"I did," Kate said, and this time allowed her face to relax into a rueful smile. "The second case isn't quite so, ah, grim. Evidently, one of your employees has married into the Park."

Truax smiled in return. It was a rather attractive smile when he wasn't forcing it, good teeth, hints of dimples on both sides, and it reached his eyes. "Nothing I can do about that, Kate. I make it a policy never to interfere in the private lives of people who work for me, so long as their private lives don't interfere with their work. Can't say I object to Suulutaq

103

workers forging closer ties with NNA shareholders and people who live in the Park, either."

"Twice," Kate said.

"I'm sorry?" Truax said.

"He married into the Park twice," Kate said. "Twice within the last five months."

There was a pause. "I'm guessing," Truax said, "that the second time was without benefit of divorce from the first wife?"

"It was," Kate said.

Truax sighed and looked at the ceiling for inspiration. "Well, Kate, you want me to fire him? Wait a minute, before I fire anyone, who is it?"

"Randy Randolph."

"Randy Randolph?" Haynes said.

"Yes," Kate said.

"Randy Randolph?" Truax said, sitting straight up in his chair. "My baker?"

"I'm afraid so," Kate said.

Truax was incredulous and not afraid to show it. "Randy Randolph married twice over the last five months? Are you sure?"

"It's who you are writing the paycheck in question to," Kate said. "What's the problem?"

"No problem," Truax said, "it's just—" There was a look of restrained hilarity on his face that made Kate curious and a little wary. Haynes, too, looked amused. He leaned over the intercom again. "Lyda, is Randy Randolph on shift yet?"

It took her a few moments, probably to look up the work schedule. "Yes, Vern."

"Thanks." Truax leaned back. "Holly, would you like to take Ms. Shugak around?"

Kate rose to her feet. "I appreciate that, but there's no need. It's not that big a camp. I'm sure I can find my way."

Truax's alarm at the prospect of Kate Shugak, Ace Detective, wandering around his mine without a keeper warred with his desire to assure Kate Shugak, chair of the board of directors of the Niniltna Native Association, that Global Harvest Resources Inc. had absolutely nothing to hide at the Suulutaq Mine. It took him a moment to reconcile these two viewpoints, during which Kate and Mutt had slipped out the door.

SIX

LYDA WAS BACK AT her desk. "Vern asked if you would show me around the mine, Ms. Blue," Kate said. "I hope you don't mind."

Mendacity was just one more service Kate offered. And she wanted to create an opportunity to speak with Lyda Blue alone.

Mutt's head popped over the top of the desk. She and Lyda examined each other again. "Wolf?" Lyda said.

"Half," Kate said.

Neither was unconscious of conversations dying natural deaths all around the large room as people took in the couple standing in front of reception. Everyone thought Mutt outweighed Kate, and everyone was right. Everyone worried over the possibility that Kate didn't control Mutt, and everyone was wrong. Mostly. Everyone was also acquiring a line of sight to the nearest window or door in the event of any emergency of a lupine kind.

Lyda nodded, unsurprised and unalarmed. If she really was from Bering, she wouldn't be either. "Vern is my boss, Ms. Shugak. What he says goes. What would you like to see first?"

"Are Dewayne Gammons's belongings still here at the mine?"

Lyda Blue hesitated for a moment too long, and knew it. "Yes," she said. "I—we didn't know where he'd gone, and he didn't fill in the next-of-kin blank on his employee form so we didn't have anyone to send them to. I didn't want to just throw them out."

"May I see them, please?"

Lyda Blue led her to one of the modular bunkhouses, the equivalent of a wide, single-story trailer with rooms on both sides, a communal bathroom at one end, and a TV lounge at the other. Lyda opened the door to a room next to the lounge, which was cleared of furniture to do duty for storage. It was about three-quarters full of haphazardly stacked cleaning supplies. Tucked next to a crooked tower of forty-eight-roll packages of toilet paper was a large six-shelf unit made of heavy, chrome-plated steel, bolted together by an inexpert hand that had left all the shelves enough out of true to be noticeable but not enough to have everything on them on the floor unless the next earthquake was a big one. The shelves were jammed with what looked like personal gear, duffels, stuff sacks, daypacks, a couple of suitcases. "This is all Gammons's stuff?" Kate said.

"No. Only this." Lyda pulled down a canvas duffel and an Eddie Bauer daypack without checking the tags.

"This all?" A nod. Kate looked back at the shelves. "Who does the rest of it belong to?"

"Wayne Gammons isn't the only employee to walk off the job at Suulutaq, Ms. Shugak," Lyda said.

"You haven't been in business out here for even a year," Kate said.

"Some guys don't last a week," Lyda said. "Maybe they miss their wives or their girlfriends. Maybe they don't like the isolation. Maybe they don't like the no drugs or booze policy. Maybe they're just pissed off they have to share the remote in the TV room."

"You'd think hauling their stuff out with them wouldn't take that much extra effort."

"They know they're coming out to the back of beyond when they take the job, and that they'll be bunking in with a bunch of strangers. Chances are they've been on jobs like this before and they're aware of what sometimes happens to personal possessions in communal living, so it's not like they've brought their most treasured belongings with them in the first place. They know Vern is going to be angry at wasting employee orientation and training on them. They're probably afraid that if they say they're quitting he'll make them walk back to Anchorage. So they leave their stuff so as not to draw attention that their last plane ride is one-way." Lyda looked down at the bags. "What do you want to do with these?"

"Is there somewhere we can take them so I can look at what's in them? A table would be good."

Still silent, Lyda Blue led her to a small vacant office at the back of the main office building, furnished only with a rectangular folding table. There was no window and the only light was a single fluorescent tube dangling from a wire in the center of the ceiling, to the imminent danger of anyone walking beneath it. The room was cold, too, and on the wall next to the door Kate spotted a bundle of wires where a thermostat might one day go. Mutt cast a disparaging eye around the space and took a seat next to the door. It was warmer outside.

Kate moved the table so that the dangling fluorescent tube hung over it and heaved the bags up. Lyda Blue lingered by the door. "Is there anything else?"

"There will be," Kate said, "but in the meantime why don't you help me unpack his bags. Don't close the door."

Lyda, who had been about to do so, said, "Why not?"

"She won't like it."

Lyda looked down at Mutt, who was watching her with a narrow yellow stare.

"Just leave it open a crack. You packed these bags, didn't you?"

"How did you know that?"

Kate shrugged. "Just a guess. You seem to be Vern's first call for everything."

Lyda hesitated for a moment longer, and then came to stand across the table. Kate didn't look up, pulling at the strap on the duffel and spreading its contents across the table. Three pairs of jeans, half a dozen shirts, jockey shorts, long underwear, wool socks, all well worn but nothing in rags. A pair of flip-flops. An electric razor, a toothbrush, toothpaste, a tube of generic shampoo, a stick of equally generic deodorant, a can of shaving cream. "How well did you know Dewayne Gammons, Lyda?"

Lyda's eyes widened. In the harsh light of the single bulb her face looked leached of all color.

In the daypack was an envelope filled with pay stubs, a checkbook with an account at the Last Frontier Bank in Ahtna showing fourteen grand to the good, and a book. Kate read the title out loud. "*The Portable Nietzsche*?" She put the book down. "At least he read." She looked up.

A tear had traced its way down Lyda Blue's cheek. "He does read," she said. "You don't know for sure yet whose body that was."

"No," Kate said, her voice as gentle as the scar on her throat would allow. "I don't. How well did you know him, Lyda?"

"How did you know?"

"You called him Wayne," Kate said.

Lyda reached up to touch her cheek and seemed surprised

to find the tear. She wiped it away, not bothering much about her mascara. "I—we met when he was first hired. He drove up from Washington State with some of the other guys looking for work. He told me they'd heard the news about Global Harvest hiring and decided to share expenses on the trip north."

"Who came with him?"

Lyda shrugged. "I remember one of them quit before Wayne did. I don't remember his name. I can probably look it up for you." She bit her lip. If the body was Dewayne Gammons, he hadn't quit. Lyda raised her chin and made an obvious effort to keep her voice steady. "Everybody's hired through the office in Anchorage and they go through their orientation there, but I process all the paperwork, get them set up with their payroll taxes and stuff, give them their room assignments, so I'm usually the first person at the mine all the employees meet. And then, you know, we all eat together in the mess hall, and play pool or foosball together in one of the lounges. We're just starting up here, so it's only week on, week off, and we're still in the early stages of exploration so the crew is still small. People tend to make friends fast."

"So you and Wayne made friends."

Lyda nodded, sniffled, and pulled a Kleenex from her pocket. She hunted in vain for a clean spot and settled for one grubby corner that nearly disintegrated under the onslaught. "He saw that I was Native, and he was curious." She looked at Kate. "You know. In a nice way."

"I know," Kate said. "Were you more than friends?"

Lyda shook her head. "No. We hadn't even met off the site."

The "yet" was unspoken but implied.

Kate hesitated. "What was his attitude before he

110

disappeared? Was he happy? Sad? Frightened? Excited?"

Lyda looked around for a trash can, didn't find one, and pocketed the very used Kleenex instead. "He told me he suffered from depression."

"Did he say he'd been diagnosed? Did he mention a doctor?"

"He didn't believe in doctors," Lyda said. "And he would never have checked himself into a hospital. He said that's where people go to die, and that when he died he wanted to be outside, in the fresh air."

Kate pulled out a piece of paper, unfolded it, and handed it to Lyda. "That's a copy of the note that was found taped to the wheel of Wayne's pickup."

Lyda read it. It took her a lot longer than it should have, as if she was reading it over and over again.

"Is that Wayne's handwriting, Lyda?"

"I—I don't know. It's just printing, isn't it. Anybody could have written that." Her hand dropped and she stared over Kate's shoulder with blank eyes, the note fluttering to the floor.

Kate stooped to pick it up. "Did he have any other friends here in camp?"

"No. Not really."

"You remember any of the other guys he drove up with?"

Lyda shrugged. It wasn't an answer but Kate let it pass for now. "Any other friends?"

"Maybe the people he worked with. On jobs like this people who work in the same department tend to hang out together, eat meals together, watch TV together. He didn't talk about anyone in particular." She sighed. "But then it was like pulling teeth to get him to talk about himself anyway. He wanted to know about me." Her lip trembled. "First time I ever met a guy who asked me questions about myself, and actually listened to the answers. You know?"

Kate was a woman. She knew.

"The thing is, he seemed to be cheering up a little, the longer he was here. At first he wouldn't talk at all about the future, but lately we'd been talking about traveling somewhere together on our week off. Seattle, maybe, or Hawaii."

Kate frowned. That certainly didn't square with the note on the steering wheel, but then suicides weren't famous for thinking linearly. "Why did you pretend not to know him?"

Lyda picked at a hangnail. "Pretty obvious I didn't know him. I sure didn't know he was going to walk out into the woods so he could lay down and die." She glanced up at Kate. "Even the elders don't do that anymore."

Kate persisted. "But you didn't want me to know you were friends. Why not?"

Lyda looked out the window of that stark, bare little room and sighed. "I don't know. Before, we were just getting to know each other. A small camp like this is such a hothouse, there's nothing to do except gossip about what everyone else is doing. I've made that mistake before. I didn't want to make it again, so we didn't spend time alone where other people could see." She was silent for a moment. "Now, if he really did this ... I don't think I want anyone to know that I could be friends with such a—"

"Such a what?"

She turned her head and Kate was surprised to see the beginnings of anger in the other woman's eyes. "Such a loser."

For the moment, Kate was silenced.

They repacked the duffel and the daypack and returned them to the storage room. Lyda had recovered most of her self-possession, although now and then she would take in a deep breath, blink hard, and let it out on a long, slow exhale. "What did you want to see next, Ms. Shugak?"

"It's Kate, Lyda. Is it possible to see his room?"

Lyda nodded. "It's still empty."

"Empty" didn't come close to describing it. It had been scoured clean of personality, not so much as a pinup of Britney Spears left on the walls.

The only thing that looked out of place was a flyer on the desk, a professionally produced glossy trifold leaflet with a circular logo on the facing page of a robed woman holding a globe. Kate opened it and bolded phrases leaped out at her: "growth mania," "conspicuous consumption," "Silent Spring," "Ban the Bomb," "Group of 10." There was a membership form, with a space for the amount of the applicant's donation. Kate flipped back to the leaflet's facing page. "Gaea," she said. "The onshore Greenpeace, the poor man's Environmental Defense Fund. We've been seeing these all over the Park. This Gaea group sure doesn't like your mine." She looked at Lyda. "Was your Wayne a closet greenie? Or maybe he was undercover for the opposition."

It had been meant as a joke but Lyda snatched up the flyer, her cheeks flushing. "There are always naysayers," she said, toeing the corporate line with what appeared to be genuine conviction. "This kind of organization is a lot more anticorporate than Global Harvest is antienvironment. It will take two years for us to put together an environmental impact statement that is going to cost Global Harvest millions of dollars to write and millions more to implement. This Gaea is just a bunch of loud nuts who figure if they make enough noise they can get other nuts to write them checks."

"Okay," Kate said. "How about showing me where Wayne worked. Maybe I could meet some of the people he worked with."

They went out to the building on the end of the back row that was serving as the warehouse. It had been gutted down to a single large room, a wall-high sliding door cut in the side facing away from camp and a rough-and-ready dock with no railing and plenty of room between the twelve-by-twelves that formed its surface. Inside the door, an overturned wooden tote served as a counter, next to which hand trucks constantly appeared and disappeared as half a dozen employees filled orders brought to the dock by other employees in pickups and on forklifts and some who just walked up in filthy coveralls, hard hats, and Xtra Tuff boots.

They were all men and while it would be unfair to say that conversation ceased abruptly when Kate and Lyda appeared on the scene, all eyes were definitely upon them as they advanced up the steps to the dock and across the floor to the tote counter. "Hi, P.J.," Lyda said. "This is Kate Shugak. Kate, this is P.J. Bourne. He was Wayne's supervisor."

"P.J.," Kate said.

"Kate," P.J. said. He was middle-aged and rotund without being soft, unshaven and not very clean. His near-together eyes were as dark as his hair, button-bright and narrowed in perpetual distrust, as if he suspected everyone he saw of having contraband duct-taped under their shirts. He wore Carhartt bibs over red flannel underwear and his cheek bulged with a wad of chewing tobacco. He spat often and without inhibition and the floor around the tote was stained a dark brown.

"They found Wayne's truck abandoned near Niniltna," Lyda said. "She wants to talk to the people he worked with."

P.J. glared at Lyda. "I don't fucking have time for this shit."

"Vern said to give her every facility," Lyda said. To her

114

credit, she did not appear intimidated.

P.J. glared at Kate. "Yeah, fuck me, Vern's not down here making sure fucking Rig 36 has enough fucking drill pipe to finish out the fucking day shift."

"Yeah, fuck me," Kate said, "like I don't have fucking anything better to do than fucking hare around after some fucking whiny little bastard who decided to fucking off himself in my fucking backyard."

Lyda sucked in a breath.

P.J. glared at Mutt, standing next to Kate, ears up. "I don't have fucking time for fucking wolves in the fucking warehouse, either."

Mutt lifted her lip to display a fine set of very large and very sharp teeth. Her growl and his sounded almost identical.

P.J. glared some more. Kate and Mutt glared right back. Standoff.

P.J. didn't go so far as to relax into a smile, but a discernible twinkle did appear in his near-together black eyes, albeit very far back, and no one would mistake it for goodwill. "Whaddya wanna know?" A forklift roared up and slid to a halt, barely missing a man in a hard hat who tripped and almost fell in his haste to get out of the way. "Harry, for fuck's sake try not to get yourself fucking run over on my fucking shift, all right? Fucking paperwork's a fucking killer on a fucking accident."

"What was he like?" Kate said. P.J.'s head whipped around and he glared at her. "Dewayne Gammons. What was he like on the job?"

"He fucking showed up on time, he fucking did what he was told. Until he fucking didn't." Harry handed P.J. a fistful of papers and P.J. snarled at him. Mutt, startled, snarled again in response, and everyone except Kate and P.J. took an involuntary step backward.

P.J. rustled through the papers. "Fucking Suulutaq Mine is fucking killing every fucking tree on the fucking planet." He consulted a laptop computer open on the tote, and hunted and pecked until another piece of paper spit out of the printer next to it. He checked a box, signed at the bottom, and shoved it at Harry, who took to his heels.

"Do you remember him saying anything, where he was going, maybe about how he was feeling, before he left work for the last time?"

The question sounded feeble even to Kate's ears, and P.J. let out a bark of laughter. "In case you ain't fucking noticed, this warehouse is responsible for supplying five fucking rigs a fucking camp and a hundred fucking employees working a fucking twenty-four-seven shift. We got no fucking time to stand fucking still, let alone go all Dr. fucking Phil."

"So, no, you don't remember him saying anything," Kate said.

"Fucking right no. He had a fucking pulse and a strong fucking back and he could carry a fucking box without fucking dropping it and push a fucking dolly without running it off the fucking dock." P.J. glared around the room. "Fucking anybody got fucking anything to fucking add?"

Nobody fucking did. It might have had something to do with the steady roar of the approaching Sikorsky helicopter, which deposited a container of freight on a pad a hundred feet from the dock, and waited just long enough for the ground crew to unhook the sling and the air crew to retract it into the helo before roaring off again in a westerly direction. Everyone flinched away from the dust produced by the rotor wash.

In the distance Kate heard the unmistakable drone of an approaching Herc, and saw that everyone on the loading dock heard it, too, probably before she had. "Thanks, P.J.," she said. "Appreciate the help. Gentlemen."

"Uh—," Lyda said as they were walking away, and then stopped when she saw the grin spreading across Kate's face.

Kate saw her expression and laughed. "Relax, Lyda. I've met P.J. before. Many times."

Lyda looked relieved. "Oh. Okay. Where next?"

"Randy Randolph."

Lyda looked surprised. "Why Randy?"

Kate explained.

"Oh," Lyda said again, and her own expression lightened for the first time that afternoon.

"What is so inherently comic in the thought of Randy Randolph?" Kate said.

"It's not Randy that's so funny," Lyda said. "It's the thought of Randy as a bigamist."

She led Kate to the mess hall at the rear of the camp and around to the back door, where there was a smaller version of the warehouse dock. Two pallets of dry goods were in the process of being torn down and the contents carried inside. Lyda and Kate dodged some fifty-pound sacks of enriched white flour on their way into the kitchen.

It was another large room that extended up into the second story of the prefab. Stainless-steel appliances and counters lined the walls, and a long gas grill and a gas-fired cooktop, with an immense stainless steel hood hanging over grill and cooktop, took up the center of the floor. Large pots steamed and knives crunched through vegetables and there was a pungent smell of garlic in the air. The four men and two women hard at work were dressed in white double-breasted jackets with mandarin collars, wrap-around white aprons tied in front, black-and-white checked pants, black nurse's shoes, and white paper cook's hats.

"Hey, Jules," Lyda said to the guy with the tallest hat.

He smiled at her, a wide, foolish, dazzled smile whose glow could have been seen in daylight from the moon. Jules, unlike P.J., had all the time in the world for Lyda, offering her a stool, apple slices layered with white cheddar, and a Diet Sprite, which Kate was given to understand was Lyda's favorite drink.

Jules was stumpy and thickset with swarthy skin and thick, untidy dark hair, but his eyes were large, brown, and liquid, and if one overlooked the spaghetti sauce and scrambled egg splatters across his broad white front and the sweat rolling down his square face, there was something rather attractive about the eager little man, with an accent that marked him down as east of the Hudson River. If he'd had a tail he would have been wagging it hard enough to power an electric generator. Kate found herself hoping the body in the woods did belong to Dewayne Gammons.

"We just need to talk to Randy for a minute, okay?" Lyda said.

"Sure, Lyda, anything you want." He cast about him for more tribute and lunged at a tray of cookies, scattering staff in front of him like marbles. He trotted back to Lyda, with what Kate had to admit looked like a fabulous chocolate chip cookie cradled reverently in his hands, at a guess six inches across. He extended it in Lyda's direction with a bona fide bow, in the manner of one sacrificing to a personal goddess.

Lyda had to take it. "Thanks, Jules. You sure there aren't any peanuts in it?"

Jules looked hurt. "You know I'll never let that happen in my kitchen."

She smiled at him and the hurt expression on his face vanished like spring mist. "Okay, thanks. I'll take it with me if you'll wrap it up."

Jules wrapped the cookie in enough wax paper to satisfy an embalmer in ancient Egypt. He presented his offering again, again with the bow. "Thanks, Jules," Lyda said again, displaying a commendable patience. "Now, if we could just talk to Randy."

Jules made an effort to pull himself together. "We're prepping dinner, don't keep him too long, okay?" He looked agonized at having to lay down even this much law to her.

"Okay." Lyda led Kate and Mutt, neither of whom had even registered on Jules's peripheral vision, deeper into the belly of the culinary beast. At the back of the room a man was taking trays of golden brown dinner rolls from an oven and replacing them with more. He was short and slight, with a potbelly that strained his apron and thinning hair, the remnants of which wrapped around the sides of his head like greasy wings, leaving a bald, sweaty dome that dampened the edges of his paper hat. He had no shoulders to speak of and less chin. He might even have been bow-legged.

Lyda walked up to him and said, "Hey, Randy. Can you take five?"

And she looked over her shoulder just so she could watch Kate's jaw drop.

THEY FOREGATHERED ON THE dock. "Kate Shugak, Randy Randolph. Randy, meet Kate. She's from Niniltna, and she needs to ask you a few questions."

Kate was still trying to come to grips with the fact that this was the Lothario breaking hearts across the Park. He did have brown eyes, with long, curling eyelashes so thick they seemed to weigh down his eyelids. Maybe the eyelashes were his secret. "Randy Randolph?" she said, just to be sure.

Lyda turned her head away but Kate saw the smile tugging

at the corners of her mouth.

Mutt, notorious for slobbering over anything with the XY chromosome pair, remained next to Kate, her head cocked to one side, regarding Randolph with a quizzical expression.

He nodded, pulling the paper cap from his head and running a hand over his scalp. It came away wet and he wiped it on his pants. "What's this about?" He looked over his shoulder. "I gotta get them rolls out pretty soon."

Kate found herself at an uncharacteristic loss for words. He was shorter than Suzy, and Bonnie had him by forty pounds. She saw Lyda watching her and while she didn't mind providing comic relief for the sake of pulling Lyda Blue out of the doldrums, enough was enough. "I work with the state trooper in Niniltna, Randy. Got a bit of a problem we thought you might be able to help us with."

He shrugged his insignificant shoulders. "I'm just a baker," he said.

"And a serial marrier," Kate said.

He was mute, but even his thick eyelashes were unable to hide the trace of alarm that appeared in the brown eyes.

"It seems you arranged for your paycheck to be sent through the mail to Suzy Moonin."

"Yeah," he said, with caution.

"The problem is that Bonnie Jeppsen is the Niniltna postmistress."

"Oh?"

"Yes," Kate said. "You remember Bonnie? She would be the other woman you married since January. She intercepted your check. Suzy came looking for it."

"Oh."

There was a flash of emotion in his eyes, something gone too quickly for Kate to identify. Fear? No, not fear. Relief?

120

Why would Randolph be relieved at being caught with two wives? When he said nothing further, she said, "That's it? 'Oh'? Anything you'd like to add?"

He shrugged his negligible shoulders again. "They're my wives."

"Yes, but most men settle for one at a time. What are you, some kind of Mormon?"

Randolph displayed emotion for the first time, in this case a wan indignation. "I'd never be a Mormon! They're against gays."

This was something of a non-sequitur, and Kate didn't quite know how to reply.

"I love them," he said. He could have said "I love NASCAR racing" with more conviction, and it took Kate a moment to realize he was referring to his wives. With the first trace of defiance, he added, "And they love me."

"As of yesterday?" Kate said. "Not so much."

Tears might have welled behind the eyelashes. "Are you going to arrest me?"

At this, Lyda stirred. "He's a very good baker," she said in tones meant only for Kate's ears. "Vern really likes Randy's crullers."

Kate dwelled for a pleasurable moment on the image of cuffing and stuffing Randolph into George's Cessna and delivering him into Chopper Jim's unwilling arms back in Niniltna, but decided that if she ever wanted to get laid again she'd probably better not. In Alaska bigamy came under the "unlawful marrying" statute, and was rated a Class A misdemeanor. Convicted, Randolph could be sentenced up to a year in jail, along with fines and community service. The trick would be in convicting him. Judge Roberta Singh, presiding judge of the Ahtna court, did not take kindly to

121

people cluttering up her docket with—and here as she was wont to do she would quote directly from the Alaska statutes—"Class A misdemeanors, which characteristically involve less severe violence against a person, less serious offenses against property interests, less serious offenses against public administration or order, or less serious offenses against public health and decency than felonies." "I wasn't hired by George W. Bush," Kate had heard her say in a rare moment of anger in response to a request for a hearing into the legality of a search and seizure in the matter of a resale amount of marijuana found growing in someone's back bedroom. "I'm a competent jurist, and competent jurists don't sit on frivolous cases."

Bobbie Singh would never issue a warrant for Randolph's arrest. Not that Jim would ever ask her for one. He, too, tried to reserve his best efforts for real criminals. "No," Kate said, not without regret. "I won't be arresting you. I don't have that authority."

He blinked. "Is the trooper going to arrest me, then?"

"Not today. Suzy and Bonnie are pretty upset with you, Mr. Randolph. You'll have to deal with them at some point. And you'd better do something about your paycheck, too." She turned to go and paused. "Mr. Randolph? Did you know Dewayne Gammons?"

Lyda stiffened. Randolph looked surprised. "Sure. Works here. Haven't seen him in a while."

"How well did you know him?"

He gestured vaguely. "He delivered supplies to the kitchen sometimes. He'd help unload the pallets, which was kinda nice. Not all those Stores people do. We talked a little."

"What about?"

He shrugged. "Not much. He was a quiet type. Seemed

kind of sad. I told him he should get married, make him feel better."

He looked at Lyda, who refused to meet his eyes.

"Yeah," Kate said, drawing out the word. "Well, thanks, Randy."

From what was apparently a hazy memory of one too many B-list noir films, Randolph said, "Can I leave camp if I wanna?"

"Sure," Kate said. "But Bonnie and Suzy are waiting for you in town. I wouldn't advise it."

• • •

KATE GATHERED UP GEORGE, protesting, from the mess hall, where he appeared bent on inhaling the better part of a tray of bear claws, and Lyda escorted them to the airstrip. "Thanks for the guide service," Kate said. "You okay?" This as Lyda started to say something, and stopped.

Lyda nodded. "Yeah, fine." But she looked worried.

Kate moved a few steps away from George and lowered her voice. "What?"

Lyda frowned at the Herc, drawn up at the end of the runway. It had dropped the clamshell to disgorge shrink-wrapped pallets of canned goods, a load of drill pipe, and a knuckleboom loader onto a semicircle of pickups and flatbeds. "There might be something else, another reason Wayne took off."

Kate thought of the suicide note. "A reason other than depression to kill himself, you mean?" As soon as she said it she knew it was the wrong thing. "I'm sorry, I didn't mean to—"

But Lyda was already shaking her head. "It's probably

nothing to waste your time over. Forget it." She smiled and extended her hand. "Nice to meet you."

There was a lack of sincerity there to rival Vernon Truax's, and Lyda's grip was cool and brief. "I've got time. I can hear anything you have to say, Lyda."

The other woman waved a dismissive hand. "Really, it was nothing. Safe journey home."

This time she turned and walked down the rise. Kate watched her pass inside the doors of the admin building with a crease between her brows.

"So, we leaving any time this century?" George said. "My time's money these days, Kate."

SEVEN

"SO," JIM SAID, "HE had a girlfriend."

"Suicides have been known to have girlfriends," Kate said.

"She also said he was depressed. His boss said he was subdued, and so did at least one of his coworkers."

"His boss said he didn't say much," Jim said. "Doesn't necessarily mean the same thing."

"His buddy the bigamist baker said he was sad."

"His buddy the bigamist baker also counseled him to marry to cheer himself up. Consider the source."

They were in his office in the post, Kate across the desk with her feet up on it and Mutt sitting next to Jim, her eyes closed in bliss as he fondled her ears. For a brief moment Kate imagined those hands fondling her own ears, and with an effort brought her attention back to the matter at hand. They were doing the devil's advocate thing, Kate taking the role of devil. Typecasting. "You don't want him to have been the victim of foul play, do you?"

"I really don't," Jim said.

"Even if he might have been?"

He looked at her, puzzled. "Kate, everything you've said points to suicide."

"Lyda Blue didn't recognize the writing on Gammons's note."

He rolled his eyes. "She didn't recognize his printing."

She was reaching and the bad part was she knew it. On a lesser woman her expression would have been called a pout. "What's really bothering you?" he said.

"Hell," she said, impatient more with her own qualms than with him questioning them. "I don't know, Jim, I guess I'm just suspicious of anything this neat. Father Smith finds the truck. We find the body. The ME finds the identity. The girlfriend and the coworkers say he was depressed. Case closed." She made a face. "We all want it to be a suicide because it's coming on summer and we're so busy we don't even have time to sleep and suicide would be so much less bother for us." She jerked her shoulders, like she was trying to shake something off. "Life is seldom neat."

"I direct your attention to the Occam's razor of police work," he said. "The simplest explanation is usually the correct one."

"What about that round I found in the pickup?"

"Kate. Come on. Show me a truck anywhere in the Bush that doesn't have a round of ammunition rolling around on the floor."

"Where's the gun? And who did it belong to?"

"Lacking evidence he was shot, that doesn't seem relevant."

"Where did he keep his truck? He couldn't get it out to the mine, he had to leave it parked somewhere in town."

"Probably," Jim said. "Again, relevance?"

She thought of whatever it was that Lyda had started to tell her at the airstrip, but she could imagine his reaction if she repeated that nonconversation to him here.

"I won't close this case if you tell me not to, Kate," he said. "I just don't see anywhere to go with it."

"Nope," Dan O'Brian said from the doorway. He flopped

126

down in the chair next to Kate and put his feet up next to hers. "Fine bunch of detectives we have here. I was eavesdropping and you didn't even notice. So you heard back from the ME?"

"Yep," Jim said. "According to Brillo, the guy you found was A positive."

"Which matches Gammons's health records in his employee file," Kate said.

"So it is him," Dan said.

"It would appear so," Jim said.

"And he marched off into the wild to kill himself."

"So he wrote."

"And Papa Grizzly took him up on his invitation."

"Looks like."

"Dumb bastard," Dan said.

"Dead dumb bastard," Jim said.

And that would seem to be that.

Jim propped his own feet up. It was his damn desk. "But at least it means I can put this one to bed. Be nice if they were all this easy."

Kate and Dan both perked up. "More bigamists?" Kate said.

Dan swiveled around to stare at Kate. "Bigamists?"

So then of course he had to be told all, and when he stopped laughing he said, "Life in the fast lane. Man, the Park is starting to look just like downtown."

Which didn't come out as quite the joke he had intended, and provoked an uneasy silence that lasted a little longer than it should have while they all thought about what looking just like downtown would mean to the trooper post, the Parks Service, and the Niniltna Native Association's resident shareholders. The silence was broken by Maggie, who appeared in the doorway to look at Jim with an expression somewhere between sorrow and pity.

"What?" Jim said with foreboding.

"Maybe nothing," Maggie said, but they could all tell she didn't really mean it. "I got a call from Cindy Bingley."

"Not Willard," Jim said, willing it to be so.

"No, not Willard," Maggie said, "but she says your presence is required to stop a riot."

So they adjourned to Bingley Mercantile down the hill and around the corner from the post, where a crowd large by Park standards was found milling near the steps that led to the double glass doors. A quick professional glance took the crowd's temperature. Edgy but not violent. Jim took his time getting out of the white Blazer with the seal of the Alaska Department of Public Safety on the door, and when he got out took a little longer to settle the trooper badge on his ball cap directly over his eyes, and a little longer than that to hitch the gun belt around his waist. The gravitas was implied.

A respectful silence fell over the crowd at this manifestation of the might and majesty of the Alaska State Troopers, followed by a definite diminution of tension. He strode forward with a ground-eating stride that caused the people in his path to simply melt away. It didn't hurt that Mutt had abandoned Kate to trot at his heels, head up, tail held at the ne plus ultra angle, adding her natural imperiousness to his state-sanctioned authority.

They mounted the steps, silver gray husky-wolf and blue-and-gold-clad Alaska State Trooper. At the top, they paused deliberately, looking over the crowd with a stern and daunting eye, a double-barreled assault from which grown men quailed.

Satisfied, Jim turned to pull open the door.

It opened outward with a gratifying vigor, in fact so gratifying that it was yanked out of his hand and banged back against the outside wall, hitting hard enough to crack the glass. The impetus shoved Jim backward, causing him to tread on Mutt's toes. She let out a series of startled yips, leaped into the air, and came down directly behind him.

What bowled out of the door resembled nothing so much as a human cannonball, very large in diameter and with many moving parts, most of them whaling on other moving parts. Punching, kicking, elbowing, kneeing, yelling, screaming, swearing, it was a mesmerizing concatenation of self-directed human energy and single-minded enthusiasm. Kate, fascinated, decided that cannonball was the wrong analogy, it was more like a fight in a *Batman* comic book. She thought she might even see "Pow!" and "Bam!" rising up out of the fracas.

That seething ball of human rage rolled right out the door and into Chopper Jim Chopin. Jim was standing in front of Mutt. Mutt was standing on the very edge of the top step. The ball hit Jim. He lost his balance. Mutt caught the backs of his knees and in another startled scramble tried to get out of the way in several different directions at once. Jim pitched back into a flawless backward somersault, any Olympic judge who wasn't sitting on the pairs competition for ice skating would have been ashamed to give it less than a 9.9.

Sergeant Jim Chopin, pride of the Alaska State Troopers, the law of the land in blue and gold, thereafter ascribed a perfect circle, his head and his feet spinning 360 degrees around a straight torso in a movement that Kate dimly remembered from some long-forgotten math class as angular motion. His constant velocity was such as to defy enough gravity to miss every single one of the eight steps leading up to the Bingley Mercantile entrance, and so in his favor were the laws of physics this day that he made a neat two-point landing with both feet smack on the ground, facing in exactly the same direction from which he had originally launched.

A long time ago Kate remembered him saying that one of the first things they taught cadets at the trooper academy was that when a trooper arrived at the scene, the first thing they must do was establish an air of authority. Today, Jim had approximately two and a half seconds to appreciate this undeniable achievement before the human cannonball boiled right down the steps, hit him with all the force of a runaway train, and flattened him on his back in the dirt and the mud and the half-melted snow.

Mutt, also a victim of physics, was already off balance when Jim flipped over her, and was sucked thereafter into the cannonball's turbulent wake. She avoided landing in the middle of it by a levitational feat heretofore only achieved by Nadia Comaneci, and managed to jump clean over the melee. She landed running, a gray streak close to light speed, and she didn't stop until she got to Kate, behind whom she promptly took refuge, uttering a distinctly un-Muttlike whine.

Those nearer to the action were too busy diving for cover to receive a clear impression of events. Kate, standing next to the door of her truck, and Dan, standing next to the door of his, got the wide-screen version and were able thereafter to replay the events of that afternoon in glorious Technicolor detail for the benefit of many, many enthralled audiences at Bernie's Roadhouse. Under pressure they would admit that their recounting of events was something of a reconstruction, as both of them had been laughing so hard at the time that their vision was somewhat blurred.

Jim, flat on his back beneath what felt like a swarm of spitting, hissing, feral cats, took a moment to realize just what had happened and just where he was. He took another moment to muster a sense of ill use, and a third to summon a swell of outrage, enhanced by the realization that the front of his heretofore immaculate uniform now had several well-outlined footprints on it, and more than a few splashes of blood. He used this as motivation to rise to his feet, attaining the vertical in a single indignant moment, then opened his mouth and gave speech. "All right. That's ENOUGH."

Mild words, maybe, but given full voice by a pissed-off state trooper in full regalia, they did not fail of effect. The human cannonball resolved into, of course, Suzy Moonin, Bonnie Jeppsen, and a third woman of whose identity he was unaware. The brief lull dissolved when Bonnie slapped Suzy and Suzy slugged the third woman. Jim grabbed Bonnie and Suzy by the scruffs of their necks, lifted them up off their feet, and banged their heads together, one time, hard.

Suzy screamed, Bonnie started to cry, and the third woman took the opportunity to kick Bonnie in the shins and elbow Suzy in the groin. Jim only had two hands and Bonnie and Suzy seemed subdued, at least for the moment, so he dropped them and picked up the third woman by a large handful of jacket, fleece vest, and turtleneck. "Lady! Calm down!" He shook her once for emphasis.

Her head rocked back hard. She stopped writhing and glared at him.

"Who the hell are you, anyway?" he said.

Tears glittered in her eyes and threatened to fall in floods. "My name," she said, her voice trembling, her breast heaving, "is Mrs! Randy! Randolph!"

He stared at her for a long moment, her feet dangling a good six inches above the ground. "Oh hell," he said, and then he dropped her, too.

And on that note, the Park's Memorial Day weekend was over.

EIGHT

FOURTH OF JULY

THERE WAS TREMENDOUS SCOPE for a fertile imagination in being the sole owner and proprietor of 160 acres in a place where daylight in summer went almost 24/7. Plants avid to exploit the photosynthetic process exploded out of the ground almost before you could step back out of their way. Every year Kate reveled in the act of throwing out a handful of seeds and telling them, "Show me what you've got." Sometimes the shrews and the sparrows got to the seeds first, but often enough she was rewarded on her rambles over the homestead by a tiny burst of color on her peripheral vision. A California poppy, say, reaching up through the surrounding grass on a single trembling stem, a triumphant shout in Creamsicle orange. Or she might stumble onto a clump of pink pussytoes curled up next to a tall, elegant delphinium, the deep blue of an Arctic summer solstice sky at midnight. Three years before she'd planted a Philippe Rivoire peony, mostly because she liked the name. Then a single, six-inch stem with four modest leaves that had cost her $2.49 at Auntie Balasha's annual spring garage sale, she'd stuck it into the ground in a clear spot next to a stand of diamond willow a mile from her cabin and walked away.

Last summer when she and Mutt had made their annual hike to the Lost Wife Mine to make sure the entrance was still securely blocked against the unwary or the reckless wilderness explorer, she was rewarded with a brilliant splash of red so bright that for just a second she had thought it was a brush fire. The single stem had morphed into a bloom-covered bush that was taller than she was and as wide as her two arms outstretched. On the way home she had cut half a dozen stems and back at the house stuck them in a decorative plastic bucket, over which Johnny pretended to warm his hands every night for a week.

The wildflowers needed no encouragement. The deep purple spire of monkshood, its cluster of closed blooms giving off an air of mystery, appeared and disappeared around every bend of trail. Dainty forget-me-nots clustered half-hidden on the shadowy edges of tree and shrub, tiny pale blue flowers delicate by contrast to almost everything else in the forest. Fireweed revealed itself in unexpected patches of blazing magenta, and western columbine spread across any otherwise unoccupied space to duke it out with chocolate lilies and Sitka roses. Military rows of arctic lupine had shouldered aside every other single living plant in their march to line the trail between road and homestead, and Kate was fighting a delaying action to prevent their conquering the clearing in front of the house.

After an idyllic month of sun leavened by comfortably spaced periods of soft, almost warm rain, the garden burst to overflowing. Rhubarb with leaves the size of elephant ears formed a lush line at the garden's edge. Strawberries, tiny scarlet gems nestled in clusters of furry leaves, enjoyed the shade of a strategic grouping of white birch. Raspberry canes leaned heavily against tomato cages co-opted for the purpose beneath the prospect of a bumper crop come August. Blueberry bushes drooped beneath the weight of fruit promising to be the size of Kate's thumb in a month's time. The potato patch was a riot of leaf, the carrots a sturdy row of feathery tops, the cabbage and cauliflower and broccoli pushing each other for room.

The half-dozen rugosa roses her mother had planted the summer following Kate's birth were now a waist-high hedge next to the rock seat at the cliff's edge and in ebullient and aromatic bloom. The rock was warm from the sun and she wriggled her backside into it with hedonistic pleasure, adjusted the throw pillow between her lower back and the natural shelf formed by the rock, and allowed herself to be seduced by the strong, sweet scent of the roses. A bee nuzzled the front of her T-shirt, a mosquito whined past her ear, and a golden-crowned sparrow trilled nearby. Water tumbled and jostled its way downstream between the narrow, rocky banks below, and she smiled without opening her eyes. If the weather held, the swimming hole would be warm enough for skinnydipping by tomorrow. Maybe even by this afternoon.

There was a low murmur from the radio perched nearby. Bobby Clark was narrating the Fourth of July parade on Park Air Live. "And here comes the veterans' float, Jeff Talbot driving his Army surplus jeep—HOO-ah!—with Demetri Totemoff and George Perry in the back throwing candy hard enough to overshoot the Kanuyaq River. Ouch! Goddammit, Perry, watch where the hell you're throwing that stuff! Ouch!"

A background murmur, probably Bobby's wife Dinah in soothe mode. One of them had to remember Bobby was on the air, although since it was a pirate radio station that changed broadcast frequency pretty much daily it wasn't like the Federal Communications Commission was ever going to catch up with him. A delighted scream too close to the mike made Kate and Mutt both jump. Bobby and Dinah's four-year-old daughter, Katya, named for Kate. Delivered by Kate, if it came to that, and on the day of her parents' wedding, no less, at which Kate had not only officiated but also stood up for both bride and groom. That had been one fraught day.

"Oh, well now." Bobby's rich baritone rolled out of the radio. "Here comes Max Chaney's flatbed bearing Miss Niniltna, whose day job is Luba Lindeman, and let me tell you gentlemen who couldn't make the parade today, you should see the red dress our own pride of Niniltna is almost wearing. All the way to China, guys, no shit—ouch! Goddammit, Dinah!"

"Goddammitdinah!" Katya said.

Park Air vanished from the airwaves for a few seconds, but Kate, veteran of many a Niniltna parade, could fill in the blanks. Luba would be perched on a pile of last year's tanned wolf, beaver, mink, and marten hides donated by local trappers who hadn't been able to unload them at the Fur Rendezvous fur auction in February. She would be wearing the gold-nugget and walrus-ivory crown made by local carver Thor Moonin. She would be attended by five other Niniltna High girls, all of them doing some combination of pageant, royal, and papal wave. They'd be giggling a lot.

They also represented six of the seven girls in the junior-senior class of Niniltna High. Vanessa would not be forming one of Luba's court, not because she wouldn't have been an ornament to float, town, and event, but because she and Johnny were both working out at Suulutaq. There at least was one reason to be grateful to the mine. Kate didn't have to go into town for the parade.

The parade would be led by a bad-tempered Maggie Montgomery in uniform driving Jim's Blazer. Jim had avoided leading the parade this time by contriving to have Kenny Hazen call him to Ahtna for an assist on an apprehension.

Park Air erupted back into life, Bobby's voice sounding disgruntled. "—there's Jimmy Moonin on his tricycle, although I don't know what the hell he's got on his head. Some kind of pad—Oh." Kate later learned that seven-year-old Jimmy had appropriated one of his mother's Kotex pads and wrapped it around one eye. In the interests of verisimilitude he'd stained it with a liberal application of red food coloring, but that was not known by the people watching the parade.

Bobby rallied. "Kid's got a hell of an arm on him, look at him field that Hershey bar! Way to go, Jimmy! Bernie Koslowski's gonna be looking serious at you when it comes time to recruit for the basketball team! I'm thinking point guard!"

Bobby's voice dropped to the low rumble that sounded like a Harley hog in neutral. A long time ago Kate had had the pleasure of hearing that rumble up close and personal, and she couldn't stop a nostalgic shiver at the memory.

"A positive rain of Hershey bars out of the back of the Suulutaq dump truck, flung personally by mine superintendent Vern Truax in company with attendant nymphs. Vern tells me he's let the nonessential employees off the chain for the day, which explains today's record crowd. Just another show of goodwill on the part of Vern and the Suulutaq Mine, and I know we all—ouch! Goddammit, Dinah!"

Dinah's voice came over the airwaves loud and clear, if more distant from the mike than Bobby's. "The Suulutaq dump truck isn't the only float in the parade."

Kate looked at the radio. No one listening could have mistaken the edge in Dinah's voice.

"Well, pardon fucking me!"

"Pardonfuckingme!" Katya said.

There was a growl and a squeal and a squawk and this time Park Air went off the air for good.

Just as well. The Grosdidiers would be bringing up the rear in their mustard yellow Silverado, Vern Truax would throw the last candy bar, and everyone would adjourn to the potluck barbecue at the gym, the games and races for the kids, and the Red Run Roustabouts playing garage band rock and roll until midnight, when there would be fireworks detonated from the Grosdidier brothers' dock. It would still be light out, so mostly people would see clouds of smoke drifting across the river in the half-light of a sun that was teetering its way around the horizon, but that was okay. Nobody expected anything different, and everyone enjoyed whining about it afterward.

She wondered if there was a chance of Jim getting back in time for a swim before they turned in for the night, and smiled to herself at the prospect.

For the moment she leaned back, closed her eyes, and wallowed in an Alaskan summer. Her enjoyment was all the richer because it was so unaccustomed. At this very moment she should have been counting fish on the deck of the *Freya* in Alaganik Bay, one boat to starboard, another to port, both crews pitching an unending silver cascade of red salmon over the gunnels and if she was lucky into the hold. Half a dozen more boats would be waiting their turn to deliver and more pulling their nets to get in line. Old Sam would be in the galley, writing out fish tickets and cursing fishermen and tender summaries and Fish and Game catch reports with a fine impartiality.

Instead, she had coerced Old Sam into hiring Petey Jeppsen in her place. Old Sam did not take kindly to newbies stumbling around his old wooden tub, tripping over head buckets and deck boards and mooring lines and incapable of telling a humpy from a dog, but after the requisite amount of grumbling, he took Petey on. When she shouted him down, he took on Phyllis Lestinkof as well. "Turning the *Freya* into a goddamn orphanage," Old Sam said, but in about seven and a half months Phyllis was going to need every dime she could lay her hands on, and she knew her way around a drifter so deckhand on a fish tender wouldn't be that big a learning curve.

Meanwhile, Kate remained on her homestead and attended to her garden, reveling in the vibrant plant life, the warm temperatures, the hours she had to potter around doing long-delayed chores, or read a book. Or lie back on her rock and enjoy the sun on her face.

Above all, there was the blissful solitude. Actual hours, connected one to the other, sometimes stretching into entire days during which she didn't have to so much as say hello to anyone. No disentangling Park rats' messy lives, no cleaning up auntie-made messes, no fighting over the goddamn Suulutaq Mine. Peace was what she had, a rare and perfect—

A polite cough. "Excuse me."

Kate came bolt upright at the same moment Mutt leaped to her feet. They both looked in the direction of the voice. Mutt growled. Kate felt like it.

She shaded her eyes against the sun. "Who—Oh. Holly, Holly Haynes, right? Suulutaq geologist?"

"Right." The other woman came forward, a tentative smile on her face, and they shook hands. Kate hadn't seen her since the case of the disappearing miner the month before. "Sorry to bother you. You looked pretty comfortable." She looked at Mutt, who was still growling.

"Mutt."

Mutt held the growl for a few seconds more before shutting it down, just so Kate would know it was her own idea. Truth was, she was as embarrassed as Kate. It had been a long time since either one of them had allowed anyone to sneak up on them.

"I didn't hear your car," Kate said.

Haynes made a vague gesture behind her. "I wasn't sure I had the right place, so I parked at the turnoff and walked in."

Kate nodded and promised herself that whoever had given Haynes directions to her homestead would pay for it one day. It wasn't like she hated the very sight of Suulutaq's staff geologist, but Kate did not approve of people dropping by uninvited. Besides, she had the uneasy feeling that her holiday had just been, if not ruined, say then shortened by press of business, and duty.

Contrary to conventional wisdom, it was not good to be queen.

She led the way back to the house. There she offered Haynes her choice of coffee or Diet 7UP and a plate of chocolate chip cookies. It was as far as she was prepared to go in hospitality, and she hoped it would discourage Haynes from a long visit. Mutt had followed them as far as the deck, and through the living room windows Kate had a clear view of her sprawled in the sun. Kate wished she were there with her. "How are things out at the mine?" she said, and thought, Me making polite conversation. Just shoot me now.

Haynes finished one cookie and reached for another. "Fine. Drill baby drill."

Kate smiled in spite of herself. "Found the limits of the deposit yet?"

Haynes, mouth full, shook her head. "Every time we think we've got to the edge, the edge moves out from under us."

Kate gave a wise nod like she knew something about gold mining, when all she really knew was that all gold miners were nuts. She didn't know if that extended to gold miners who pulled it out of the ground in commercial quantities, but she wouldn't bet against it. "So, that must make you happy," she said.

"It makes Global Harvest happy," Haynes said. "I'm just doing my job."

Haynes was devouring the plate of cookies as if she wasn't expecting to eat ever again. She was thin to the point of gauntness, something that hadn't registered on Kate at their first meeting, which gave Haynes the hollow-eyed look of either an insomniac or a fanatic. "Not a job after your own heart?" Kate said.

Haynes paused in the act of reaching for a fifth cookie, met Kate's eyes, and seemed to recollect herself. "Oh yes. I love geology, I never wanted to study or work at anything else. It's just—"

"Yes?" Kate said, when Haynes hesitated.

Haynes shrugged. "I just don't know if the world needs another gold mine."

"It's a pretty useful metal," Kate said.

Haynes shrugged again. "Jewelry."

"A good conductor of electricity, too," Kate said.

"Embroidery thread," Haynes said, wincing around a bite of cookie.

"Reflects electromagnetic radiation," Kate said, "they use it on satellites, and astronauts' space suits, and airplanes." An inner voice did wonder who she was trying to convince.

Haynes polished off the last cookie, licked her forefinger, and used it to pick the plate clean of crumbs. "I know."

"What would you rather be mining, and why aren't you?"

Kate had no time at all for anyone who worked at a job they didn't like.

Haynes looked up at that. "Oh, I love my job. Especially the travel. I get to go all over the world, places I'd never get to on my own. Russia, China, Peru, Madagascar. A couple of times we were the first Americans the people we met had ever seen."

Kate had heard avowals with more conviction, but then Haynes wouldn't be the first person talking herself into believing that she didn't hate her job. Hard to bite the hand that feeds you, and Global Harvest fed very well indeed.

Haynes brushed her hands, gulped down the rest of her drink, and sat up straight in her chair, folding her hands on the table in front of her. "The cookies were great, thanks."

Kate made a deprecating noise, and waited.

"Vern gave most of the nonessential personnel the day off and brought us into town on George's Otter. He wanted me to drop by and, well, touch base, so to speak, with the chair of the board of the Niniltna Native Association. Which would be you."

She smiled. Kate smiled back. Both smiles lacked conviction.

"I didn't want to come," Haynes said, "it being a holiday and all."

And being uninvited and all, Kate thought.

"But Vern insisted. He—We want to assure you that you're welcome out at the mine at any time, that there is no question you have that we won't answer. We know there are plenty of people in the Park who aren't necessarily overjoyed about the mine going in here. Vern wants you to know that we're prepared to be completely transparent about the operation."

She picked up her glass, forgetting that she'd already drained it, and sucked at the one or two remaining drops. She declined Kate's honor-bound offer of another. "Vern wants you to know that you're our first call when something happens at the site."

"You can tell Vern I appreciate that," Kate said.

Conversation wandered around a little after that, from the computer installation just begun at the school to the ongoing talks with three different communications companies vying with one another to provide cell phone access to the Park. At one point, Haynes said, "Sergeant Chopin told us that the body in the woods was confirmed as Dewayne Gammons."

Whatever misgivings Kate had had over the gentleman who had walked into the Park to make of himself a bear's breakfast, they had waned over the intervening month, to the point that it took her a moment to place the name. "Oh yeah," she said, "the blood matched the employee record. What with the note and his girlfriend and his coworkers saying he was depressed, the coroner came back with suicide."

"He had a girlfriend?"

"Yeah, maybe not girlfriend," Kate said, "but I got the feeling it might have been if he hadn't gone into the woods. But I suppose if he'd had any real feeling for her he wouldn't have gone into the woods in the first place." She shook her head. "I don't know, I guess it's one of the more environmentally friendly ways to off yourself."

"Was the, what, the un-girlfriend very upset?"

Kate looked at her. "You know, for a workforce of only a hundred you people sure don't talk to each other a lot."

Haynes looked startled. "What do you mean?"

"You didn't even know who Gammons was when Sergeant Chopin asked you about him." Haynes looked blank, and Kate reminded her. "At the café the day his body was found."

Haynes shifted in her seat and looked defensive. "The

143

work's pretty intense, especially when they're pulling five core samples out of the ground every day. Rick Allen was the only worker who wasn't staff who I had a lot to do with."

"He 'was'? What, you lose another employee?"

Haynes grimaced. "We lose some with every paycheck. Attrition is always a problem on a job like this. Working out in the middle of nowhere isn't everyone's cup of tea. It'll get better when we go into production and the camp gets bigger, more amenities, a movie theater, a swimming pool."

Kate remembered Lyda saying more or less the same thing. "Did the mine notify Gammons's next of kin?"

"He didn't have any," Haynes said.

Kate stared at her. "None?"

"He didn't put an emergency contact on his employee form." Kate already knew that from Lyda Blue. "Lyda called his high school and the principal barely remembered him, much less his parents. She called his voc-ed school and they barely remembered Gammons, either. Vern and I talked it over and decided we'd done as much as we could. Maybe someone will come looking."

Kate wondered what it would be like to have no one looking for you if you disappeared. "How's Lyda doing?"

Haynes looked surprised. "Fine. One of the best exec assistants I've ever worked with, smart, takes the initiative, never makes the same mistake twice. Why?" Then in sudden realization, "Lyda was Gammons's girlfriend?"

Kate raised a hand. "Not quite girlfriend, but she was upset at his death. And don't hassle her about it."

"Of course not," Haynes said. "I'm just surprised. I didn't realize they were close."

No reason you should, Kate thought, you don't appear to have known Gammons even existed.

Out on the deck Mutt stretched out and gave a voluptuous groan.

"Who's your second call?" Kate said.

"I beg your pardon?"

"You say we're Suulutaq's first call. I was just wondering who your second call was. The boss in Anchorage, maybe?"

Haynes, thrown off her game, said, "Well, I … well, of course, we—"

She was spared further inarticulation by the arrival of a vehicle in the clearing. Kate stood up to look out the window. "Ah. Here's another one of your First Callers."

She went outside, trailed by a still stuttering Haynes, as the powder blue Ford Explorer, driven with dash and style, slid to a halt not quite eighteen inches away from the foot of the stairs. A diminutive octogenarian hopped out with a spryness that belied her years. "Katya!"

"Hi, Auntie Vi," Kate said.

Mutt, through long experience wary of whatever mood Auntie Vi might be in, remained at Kate's side.

Shorter than Kate and thicker through the middle, Auntie Vi had bright button eyes of a piercing brown, a tousled bob of hair in which not a strand of gray dared show its face, and skin the color and smoothness of a walnut shell. "Ha, Katya," she said again, moderating her tone as Haynes moved into her sights and she realized they had an audience. She bent an accusing stare on Kate, aggravated at this thwarting of her natural inclination.

"Hello again, Vi," Haynes said. To Kate she said, "Vern and I are both spending the night in town."

Kate wondered if they'd taken adjoining rooms.

Her thought was immediately confounded when Haynes added, "Vern's wife flew in for the weekend."

Kate raised her eyebrows. "Really? Nice for them both."

"Yes." But Haynes's jawline looked taut. She was able to hold Kate's gaze for only a few seconds before she said in a false, bright tone, "Is that what you call a cache? I've never seen a real one before." She walked to the edge of the clearing to examine the little house on peeled-log stilts with a wholly unmerited attention to detail.

Auntie Vi took the opportunity to say in a tone that approximated a hiss, "Board meeting next week. You be there?"

Kate repressed the shudder along her flesh. "Actually, it's not until week after next, but yes, I'll be there, Auntie."

Auntie Vi looked hard at Kate. "Why not you down Alaganik way with Old Sam?"

"I decided to spend a summer at home for a change."

Auntie Vi dismissed this with a wave of her hand. "But you be in town for board meeting."

"Yes, Auntie," Kate said. "I. Will. Be. There."

"Demetri say he might maybe be up at lodge. So maybe he not there either."

"Yes, Auntie," Kate said. "That's why we made the board larger, so we'd still have a quorum when some of the board members are absent."

Auntie Vi snorted. It was a trademark expression, and one eloquent of feeling. "You make. Not we."

This was not true. In January on Kate's recommendation the Association shareholders had voted to expand the board from five members to nine. Afterward, Annie Mike orchestrated a one-time-only write-in campaign to fill the four new seats. They were announced at the April board meeting and in letters that went out to every shareholder. When Kate looked at the names, she almost wished the amendment to the bylaws had failed. Her only consolation was that Auntie Vi didn't like them any better than Kate did. Only one of the four, Herbie Topkok, lived in the Park. Einar Carlson was from Cordova, Ulanie Anahonak from Tok, and Marlene Colberg from Kanuyaq Center.

"We had to open it up to people who didn't live in the Park, Auntie," Kate said. "We'd never have been able to fill nine seats otherwise. And they are shareholders." She looked at Auntie Vi and her smile was ever so sweet. "You could have run for a seat on the board yourself, Auntie."

Auntie Vi snorted again, and threw in another glare for good measure. They both knew that Auntie Vi was a behind-the-scenes kind of gal. She wanted to pull strings, all right, but only in the background, where no one could see.

Kate had a feeling that the board meeting was only a red herring. Auntie Vi proved her right when she looked over her shoulder at Haynes, who was still rapt in contemplation of the cache, and said, in a lower voice, "You let those kids go to work at mine!"

"Yes," Kate said. Mutt looked up, the wag of her tail slowing. "Yes, I did. You could even say I encouraged them. They wanted to work, which I consider a minor miracle in sixteen-year-olds, and this was hands down the best opportunity going. You got a problem with that?"

It came out a little more in-your-face than Kate had meant, and it only fanned the flames. Auntie Vi forgot their audience, opened her mouth, and prepared to wax even more eloquent.

"Auntie," Kate said. Something in her tone of voice arrested Auntie Vi in mid-peroration. "The Suulutaq Mine might be this generation's Prudhoe Bay. Who am I to say they can't have their paycheck?"

Auntie Vi stared at her, mouth still open.

"Besides," Kate said, unable to stop herself, "look who's talking. You sold out at the first offer."

Fortunately or unfortunately, at that moment Old Sam chugged into the clearing in his International pickup, a vehicle that wasn't as old as he was only because he had been born before they started building them. He climbed out of the cab on his spider legs and stood surveying the tableau with a sardonic expression on his face. "Vi," he said.

Auntie Vi's mouth closed with a snap, and her hand, half raised to do who knew what, fell again to her side.

Old Sam smiled at Kate. "Hey, girl."

"Uncle, what are you doing here? Why aren't you in Alaganik? Who's got the *Freya*?"

"Got some king salmon for you, girl," he said.

"Kings?" Kate said. "Where'd you get—"

She quit before she got them all into trouble. Due to three years' worth of low returns, king season wasn't open anywhere on the Kanuyaq, or in Alaganik Bay, either, not even for subsistence fishers.

The other shoe dropped and she glared at him. It was so typical of Old Sam to apologize for the whole body-as-bear-bait affair with salmon that were illegally caught. She had thought that business concluded with his hiring of Petey Jeppsen and Phyllis Lestinkof. Her mistake.

Old Sam followed her train of thought without difficulty, and gave her his patently could-give-a-shit grin. Where was Mary Balashoff when Kate really needed her? "Where's Mary?" Kate said.

Mary Balashoff was Old Sam's longtime squeeze. She had a set net site on Alaganik Bay and the two were inseparable on off periods during the summer.

"She's minding my girl," Old Sam said. "Since my regular

deckhand saw fit to run out on me this summer."

This was unanswerable, so Kate said, "Petey working out?"

"He's almost worth cutting up for bait."

From Old Sam this was a compliment.

"And Phyllis?"

"Some of what she cooks is almost fit to eat."

All well, then.

"You want the kings or don't you?" Old Sam said.

Kate looked at Auntie Vi. With unspoken agreement neither looked at Holly Haynes, the Outsider who stood there, clueless, and who should for all their sakes depart as unenlightened as she had arrived. "Let's see 'em."

Old Sam pulled down the tailgate of the International to reveal a wet-lock box. With some ceremony, he opened it.

Inside were half a dozen kings, which Kate eyeballed at about thirty pounds each. They'd been blooded and gutted, and from where she was standing Kate could see the thick line of fat between skin and meat.

Drool pooled in her mouth. These kings had never seen fresh water. She looked at Old Sam, who looked back at her, radiating all the innocence of the devil himself. "What do you want to do with them, girl?"

"We're going to eat one right now," Kate said. "I'll smoke and can the rest."

"I guess I'd better be going," Holly Haynes said, without moving.

"You're welcome to stay," Kate lied.

Auntie Vi, constrained by Bush hospitality, said with a false heartiness anyone but a moron would have recognized, "Stay, stay! You got to eat!"

Haynes, alas, hesitated, and then, eyeing the salmon, capitulated. Her capitulation could also, Kate realized after the fact, have something to do with Haynes not wanting to go back to Niniltna and the B and B where Mr. and Mrs. Truax were enjoying a rare moment of connubial bliss.

Kate set up a stained sheet of plywood on two sawhorses and got out the filet knives and the garden hose. Auntie Vi filled a couple of five-gallon plastic buckets with water and stirred in quantities of salt. Old Sam headed and fileted the kings with deft, sure motions, and all the filets but one went into the brine. The heads went into the freezer for fish head soup in the winter.

Old Sam had brought the eggs from the females along in a plastic bag, and Auntie Vi pulled out one of the sacs, tore off some of the eggs, and popped them in her mouth. She closed her eyes and chewed, humming her approval. She opened her eyes again and saw Haynes looking appalled. "You try? You like!"

Haynes stuttered a refusal, trying to be polite about it and failing, and Kate laughed.

Auntie Vi laughed, too. It transformed her face, and Kate saw Haynes looking at her, marveling. It was good to be reminded that as cranky as Auntie Vi was determined to appear, said crankiness was a tool used to intimidate, and not or at least not always her prime characteristic.

Kate lit the charcoal in the cement block grill between the house and the garage. She brought out wasabi, soy sauce, and ginger paste, mixed them into a sauce and brushed it on the salmon filet. When the grill was hotter than hot she laid the filet skin side down on a sheet of foil across the coals. The smell of roasting king salmon was immediate and irresistible. They crowded around the grill like seagulls ready to fight over their next meal. Mutt even started barking again.

"What matter with that dog, Katya?" Auntie Vi said irritably, eyes fixed on the grill. "She want her fish raw or what?"

"Mutt!" Kate said.

Mutt looked at her and barked again, looking exasperated.

Then Kate heard it, too, a not-so-distant crashing through the brush beyond the clearing. Kate and Old Sam had heard that same sound just a month before.

"Bear," Old Sam said. "Must have smelled the fish."

NINE

"EVERYBODY INSIDE!" KATE SAID. "Mutt! Guard!"

She ran for the house and the .30-06 in the gun rack next to the door. She was back on the deck before anyone else had hit the stairs. Old Sam, who didn't hold with outmoded notions like chivalry, was well in the lead.

"Mutt!" Kate said. "To me!"

Mutt ignored her, ears back, half crouching in the center of the clearing, barking ferociously at the increasing noise from the brush, which was loud now and getting louder.

"Mutt!"

Mutt gave one last warning bark and loped to the stairs, took them in a single leap, and in another leap was at the railing at Kate's side. Her mane was standing straight up, her ears were still back, and a low, menacing growl issued steadily from her throat at a volume that by rights should have frightened off every living being within half a mile.

Inexplicably, it did not. Branches crashed and cracked beneath the onslaught of whatever creature was advancing on the homestead. Kate planted her feet, worked the bolt on the .30-06, and raised it to pull the stock into her shoulder. She sighted down the barrel at the tiny bead welded on the end. It steadied on that section of brush from which came the approaching noise.

All of this was happening again all too soon. Behind her

she could hear murmuring, and between clenched teeth she said, "Get. Inside."

How much damage it would do would depend on if it was black or brown, how large, and how either pissed off or hungry it was. Someone had once likened a bear moving across the ground to a lightning bolt shooting sideways. When they got going they were hard to stop, and when they were pissed off they were even harder to calm down. Most of the time they'd make a false charge, and back off. Most of the time.

Empirical experience recently obtained had proved beyond any doubt that "most of the time" didn't count in the Park. If this was one of those years for close encounters of the bear kind, Kate wanted to make sure it was two for two for her side.

A branch snapped. Brush shuddered.

Unless it was a moose. If it was moose, it was running from something, and barring obstruction or human interference it would just gallop through the clearing and keep on going out the other side. Probably. Of course, whatever had startled the moose might be right behind it. She couldn't think of anything else that would make that much noise coming through the woods, but whatever it was it had to be big to be that loud.

Just before the edge of the clearing the lowest branch of a spruce caught on something, jerked free, and flapped wildly. A piece of wood broke with a sound like a gunshot.

Big and clumsy. Her finger tightened on the trigger.

"Kate, no!" Old Sam's shout came at the same moment as the approaching menace smashed into the clearing.

Very, very carefully, Kate unbent her forefinger from around the trigger. She lowered the rifle with stiff arms. The tiny click of the safety was audible to everyone.

For a very long moment there was no other sound in the little clearing, all participants frozen in shocked silence.

Then behind her Holly Haynes made a noise, Auntie Vi exclaimed in horror, and Old Sam swore. Kate let go of the breath she didn't know she'd been holding. Mutt looked up at her and gave a soft whine.

The apparition stood on two legs, all right, but they were clad in jeans that were torn and shredded to above the knee. The legs beneath were a welter of bleeding scratches and oozing wounds. These matched the ones on his arms, bare beneath the fragments of what once had been a dark blue Goretex jacket and a T-shirt so ripped and stained the logo was illegible. His right foot was bare, wrapped in what was probably one of the sleeves of the jacket. The other foot was clad in the remnants of a boot, leather laces wrapped around the sole to hold it in place.

His face looked like something off the cornice of Notre Dame. One eye was swollen shut and sealed by a rusty brown flow of blood that had cascaded from a crusty slash that had opened his forehead from between his eyebrows to the hairline on his left temple. The other eye was the merest slit, through which he peered around him as if he were shortsighted.

He was bearded and filthy and so emaciated it was impossible to tell his age. He could have been fifteen or fifty. They could smell him from the deck. Mutt, recovering her composure, streaked down the stairs and halted in front of him on stiff legs, head between her shoulders, ears flat, her patented threatening growl issuing from deep in her throat. Kate heard Auntie Vi suck in her breath. She said, keeping her voice low and soothing, "Mister?"

He'd been backing away from Mutt's growl. Now he jerked around at the sound of her voice, tripped over one of the buckets of brined salmon, and almost fell.

"Uncle," Kate said in a soft voice. When he came to stand

beside her she handed him the rifle. "Cover me."

"All right, girl."

She came down the steps very slowly, talking all the while in a low, nonthreatening voice. "You been lost in the woods, mister, right? You're okay now. You're found. We'll take care of you."

He let her get within ten feet before he flung himself backward again. He tripped over a pile of alder kindling, scattering it everywhere, and this time he did fall. He landed hard, then pulled himself into a fetal position, hands over his head, uttering a high, thin, continuous cry.

"Jesus," Kate heard Old Sam say. She glanced at him and saw that he looked as unnerved as she felt. In itself that was almost as shocking as the sight of the apparition in front of them.

Mutt had stopped growling. Mutt was a better threat indicator than Homeland Security. If she had ceased to perceive their uninvited guest as dangerous, then he wasn't. Of course, it wasn't like she wasn't still on alert, ears flattened, lips drawn back, drawn up on tiptoe and ready to protect and defend.

Kate took small, slow steps forward, continuing to speak in a husky and she hoped soothing monotone. "Mister, it's all right now, it's okay, you're back in the world. We're going to take care of you. You're cold, and you're hungry, and you're tired. We're going to take care of all that."

She continued to croon, scarcely knowing what she was saying, as she knelt next to him. A tentative hand on his shoulder caused him to shriek. Everyone jumped, and Old Sam swore again.

"It's okay," Kate said, "it's all right."

He lay there on the ground, a quivering knot of misery,

unwilling or unable to look at her. She wasn't even sure if he could hear her, but she kept talking, and began to pat his shoulder, accustoming him to being touched. Close up, his wounds looked far worse. Some of them were infected, others well on their way. The putrid aroma of decomposition made her swallow hard, but his eyes were fixed on her face, wide, unblinking. For the first time in her life Kate thought that a working cell phone system in the Park might not be such a bad thing.

"Can you stand up, mister? Come on, let me help you. Let's get you inside so we can help you clean up. You must be hungry. I bet you'd like something to eat. We've got fresh salmon. Did you smell it cooking? Would you like some?"

He seemed to calm down again. Kate continued her undemanding patter as Old Sam went back to the house to rack the rifle and returned to help haul the man to trembling legs. He was taller than Kate but shorter than Old Sam. He moved in an awkward and disjointed fashion, with no sense of balance, so that he would lurch from Kate to Old Sam and back again, walking as if his feet hurt him. From the look of them Kate thought they had to. There didn't seem to be a square inch of any part of him left whole.

Together the three of them navigated a careful path to the house. The stairs were negotiated with the maximum amount of difficulty. When they got him inside they found that Auntie Vi had been busy. She'd covered one of the dining table chairs with a sheet and directed them to ease him down onto it. She'd found some leftover moose stew in the refrigerator, pureed it in the blender, and poured it into a saucepan to heat. She thinned it with some instant beef broth and poured it into a mug.

She brought it steaming to the table, where Kate and Old

Sam had been working with clean sponges and a bowl of warm water to clear some of the crusts from the man's more serious wounds. "This guy needs the docs," Kate said.

Old Sam, lips compressed in a grim line, shook his head. "He needs an emergency room."

"He maybe not make it that far," Auntie Vi said. It was what they were all thinking.

It wasn't just his eyes, his whole face was swollen, and as they cleared away the blood and the dirt they could see hard angry lumps on his arms and legs as well. "Jesus, the mosquitoes really got to him," Old Sam said.

The man made a sudden swipe with his hand and Kate ducked to avoid being hit.

He slapped again, and this time Old Sam caught his hand in a firm grip. "Hey, buddy," he said. "Calm down. You're fine. No bugs in here."

The man opened his mouth and made an effort. "Aaar," he said.

Kate's eyes met Old Sam's. For some reason, the man's inability to speak shook them both more than anything that had come before.

"Maybe we should just put him in the tub," Kate said.

"Only get him into tub one time," Auntie Vi said. "Clean off first much as we can."

"He's in shock," Old Sam said. "Should we get him wet?"

"Clean feel better," Auntie Vi said. "Half the battle."

Holly Haynes wasn't much use. Every now and then Auntie Vi would give her a chore, like go get another sponge or warm up some more broth, but mostly she hovered and got in the way. She might have been hell on wheels as a geologist but she wasn't much for first aid. Kate, looking up once, saw her face. She looked frightened, and sick, but then they all felt like that.

The bowl of water turned dark with dirt and blood. While Kate changed it, Auntie Vi tried to get some of the soup into him. Some made it down his throat, although it seemed to hurt him to swallow. The rest trickled down his neck. His first cry had been his last. After that, he remained silent, staring into space, taking no notice of their efforts.

At least he wasn't fighting them.

Kate brought more clean water and Auntie Vi and Old Sam started in again. Kate found some clean clothes belonging to Jim, measured them against the stranger's frame, and exchanged them for some of Johnny's instead.

Kate ran Johnny's tub full of warm water, thinking hot might be too much of a shock for him. The man came alive when they tried to remove the remnants of his clothes, until Old Sam lost his temper and said, "You two broads get the hell out of here."

Kate and Auntie Vi retreated to the kitchen. In the bathroom Old Sam swore. Auntie Vi made coffee with hands that seemed less deft than usual.

Kate watched her for a moment, and then remembered. "Oh hell," she said, and went out to find the king filet burned to a crisp on the grill. She put the lid down and closed the dampers and went back inside. Water was gurgling out of the tub, and the faucet was turned on again full bore.

"That boy plenty dirty," Auntie Vi said. "Old Sam changing the water."

Kate hoped the well held out.

They drank their coffee and felt better. Kate bundled the disgusting sheet the stranger had been sitting on into the laundry room. She knocked on the bathroom door and said, "Give me his clothes."

A bundle of rags was thrust at her, and she took them

outside and put them in the burn barrel. They had no identifying marks on them, Levi's jeans, Jockey underwear, what proved to be an All Gone Dead T-shirt, a JCPenney blue plaid shirt, a North Face jacket. Nothing that couldn't have been purchased from any of a hundred catalogs or department stores.

She put it all in the barrel save the remaining boot, squirted it with lighter fluid from the barbecue, and torched it off. If the guy never spoke again, she would get serious shit from Jim for disposing of evidence that might help identify him, but the clothes were filthy and crawling with livestock and she wanted them gone.

The boot looked as if it had been well made, sturdy construction, thick soles. It had a steel toe, too. That she kept.

She went into Johnny's room and cleared the twin bed by the simple expedient of lifting up the mattress and letting everything on it slide to the floor: clothes, books, CDs, headphones, copies of *Maxim* and *Outside* and *National Geographic*, a half-empty bag of Doritos, a plastic sleeve with one remaining saltine cracker, a bowl that looked like it might once have held a generous portion of Cherry Garcia ice cream, and a thumb drive. She rescued the bowl, although cleaning it would take a hammer and chisel, and the thumb drive and swept the rest into a pile and put it in a trash bag which she stowed on the back deck. Either Johnny would never miss it all or he'd look until he found it. If he didn't find it Kate would cart it out to the dump west of the house. Kate didn't usually clean up after Johnny, as had been agreed when he moved in. The most she was willing to do was limit the chaos by closing the door on it. These circumstances, however, were extraordinary.

She remade the bed with clean sheets and came out of the

bedroom to find the bathroom door opening. The stranger shuffled out, Old Sam holding him up with both hands. The man was dressed in jeans that were two inches too long and a T-shirt from Johnny's Kanye West period. He had about as much mass as a scarecrow and the clothes hung on him. Old Sam had threaded a double strand of what looked like dental floss through the belt loops of the jeans. It was the only thing keeping them from sliding to the floor.

"In here," she said.

Old Sam laid him down on the bed, and Kate covered him up. He stared unblinking at the ceiling.

"Mister," Kate said. "Who are you?"

He said nothing.

"Can you tell us your name? Your family's bound to be worried. We could call them, tell them you're all right."

The man stared past Kate and his face twisted. "Aaaah," he said, starting to shake again. "Aaaaaaaaaaah."

"It's okay, buddy," Old Sam said. "You're all right. No bogeymen here, just us."

Old Sam's rough voice seemed to calm the stranger more than Kate's raspy monotone. He quieted.

"You're safe here," Old Sam said. "You're safe. You're safe."

The man's eyes closed, perhaps lulled by Old Sam's litany.

There was silence. "He's not dead, is he?" Kate said.

"Sssshh." Old Sam put his gnarled hand down gently on the man's chest. After a moment, it rose and fell with the man's breathing.

"He's sleeping, right?" Kate said in a whisper. "Not in a coma, or anything?"

"Jesus Christ," Old Sam whispered back. "Of course the man's asleep. He's been lost in the Bush for what looks like the hell of a while, he's clean and fed for the first time in who knows how long, you'd be sleeping, too. Go on, get out of here."

"Maybe somebody should stay with him," Kate said, looking over her shoulder.

"Maybe somebody should leave him the hell alone," Old Sam said, shoving her out the door in front of him and closing it firmly in Auntie Vi and Holly Haynes's faces.

"He never told us his name," Kate said.

Holly Haynes took a shaky breath and let it out again. "Um—"

"You know him?" Kate said. She thought of the steel-toed boot, the boot of someone who worked around heavy equipment. "Someone from the mine?"

Haynes hesitated, and shook her head. "I was going to say, what happened to that hiker that the ranger was so upset about?"

"What hiker?"

"Remember, in the café? Memorial Day weekend?"

Memory came flooding back, of the wannabe backwoodsman in Dan's office on the Step, of his raggedy-ass gear and his romantic notion to hike up to Bright Lake. "If anyone had gone missing, everyone would have heard before now. And Dan's guy—" She hesitated, thinking back. "The toe of one of his boots had been punctured." She shook her head. "No, it was the right boot. This guy had his left one."

She looked at Old Sam. "But it couldn't be, anyway. Dan's guy said he was headed for Bright Lake."

Old Sam snorted. "Bright Lake's in about exactly the opposite direction from here. If this is him, bastard sure took the scenic route."

Haynes persisted. "It's been a month. I know it's a long

way, but anybody can go pretty far in a month."

True enough. Kate compared her memory of the man in Dan's office that day to the one sleeping in Johnny's bed. If memory served, this guy seemed to be about the same height. His own mother wouldn't have been able to identify him from the mess of his face.

"Probably should get him to Anchorage, have him checked out," Haynes said. "I've got a pickup. If we put some padding in the back we can take him in in that."

"Let him sleep," Auntie Vi said. "Best thing for him."

"Damn straight," Old Sam said. "Dumb bastard."

TEN

"IT'S NOT DAVIS," DAN said that evening.

"Why not?"

Dan's eyes were red-rimmed, his face sported a grayish red stubble, and his clothes looked slept in, but regardless he spread his arms and burst into song. "He once was lost, but now is found …"

Kate flinched. Old Sam winced. Mutt put her nose up in the air and howled.

"Thanks, Mutt, another country heard from," Dan told her, and looked up again. "Davis did go missing. Wasn't anything we didn't expect. You saw him," he said to Kate. "He was either gonna die or get rescued."

"He got rescued?"

"He's three days out and he stumbles over his own feet, falls down a couloir on the trail up to Bright Lake, and breaks his leg. He trips his beacon and I had to call in the goddamn Air Guard out of Eielson to pick him up. Cost sixty fucking grand. Our tax dollars at work. This guy ain't him. I personally put him on a plane for Anchorage and told him to stay the hell out of my Park."

There was a brief, charged silence. Kate and Old Sam looked at each other. "You aren't missing anyone else?" Kate said.

Dan had to smile at the hopeful note in her voice. "Sorry."

"So," Old Sam said, putting into words what they were all thinking, "who the hell is this guy?"

A DAY LATER THE Grosdidier brothers had their patient at the airstrip, bandaged like a mummy and ready to load on George's Otter turbo for transshipment to Providence Hospital in Anchorage. Out of what she assured herself was a misplaced sense of responsibility, Kate was there to see him off. Peter Grosdidier roughhoused with Mutt while the other three brothers stood talking to Kate. Old Sam, who had taken a proprietary interest in the stranger, was present, too.

"He's still not talking?" Kate said.

Matt shook his head.

"What's wrong with him?"

Matt shrugged. "It could be post-traumatic amnesia. Or maybe dissociative amnesia, or even repressed memory."

"What's any of that goddamn medical mumbo jumbo mean in English?" Old Sam said.

Matt made a vague gesture that encompassed the Park. "His mind might be repressing something that happened to him out there. Hell, everything that happened to him out there. Pretty fair guess that it wasn't a walk in the, well, Park for him. How long post-traumatic amnesia lasts is usually related to how serious the injury is."

"Do people usually come out of it?"

"Yeah," Matt said. "Usually."

The corollary to that being sometimes they didn't. "He had a lot of injuries," Kate said.

"Tell me about it," Matt said with feeling. "I had to order in a new supply of four-by-fours."

Kate looked down at the unknown woods warrior. "If he does come out of it, how long will it take?"

Matt looked down at the guy, too. "No idea. But you don't get over that amount of trauma in a day or two. One thing for sure, he probably isn't a Park rat or he would have survived his trek in better shape."

"And he woulda got himself found a lot quicker," Old Sam said.

Maybe, Kate thought, and maybe not. Not every Park rat was as backwoods apt as Old Sam.

Everyone looked at the unknown hiker wrapped in olive green Army blankets, his one good eye open and fixed in a thousand-mile stare on something over his head that none of the rest of them could see. They all looked away again with the half-ashamed, half-relieved embarrassment the sane felt in the present of the not so. Kate had been relieved to see that the swelling on his face was reduced to the point where the shape of his features had returned to something less gargoylian, although it was still a roadmap of what he'd been through.

It was with relief they heard the approach of the Otter, and turned to watch it touch down at the end of the strip. It pulled to a halt in front of the Chugach Air Taxi hangar and George came out to open the door and pull up a step stool for the passengers to disembark. Mine workers got off the plane in less of a hurry to go back to work than they had got on to go on R & R. Many looked rather the worse for wear, and Kate hoped none of them would be operating heavy equipment any time in the near future.

Lyda Blue was last out, slinging a daypack over her shoulder. Kate caught her eye and raised a hand.

Lyda nodded and walked over to say hello. Her eyes dropped to the lost guy and the daypack slid from her shoulder to the ground.

"What?" Kate said.

Lyda opened her mouth and nothing came out. The color drained from her face and she started to go down.

"Whoa," Kate said, catching her. "Guys. Guys! Help me out here."

The Grosdidier brothers scampered around and caught Lyda before she went splat. The Otter's step stool was confiscated and slid beneath Lyda's butt, and her head was pushed gently but firmly between her knees. She submitted for several deep gasps of air, and then she struggled free, coming down on her knees next to the stretcher. A shaking hand reached out, a fingertip touched the lost guy's cheek.

"Lyda?"

Lyda Blue looked up, her face frozen but for the tears spilling down her cheeks. Through numb lips she said, "It's Wayne."

Between them the lost guy stared unblinking at the sky.

And Sergeant Jim Chopin of the Alaska State Troopers chose this moment to set his Cessna down light as a feather at the end of the runway. He taxied to the much smaller hangar next to Chugach Air, killed the engine, and got out, to be greeted by an ecstatic Mutt who had identified the sound of his engine when he was still a mile out.

She escorted him back to the group at very nearly a prance. He studied Kate's expression, eyed Lyda Blue's crumpled face, passed briefly over Old Sam and the four Grosdidiers, and came to rest on the man on the stretcher. "What seems to be the problem here?"

"BUT DEWAYNE GAMMONS IS dead," Jim said.

Kate had never heard him sound more at a loss. She didn't blame him. "I know."

"You found his body," Jim said, reminding her, reminding

everyone in the room. "Bear snack."

"I know," Kate said again.

"This girl—" Jim looked at Lyda, who was sitting in a chair looking pale and strained.

"Lyda," Kate said. "Lyda Blue."

"You know him well enough to make a positive identification?"

Since Lyda seemed incapable of speech, Kate said, "She works admin out at the mine. Plus they were friends."

"She just identified him today?"

"She just got back from her week off. It's the first time she's seen him since he showed up."

Jim was determined to be obtuse on the subject for as long as possible, because he knew what was going to happen when he stopped. "When, again, did you say this guy came out of the woods?"

"Yesterday," Kate said. She knew what was coming, too, and she wasn't any happier about it than he was. "Fourth of July."

"Wait a minute," he said. "Didn't you say what's her name, Hollister, Haversham—"

"Haynes," Kate said.

"Yeah, Haynes, the goddamn Suulutaq staff geologist, didn't you say she was at the homestead when this guy came crashing out of the woods?"

"Yes."

"And she didn't recognize him?"

"Jesus, Jim," Old Sam said, defying all efforts to exclude him from what he knew was a hell of a story in the making. "He wasn't hardly human when he come out of the woods. His own mother wouldn't a recognized him."

"Okay," Jim said. "So now he's on his way to—"

167

"Anchorage. Matt said he needed a big hospital, preferably one with a stable full of shrinks."

"Okay," Jim said again. "Say he is Gammons. He parked his truck, hiked out into the Bush, got lost returning his body to nature—"

Lyda flinched at the sarcasm in his tone.

"—evidently nature turns him down, and a month later he staggers onto Kate's homestead. That about it?"

Nods all around.

"Okay," he said for the third time, and there was no mistaking his irritation now. "Just fan-fucking-tastic. If Gammons is alive—more or less, from what I saw—then who the hell belonged to those pieces you people pulled out of the woods a month ago?"

And he glared at Kate and Old Sam and Lyda like it was all their fault.

ELEVEN

IT WAS COMING ON seven o'clock at night, and Niniltna was in post-holiday mode, with crooked bunting hanging from the eaves of houses and Alaska and USA flags fluttering from porches. Everyone who wasn't at fish camp or waiting on Alaganik Bay for the Fish and Game to announce an opener or working at the Suulutaq was out in force. Many of them had been drinking since the day before and were full to the brim with good spirits and bonhomie. Jim turned a blind eye to any and all lingering fireworks, and against all expectation on his way home did not actually see anyone driving under the influence, for which he was profoundly thankful.

He and Kenny had caught their bad guy in Ahtna, although the bad guy had not given up without a fight. Jim, not a small man, and Kenny, a very large man indeed, had both been put to strenuous effort to subdue one guy maybe five eight weighing maybe 150 pounds. All he had to do was resist and keep on resisting, and this he did with vigor and enthusiasm. The trailer park mob that poured outdoors to watch didn't help, many of them previously known to both Kenny and Jim and many more well lubricated in celebration of the day. For a while the arrest appeared to be teetering on the edge of precipitating a riot. Kenny was finally driven to putting his hand on his sidearm in a show of force. He didn't pull it, he didn't go that far, he just let it sit on the butt of the .357

Magnum. Jim was fully occupied in hanging on to their bad guy and couldn't even hitch his gun belt in support, but that was okay. Enough of the crowd had seen *Dirty Harry* and were ready to abandon their fellow to his fate on the strength of it.

Their guy's energy leached away with them and Kenny and Jim bagged him along with a trailer full of stolen property, including a closet full of weapons. The most interesting of these was an assault rifle with a canvas grip full of loaded clips. "Ah, Mr. Kalashnikov, I presume," Kenny had said. "And if I'm not mistaken, a Type 81. I wonder where the hell that came from." He looked at Jim. "Other than China originally, I mean."

Jim didn't care. He wasn't a gun nut. He could clean and load a 9 mm Smith & Wesson automatic and his backup piece, an M&P .357, and produce a respectable grouping of shots on the police silhouette target he printed out on his computer once a month. He wasn't a hunter, he didn't own a rifle, and he owned no recreational weapons. A closet full of probably stolen and certainly unpermitted weapons, a majority of which appeared to qualify under AS 11.61.200(h)(1)(C) as prohibited, looked to him like a Class C felony and nothing more.

The good news was Bobbie Singh was going to be able to keep the perp out of his hair for at least five years and probably more if Jim was any judge of his character. The gentleman did not appear to him to be a viable candidate for time off with good behavior.

Still, yesterday's had been a tense afternoon, made more so by a close encounter of the newspaper kind, this in the form of an interview by one Benjamin Franklin Gunn of the *Ahtna Adit*, the town's weekly newspaper. He made Kenny and Jim pose for a photograph in front of the pile of illegal weapons. Jim liked trophy shots about as much as he liked interviews. He was left feeling sore in body and in spirit, neither of which was alleviated by the necessity of reopening an investigation into a case that had been disposed of a full month before. While he did not grudge Dewayne Gammons his return to the ranks of the living, he was seriously pissed off over the prospect of trying to identify the month-old remains of yet another idiot who had gone wandering off in the Park without a clue as to what was lying in wait for him there.

The only way to make something foolproof was to keep it away from fools. He didn't know who'd said that but it was a rule to by god live by if he'd ever heard one. He wondered when science would invent a buzzer that would go off on Maggie's desk when a fool stepped off a plane at the Niniltna airstrip.

All he wanted now was food, a hot shower, and a bed. And the promise of at least a few fool-free moments.

Kate was on her way home, too, by prior arrangement detouring first by Auntie Edna's. The best bulk cook among the four aunties, she always had something on the stove in a quantity large enough to feed the crew of an aircraft carrier. Her father had been a Filipino and a damn fine cook and he had taught Auntie Edna well, and today what was on the stove was lumpia, chicken adobo, and rice.

None of that was new. What was new was the line at the door, made up mostly of, you guessed it, Suulutaq Mine workers. Kate arrived to find Auntie Edna in the act of exchanging a recycled garbage bag containing four white Styrofoam containers for a fistful of cash from a young mine worker who might have been drooling a little out of the corner of his mouth. Kate didn't blame him, given the collection of

171

aromas wafting from Auntie Edna's kitchen.

Auntie Edna looked up to see Kate take her place at the end of the line, and waved her forward with an imperial gesture. "My niece," she said, "very important, busy person." Everyone else shifted their feet and sighed and sulked and Kate could feel their resentful glances boring into her back, but none of them was so foolish as to walk away and lose their place in line.

"When did you get started in the take-out business, Auntie?"

Auntie Edna, normally an Olympic-class grump and hands down the sourest of the four aunties, this fair summer evening looked happier than Kate had ever seen her. "Some boys follow their noses to my kitchen on Memorial Day," she said, aiming a beam of Auntie Joy–wattage at the line. "Other boys follow. Good eaters, all them boys." She lowered her voice. "And good payers, too."

Over her shoulder Kate saw that Auntie Edna had borrowed some of the larger pots from the school cafeteria, which sat steaming on a stove with all four burners on high. Tacked next to the door was a hand-lettered menu, beginning with bagoong. Kate toted up her order and was ready with her tab when Auntie Edna handed out a full bag, and almost went into shock when Auntie Edna waived payment. "My niece," she told the line, turning Kate to face them, hands on her shoulders holding her on the top step. "She make mine happen. She why you here. Okay, next?" A firm shove and Kate was displaced on the top step by the next in line.

The combined smells liked to drive Kate insane before she got to the homestead, and she was conscious enough to look guilty when Jim raised an eyebrow at how few lumpia had survived the trip. It wasn't her fault. Lumpia was finger food.

You can't eat long rice and drive at the same time. "Did you know Auntie Edna is running a take-out restaurant out of her kitchen?"

He nodded. "I'd heard something about it."

She shook her head. "Auntie Vi sells her B and B, Auntie Balasha is selling kuspuks at the Riverside Café, now Auntie Edna is selling Filipino takeout out her back door. What next?"

"I'll set the table while you shower," he said, and picked her up and kissed her. She kicked him in the shins with one of her dangling feet, but not very hard.

Jim pulled all the leftovers out of the refrigerator to join what Kate had brought home, which didn't look like anywhere near enough to either his eye or his stomach. Fifteen minutes later they sat down to a meal that while it adhered to no particular nutritional guideline was immensely satisfying. Jim had even sliced some sashimi from a fresh king filet he found in the refrigerator and mixed up a wasabi-soy sauce accompaniment.

All was quiet for a time, and then Jim sat back and burped in a very satisfied manner. "I might live."

"Me, too. So how was your day, dear?"

He told her. "How was yours?"

She fetched the boot remnant that was still sitting on the deck.

He studied it, turning it over in his hands. "Suulutaq buys gear for their employees, right?"

"Outside gear. Parkas, jackets, bibs, overalls."

"And boots?"

"And boots."

"Boots like this one?"

"Almost exactly like this one, I'd say."

He grunted, and set the boot aside.

"Bed?" she said.

"God, yes," he said, and followed her up the stairs. They stripped off their clothes and tumbled down together and were instantly asleep.

THE NEXT MORNING KATE woke up, sat up, and said, "Who else hasn't shown up for work at Suulutaq in the past month?"

Jim opened one sleepy blue eye and considered. "Good question. You're back on the clock."

She threw back the covers and swung a leg over the edge of the bed.

A long arm snaked out and grabbed her before she got both feet on the floor. "Where do you think you're going?"

She let herself fall back onto the mattress. "I think I'm staying right here."

He pulled her beneath him. "Good decision."

That it was.

AFTER CHECKING IN WITH Maggie at the post and turning a blind eye to the accumulating pile of pink call slips she had left in the exact center of his desk, Jim went to Old Sam's house. This was a log cabin on the very edge of the Kanuyaq River, about five hundred feet north of Ekaterina Shugak's old house, now occupied by Martha Barnes and her large brood of children, six or eight of which he could hear whooping and hollering in a game of cowboys and Indians. Sounded like the Indians were winning.

Old Sam's cabin was very much lost in the tall grass, and the forget-me-nots, columbine, and moss campion that were running riot over the sod roof provided a much-needed homing beacon. A path led to a weathered but sound wooden walkway that led in turn to the cabin door, and from there down to a small dock. At the end of the dock there was a bench made from lengths of alder woven together in a sturdy frame that had achieved the patina of old pewter. On that bench sat Old Sam, coffee mug in hand and feet crossed on an overturned galvanized steel bucket. He'd heard Jim's footsteps on the dock. "Go on in, get yourself a mug up if you want."

Jim had to duck to get in the door. Inside, there was a counter with a sink and a pump handle, an oil stove for cooking, a wood stove for heat, a beat-up brown leather Barcalounger and shelves made of two-by-twelves fixed to every inch of available wall space. Jim, perforce, paused to look at some of the books on the shelves. Old Sam's taste in reading was catholic, he'd give him that. He had everything ever written by Robert Ruark, including three different editions of *Use Enough Gun*. Wilbur Smith and Peter Capstick were well represented, and Zane Grey and Louis L'Amour very much in evidence. Jim pulled down a book with a leopard-print cover that revealed itself to be a much-thumbed copy of *The Truth About Hunting in Today's Africa*, which fell open to a black-and-white photo of "the dreaded tsetse fly."

He closed the book and replaced it on the shelf. So far as he knew Old Sam had never left Alaska.

The next shelf was dedicated to Captain Cook, including a venerable edition of Cook's three-volume log bound in worn maroon leather with gilt titles, a copy of Tony Horwitz's *Blue Latitudes*, a favorite of Jim's, and the Cook biography by Alistair MacLean. The next shelf was reserved for Alaskana, autobiographies by Wickersham and Gruening and Hammond, histories of the war in the Aleutians and the gold rush, bios of Bush pilots. He opened one at random and found dog-eared pages with copious notes in the margins.

He'd never thought of Old Sam as a reader. The old man had always seemed to him to be more a man of action than reflection. He shrugged and replaced the volume on the shelf. No law said a man couldn't be both.

A chrome-legged dining room table and chairs that would have been new around 1957 took up the center of the room. Overhead was a narrow sleeping loft, reached by a homemade ladder whose uprights were worn smooth from long use.

It felt very familiar, and after a moment Jim knew why. Although older and smaller, Old Sam's cabin looked a lot like Kate's old cabin. Well, why not? Old Sam must have known Kate's father. They might even have helped put up each other's cabins. Why screw with a floor plan that worked.

This cabin had electricity, though, and a plug-in coffeepot. Jim poured a fluid the viscosity of thirty-weight into a boat mug he found on a shelf and added a precautionary dose from the can of evaporated milk standing providentially near to hand.

The sun was warm on his face as he walked down the dock. The current was running strongly downstream, where other cabins and houses and docks could be seen with their toes in the swift-running water. Old Sam moved over on the bench, which creaked, but not alarmingly. Jim sat down next to him and crossed his heels on the edge of the dock. He took a sip of coffee and hid his wince. "Meant to say yesterday, aren't you supposed to be down Alaganik way this time of year?"

"I would be if the goddamn fish hawks would call an opener."

"Who's minding the *Freya*?"

"That Jeppsen boy and the Lestinkof girl Kate wished on me."

"Who's minding them?"

"Got her anchored up just offshore of Mary's site. She's keeping an eye out."

The two men contemplated the passing river in companionable silence. A pair of eagles chittered from the top of a nearby scrag, three ravens chased each other in a madcap spiral, and a lone seagull zeroed in on the carcass of a spawned-out salmon cast up on a nearby sandbank. Almost immediately half a dozen other seagulls materialized to fight for their share.

Martin Shugak went by in an ancient, paintless dory powered by a seventy-five-horsepower Mercury outboard engine that looked brand-new. He raised a hand in greeting to Old Sam, saw Jim and hunched his shoulders and looked the other way.

"Nice outboard," Old Sam said.

"Don't go there," Jim said.

A little while later Edna Aguilar came upriver in an olive-green inflatable boat with a two-horsepower Evinrude on the back that looked like a large mosquito. It sounded like one, too.

"Is it just me or does she always look pissed off?" Jim said.

"It ain't just you," Old Sam said.

The proper thing would be to compliment Edna on last night's meal but Jim was too scared to. Both men gave perfunctory waves and prayed silently that she would go on by. They breathed more easily when she had.

Andy Martushev appeared in his canoe, paddle moving through the water at a steady beat, the sun illuminating the crystalline drops of spray over the bow when he changed sides.

"Andy," Old Sam said when Andy was in earshot.

"Sam," Andy said.

"Want some coffee?"

"Got some waiting on me at the café."

"And somebody a lot prettier to wait on you," Old Sam said.

Andy grinned and paddled on by. "He's dreaming," Old Sam said.

"Why?" Jim said. "Andy's all right. Laurel could do a lot worse."

"I hear she and Matt Grosdidier might maybe got a thing," Old Sam said, always a step ahead of everybody else on Park gossip. "Besides, Laurel's not about to throw herself away on a fuckup like Andy. She's too much her mother's daughter." Old Sam drank coffee. "Things going okay with the girl?"

Grunt.

"Looking like it's going to last?"

"Jesus, Old Sam, I don't even talk about this stuff with Kate."

"Maybe you oughta."

With what he felt was pardonable indignation, Jim said, "Whose coffee am I drinking here, Dear Abby's?"

"The NNA chair knows that mine's a good thing for the Park. Industry, jobs, a tax base so they can start picking up where the state's falling off."

Jim looked at the old man, startled by a comment that seemed right out of left field.

Old Sam wore an uncompromising expression. He was going to say what he had to say and Jim was going to hear it. "The Park rat's a different story. The Park rat, she hates the mine and everything to do with it. The mine's invading the place that healed her when she was wounded body and soul after that job in Anchorage. It's a violation of the peace and

178

the privacy she's taken as her birthright. This mine will change the face of the land itself, scar it so that it will never be the same again." Old Sam looked down into his mug. "This ain't easy times for the Park rat. Just saying you should keep it in mind, is all."

His peaceful mood shattered, Jim finished his coffee and set the mug down on the dock. "You remember where you guys found that body in May?"

Old Sam scratched his chin and pretended to think about it. "The body that was previously identified as this guy who staggered out of the woods day before yesterday?"

"Yeah."

Old Sam thought some more. "I reckon I could find it again, was I asked."

This was the purest sophistry, of course. Old Sam Dementieff had more time served in the Park than any ten other Park rats you could name. He'd covered most of its twenty million acres on the ground, on either foot, four-wheeler, or snowmobile, not to mention cross-country skis, snowshoes, pickup, and the ever and omnipresent airplane. There wasn't a grizzly den or a caribou calving ground within a hundred miles that Old Sam couldn't have found in his sleep. He'd walked out of at least one plane crash in the dead of winter when everyone else on board including the pilot had died, showing up in Niniltna a week later. "Didn't look like he'd missed a meal," Kate had said. "What's more, he led them straight back to it, no passing Go, no collecting two hundred dollars." She'd shaken her head. "I'm a pretty good backwoodsman, but Old Sam ..."

Jim knew it, and Old Sam knew he knew it, but Jim wasn't going to say it, partly because it would just pander to the old fart's ego, which justifiably or not was already the size of Big

Bump, and partly because saying so might then necessitate a discussion about what Old Sam had really been doing out in the woods the day the search party had tripped over him. Like Kate, Jim thought the less official notice taken of that, the better for all concerned. So he said only, "I'd appreciate it if you could guide me out there."

"What for?"

"Well." Jim squinted into the sun. "Kate tells me the bunch of you were in something of a hurry when you left."

"We were at first." Old Sam grinned that saturnine grin. "After, of course, Dan insisted we skin out that ol' griz and take his bladder so no one else would and sell 'em off on the black market."

"Yeah, Kate said. She is especially torqued that Dan wouldn't let her keep the hide. Anyway, I was thinking there might be something there that got missed in all the excitement." Jim looked back across the river, wishing he could sit next to its calm serenity for the rest of the day. "The thing is, I'm going to need a hell of a lot more than I've got now if I'm ever going to identify that body."

OLD SAM DROVE THEM to the place where they'd found Gammons's pickup. He parked and they got out. He had his Model 70 slung over his shoulder. At Jim's look he said tersely, "Fish are hitting fresh water. The bears'll all be down on the creeks by now."

Jim had brought the shotgun from his Blazer anyway.

They moved through the woods, Jim following Old Sam. To Jim it looked like your average forest, dark, impenetrable to the sun, and possessed of a malevolent spirit that was out to get him and only him. Scrub spruce flung up roots for him to trip over and then slapped him in the face with their branches, if they didn't outright leap into his path. Diamond willow wound themselves into a tangle that would have put the Gordian knot to shame. Where the willow left off the alder began, and when he managed to fight off the alder a grove of birch trees was lurking in a dense fence with no bole more than six inches from the next. Biting flies and mosquitoes gathered around this heaven-sent infusion of fresh blood and in spite of the bug dope he had slathered on himself before they went in he was attacked with the enthusiastic, single-minded dedication only genus *Aedes* can bring to their duty. The one place they didn't bite was where the spruce sap had attached itself to his skin, and he knew from bitter experience the only way to remove spruce sap was to grow a new epidermis.

There was a reason for the invention of airplanes, and it was so you could fly over this crap instead of walk through it. Jim knuckled a drop of sweat depending from the tip of his nose and soldiered on.

Ahead of him, by contrast, Old Sam ambled forward with all the air of a man taking a walk down a country lane on a mild Sunday morning. He didn't trip or stumble, he didn't sweat or swear, he didn't swat or slap, no, he simply slid through the brush as if it had been greased specifically for his passage, while the bugs kept a respectful distance.

It felt as if hours and miles had passed before Old Sam said at long last, "Here," and Jim emerged into a clearing, blinking in the rediscovered sun that had been there all the time and that beamed down on them now like an old friend. He stood there for a moment to let his eyes adjust to daylight again. A raven croaked from the top of a tree, and a couple of crows cawed from another. Even the birds had attitude today. He pulled out a bottle of water, uncapped it, and drank it down in one long continual swallow.

Old Sam stood to one side, one hand hooked on the sling of his rifle, the other in the pocket of his jacket, watching with a quizzical expression on his seamed face. Fucker wasn't even sweating.

Jim crushed the bottle, replaced the cap, and put it back in his pocket. "Okay, let's take a look around."

"You want help, or you want me to stay out of the way?"

"Help, definitely. We'll walk it in a straight line, side by side about six feet apart. Walk slow and watch where you put your feet."

Old Sam surveyed the area. "You really expecting to find anything?"

He had a point. When they'd been there the month before, Old Sam said, the grass had just been beginning to green up. Now it was four feet high and under the influence of twenty hours of daylight leaping even farther skyward with boundless enthusiasm. Jim could wish it were a little less healthy.

The raven croaked again and then changed dialects like they sometimes did, producing a series of clicks and taps and claps. Two more ravens arrived and joined in the chorus.

"Great, we've got an audience," Jim said.

Old Sam said nothing, eyeing the ravens with a narrow stare.

"Okay, let's get it done," Jim said.

It took them a full fifteen minutes to wade slowly the length of the clearing. About halfway across on the return trip Jim tripped over something. He rooted around until he found whatever it was, and froze in a bent-over position, his eyes wide.

"What?" Old Sam came up to stand next to him and peer into the grass. "Oh," he said. "Yeah, that'll be the bones left from that griz Kate shot. We skinned 'em and left the rest." He admired the pile of bones, stripped clean of any shred of flesh or gristle, leaving nothing behind but tooth marks in varying sizes. "Got to admire the efficiency."

Jim straightened up and passed a shirtsleeve over a sweaty forehead. "Right. Sure. Of course." He would never have admitted it, especially not to Old Sam, but he didn't like the tall grass any better than he'd liked the impenetrable forest. A clear view in every direction was the best defense against predators, whether they had two feet or four.

"Hell," Old Sam said, still peering at the bones, barely visible in the abundant new growth. "I'm not sure I'm even seeing all the way to the ground. Shoulda brought Mutt. She could sniff out anything."

Jim reined in his imagination. "Let's move down twelve feet and do it again."

This time, two-thirds of the way across the clearing Jim's toe hit something hard, and he tripped and nearly fell again. He swore and caught his balance.

"What?" Old Sam said.

"I don't know," Jim said, parting the grass and peering down. "I kicked something."

He moved some more grass aside, and paused.

"What?"

Jim pulled a thin rubber glove from his pocket and pulled it on. From another pocket he pulled an evidence bag. With the gloved hand he reached down and picked up a small pistol, a revolver with a brown grip that wasn't wood, with the little silver Smith & Wesson badge on both sides.

He looked at Old Sam, who looked from the pistol to where they'd come out of the woods into the clearing. "I be damn," he said.

"What?" Jim said.

"I bet that sumbitch is what tripped me up," Old Sam said. "Lost my goddamn rifle, too, which is why Kate got my bear."

" 'My' bear?" Jim said.

Old Sam grinned. "Did I say 'my' bear? Slip of the tongue."

"That's what I thought," Jim said, and they both looked back at the pistol. "Twenty-two Long Rifle CTG."

"I'm impressed," Old Sam said.

"It says so on the barrel," Jim said. He smelled the muzzle. Old Sam raised an eyebrow, and Jim shook his head. "It's got green stuff starting to grow on it. Been here a while."

"Long as the body?"

"That would be the question." The revolver had a swing-out cylinder, and Jim broke it open and held it up to look through it.

It had been fully loaded. All six rounds were spent. He remembered the loose round Kate had found on the floor of Gammons's pickup.

The ravens sent up a chorus of whistles and clicks. Jim looked up to find that the treetops had taken on a Hitchcockian air, with black birds perched in every second tree. "Okay, this doesn't give me the creeps or anything."

Old Sam was looking up at the ravens, head cocked to one side.

"What?" Jim said.

"They're not here for no reason," the old man said.

"What—" Jim stopped. "Oh."

Old Sam looked at him, his face grim. "See how they're grouping up on that side?"

Jim did. "Probably just a dead rabbit or something."

"Maybe." Old Sam waded through the grass in that direction. "Maybe not."

They found the dead moose calf. They also found the human skull.

It had been reduced mostly to bone, with a few strips of gristle and skin left to it, which explained the ravens and crows. A distinctive squawk made Jim look up at the trees again. And the magpies. Grass had grown through the one unbroken eye socket. The brain cavity had been picked and sucked and licked clean. The hair was gone, probably plucked by innumerable beaks and used for bird nests.

Jim looked at Old Sam. No one had told him the month before that the skull hadn't been found, and he hadn't thought to ask. No wonder the ME had been so focused on blood types. "You didn't look for the skull?"

Old Sam squinted at the ravens. "Yeah, well, like you said. We were in a bit of a hurry."

Jim used a pen to hook the skull through the eye socket and drop it into another evidence bag. He sealed it and raised it to eye level.

His heart lifted. There were still some teeth attached to the jaw, and a couple of the teeth had fillings.

TWELVE

KATE HAD TO WAIT until noon for a seat on a flight out to the mine, and this time she flew in the Beaver with the new guy. He was in his late twenties, cocky and capable, and was hitting on Kate before they'd been in the air five minutes, Mutt sitting just behind them notwithstanding. Kate advised him to attend to his flying. He gave her a comprehensive once-over, a cheerful grin. "Can't blame a guy for trying."

The reappearance of Dewayne Gammons a month after he'd been pronounced dead had reawakened all of the niggling little doubts she'd had a month ago over the presumption of suicide. There was no real reason for this, since it didn't appear that the body in question had been the victim of foul play. It didn't stop her from reviewing the points one by one as the land passed beneath them and the rocky arms of the Quilaks rose up before them.

The round of .22 ammunition found rolling around in the truck. Where was the box it came from? Where was the firearm it was made for? Who did both belong to?

It was Gammons's truck, which argued the ammunition was his. He'd had no pistol on him when he had crashed headlong into Kate's yard, although he could have dropped it somewhere in the past month. But why take a pistol if you were planning to die? Unless you were going to shoot yourself with it. But he hadn't.

Maybe he'd tried to, and missed.

The size of the round and the size of the firearm it was made for led to another question. Who in their right minds took only a .22 into the Park with the bears just up? A .22 would most emphatically not stop anything bigger than a lemming.

It would, however, be useful against another human being.

Lyda Blue had not recognized the writing on the suicide note. Okay, Jim was right, it was a printed note. The crime lab had compared it with the little of his handwriting to be found in his personnel file and declared that there wasn't enough of a sample to say one way or another. Nor had they been able to find enough left of a fingerprint either in the file or on the note to make a match. Still, Kate remembered that split-second moment of hesitation between when Lyda had first seen the note and when she had dissolved into tears. Kate was sure Lyda had seen something in that note, something she had chosen not to share.

Or maybe Jim was right and all of this was just a product of her fevered imagination.

The round, the missing gun, the note. What else?

The truck. There was no road between the mine and Niniltna. Gammons had to have parked the truck in Niniltna and taken the company flight to the mine. Which meant the truck had to have been parked somewhere secure or Howie Katelnikof or Martin Shugak would have made it their business to acquire it, either one piece at a time with a lug wrench or more probably all at once with a tow bar.

In any event, finding out where Gammons had parked the truck between shifts wouldn't prove anything about the body one way or another. It was just another piece of information, and you never knew which piece would cause the whole puzzle to fall into place. A while back Kate had worked a case that had hung on the different colors of aviation gas through the ages. Details were important.

When Gammons came out of his funk she could put all of these questions to him. When she was done today she expected to have more.

The pilot, who had introduced himself as Bud, set the Beaver down on the mine's airstrip with a bounce that told anyone watching he wasn't flying his own plane. They rolled to a stop and someone popped the pilot's door before the prop had stopped rotating. Vern Truax was on the other side and he did not look as if his wife's weekend booty call had been a success. He saw Kate and his mouth tightened. "I've got someone I want you to take back to Niniltna immediately."

Bud looked confused. "What about the off-shifters?"

Truax leaned in. "I want your ass and his ass in the air going northwest. Immediately."

Bud lost color. "Yessir, Mr. Truax."

"You can come back for the shift change when you dump his ass in Niniltna. Clear?"

"Yessir, Mr. Truax."

Truax gave Kate a barely civil nod. "Kate."

"Vern," Kate said, and climbed back through the plane and out onto the ground, Mutt jumping down next to her.

Truax was clearly in a white-hot fury. Kate thought it might have something to do with the man standing next to him, who stepped forward with an outstretched hand. "Kostas McKenzie, Ms. Shugak. I've heard a lot about you. I expect everyone has."

She took it. He hung on a little too long and he gripped a little too hard, like maybe he had something to prove. Mutt took a step forward. McKenzie looked at her and held on a

188

little longer, just to make his point.

"Have we met?" Kate said when she'd managed to free herself.

"I'm with Gaea," he said.

He looked to be in his late thirties, medium all over, height, girth, and weight, brown/brown, perfect American teeth displayed in a genial smile that looked practiced, a ruddy complexion that indicated a life spent mostly outdoors, and attire that inferred money spent. He didn't give off the impression of a Suulutaq Mine employee, or at least not one paid by the hour.

After a minute she had it. He'd been in the café on Memorial Day. When he didn't say anything else she said, "And Gaea is …"

He laughed, throwing his head back and baring all of his beautiful orthodonture. He had a kind of animal magnetism that Kate recognized and mistrusted in the same moment. Louis Deem, the nearest thing the Park had ever produced to a Ted Bundy, had had a similar quality.

Meantime, McKenzie reined in his guffaw to a genial chuckle that Kate heard as produced. "Gaea is an environmental activist nonprofit group. Like the Wilderness Society, or the Sierra Club." There was a twinkle in his eyes, albeit one devoid of patronage, as if he was aware of his organization's low profile and unconcerned and even amused at it. It argued a less self-involved personality than she had first thought. "Only newer."

"And I would guess with a much smaller membership and virtually no public profile," Kate said, "because I'd never heard of you before this summer."

The twinkle persisted. "For now, yes. Anyway, I took the liberty of introducing myself because we've taken an interest in the Suulutaq Mine."

"You and Greenpeace and Friends of the Earth, oh my," Kate said.

"And because you are the chair of the board of the Niniltna Native Association, and because the NNA is the closest thing to a governing body the Park has, I thought we should at the very least be acquainted." He produced a business card. She looked at it. There was a tiny logo in one corner, a dark-haired woman in flowing draperies cradling a ball. It was the same logo she had seen on the flyer in Gammons's room a month before. "This is the address of our local office. I'd be happy to show you around the next time you're in Anchorage."

"You have a local office?" Kate said.

"Sure do." He turned his smile on Truax, who scowled. "We even plan to open an office in Niniltna." He took a moment to bask in the reaction to his last statement before turning and climbing into the plane. An unnerved Bud wasted no time in getting airborne. McKenzie tossed them a jaunty wave as they lifted off the end of the airstrip.

"Well, this just gets better and better," Kate said. When PETA tried to change fish into kittens she'd pretty much tuned out of the environmental movement for the foreseeable future. "You invite him out here?"

A bark of angry laughter. "Hell, no! Fucker sneaked in on one of the crew-change flights. Somebody didn't show up, there was an empty seat, and he just climbed on board and rode in and started snooping around."

That took a certain amount of gall. It was something Kate might have done herself. "What did he want?"

Vern exploded. "What do those bastards ever want? Evidence that we're poisoning the land with toxic waste and slaughtering all the animals and for all I know causing the earth to rotate in reverse. Jesus!" He fixed her with a furious eye. "There are legally required environmental standards and we adhere to all of them, Kate."

"Okay," she said.

"Even the ones we don't agree with, even the ones that seem ridiculous, like filing paperwork when somebody spills a quart of oil when they're changing the filter on a truck."

"Okay," she said.

"I will go so far as to say that in certain cases we exceed those standards because we don't think they're strict enough. It's not like we go out shopping for ways for assholes like that to come down on us." He made a gesture that was perilously close to giving the finger to the rapidly receding aircraft.

"Okay," she said.

He took a deep breath and made a visible effort at calm. She admired his self-control. "He was here for four hours before Holly overheard him asking too many of the wrong questions."

"Tell me something, Vern. If he'd asked for a tour, would you have given him one?"

"We run regular tours one Sunday every month during the summer for journalists and spouses," Vern said, so prompt it sounded rehearsed. "Anyone who wants to join it, all they have to do is fill out a form at the office in Anchorage."

Kate raised an eyebrow. "Representatives of outfits like Gaea get priority seating on those tours?"

For a moment she thought he was going to explode again. Instead he burst out laughing. "Okay, you got me. Maybe not priority seating." He shook his head. "What can I do for you today, Kate?"

"I need a list of every male employee who walked out on their jobs here for the last two months. Say three months, just to be safe."

"Why?"

"Remember Dewayne Gammons?"

"Who could forget? He was the dumb fu—the guy who returned his body to nature."

"Yeah, well, it turns out not so much. He's alive."

Truax's head came up. "What?"

"Didn't Lyda tell you?"

"Tell me what?"

Kate could understand Lyda not wanting to talk about Dewayne Gammons's return from the dead. *Such a loser*, she had said. Once recovered from the shock of seeing him alive, she had probably been angry with herself for showing so much emotion.

As for everyone else on her plane, true to form Gammons's presence on the airstrip had not registered with his coworkers. He'd erased himself from the camp's consciousness before he'd even left. "He's alive," she said. "He walked out of the woods on the Fourth of July."

Truax stared at her for a moment. "Gammons is alive."

"Yes."

"And you want the files because—"

"Because our best guess is still that the body is one of your ex-workers. Just not Gammons."

"Great. Yeah, okay, I'll get Lyda to pull the files for you. I sure hope—"

He broke off when Holly Haynes came running up over the rise to where they were standing. She looked wild and she was breathing hard, and she rushed straight at Truax like he was her last hope of heaven, certain of succor, of comfort. "Vern, come quick, something awful."

He gave Kate a fleeting glance and caught Haynes by her arms, holding her away from him. "Holly, what's wrong?"

When she didn't immediately answer he gave her a shake that was less than loverlike. "Holly. What's wrong?"

She struggled free of his hands and bent over, hands on her knees, and tried to catch her breath. She said something without looking up.

Vern frowned, bending down to catch what she was saying. "What? I can't hear you. What did you say?"

Haynes stood up straight, face red from the blood rushing to it. "It's Lyda."

Vern stood up with her. "What about her?"

"She's dead."

Kate went cold all over. Mutt looked up at her and gave a soft whine.

"What do you mean, she's dead?" Truax said. "Holly, if this is some kind of joke I have to say I don't find it a bit funny."

"It's not a joke." Haynes was trembling and there were tears in her eyes. She took Truax's hand and stared up at him. "She's dead. I saw her."

"Where is she?" Kate said.

Haynes looked at Kate. "What? I—"

"Where is she?" Kate said.

The hard, inflexible voice had its effect. Haynes stiffened, almost to attention. "In her room."

"Did you lock the door when you left?"

"I—No, I didn't, I—"

"Who has been in it, besides you?"

"Just me. She didn't come into work this morning. Everybody was out of the office and no one knew she wasn't there until I got back from Rig 36. I went to check on her."

"And no one else has been in the room since?"

"No. I don't think so."

Before Kate could say anything else Truax was double-timing it down the side of the airstrip. Kate followed through the buildings, up the steps and into the trailer and down the hall to Lyda's room. "Stay," she told Mutt, and Mutt took up station a few feet away from the door.

There were people standing around, among them Jules the chef, who had tears streaming down his face. "Break it up, folks," Truax said. "Go on, get back to your jobs."

"I can't believe it," Jules said, smearing snot and tears with his hand, "I just saw her at dinner last night, and she was fine then. What—"

Vern thumped him on his shoulder and turned it into a shove toward the exit. "We all saw her at dinner last night, Jules. Go on, get back to the kitchen. God knows what the rest of the kitchen crew's getting up to without you there to keep an eye on them."

Jules stumbled off, the last one out, his face a picture of misery.

"Open it," Kate said.

Vern did, and took an involuntary step back.

The smell hit them first, like it always did. The dead void themselves as their last living act, death's first triumph before decomposition kicks in. Way down deep in that subconscious swamp, the one filled with snakes and heights and airplane crashes and commitment, the smell of our own mortality is the fear most immediate and most visceral. It wasn't the first time Kate had smelled it and it wasn't something she ever got used to. She had often thought that that smell alone validated the larger part of the salary any practicing policeman earned.

The room reminded her of her dorm room at Lathrop, single bed, pressboard closet and desk, single upright chair. One window looked onto its twin in the next building over, the blackout blind drawn firmly down to present a bland blank face to the world. Lyda was lying half on her bed, half on the floor, the covers tangled around her legs. Her nightgown had ridden up her thighs. Kate went into the room, stepping with care, and laid two fingers against Lyda's throat. The flesh was cold and motionless. She put the same two fingers beneath Lyda's left wrist and tried to push it up. It remained locked in place. She looked around the room, eyes pausing for a moment here and there, and then came out into the hall. The lock on the door was of the button-on-the-knob variety. She pushed it in and closed the door behind her, testing to see that it was secure. "There's a key?" she said.

Vern, looking shaken, nodded. "There are master keys for all the doors back in the office."

"All right, let's go there. Mutt." She pointed. "Guard."

Mutt sat in front of Lyda's door, lips drawn back in a snarl at the smell of death.

IN HIS OFFICE VERN sorted through keys on a ring, detached one, and handed it over. "Was the door locked when you got to the room?" Kate said to Haynes.

The geologist looked as if she were going to faint. Kate pushed her into a chair and shoved her head between her knees, remembering with a pang having to do the same thing for Lyda the day before. "Was the door locked when you got to the room?" she said again.

Haynes shook her head. "Open."

Kate looked at Vern. "May I use your sat phone?"

She had to ask him how to use it. Maggie came on. "Maggie, it's Kate. Is Jim there?"

"No, he took off somewhere with Old Sam Dementieff, I don't—"

"I'm out at Suulutaq. Tell Jim I said he needs to get here as soon as he can."

"Why, what's going on?"

"There's been a death. Tell him I said right away, and to bring his crime scene kit." From the corner of her eye she saw Haynes sit up and look at Truax.

"What—" Maggie bit back whatever she'd been about to say. "Can't talk?"

"Don't want to."

"Gotcha. Jim, head for Suulutaq ASAP, bring murder bag."

"Thanks, Maggie." She handed the phone to Truax.

"Crime scene kit?" Haynes said. "But—"

"But what?" Kate said.

"It's not a crime, is it?" Haynes looked from Kate to Vern. "You saw the note, right?"

"Note?" Vern said. "What note?" He had seen the body of his executive assistant and nothing more.

Kate said, "Yes, I saw the note."

"Well, then—"

"State law requires the investigation of all unexplained deaths," Kate said. "While we're waiting for Sergeant Chopin, I'd like to talk to some of the employees, the ones who knew her well, and especially the people who lived on either side of her and across the hall from her."

"We'll have to pull some of them off work," Truax said, protesting.

"Then you'll pull some off work," Kate said.

"Maybe we'll just wait to see what the trooper says."

Kate's expression lightened briefly. "Yeah. You should definitely do that."

They had to go to Lyda's desk. Vern turned on her computer

to click through her files. "I'll have to print out the resident list for that trailer." He clicked and the printer hummed into action. "Holly? Round these guys up and send them over to the mess hall, okay?"

Haynes, still visibly shaken, stepped forward to take the piece of paper, and departed without a word.

Haynes assembled twenty-three people in the mess hall, and Kate spoke to them one at a time at a table in the corner, she hoped out of earshot of the rest. They'd all seen Lyda at dinner the night before. She had seemed to be her usual calm self. "She wasn't normally a jokey kind of person to begin with," one of them said, "but she seemed fine to me."

That seemed to be the general consensus.

Kate went back to the kitchen to talk to Jules, who was assembling ham hocks and beans in a stainless steel pot the size of a small water tower. He was still upset, with the occasional tear dropping into the beans. His staff was giving him plenty of room.

"Jules, when I was here last time," Kate said, "you gave Lyda a cookie."

He nodded. "Chocolate chip. I remember. That was a good batch. She told me over the serving line at dinner the next night she really liked it." He began to dissolve again. "You know," he said, a sob catching in his voice, "they're different every batch. No matter how much you stick to a recipe."

"Jules, I need you to hold it together for me," Kate said, her voice gentle. "I need some answers only you can give me, so I can figure out what happened to her."

He brought out a red kerchief the size of a mainsail and blew his nose. "Anything," he said. "Anything you need."

"When you gave her the cookie, she asked if there were

any peanuts in it."

"Yes. She didn't have to. I was always very careful, because of her allergy."

"She was allergic to peanuts?"

He nodded. "I stopped ordering snack packs with peanuts in them after she told me. I even got rid of all the peanut oil, even though there's nothing better for deep-frying chicken and French fries. But we made do."

"You don't have peanut anything in this kitchen?"

"Peanut butter," he said, "and three kinds of jam, because people get cranky when they can't have their PBJs, especially the night shift when they come in for mid-rats."

"Do you make peanut butter cookies?"

"They're a staple," he said. "But they are clearly marked and the baker knows not to mix the doughs and to scour the mixing bowls and the baking sheets between batches." Jules gulped and sniffed. "Are you saying Lyda had an allergic reaction to peanuts? That that's what killed her?"

"We don't know yet how she died," Kate said. "I'm talking to everyone who knew her, getting all the details I can. It's just routine." She heard the engine of the Cessna pass overhead, and left Jules with more tears rolling down his plump cheeks.

She and Vern arrived on the airstrip at the same time. From the moment Jim climbed out on the strip Vern spoke to him and only to him, as if Kate no longer existed. He walked them back to Lyda's room. Kate unlocked the door.

Jim put his kit down and opened it to extract his camera. He took several shots of the room and donned gloves before stepping inside.

"Go on back to your office," Kate said to Truax. "We'll come to you when we're done."

He didn't like it, especially not coming from Kate, but once the door was open again he wasn't enjoying himself so he left.

The first thing Jim did was check for a pulse. "She's cold," he said.

"Yeah. And rigor's fully established."

Jim tried to raise Lyda's arm.

"See her face?" Kate said.

"Yeah. She was definitely having trouble breathing." He raised a corner of the blanket.

"Diarrhea?"

"And vomiting." He let the blanket fall again. "Are those hives?"

"Looks like it."

"Anaphylaxis, you think?"

"She was allergic to peanuts," Kate said. "Bag the napkin with the crumbs on it."

"Death by what, peanut butter cookie?" Jim said. "Christ." He bagged the napkin and the crumbs on it. He picked up the note that was sitting next to the napkin. " 'I'm sorry. I never should have helped. Tell Dewayne I said good-bye.' " Jim looked up. " 'Never should have helped' what?"

"I don't know yet."

"Typed," he said.

"Yes," she said. She held out a bag and he slipped the note inside.

Jim took notes and more photos. "You take the desk, I'll take the closet."

Kate stepped over Lyda Blue's sprawled leg and started opening drawers. There were three on the left side and a wider, shallow drawer in the desktop, the right side of which was fixed to the wall. The side drawers held toiletries, underwear, T-shirts, socks, sweaters.

Nothing unexpected or unusual. Kate pulled open the

middle drawer. Pencils, pens, envelopes, stamps. A checkbook. Kate opened it. "She had about twenty-five hundred in checking, and almost ten thousand in savings."

"Is there a statement?" Jim was patting down the clothes hanging in the closet.

"No."

He grunted. "She might have had those sent to her home address. They'll have it at the office. Bag it and tag it."

Kate tried to close the middle drawer and it stuck halfway in. She tugged on it. Now it was completely stuck. She bent over to peer inside. There was a large, elongated object in the back that was catching on the bottom of the desktop. She reached inside to grab it while she jiggled the drawer.

When the drawer finally came all the way out, she was holding a leather holster in her hand. "Hey," she said.

Jim was just closing up the closet, and looked over at her. "Well," he said.

"Empty," she said.

"I noticed." He raised his head. "This morning, Old Sam and I found a .22 revolver in the clearing where you guys found the body."

"What?"

He nodded. " 'Fraid so."

"Goddammit," she said. "It's not that big a clearing, how could I have missed it?"

"Also the skull I'm going to assume belongs to that same body."

"Shit," she said.

He waited.

"I should have made another sweep after I shot that bear." She looked at him, anger warring with embarrassment on her face. "I'm sorry, Jim."

"Facing down a charging grizzly takes pretty much all your attention," he said, "and afterward it's all you can do to stand upright. Don't beat yourself up about it. Besides, I don't know that it would have made any difference. Guy wasn't shot, so far as we know."

The overhead light had a very low wattage bulb. She held the holster to the window. It was a brown leather side holster, right-hand draw. Kate turned it over. "Challenger 1-C."

"George Lawrence, leather crafter to the stars." At her look he said, "Okay, I admit I know less than nothing about guns and gun paraphernalia, but I know that much."

The light from the window wasn't enough. She turned on the desk light and held the holster directly beneath it so they could see inside. "The front and rear sights have left indentations in the leather."

"The trigger guard and the cylinder, too."

Kate regarded the holster with a somber expression. "You think the pistol belonged to Lyda?"

Jim shook his head. "Let's leave that up to Brillo's boys. I'll send it in with the pistol and the body."

Kate bagged the holster, and the small shoulder bag Jim had found suspended from a hanger beneath a down jacket. It contained a wallet with Lyda's driver's license, a credit card and a debit card, a lipstick, a comb, and some peppermints.

Jim shook his head. "It's no wonder the American economy went broke. None of the people involved in whatever the hell we're calling this were into conspicuous consumption, that's for damn sure. Let's bag her and get her to town."

A small crowd gathered to watch as the two of them brought the black body bag down the steps and set it gently into the back of the pickup that someone had backed to the door. Mutt escorted them down the stairs and gave the crowd the business end of her yellow stare. They took an instinctive giant step back. At the back of it Kate saw Johnny and Van. She knew they were working days, and realized that it must be past six o'clock.

Jim sealed the door to Lyda's room. They left Mutt on guard and walked over to the admin building. Kate gave Johnny and Van the high sign to follow at a discreet distance.

Truax came downstairs to meet them. Haynes was not in evidence. The room was hushed, people speaking in whispers and sneaking covert glances at Jim. It wasn't every day you saw a state trooper march into your office and take charge. It wasn't every day, Kate thought, that these people saw Vern Truax take orders.

She was unaware of how much she and Mutt added to the respectful, uneasy, and expectant silence.

"Who lived in the rooms on either side of her?" Jim said.

"No one, they were both empty. The camp's not anywhere near full capacity. Lyda has been ... Lyda was assigning every other room where she could, to give people some privacy."

"I found a guy who lived a couple of doors down," Kate said. "He says he heard female voices in the hall about ten o'clock, but he didn't recognize them. There are two other women bunking in the same trailer. Both of them were watching a movie in the TV lounge in the trailer next door, and got back about then, they think. I talked to them, and they said they didn't see Lyda after dinner last night."

Jim nodded. "I want to go through her desk. And we'll need her personnel file."

Truax opened a file drawer and tabbed through it, producing a folder and handing it over.

"Vern, you said you'd worked with her on other jobs," Kate said as Jim opened and closed drawers in methodical fashion, tagging and bagging some of the contents, discarding others. "Do you know her family?"

Truax shook his head. "No. One of the things I liked about working with Lyda was that it was all about the job. I never had to worry that she would allow personal problems to get in the way of what we had to do every day. She was a good worker. Damn it." He smacked the desk. "Damn it! She made this camp run. She processed new employees, she assigned rooms, she ordered supplies. I don't know how the hell I'm going to keep to schedule without her." He looked up. "If she was in trouble why didn't she say something to me? She should have said something."

She wouldn't have, not to a boss who was so pleased that she kept it all business all the time on the job, Kate thought. She could have said it out loud but what was the point other than making Truax squirm, and that wouldn't help. "On another topic. Since Dewayne Gammons is alive, it follows that we have to identify the body we found. Best bet is he was another of your employees. I've been asking around today. You had an employee, a Rick Allen, who walked off the job the same time Dewayne Gammons did. Do you remember him?"

"Rick Allen? I don't—Wait a minute, was that Holly's gopher?" He consulted a computer, and after a few blasphemous moments managed to locate Rick Allen's room. Kate made Vern hand over Allen's personnel file and declined his escort to the room. They left him staring after them with a pronounced set to his jaw.

Johnny and Van were waiting outside the doors to the admin building. "Walk with us," Kate said, and they fell into step next to her. "Did you know Lyda Blue?"

Johnny and Van exchanged glances. "Sure. She processed

all of the roustabouts from Niniltna in, helped us with the forms, introduced us to our bosses."

"You spend any time with her?"

They both shook their heads.

"Anybody say anything about her?"

"I heard somebody say that she looked pretty friendly with the dead guy you found off the Step road."

"Turns out he's not so dead after all," Kate said. "Who was it said that?"

Johnny shook his head. "I don't know who said it. It was a bunch of guys sitting around the TV room talking about the women in camp." He glanced at Vanessa. "When the women weren't around. Hers wasn't the only name mentioned."

"Okay. Keep your heads down and your eyes open. Job okay?"

They both nodded. "It's not make-work, we're really doing stuff. We're busy all the time and we're outside a lot. It's all good, Kate."

"All right. Scoot."

They headed for the mess hall and their dinners and Jim and Kate went to what had been Rick Allen's room.

"So Rick Allen went missing the same time as Dewayne Gammons?"

"It's not much."

"It's more than we had before. Let's see what's in his room."

But the ever-efficient Lyda Blue had long since emptied it out and they found nothing, no loose floorboards or ceiling tiles behind which Allen had concealed even so much as a secret stash of girlie magazines.

Kate found her way back to the bakery. Jim's expression when he saw Randy Randolph for the first time reminded her that no matter how tragic and terrible life could sometimes be, sooner or later it would be leavened with a glimpse however transient of the eternal comedy.

"You're Randy Randolph?" Jim said.

Randy nodded, looking resigned. "Are you arresting me, officer?"

"What? Oh. Uh, no, uh, no no, of course not." Jim glared at Kate, who was looking preternaturally solemn, and pulled himself together. "I mean, not yet, Randy. Bigamy is a crime, a Class A misdemeanor in the state of Alaska. You're going to need to get your personal life in some kind of order or—"

Kate saw that Jim was trying to recollect the penalties for bigamy and, ever helpful, said, "You could be fined."

Jim turned his shoulder on her in pointed fashion. "Randy, you've heard about the death in camp, haven't you?"

"Lyda Blue." Randy nodded, his pasty face set in grave lines. "She was a nice lady. I liked her a lot."

Jim gave Kate a look that stopped whatever she had been about to say dead in its tracks. "You knew about her peanut allergy?"

"Oh yeah. Jules made sure everyone knew about it. He had kind of a crush on her, you know."

"Yes, we know. Is there any way that ground peanuts or peanut oil or anything made from peanuts could have gotten into something it shouldn't have?"

Randy shook his head. "No," he said, and he was very firm. "We haven't used peanut oil for months. The peanut butter and jelly is on its own tray, and Jules is rabid about reading the ingredients on packaged foods before he uses them on the line."

He pulled a tray of croissants out of the oven. They were pale gold perfection, and Kate wondered if it was perhaps his baking skills—along with the eyelashes—that were the attraction here. "Randy, you know Sergeant Chopin found another one of your wives, right?"

He looked glum. "Yeah, I heard about it."

"She's not happy. Neither is Suzy or Bonnie. Might maybe want to get yourself a good lawyer."

"Why?" He looked like he might burst into tears. "I don't want to divorce them. I love them all, I want to take care of them all."

Whatever. "Randy, you remember you said you knew Dewayne Gammons?"

"Yeah." He looked a little whipsawed at the change of subject, which was what she'd intended.

"You said he didn't have any friends."

"No. Well, not to speak of, not like I saw him hanging around with the same guy all the time."

"Do you remember a roustabout named Richard Allen?"

"Hell, sure I remember Rick," Randy said. "Worked with the geologist out on the rigs, pulling core samples? That gang works all hours, they're in and outta the mess hall all the time. Rick was a nice fella." He chuckled. "Had a pile of dirty jokes he could tell, never the same one in a row. And big dreams, always talking about making a pile and retiring to a tropical island."

"Did you ever see him with Dewayne Gammons?" It was a long shot, but Gammons and Allen going missing at what from the pay records looked like very near the same day seemed entirely too coincidental to her.

He sucked at his teeth. "I remember one time, middle of the night, I was just coming on shift, and Rick come through the loading dock. Gammons was with him. They were both looking to score something fresh outta the oven." He shrugged. "Lotta guys do that. I generally give 'em whatever they want.

206

Food is about all a guy's got to look forward to on a remote job site like this one."

"Were they talking to each other? Did you hear them?"

He shrugged again. "They was talking, sure." He reflected. "Kind of weird conversation, now I think of it."

"Weird how?"

"Talking about the best way to die. Drowning, plane crash, shooting." Randy gave a mock shudder. "Creepy, but I don't mean like they was planning any of this. Just speculating. And hell, I was busy mixing dough and cutting cookies. Dint have no time to listen in." He brightened. "I give 'em some of my lemon cookies, they're a specialty. I just made some more last night, you want some?"

"No," Kate said, giving up, "but I'll take one of those croissants."

"Okay, Randy," Jim said, "appreciate your help. Oh. And, uh, you should do something about that situation with your wife. Uh, wives. Anyway, do something about that before I have to come arrest you, okay?"

"But I don't want to do anything about it, Sergeant, don't you understand? I love them all—"

On the dock Kate said, "So now we know Rick Allen and Dewayne Gammons disappeared on the same day, and we know they were friends."

"It's still not much."

"We also know they were both obsessing over ways to die."

"We know they had one conversation about ways to die," he said. "One conversation does not equal an obsession."

She led him to the room that served as Suulutaq's left-luggage locker, used the master key to open it, and switched on the light. She pulled down Gammons's duffel and daypack and said, "Take those out to the pickup and come back here."

It was an order, not a request, and Jim smothered a grin as he did what he was told. When he got back to the room, she had pulled down another duffel, a roll-on suitcase, and a briefcase. She took the briefcase and the roll-on and he shouldered the duffel. "Who does all that stuff belong to?"

"Gear left by workers who never come back."

"Ah. The first load of luggage—"

"Belonged to Gammons. According to the tags, this load belonged to Richard Allen."

Haynes was at the truck with Lyda's body in the back, face now drawn and tired. "Figured somebody should keep watch."

"Somebody was," Kate said. "Mutt, up!" Mutt jumped into the back of the truck, landing light of foot and not coming within a toe-nail of any of what was back there with her.

"Wait a minute, what's all this stuff?" Haynes said.

"Evidence in an ongoing investigation," Jim said, scribbling a receipt and handing it to her. "We'll get it back to you as soon as we can."

"I don't know if I can let you take all that," she said, staring at the pile of luggage. "It's someone's personal property, the mine could be liable for—"

"Investigation of a potential felony supersedes pretty much everything, including private property rights," Jim said, and gave her a cheerful smile. "You want to ride up to the strip with us? You can bring the truck back."

"I—" She cast a glance over her shoulder in the direction of the admin building. "All right." Haynes climbed in after Kate. "You pretty much cleaned out Lyda's desk. We might need some of it for day-to-day operations, especially the hard drive on her computer."

"We'll return everything when we're satisfied we have all the evidence we need to close the case," Kate said.

Haynes frowned, not liking the answer. "It's not too much to say that she ran this camp. There will be a lot of operational stuff on that hard drive, pay sheets, meal plans, work schedules, flight manifests, equipment maintenance."

"Surely you have backups of the files and programs you need for the day-to-day business," Jim said.

Haynes gave a heavy sigh. "Yeah, of course. It's just that Lyda handled most of them through her computer. She'll have a lot of shortcuts that the rest of us don't."

Kate was beginning to wonder just how competent Vern Truax and Holly Haynes were as managers.

"We'll get it back to you as soon as possible," Jim said. They came up over the rise and stopped next to the Cessna.

When everything had been loaded, Jim slammed the tailgate. "Okay, we're good to go."

Kate, Mutt, and Jim got into the aircraft. Haynes stood next to the pickup, watching them, still subdued and pale.

They had to wait for the Beaver to land, and it was unloading before they began to taxi for takeoff. "What the hell?" Kate craned her neck to see as they went by.

"What?" Jim said.

"What the hell is she doing here?" Vern Truax himself came up the hill to meet her, holding out both hands to clasp hers.

"Who?"

"Ulanie Anahonak," Kate said. "And Vern Truax is greeting her like a long-lost friend."

"Other board members aren't allowed to visit the mine without the chair's say-so?"

"No," Kate said.

"Think Harvey Meganack tells you every time he comes out here?"

"No."

"Then give it a rest."

She watched Ulanie and Vern disappear into the admin building, before facing forward again and readjusting her headset. "Jim, Lyda Blue did not kill herself."

"How many times did you see her, Kate?"

"Once. Well, twice, if I include on the airstrip yesterday."

"How long ago was the first time?"

"A month."

"When you spent how much time with her?"

"A couple of hours."

The Cessna rolled forward, jolting over the gravel. Sitting as far forward as she could get without actually occupying one of the two front seats, Mutt's head bumped Kate's shoulder. "A lot can happen in a month, Kate. And her self-acknowledged best friend was a guy who was by all accounts unconditionally suicidal."

"Jim—"

"We've got a preexisting allergic condition, crumbs from cookies that I'm betting aggravated the condition, and a note. Notice I'm not even mentioning the empty holster. If it matches the gun I found, what was Lyda Blue's gun doing out in that clearing? Was Lyda involved somehow in Gammons's disappearance? And did that involvement lead her to take her own life?"

"When I was talking to the people who knew Lyda Blue," Kate said, "I asked them if anyone else hadn't come back to work at the same time Dewayne Gammons didn't come back. Three of them said this guy Rick Allen."

"You think he might be our DB?"

"Jim! We got a guy eaten by a bear, only it turns out the bear ate somebody else, and the guy who we thought got eaten is alive. Now we got the live guy's girlfriend dead, only she's got a holster that is probably going to match the pistol you found by the dead guy." Kate shook her head. "At this point I'm willing to swear in court that the dead guy is Jimmy Hoffa, just so I can get off this merry-go-round before I throw up."

The Cessna rose into the air. Jim put the nose on Niniltna and pulled the throttle out. George's last flight for Anchorage on the new schedule left in forty-five minutes. The day had gone cloudy, with the tallest peaks in the back range obscured and the nearer mountains muted to a dull olive by lack of sunshine. It looked cold. It felt cold. Kate shivered.

She was still unhappy at the thought of Lyda's suicide, and Jim was not unsympathetic. "You liked her, Kate, I get that. But if you're convinced it wasn't an accident, and I admit there is enough circumstantial evidence to at least support the possibility that no way did she eat a peanut butter cookie by mistake, then it was suicide, or it was murder."

Their tailwind caught them a good jolt and Kate was thrown up against her seat belt. Another lumpity bump and she pressed her hand flat against the ceiling to keep her butt in her seat.

Jim corrected for drift and said, "Either way, we'll have to wait on the autopsy. In the meantime, nobody's going anywhere, and we've got a pile of evidence to sift through."

She was silent, and it made him nervous. "What?" he said. "I can hear you thinking."

"Let's get the body to Anchorage and see what we've got," she said.

THIRTEEN

JIM'S OFFICE LOOKED LIKE someone had detonated a bomb. There were files and paper forms everywhere, and the map tacked to the wall had become a de facto bulletin board, with sheets of paper pinned all over it. A whiteboard was filled from one edge of the frame to the other with notes illegible to anyone who hadn't written them. The smell of coffee heating too long in the carafe burned the back of the throat. Mutt had long since thrown in the towel and had gone outside to sprawl in the clear air.

They'd spent the early part of the morning going through the personal belongings of Lyda Blue, Richard Allen, and Dewayne Gammons. To Kate's increasing exasperation, they had found precisely nothing. Allen's personal possessions amounted to toiletries, half a dozen changes of clothes, a traveling clock, assorted *Penthouses* and *Playboys*, and an MP3 player loaded with Clint Black, Brad Paisley, and Big & Rich. If Allen had had a wallet, he'd left with it and the bear must have gobbled it up right along with Allen, hip pocket and all. Bears were not known for their discriminating palates.

Neither Gammons's duffel nor his daypack had acquired anything new since she last examined them. Lyda at least had the saving grace of family photos and a file folder that held her Bering High School and Charter College associate's diplomas, as well as a certificate naming her Employee of the

Year at the Bravo Mine, Montana, two years before. It was signed by Vernon Truax, Mine Superintendent.

"Explain to me again how so many of their employees just disappear," Jim said without looking up from the monitor, where he was scrolling through the files on Lyda Blue's hard drive.

"We got a bunch of young people, mostly male, working out here in the back of beyond, making more money in a month than most people see in six. The mine loses at least one every pay period, right after paychecks are issued. I'll bet that's why they only pay them once a month."

"And you are looking at all the files instead of just the guy who went at the same time Gammons did, why?"

"Because we still don't know whose body we found in the woods. It could be any of them."

"It could be none of them."

"True." Kate didn't believe it, but that didn't mean he was wrong. "But, I remind you, there aren't any missing Park rats. Our best operational theory is the probability that the dead guy worked at the mine."

Jim clicked on a folder marked PERSONAL.

"Three, because I don't know how he died."

Jim looked up at that. "He was attacked by a bear. That'll pretty much get the job done."

"We don't know that, Jim. No, wait, listen. We don't know that. We found the remains, that's all. He could have been killed and the body eaten afterward. Wouldn't be the first time that happened. Ravens, eagles, foxes, grizzlies, none of them turn up their noses at carrion, especially before fish hit fresh water."

"Okay," he said, turning his attention back to the monitor. FINANCE, LETTERS, CONTACTS, FUN, and another folder marked MINE. Why would Lyda have a file on the mine in her personal folder? Or maybe it was "mine" in the lower case personal pronoun sense. Love letters, X-rated Web site shortcuts, bad poems written in praise of the hair on the backs of her lover's hands.

He clicked on it. It was password protected. He looked up her birth date and typed it into the space. He was in. Pitiful.

Kate returned to the personnel folders. There were a dozen of them, all men, none over forty, five married. Notes in what Kate guessed was Lyda's handwriting logged calls to the married employees' home phones, termination of employment documents, and final paychecks mailed.

Five of the remaining seven employees were equally straightforward. Three had their parents listed as their emergency contacts and the other two their girlfriends. All were eventually found, officially terminated, and paid off.

Two of the twelve files remained.

The first was of course Dewayne Gammons, twenty-nine, work history varied, mostly construction. He'd listed Roy, Washington, as his birthplace, and that was about the extent of the personal information he'd cared to share. There was no emergency contact, no listed friends or relatives. His check had been direct-deposited to a bank account in Anchorage, which as of the last time Lyda had checked—two days before the body in the clearing had been found—had not been touched since his final R & R to town. Lyda had gone so far as to call the police department of Roy, Washington, who told her they didn't know Dewayne Gammons from Adam. The cop who had answered the phone had called the state bureau of vital statistics for a copy of Gammons's birth certificate, which yielded the names of his parents, Sylvia and Francis Gammons, neither of whom were listed in the phone book or had any record of contact with the police. The cop must have liked the sound of Lyda's voice, because he had even attempted to contact the doctor on the birth certificate (also dead, practice dissolved, patient files destroyed) and called round to the local Roy churches, again drawing a blank.

Kate, as family-ridden as she sometimes felt, found it in herself to be grateful that she wasn't that much of a blank space in the firmament. She looked at the employee photo clipped to the inside of the folder, taken with what appeared to be all the artistic talent of a clerk at the DMV, and said out loud, "You've been disappearing practically since the day you were born. No wonder you were depressed."

"Huh?" Jim said, intent on the monitor screen.

"Nothing." Lyda's last entry in Gammons's file was a note stating she had copied his medical records for sending to the medical examiner in Anchorage, as per the request of the state trooper office in Niniltna. Kate looked at Gammons's medical records. Nothing there. Suulutaq's in-house physician's barely decipherable scrawl read, as near as Kate could make out, "All tests/reactions in the green, good to go." All he would have seen, all he did see was another warm body. He wouldn't have investigated any further. To be fair, he wasn't paid to. Probably all Suulutaq was interested in on the medical side of things was any indication of preexisting conditions for which the employee might later claim workmen's comp.

She turned to the last file with a sense of anticipation. The twelfth missing employee and the only one unaccounted for was Richard Henry Allen, thirty-four, born Minneapolis, Minnesota, graduated from Coon Rapids High, worked as an apprentice lineman in Minnesota, Missouri, and Washington before coming to Alaska and going to work for Suulutaq. His medical record was as average as Gammons's, with a similar build and a face the employee photo revealed to be just as nondescript.

The difference was Allen had an emergency phone contact. Lyda had called it and a business of some kind had answered. She hadn't written down their name, probably since they had claimed no knowledge of a Richard Henry Allen. Lyda's note read, "Wrote the number down wrong?"

Kate was growing exasperated. Surely to god if there was one thing you could count on in modern life it was a paper trail.

She compared Allen's file to Gammons's, spread out on the floor side by side, page for page. A couple of average guys, similar in age, height, weight, health, and, evidently, lack of ties. It wasn't an unusual story in Alaska, the state was a magnet for the rootless adventurer every bit as much as it was for those on the run from past lives. About the rudest thing you could say to an Alaskan was, "Where are you from?" Many cheechakos embraced anonymity as a rite of Alaskan passage, and all sourdoughs respected it as a simple right.

Jim could run a wants or warrants on Allen, which might tell them something. But it would take time. "The ME ID'd the body as Gammons's," she said out loud. "If I'm right, it's Allen's. Which means the files got mixed up."

She sat back on her heels and surveyed the disassembled files. Before she'd ripped them apart, they had been neat and orderly. Lyda had had a system for the personnel files, each required form in the same place in each file, organized with colored tabs so the relevant part could be accessed without hesitation. The medical section was the second section in each file, marked with a red tab, with patient history, tests, results, and physician's evaluation in the same order in every file. Blood tests were the third page down in the medical section.

"Jim."

He grunted.

"Did you hear me? The files got mixed up. That's how the body was misidentified."

"Yeah, I heard you."

"The problem is, no way did Lyda mix them up. I've never seen files like this. Woman could have given lessons in organization to Genghis Khan."

"Problem with that is," he said, "it would be just as easy for an unauthorized person to find something in the files as it would be for Lyda."

It wasn't quite a question. "Yes."

He looked up from the monitor to meet her eyes. "So someone switched out the blood tests."

"Easier just to swap out the entire med section. But yeah. Just as easy for someone to switch the blood tests."

"Gammons and Allen pretty similar, physically?"

Kate looked down at the two employee head shots, Allen on the left, Gammons on the right, and their physical data. "White, brown/brown, medium/medium. Faces are similar enough, I suppose. Always hard to tell from a head shot."

Jim sat back and linked his hands behind his head. "Okay. So the DB has Gammons's blood type."

"Yes."

"But the DB isn't Gammons."

"No."

"Allen went missing the same time as Gammons."

"Yes."

"And our favorite bigamist overheard a conversation where the two of them were talking about ways to die."

"Yes."

"A suicide pact?" He couldn't believe the words coming

out of his own mouth, but if you didn't enjoy the weird you had no business becoming a cop in the first place.

Kate shook her head. "Then why switch the files?"

He nodded. "Why, indeed. And who?" He reflected. "So, logically …" His voice trailed off. Logic, thus far, was in this case notable only by its absence.

"It would help to know when the files were switched."

"You mean—"

She nodded. "Before they went into the woods? Or after?"

"Crap. I hadn't thought of that." He stared at the ceiling. "The one person who might have been able to figure that out is dead."

"Yes, she is," Kate said.

"And is looking less like a suicide by the moment." He unlinked his hands and turned the monitor. "Come look at this."

Kate leaned over his shoulder to look at the screen. It displayed two columns of numbers. First column was a date. Second column was a very long string of numbers separated by dashes. The first date was in April, the latest the first of July. There were four entries.

"It's in her personal file, in a folder marked 'Mine' that was password protected."

"You figured out her password?"

"It was her birthday."

Kate closed her eyes and shook her head.

"Yeah, I know. She was keeping track of something, Kate. The question is, what?"

"The dates aren't at regular intervals. One in April, two in June, one in July."

"The numbers on the right … they're in sequence."

"Core samples, maybe? Those middle numbers could be

depths. The last numbers are so similar I'm thinking they're coordinates. You know, maybe latitude and longitude?"

He looked at her, her face so close to his that his breath disturbed a strand of short dark hair that lay across her cheekbone. He was seized by a sudden impulse to bite her earlobe. "Why core samples?"

Their eyes met, a faint smile in hers. She knew. Oh yeah, she always knew. "There's a lot of proprietary information being accumulated at the Suulutaq Mine, Jim." She tapped the screen, drawing his attention back to the monitor. "Scroll down."

"Huh?"

"Look at the doohickey on the vertical scroll bar. With the cursor on the bottom row of numbers, it's nowhere near the bottom of the document. Scroll down."

He scrolled down. The columns disappeared off the top of the screen, and three lines of type rolled up on the bottom.

As far back as I'm able to go with the records available here.

There may be others.

The cursor blinked steadily at them from the end of the page.

Jim stirred. "Okay," he said. "Looking less like an accident, and a lot less like suicide."

Kate's grin was fierce. She checked the clock on the wall. "George has a crew-change flight going into Anchorage in fifteen minutes."

"What? Why do you need to go into Anchorage?"

"For one thing, I can take Gammons's and Allen's files to the ME, see which matches who. If Gammons's file matches the DB, and we know Gammons is alive, then I'll take Allen's file to the hospital and make them check it against him. Once we have confirmation that someone switched the files, we can work on why."

"What do Allen and Gammons have to do with Lyda Blue's death?"

She looked at him. He raised an eyebrow. If the state was paying her way to town, he wanted to lay out why. She huffed out an impatient sigh and ticked off on her fingers. "One, all three worked at the mine. Two, Lyda had a relationship with Gammons. Three, Allen was a gofer for Holly Haynes, which would have put him in the office a lot and therefore Lyda would have known him pretty well, too."

"Fine so far as it goes, but according to your scenario Allen was dead for over a month and Gammons was in the hospital in Anchorage when Lyda died."

"It's all connected, Jim, it has to be."

He sighed. "Why not just let George take the file in?"

"I can harass Brillo to hurry the autopsy."

"You're in a hurry."

"You should be, too, Jim," she said. "If Lyda found someone spying on Suulutaq's operations, the longer we take to put this case together the more time they'll have to cover their tracks, and the harder it'll be to prove they killed her before she could turn them in. Another reason I want to go to town is I want to talk to Gammons, if he's come out of it. And I've got one other thing that will be easier to check out in town, too."

"The contact number in Allen's file?"

"Yes."

"Lyda's note said it was a wrong number."

"Maybe it was, maybe it wasn't. I want you to let me give it to Kurt Pletnikoff."

"Ah. This would be the guy you blue-ticketed out of the Park and set up in Anchorage as a PI."

"Yes."

"He any good?"

"Hey, he's the Meyer to my Travis, the Mouse to my Easy, the Hugh to my Cadfael."

"Not to mention the Costello to your Abbott," Jim said, who had not forgotten why Kurt Pletnikoff had been blue-ticketed out of the Park in the first place.

"He's good, Jim," Kate said. "He took some kind of a data mining class, or whatever they call it, and I won't say he's a genius but he is damn good at trolling for information on the Internet. He's also fast, and we won't have to sit around waiting for him to call back. I'm going to give him everyone's Social Security numbers and tell him to get me everything he can on them, too." He didn't say anything. "A screwup doesn't have to stay a screwup forever, Jim." She thought of Petey Jeppsen.

"He's not going to break any constitutional amendments, is he?"

She knew she'd won then. "Cross my heart and hope to die."

He recognized and admired the determination in the square set of her shoulders, the stubborn jut of her chin, the militant look in her eye. She was pissed off at Lyda's death, and she would not rest until she knew what had happened in every detail, and the perpetrator, if there was one, had been brought as near to justice as possible.

It didn't matter that she'd liked Lyda. She would have reacted the same way to any wrongful death. Lancelot, that's who Kate reminded Jim of, and while she might not be able to swim a moat in a coat of heavy iron mail, she was sure as hell blessed with an iron will. God help anyone who got in her way in this mood.

It wasn't going to be him, that was for sure, and besides, she was making enough sense for him to let her run out the string and see what was there. "I suppose you'll be billing the state for the work."

She grinned. "You suppose right."

"You taking Mutt?"

Kate glanced out the window, where Mutt lay beneath the wide branches of one of the few healthy spruce trees left in the Park. "No."

"She won't like that."

"I'll be back before she knows I'm gone. I'm going to go see Brendan, too. He might be able to dig up something we can use, too."

"Are you now." He grabbed the back of her neck and pulled her into a long, thorough kiss. "Just marking my spot."

FOURTEEN

CALM AND CLEAR HAD followed the previous night's brisk blow, every pilot's dream weather conditions, and every passenger's dream ride. Kate sat up front, riding shotgun next to George, and admired the way he flew as if he and his craft were one being. She always felt safer in small planes, anyway, with pilots and mechanics she knew on a first-name basis. She adjusted the muffs over her ears and pursed her lips to make sure the mike would pick up her voice. "A regularly scheduled airline. Who'd a thunk it?"

His grin was wry. "The bank is who. I got loan payments to make every month now, Kate."

At five hundred dollars round trip Niniltna to Anchorage, running full most flights, chances were he'd have no trouble making them. "How long is the flight?"

"Little over an hour."

She was impressed. It would have taken two hours in the Cessna. "She's a beauty," she said, looking around at the spotless interior. There wasn't a speck of caribou blood or a tuft of beaver fur anywhere, no duct tape as yet holding up the interior fabric or holding on the exterior shell, all the buttons and levers on the instrument panel still buttons and levers instead of clips and grips scavenged out of the toolbox. The GPS mounted to George's right on the dash mimicked in electronic pixels the landscape moving beneath them. The sun was high and north, throwing the isolated peaks of Mounts Sandford and Drum into stark relief, and the sky was a gold-washed blue.

"You should start giving out frequent-flier miles," she said.

She was shocked into near speechlessness when he replied, "Way ahead of you. We're in talks with Alaska Airlines about a code-share agreement."

Her mouth opened and closed, and the most she could muster up was, "Who's we?"

"Bruce O'Malley. He figures it'd be a nice perk for the mine workers, plus something else he can offer prospective Alaskan employees. You know we like our mileage."

She thought about this. "You're going to need more pilots."

"I know. Bobby Clark's going to pick up the mail route, for the summer anyway."

"He going to be able to unload the mail?"

"He said he'd put his legs on for the duration. Course, he's charging me the equivalent of highway robbery for a salary, and Dinah's not feeding me because I stole her husband, and Katya's pissed 'cause I stole her daddy."

Good for Bobby, Kate thought. "Bet he's just happy he doesn't have to deal with passengers."

George laughed. "Always the worst part of the job. And I found a guy who spent the winter in Prudhoe Bay, flying supplies and crew to drilling rigs out on the ice. I put him on the Niniltna-mine run, turnabout with the other new guy, Bud Schaefer."

"Flew over with Schaefer yesterday. Haven't met the other guy yet."

"Her. Name's Sabine, for crissake."

"Can she fly?" Kate said.

"Wouldn'ta hired her otherwise. Oh. Sorry, my sarcasm

button kicked off there for a second." He made a minute and probably unnecessary adjustment to the trim. "Doesn't mean Sabine ain't no name for a pilot."

Kate made a silent vow to introduce the name "Sabine" into every conversation she had with George from that day forward.

It was quiet in back, and Kate looked over her shoulder to behold all ten passengers sound asleep in uncomfortable positions. Holly Haynes was sitting in the seat behind her, her jacket jammed between her head and the window. Ferrying paperwork into the Anchorage office, she'd said on the strip. Her expression was bleak and there were shadows under her eyes.

Probably reporting in person on Lyda's death, too. Kate thought less of Truax for handing off that job.

She faced forward again and George spent the rest of the flight in Park gossip. She heard all about Gene Clauson getting caught with a case of beer and a fifth of whiskey in his plane on the ground at King City, a currently dry town. "Plus," George said, relishing the story because it wasn't about him, "all three of his passengers had booze in their luggage, including airline bottles stuffed in their shoes, a suitcase full of whiskey and rum, and three bottles of Kahlua in a Dora the Explorer knapsack."

"Not feeling his pain," Kate said.

"Fifty-five-thousand-dollar fine," George said. "Twenty days in jail."

"Still not feeling it," she said, and retaliated with a libelous description of Randy Randolph, heartbreaker to the Park, and his career approach to marriage. George had been so busy he'd missed the story entirely, and by the time he'd stopped laughing they were on approach to Merrill Field. He put them down in landing that was a runway paint job and taxied over to a hangar Kate remembered from past arrivals. This one seemed bigger somehow. Possibly because it had a brand-new coat of paint, a new sign, and the old gas pump had been replaced by a new one, shiny in chrome and red enamel. When they rolled to a stop a young woman in Chugach Air colors came trotting out with a step stool, and a young man in like colors whizzed out on a four-wheeler hauling a trailer for the baggage and freight. The door popped open, the stairs were let down, and passengers and pilot were on the tarmac marching toward the office attached to the hangar mere moments later. Slick.

Kate didn't like it at all.

"When you coming home?" George said, waving the waiting crew on board.

"Tonight if I can, tomorrow if I can't."

He nodded. "I'll keep a seat open for you every flight until we're ready to button 'er up. You be careful out among the English."

It was his favorite line from his favorite actor from his favorite film. Kate laughed and waved him off.

She called a cab from the office and fifteen minutes later was unlocking the door to the Westchester Lagoon townhouse.

The townhouse had belonged to Jack Morgan. Kate now held it in trust for his son, Johnny. They'd talked about renting it out or even selling it off, but Jack had carried an insurance policy that had paid off the mortgage when he died. Monthly fees, annual taxes, and occasional maintenance came to less than what they would spend on a hotel room every time they came to town, especially in the summer, and besides, she liked the idea of Johnny having some property of his very own.

An unoccupied condominium was also less at risk of

break-in than an unoccupied house would be, and Kate made sure to bring smoked fish in for the neighbors on both sides at the end of every summer in hopes that they'd keep an eye on the place. It came very well furnished, including the Forester in the garage. Seven years old, hadn't been driven in months, it started on the first turn of the key that was left in the ignition. As she always did, she took a moment to enjoy the electric garage door opener before putting the car in first and heading out.

The crime lab was a square gray building on Tudor Road that looked as all business on the outside as it did on the inside. Kate handed over the holster and Gammons's file and told Brillo what she wanted. He kicked when she said she wanted it by that evening ("Do you know the backlog we've got already, Shugak?") but he'd worked with her before and he knew it would be easier to make her go away if he just gave her what she wanted. She left him yelling for someone from ballistics to get their ass in there.

Kurt and Brendan's offices were downtown and Providence on the way there, so she turned off Tudor on Bragaw. As expected, she found a parking space in the hospital parking lot in the row nearest the door, because during an Alaskan summer no one had time to be sick. Inside, she asked her way to Dewayne Gammons's room, and found him a building over and a couple of floors up, on a small, hushed ward which, if brief glimpses through open room doors were any indication, seemed to cater to silent, unhappy people who didn't get a lot of visitors.

Gammons himself was sitting in a chair, clad in hospital pajamas and robe and those horrible hospital slippers consisting of a thin sole and a wide band over the instep that were guaranteed to either fall off or, worse, trip you at the first step. He was staring out the window at the Chugach Mountains, green and lush in the bold, brash light of an Arctic summer day. There was more animation in the still scene on the other side of the glass than there was on his face.

"Mr. Gammons?" Kate said. "Dewayne?"

He didn't look around, didn't twitch, didn't react in any way.

She knelt down next to him. "Dewayne, I'm Kate Shugak. Do you remember me? You walked out of the woods into my yard. Do you remember? It was the Fourth of July, and we had salmon on the grill. I was there with my auntie Vi and my uncle Old Sam, and you remember Holly Haynes from the mine, she was there, too."

Gammons was silent.

"We found your truck," Kate said. "It's back in Niniltna, safe with the trooper. You can pick it up any time."

Nothing.

"Did you go into the woods alone, Dewayne?"

Silence.

"Did you go with a friend, maybe? Rick Allen, did he go with you?"

His chest moved up and down with his breathing. Otherwise, he didn't move.

Kate bit her lip. There was no other way to put this. "We have your note, Dewayne. We know what you meant to do. Did your friend Rick maybe come after you, to stop you?"

He stared out the window. There was a stubble of beard on his chin, his hands lay loosely along his thighs, and he looked somehow weary, drained of any energy for life, love, or laughter. His wounds were healing, and the bug bites, the ones he hadn't scratched into infection, had shrunk to dark red spots. He almost looked like the photograph in his personnel file. Of course, he almost looked like the one in Richard Henry Allen's, too.

Not without a twinge of conscience, Kate said, "Do you remember your friend Lyda, Dewayne? She worked out at the mine with you? You were friends, remember?"

For the first time she saw something in his eyes that might have been a flicker of awareness.

"Dewayne?" she said, pulling herself up by the arm of his wheel-chair so she could look directly into his eyes. "Dewayne, do you remember Lyda Blue?" she said, her voice urgent. "You liked her, didn't you? She liked you, too. She was very upset when you went away."

But it was gone, that flash of intelligence, and she had to admit that it might never have been there in the first place, but for her wanting it to be so very much.

A movement caught the corner of her eye and she looked around to find a doctor in the doorway. He was a heavy, balding white man in his midforties who smelled of cigarette smoke and antiseptic solution. He looked like he'd been on his feet for days with no sleep. He was wearing a white coat with the inevitable stethoscope around his neck and carrying a chart, which he opened to scan and then closed it again, shaking his head. "He eats if we feed him. He'll wet the bed if we don't put a diaper on him. He hasn't said one word since he got here."

"When is he going to come out of it?"

The doc shook his head. "My official diagnosis, Miss Shugak? Beats the hell out of me. He's retreated so far inside himself that I don't know if he's ever going to see the light of day again."

"You know me," she said, rising to her feet. "Have we met?"

He shook his head. "We've never met. I'm Dick Lempe, Mr. Gammons's default attending physician. We haven't met, no, but we've all heard the stories. You cut quite the dash when you were working for the DA's office. The ER staff speak of you with"—he paused—"great feeling. You are remembered as being good for business." He looked around. "There is supposed to be a dog."

"She stayed home this trip," Kate said. "You've been told that Dewayne Gammons was in a depressed state prior to his disappearance?"

"Yeah. We're only just now finding out about depression, what causes it, what we can do about it. We know that—"

"What causes it? You mean something physical? I thought it was a psychological thing. A state of mind."

The doc shook his head again. "There are a lot of identified causes, family history, pessimistic personality, illness, trauma." He looked at her. "Stress. I understood he had been found in pretty severe conditions."

Kate remembered the starving, gibbering scarecrow who had burst into her clearing on the Fourth of July. "You could definitely say that."

"Well, that would tend to aggravate an already depressive condition."

"So he was depressed before, and his adventure in the Bush pushed him into catatonia."

"You diagnosing my patient, Ms. Shugak?"

"Sorry, doc," she said. "Just trying to get a handle on his condition. A body was found where we think he went into the woods. We thought it was him, until he showed up a month later. There was only one vehicle at the scene, his, so we're guessing they drove out together, but it is just a guess. I really need to talk to him, get him to tell me what happened."

The doc yawned hugely, jaws cracking. "Sorry, I've been up all night with another patient. Mr. Gammons is not talking, Ms. Shugak. I don't think he's going to talk until he's good and ready." He looked across the room again at the silent man. "And I think you'd better be prepared for that to take a long time."

"Why do you say that?"

He smiled his tired smile again. "I've been doing this a long time. Oh, I almost forgot." He pulled out a buff file folder and handed it to her.

"What's this?" she said.

"A picture of one of the wounds he came in with."

She opened the folder and stared down at the photograph. She looked up, a question in her eyes.

He nodded. "We think he was shot. It was low on his abdomen and to the right. It didn't hit anything important and it went right through. It had actually healed up pretty well by the time he got to us, nice healthy scabbing, one of the few wounds he had that wasn't infected." The doc shook his head again, too experienced to question the vagaries of the human body. "We flooded him with intravenous fluids and antibiotics. I swear he fought back. It was like he was willing himself to die. We only let him up today."

Kate closed the file with a snap. "Was he shot from the front or the back?"

"The back. Bigger hole in front where the bullet exited, as is generally the case. Pretty sure you show that to a forensic pathologist, they'll tell you it was caused by a small bullet. Not my area of expertise, but I have seen a few gunshot wounds in my time and that's my guess."

And back to Brillo she would go. "Something else." She pulled Richard Allen's blood workup from her daypack. "Can you tell me if this is his blood type?"

He looked first at the name. "But this isn't—"

"Never mind the name. Is it the same?"

"Yes, but—"

"I need to know if the blood sample from that file is from Dewayne Gammons. If I have to I can take it to the crime lab, but they're pretty backed up and it'll take time."

"Crime lab?" The doc looked startled.

"I'm working a murder investigation," Kate said. "I figured since we're standing in the middle of a hospital with all the modern conveniences, you could get it done quicker. And I need quicker."

Her face was stern, her manner brisk and no-nonsense, one professional to another. The doc stood up straighter and said, "I'll take it down to the lab myself. I've got a friend down there, and it's a simple test. Have you got a cell number?"

Kate had found her cell phone along with its charger behind the seat in her pickup the month before. She'd left it there and remembered to grab it when she was running to catch the plane that morning. She'd tried it when they'd landed and was amazed that it still worked. That didn't necessarily mean she knew the number. She fumbled it out of her pocket and looked at the keys. Green phone, green phone, ah, there it was. She pushed it, waited for her number to come up, and read it off to the doc, who scribbled it down.

She stopped at the nurse's station on her way out. "Have you got a piece of paper and a pencil I could use?"

She wrote down her telephone number and asked for a piece of tape. The nurse, a pleasant woman in pink scrubs, watched with a bemused expression as she taped the number to the back of the phone.

She went back to the crime lab, endured Brillo's invective

until he had to pause for breath and she could show him the photograph of the putative bullet wound. It caught his interest, and she left him yelling for ballistics again.

She pointed the Forester downtown.

Not long ago Kurt Pletnikoff had been in the Park poaching bears for their gallbladders. What a difference two years could make. His office was on the seventh floor of a building that catered to the attorneys who practiced their trade at the courthouse two blocks away. The brass sign was small with a plain font. The door was solid and heavy and closed behind her on a discreet hydraulic hinge. Painted gray and furnished in teakwood and maroon leather or a reasonable facsimile thereof, the outer office also sported a receptionist. She was, at a guess, Yupik or Inupiat, short and plump with round cheeks, dark eyes, and thick black hair so shiny it looked oiled, cut short in the very latest style. She was dressed in a single-breasted dark red suit over a cream silk blouse with discreet cleavage. Around her neck was a thin gold chain with a tiny diamond pendant, which matched the tiny diamond studs in her ears.

She reminded Kate of Lyda Blue, if Lyda had worked in town and shopped at Nordstrom.

She took in Kate with a cool, steady gaze. The phone rang and she picked it up. "Pletnikoff Investigations." Her voice was low and pleasant. "One moment please." She waited for a reply and pressed the Hold button. She looked at Kate.

"Kate Shugak," Kate said. "I called ahead."

The receptionist, who according to the brass nameplate on her desk went by the name of Agrifina Fancyboy, pressed another button and murmured into the phone. She waited for a response.

The single door in the wall to her right opened and a firm

step was heard. "Kate!" Kurt walked forward and enveloped Kate in a bear hug that raised her right off her feet.

"Oof," Kate said. "Lemme go, I can't breathe."

He laughed and dumped her back on the floor, beaming down at her as if she was the best thing he'd seen in a month of Sundays.

"You look great," they both said at the same time, and they both laughed.

"Hold my calls," Kurt told Agrifina, and led Kate into the inner sanctum.

This room was three times the size of the outer office and decorated in the same colors, with some brass and glass thrown in. It was a corner office with dovetailed windows looking north and west, before which Kurt's desk sat with two visitor chairs arranged in front of it. In another corner was a couch and two armchairs around a coffee table, and in a third corner was, if Kate's eyes did not deceive her, a wet bar.

She blinked. "Just tell me we've still got some money left in the operating account."

He grinned and flopped down on the couch, pointing to one of the chairs. On the table was a faux silver (hell, it might even be sterling) tray with two glasses of cracked ice and a large bottle of Diet 7UP. "Something to drink?"

"Sure." Kate sat down and watched him open the bottle and fill up the glasses.

Their first significant encounter had been in a cabin in the Park. He'd had a hatchet on his side, she'd had quick and tricky on hers. Their next encounter, in Anchorage this time, had encouraged her to believe that he might not be the loser she'd thought, and had led her to start him down the road toward becoming a private investigator. Later on, she'd helped bankroll his first office, which she recalled being in the corner of a shabby strip mall in Spenard.

Attired in a black suit that did not look off the rack, a white button-down shirt with a dark blue silk tie, and black leather shoes gleaming with polish, he looked as if he'd been decorated with the same fine hand as the office and the receptionist sitting out front.

But that was only on the surface. It was what was beneath that surface that she found most interesting, and gratifying. Where before there had been a subdued despair, now there was a quiet confidence. He was going to be okay. Who'd have thought Kurt Pletnikoff, Park rat, poacher, and all-purpose super-duper utility screwup, would have a happy ending?

He handed her a glass and caught her looking at him. "You look good," she said again.

"Thanks," he said, and the fact that he didn't try to aw shucks it off told her that Kurt had come to a certain sense of his own worth. It was good to see.

"When did you move into the new office?"

"Remember I told you about that case last year?"

"The banker?"

"Yeah."

"A moneymaker, was it?"

He held up one hand and rubbed finger and thumb together. "Turns out I'm a natural-born peeper."

"Private investigator," she said.

"Yeah, yeah. Anyway, I found most of the embezzled funds and we got a percentage. I got a lot of referrals after that, too, and I could see on the expression of clients' faces that it was time to trade up."

She hooked a thumb over her shoulder. "Agrifina?"

"Found her at Bean's."

"She was on the street?"

He nodded. "Fresh in from Chuathbaluk, on the run from a home life she won't talk about." Their eyes met. "I could relate, and she seemed clean."

"She sure does."

He grinned again. "Yeah, she's seen a lot of Lauren Bacall movies." He hesitated. "I gave her a clothing allowance."

"So? I gave you one, too, if you remember." She raised her glass. "Here's to all the richest murder suspects walking in your door."

"Hear, hear." They drank and he put his glass down. "What can I do for you, Kate?"

"How are you with industrial espionage?"

"You're kidding." He leaned forward. "Tell me."

She told him the whole story, leaving nothing out. At the end, she handed him the phone number Allen had listed, the three Social Security numbers, and her cell phone number. "I need anything you can get me and I need it fast. I'm especially interested in anything you can dig up on Allen. Gammons, yeah, but not as urgent."

"How fast?"

"End of the day if possible, tomorrow if not. My phone doesn't work in the Park."

He grimaced. "I can call in a few favors."

She drained her glass and got to her feet. "Please do. And you'll be billing me at the usual rates." He was about to protest and she said, "I'm working for Jim."

"Oh well, that's different, then," he said.

They shook hands, and she left with the warm feeling that here at least was a quarterly shareholder dividend being put to good use.

• • •

236

FROM PLETNIKOFF INVESTIGATIONS IT was only an elevator ride and a block's walk to the offices of the district attorney. Ten minutes later she was having the stuffing hugged out of her for the second time that day by Brendan McCord, a large, untidy man with a mop of red hair and a tie that invariably announced what he'd had for breakfast. Again she told her story, and asked him to run what little she had on Gammons and Allen through every database he had access to. They hadn't called her "Two-source Shugak" for nothing back in the day.

"Okay," Brendan said, "but only because I've been trying to seduce you for eight years and this might get me to first base."

"In your dreams," she said. "Besides, you owe me."

"For what?" he said in mock outrage.

"For serving paper on the Smiths last year," she said, ignoring for the purposes of the current conversation that she'd been well paid for the task.

"I thought you did that because you were secretly in love with me and wanted to bend me to your purpose," he said, hurt.

Kate left with a grin on her face.

THE NEXT STOP REQUIRED the Subaru and a lot more self-control.

The house was in a quietly affluent cul-de-sac off 100th Avenue in south Anchorage, with a finely tuned yard back and front. Axenia answered the door, baby on her hip, and after a startled moment invited Kate inside with a politeness designed to freeze the marrow in Kate's bones. It failed of effect because it was nothing more than she had expected.

Kate and her cousin Axenia had been stuck in a cold war

237

for years. Kate, the elder, had been the one tasked by Emaa to look out for Axenia all through school. The plan—Emaa's plan—had been for Axenia to follow Kate to the University of Alaska Fairbanks, there to study some discipline that she could bring back to the Park, to better serve her tribe. That had been the big idea for Kate as well, but Kate had moved to Anchorage instead and gone to work as an investigator for the Anchorage district attorney. Axenia had never gone to college, instead remaining home to run through a series of boyfriends, each of whom she hoped would get her out of the Park and each one of whom proved less worthwhile than the last.

The case that had brought Kate out of retirement on her homestead, following five and a half harrowing years working sex crimes in Anchorage, had concerned the disappearance of Axenia's most recent boyfriend, one of Dan's rangers and Axenia's best prospect to date. When the case ended, Kate went behind their grandmother's back and got Axenia a job in Anchorage. Anchorage could be a large, lonely place to someone raised in the Bush, but Kate called in a lot of favors and saw to it that Axenia landed in a preselected social circle.

It turned out that Axenia, in spite of an impassioned plea that Kate help her get out of Dodge, was less than grateful for this masterful orchestration of her life. She became even less grateful as time went on. Raised in the shadow of her legendary cousin, she had always been a little jealous of Kate's seniority and of her status within the tribe. Free from the Park's parochial vigilance for the first time in her life, Axenia had struck out on her own.

Kate followed her cousin into the kitchen, perched on the proffered stool, and accepted the cup of coffee and the plate of assorted cookies Axenia was honor-bound to offer. One thing about Bush hospitality, if you were raised in it it stuck even after you moved to the big city. Kate ate, drank, and attacked. "I wanted to talk to you about the mine," she said, pushing away her cup. "The board is—"

"Actually," Axenia said with a thin smile, "I wanted to talk to you about the mine, too. Mathisen, Dischner has been retained by Global Harvest."

Axenia was married to an Alaskan lawyer and lobbyist named Lou Mathisen. Lou and Kate didn't get along for many reasons, not least of which was her conviction that he'd married Axenia because he was white and she was Alaska Native. There had been a lot of that going around Alaska ever since ANCSA, Natives suddenly becoming desirable mates to whites who wanted a share of the money, the land, and the political influence the act had granted them.

"Oh," she said, thrown off stride. "I didn't know."

"Lou says Global Harvest thinks you're in their pocket. One hundred percent pro-mine. Don't have to worry about the chair of the Niniltna Native Association board of directors, boys, she's got her hand out just like the rest of them."

Kate set her teeth and said nothing.

Determined to provoke a response, Axenia said, "You might not have won if people had known all that before the election in January."

The baby was sucking on its fist and the toddler was drowsing in a playpen in a corner of the large, expensively furnished kitchen, so Kate didn't do what she wanted to do, which was reach across the counter and separate her cousin's head from its body. "Axenia," she said, keeping her voice calm, "you know it's not anything I ever wanted."

Axenia snorted her disbelief and hitched up her baby. "What did you come here for, anyway? I have to put the baby down for a nap, and then I've got some errands."

Here's your hat, what's your hurry. "I was hoping to talk you into organizing the NNA shareholders who live in town."

"Organize them to do what? Support your moves on the board?"

"Nothing like that," Kate said. She took a breath and moderated her tone. "Start a regular shareholder meeting here."

"In Anchorage?"

"Yes. I—We were thinking you could maybe have monthly or even weekly meetings, the people getting together to say hi and exchange news and introduce the grandbabies. The aunties could come in and teach a quilting class. You could get somebody else in to teach beading or basket weaving. Ask Ossie to teach dance classes. People could bring food. I—we could get Park rats to send in meat and fish. It doesn't have to be political, Axenia, it could just be about family, visiting, keeping in touch."

"And where would this meeting take place? A lot of NNA shareholders I wouldn't have in my house." Her expression indicated present company not excepted.

One of the great things about a tribe was that it was all about family, Kate thought. And one of the worst things about a tribe was that it was all about family. There was no bloodier warfare than brother against brother. Or cousin against cousin. "I managed to talk a few bucks out of the board. It'd be enough to rent the Alaska Native Heritage Center once a month for six months."

"And what would we do at these meetings?"

"It would be your show." Kate shrugged. "They've got a theater, you could even watch movies if you want."

Axenia examined this proposal with suspicion bordering on scorn. "Why? What's in it for you?"

"Over a third of NNA shareholders live in Anchorage, Axenia. Half or more of them never make it back to the Park for the annual shareholder meetings. I—The board feels like the Anchorage shareholders have been orphaned. This is a way to, I don't know, bring them back into the family, I guess." Maybe not such a desirable objective, Kate was thinking now. "Auntie Joy thinks we should send a board member into town to attend, so they can answer questions and hear about problems."

"What do you get out of it?"

Kate looked at Axenia. If she stayed, Axenia would just keep asking that question over and over again. "Think about it, Axenia," she said, sliding to the floor. "If it sounds like something you'd like to do, let Annie know and she'll get you contact information for the Anchorage people."

"Or maybe I'll just run for the board myself," Axenia said, her voice rising as Kate walked away. "Maybe I'll run for president!"

"Feel free," Kate said. "Thanks for the coffee and cookies, and say hi to Lou. I'll find my own way out."

She was proud she didn't slam the door.

FIFTEEN

SHE CHECKED HER PHONE for messages. None. She cursed Brillo, the doc at Providence, Kurt, and Brendan with a fine impartiality, and felt better, if a little guilty. They were all capable guys but they weren't miracle workers.

Where next? She should drop in at the Raven offices, she really should. Instead she drove right by the building on Dimond and went to Costco, there to spend a productive hour buying flour by the twenty-pound bag, olive oil by the gallon, and Tampax forty-eight to the box. Kate was so done with fertility, she didn't know why it couldn't be done with her. As a bow to that fertility, however, she included a box of condoms, and filled the cart with other necessities, finishing up at the book table. The books were cheap but every third one seemed to be by the same author. She trundled the cart around to the other side. Ah, lots of Alaska books. She went in, and surfaced half an hour later when her phone rang.

It was Brendan. "Is this some kind of test?"

"What?"

"Is there a camera on me, waiting to record the moment when I tear my hair and burst into tears?"

"What did you find out?"

"Not a goddamn thing on Gammons."

"Nothing?"

"Other than I'm reliably informed that he was in fact born.

Where the hell do you come up with these people, Kate?"

"The 'born in Roy' holds up?"

"Yup, but I can't find his parents, where he went to school, nothing. I talked to the same cop your girl talked to. He says he's found a few people who maybe remember the parents, but they're not sure, and they can't remember anything about them other than they were thought to have died young." There was a brief silence. "Kate?"

"I suppose he could have been an orphan who lived a very clean life."

"Try sanitary. Hell, try sterile."

"Some people do. What about Allen?"

Brendan's voice changed, grew deeper, richer, the vowels resounding with resonance and meaning, the consonants crisp in contrast. Kate knew that tone. Someone's cart bumped her in the butt. It was another book lover, and she moved over to a deserted corner between the bicycles and the garden tools.

"Ah, well now, Mr. Allen," Brendan said, rolling out the words like GM would a new car, if they hadn't gone belly-up by then. "Mr. Richard Henry Allen, native of Minnesota, *L'etoile du Nord.*"

"Okay," Kate said.

"The Star of the North, the state motto. State bird the common loon, but state flower the showy lady slipper."

When Brendan had something really juicy he liked to milk it for all it was worth. Kate leaned against a stack of wheelbarrows and prepared to wait him out. "Okay."

"Official state song? 'Hail, Minnesota.' "

Kate closed her eyes and hung her head.

"Minnesota's exports were up thirteen percent in the last quarter. Their number-one biggest trading partner? Canada. Australia's way down there at sixteen."

"Brendan—"

"They're pretty industrious, Minnesota. Never mind what Garrison Keillor says, they're not all Norwegian bachelor farmers. Some of them are Norwegian bachelor geeks. They exported over a billion dollars in computer and electronic goods last year, three-quarters of a billion in machinery, and a quarter of a billion in chemicals." He paused. "You still there, Kate?"

"Never mind me, Brendan. There's a hoe here I'm thinking of using to cut my throat."

He chuckled. It sounded less than avuncular. "I found our boy's bank account in Minneapolis." Brendan always got proprietary when he liked them for something.

Kate opened her eyes. "Did you?"

"I did. He used a different name but his own Social Security number. Guess he wanted to be sure he was eligible to collect those benefit checks come sixty-two. He was thinking ahead, our boy, just not far enough ahead of me."

"And?"

"And the account shows regular direct deposits from the Suulutaq Mine. One every two weeks, same amount every time."

After all this there had to be more. "And?"

"And," Brendan said, "there are other deposits."

"Where from?"

"First you want to know how much."

"Oh." Kate was silent for a moment. "Oh. Okay. How much?"

"You know if you're moving large chunks of cash around you have to report anything over ten grand."

"Yeah."

"These amounts varied between seven and nine thousand,

so I'm thinking our Mr. Allen knew that, too."

"Where'd the money come from? And how often?"

"Well." Brendan cleared his throat. "I don't know yet, Kate. The amount was funneled through a lot of banks, different ones each time, and half the time including an offshore bank. Four times a month. Almost like a salary, except the amount changed every time."

They listened to each other think for a few moments. "Someone was paying him off," Kate said.

"Ah, but what was he selling?"

"Good question. Thanks, Brendan, I—"

"Not so hasty, Ms. Shugak, ma'am. That was just the first unaccounted-for thing in his bank records."

"Do tell."

"Indeed."

"No, Brendan, I mean really, do tell me."

"He had another regular payment coming into his account. Same level of amounts, this payment twice a month like clockwork."

"Jesus, Brendan, how much money did this guy have squirreled away?"

"Just under three hundred thousand dollars."

Someone banged into her cart and apologized. Kate waved them off—she could barely make out their faces through suddenly blurred vision—and said, "Are you kidding me?"

"Nope. Here's the best part, Kate."

"What? What!"

"This payer wasn't quite as careful. We traced that sucker right back to its source. Took my guy approximately seventeen and a half minutes."

"Who was it?"

He told her.

SIXTEEN

IT HAD BEEN A long time since she'd been in the RPetCo building, almost five years since she'd been hired to find a drug dealer at their camp in the Prudhoe Bay oil fields. A lot had changed since then. For one thing, there was now a veritable bank of security guards in the lobby, dressed alike in polyester blazers with the RPetCo logo embroidered discreetly over their hearts. One of them took her name, asked to see some picture ID, and made a phone call.

"Have you got a fax here?" she asked another of the guards. They did. "Okay if I have something sent over? Your boss is going to want to see it."

He thought this over with a gravity better befitting the weighty cares of an agent of the Secret Service, decided it would be difficult to fax a bomb, and agreed. She called Brendan and gave him the number. A moment later the fax hummed into operation.

While the fax was printing out the bank of elevators opened to disgorge hundreds of employees heading home at what Kate guessed would be a much smarter clip than they had come in that morning. She searched the faces, looking for someone she knew. No one looked familiar, no one said, "Hey, Kate Shugak!" She would have liked to have seen Sue Jordan, hear what diabolical new methods she had thought up to terrorize all the men in the RPetCo Hilton, but Sue was probably in Prudhoe Bay doing just that at this very moment, and Kate wouldn't have wished otherwise.

"Ms. Shugak? This way, please." Someone in the building must have remembered her, because she was escorted without further delay into an elevator that wafted them to the top floor.

Yes, someone must have remembered her, because a security guard accompanied her every step of the way.

The elevator debouched into a massive suite of offices on the penthouse floor. The guard led the way between a dozen desks, most of them abandoned by now. The boss's door was guarded by a grayhaired woman in expensive tweeds and sensible shoes. The guard said, "Kate Shugak, Mrs. Podhoretz," and turned Kate over with the air of having successfully handed off a very hot potato.

"This way, Ms. Shugak," Mrs. Podhoretz said. One of Mrs. Podhoretz's sensible shoes squeaked. She led Kate to the grand set of double doors, mahogany by the look of them. She knocked and said, "Ms. Shugak, Mr. King," and stepped back to let Kate inside. The door closed behind her.

The man at the desk might have lost most of his hair but he hadn't changed much otherwise. He still had the same general build as a fireplug, his face was the same freckled square, he had the same baleful glare. The glasses had been updated, he'd lost the aviator frames with the Coke-bottle lenses and replaced them with rimless. It made his eyes look bigger and his glare meaner.

"Hey, John," Kate said.

He stood to shake her hand, a hard, dry, hot grip. "Jack Morgan was a good man. I was sorry to hear he was gone."

"Thank you."

He sat down again in his high-backed black leather chair.

That was all she was going to get in the way of greeting or sympathy from John King, president and CEO of the Royal Petroleum Corporation, and that was fine with Kate.

"You remodeled," she said, looking around the office. "Nice."

"What do you want, Shugak?" he said, proving her point. "I only agreed to see you because you said it was urgent and that it affected the company."

"What's the price of a barrel of Prudhoe Bay crude lately, John?"

The glare increased in wattage. "Why the fuck do you care?"

At their first meeting five years ago, when Jack had brought her to this same office so the president and CEO of RPetCo Alaska could look her over and decide if she was up to the job, she had learned that John King respected only those hardy souls who stood up to him. If he saw you flinch, cringe, or cry, he would bully you without mercy. Therefore Kate matched him attitude for attitude, saying in the same unyielding voice, "How much?"

"Forty-two twenty-four," he said. "Up two bucks from yesterday."

"But down about fifty bucks from a year ago," she said.

Again with the increase in wattage. "What of it?"

"Five years," Kate said, "that's a long time as CEO."

"What the fuck do you want, Shugak?"

"I made a few phone calls before I came here. There's an RPetCo shareholders meeting coming up, next month, isn't there? There are rumors that they're angry about the decrease in their dividend. There are more rumors that they're going to orchestrate a vote of no confidence in the corporation's officers."

"You're awful goddamn knowledgeable about the oil business all of a sudden."

No, she thought, I've just recently acquired some experience in running a corporation. Big or small, the politics were bound to be much the same. "So it follows that you'd want to roll something out, some plan to increase RPetCo's share of potential resources, to convince the shareholders you're still on top of the game. I figure you've probably already written that part of the speech, about how the recession's hurt us all and it's going to take a while to come back, and in the meantime RPetCo is making long-term plans to expand their presence in the resource industry."

He leaned back in his chair. "If you can get to a fucking point any time before the end of the year, I won't throw you out on your cute little ass."

She almost said she was glad he thought it was cute and thought better of it just in time. Like the bullying and the profanity, sexual innuendo and harassment were part of John King's stock in trade. She remembered P.J. on the Stores loading dock at the mine, and Lyda, who had been so apprehensive of Kate's reaction. *I've met P.J. before.* She put the fax on his desk.

He didn't touch it. "What the fuck is that?"

"It's a record of a series of bank deposits going back over the last six months, paid by various illegal stratagems into the account of one Richard Henry Allen. Allen is, or was, an employee at the Suulutaq Mine. What was he selling that you were buying?"

He stared at the paper without touching it. "I don't know what the fuck you're talking about."

"Yeah, you do," she said, "and you're going to tell me all about it."

"Why the fuck would I do that?"

"Because you owe me," Kate said, fixing him with her own glare. "I damn near got killed on that job up in Prudhoe and I put down your bad guy anyway." She raised an eyebrow. "I had you figured as someone who didn't welsh on his debts. Prove me wrong and I'm out of here."

They glared at each other.

King broke first, picking up the fax and scanning it. She watched him but his expression didn't change. He tossed the fax back down on the desk and punched a button on his phone. "Get in here."

The door opened so quickly Kate knew the person had probably been listening on the other side of it.

"Ms. Shugak."

"Mr. Childress," Kate said to RPetCo Alaska's security boss. A retired Army officer with a brush cut and a habit of command, he was more polished than his boss.

"John?" he said.

"You heard?"

Childress didn't pretend not to understand. He nodded.

John King glared at Kate one more time. "Tell her."

"All of it?"

"All of it," King said.

Kate crossed her legs, folded her hands, and settled back to listen.

They had hired Allen in October, after Global Harvest announced they would be hiring for the mine in December.

"Why Allen?" Kate said.

Childress exchanged a glance with King. "He had what we felt were certain talents that would help him get the job done successfully."

"What was he, an actor? A con man?"

Another glance told her she had come close to the truth. If Kurt couldn't ante up, she resolved to have Brendan go a little deeper into Richard Henry Allen's personal history.

They'd told Allen to come to Alaska and apply for work at the Suulutaq Mine. "He was to draw no attention to himself, other than to work hard enough to earn promotion and responsibility. The end goal was to work with the geologists, so he would have access to the core samples."

"And get copies of the core samples to you."

"Yes."

Data that could inform either a buyout or an unfriendly takeover, Kate thought, meditating on her clasped hands. "When is the last time you heard from him?"

"Over six weeks now," Childress said.

"Did he quit?"

"No. He just stopped sending us core sample reports."

"Did you try to contact him?"

Childress shook his head. "That's not the way it worked. There was to be no direct contact, ever."

"How did you get the reports?"

"He brought them with him when he came to town on his shift off and mailed them to a post office box in Houston. Someone in the Houston office would pick them up and courier them to my office."

"You paid him on delivery."

They both looked at her as if she had suggested they vote Democrat. "Yes."

That explained the regular payments every two weeks, Kate thought.

"How did you trace the payments to us, Shugak?"

She stood. "It took a friend a couple of minutes on a computer," she said. "You guys aren't exactly James Bond, are you?"

She walked to the door. "Oh," she said, hand on the knob, "probably no harm in telling you." She smiled at King. "You weren't the only people he was selling information to."

She pulled the door closed behind her with the gentlest possible click, grinned at Mrs. Podhoretz, and sauntered to the elevator.

She'd leave the news that their spy was dead for another time.

SHE SAT IN HER car while she tried to figure out where she should go next.

"I probably should stop by Raven."

Raven Inc. was a regional Native corporation, one of the thirteen created with the passage of the Alaska Native Claims Settlement Act to administer the money and lands granted to Natives in that act. The thirteen regional corporations were the umbrella organizations for the two hundred plus tribal organizations, like the Niniltna Native Association. Raven Inc. headquarters was ordinarily a place the pre-chair apolitical Kate would shun like the plague, but things were different now. And it wasn't like Anchorage was the world's biggest city. Someone would have seen her and word would go around, especially if it got to be known she'd come to town and snubbed her fellow executives.

Now, there was a job right up Axenia's alley.

Really, it only made diplomatic sense, as the head of a small but powerful association, as Emaa's granddaughter and the (temporary) leader of hundreds of Native shareholders, she should at least drop in to show the flag.

Her cell phone rang. She'd never been happier to hear it.

It was Lempe. "My friend says the blood types match exactly." When she was silent, the doc said, "Ms. Shugak, does this mean that Mr. Gammons is actually this person named Allen?"

"No," Kate said, "no, the man in your hospital is Dewayne Gammons, all right."

He was silent. "We're transferring him to API. We need the bed on the ward for more critical patients."

"He's still not talking?"

"No."

Some of Kate's best perps had been cycled through the Alaska Psychiatric Institute. "I could have sworn I saw something when I mentioned his girlfriend."

"Could you get her to come in and talk to him? He might respond to her."

Kate took a deep breath and let it out slowly. "I'm afraid that's impossible. Lyda Blue is dead."

"I ... see." A brief pause, and when he spoke again his voice was cooler. "Ms. Shugak, I am aware of your propensity for getting information by any means. Some people find that admirable. I find it reprehensible. Don't ever lie to a patient of mine again, even if that lie is only one of omission."

"He couldn't even hear me," she said.

"And if he could? And if he remembers you asking about her? And if he comes out of this and asks for her? And I have to tell him she's dead? It could throw him right back where he was before. I will see to it that you are stricken from his guest list."

She was ashamed of herself, she had been when she'd asked Gammons about Lyda. "Doc," she said, "Lyda Blue was murdered yesterday." She was momentarily surprised to hear how certain she was. "I'm sorry for Dewayne Gammons's condition, and I'm sorry as hell if I've exacerbated it, but he may be in possession of knowledge that will allow me to find out who did it, and why. If he regains consciousness or wakes up or even gets up to pee on his own, you will call me immediately, do you understand?"

A brief and frigid silence. "Is that all?"

"It is," she said. And added, trying to keep the lines of communication open, "Thanks, doc. I owe you one."

She was speaking into a dead phone. How to win friends and influence people. She looked at the time. Six o'clock. It took her five minutes but she finally figured out how to check her voice mail. Nothing. She thought about calling Kurt but she knew if he'd had anything to report he would have called her.

Wait a minute, who was that guy Truax had thrown off the mine yesterday? She still had his card in the back pocket of her jeans. Kostas McKenzie. Well, there was a suspicious name right there, Greek and Irish, or maybe the McKenzie was Scots, even worse, absolutely have to check that out.

Besides, she thought more soberly, if the Park was going to be the scene of future environmental protests, best to know as much as possible about it in advance.

She dialed the number on the card. It was picked up on the first ring, a breathless young voice very impressed with the urgent importance of the job her organization was doing. Would Kate like to donate to the cause? Well then, would she like to volunteer? Mother Earth was at grave risk from wholesale, environmentally unsafe resource extraction by conscienceless corporate giants interested only in gross profit and executive bonuses. Kate could answer phones, stuff envelopes, knock on doors, conduct surveys, write letters to her legislators and to her congressmen. There was so much to do if the planet was to be saved. The time to act was now. If you weren't a part of the solution, you were part of the problem.

When she was able to get a word in edgewise Kate asked if the office would be open for much longer that evening. Office hours were from ten in the morning until nine at night, this information given to her in a voice thrilled at the prospect of recruiting another true believer into the army of the righteous. When she managed finally to get off the phone Kate pulled the Anchorage map out of the side pocket, found the street name on the card, and set off.

They were located on one of those ubiquitous four-space Anchorage strip malls. Gaea took up the middle two spaces, and everything looked very bright and shiny and new through the floor-to-ceiling windows that made up the wall that faced the street. Kate pulled the Subaru into a spot in front of the double glass doors and looked at the logo printed in translucent paint across them both. It was a larger drawing of the logo on McKenzie's business card and the leaflet in Gammons's room, a kneeling goddess dressed in flowing blue-green robes, head bent over a globe cradled in her hands. The goddess was sort of a Euraisamerind racial blend designed to offend as few as possible. The Earth was resplendent in its customary blue-and-white regalia. Beneath the image was the name GAEA, and beneath it the slogan, "One people, one planet."

It was a clean image, unfussy, the artist had been restrained from doing too much, and it was very attractive. Kate was reminded again that the Niniltna Native Association had yet to decide upon its own new logo, following the grand plan she had instigated at the last annual shareholders' meeting in January. She sighed.

The glass door with half a goddess on it swung out smoothly

and heavily, all by itself announcing Gaea to be an organization with weight and gravitas. Money well spent. Inside, the front two-thirds of the room was filled with desks and tables. Volunteers were on the phones and computers. It wasn't a hive of industry but there was enough of a hum of activity so as to give the impression that Gaea was an organization with a serious base of support.

The last third of the space against the back wall was partitioned into a small kitchen, a bathroom, and the boss's office. Only the bathroom had a door you couldn't see through. The first impression you got walking in was transparency. Kate applauded their decorator.

"May I help you?"

It was the same voice that had answered the phone, and it belonged to a sweet young thing in a cropped top and low-rider jeans, who wore far too much black eyeliner and had punked purple hair shorter than Kate's held back by a wide band of rainbow spangles. Small silver hoops traveled from one lobe to the top of her ear, while its fellow sported a single hoop six inches in diameter that kept catching on the shoulder of her top.

She was totally styling, and Kate almost said so but caught herself in time. "Hi, I'm looking for—"

"Kate Shugak!"

She looked around and found the man himself emerging from the one enclosed office, hand outstretched and a beaming smile on his face. "I'm so glad you could drop by." He looked around. "Where's Mutt?"

This remark bespoke a personal knowledge of Kate's personal life that alarmed her a great deal. Before she could snub him for his presumption he put a hand beneath her elbow. "Let me show you around."

He escorted her through the room, introducing her to everyone as "Kate Shugak, chair of the board of the Niniltna Native Association, the largest village closest to the Suulutaq Mine." The words "Suulutaq Mine" appeared to be the most relevant ones, as people's eyes lit up and she was welcomed warmly into the fold. When the royal progress was complete, Kate looked at McKenzie and said, "You do know I'm not against the mine."

He grinned again. "Not yet you're not. Give us a little time and we'll convince you."

She cocked her head. "Well, I haven't met any bomb-throwing fanatics today, I'll give you that much."

"We keep them in the basement," he said.

Much against her will, it drew out a smile. "Okay. Make your pitch."

A map of Alaska covered the entire eastern wall, with an inset of the Park superimposed on it. "Okay if I start from go?"

"Sure. I'd like to hear what everyone hears."

He nodded and in an instant shifted from genial host to crusader. He positioned himself in front of the map without obscuring the area in question and pointed to locations when he mentioned their names. "The Suulutaq Mine is a proposal by Global Harvest Resources Incorporated to build one of the world's largest gold mines in interior Alaska, approximately fifty miles north of the shores of Prince William Sound."

Good sound bite, Kate thought. Everyone hearing the words "Prince William Sound" immediately flashed on a picture of a dying sea otter covered in some of the eleven million gallons of crude oil spilled there thirty years before by the RPetCo Anchorage. A subtle tarring of GHRI with RPetCo's brush. Work with what you've got.

"Global Harvest has not yet applied for permits, but they are in the process of drilling for core samples to determine the extent of the deposit and the amount of recoverable ore. So far, estimated deposits include over forty-two billion pounds of copper, almost three billion pounds of molybdenum, and almost forty million ounces of gold, which would make it the second largest gold mine in the world."

Clever again, Kate thought. While gold had its practical application in electronics and aerospace, it was best known for its luxury use in jewelry. Who cared if Donald Trump's thirteenth wife got her Cartier wedding set? Especially if it came at the expense of something that you could be convinced was far more precious. Guilt by useless luxury association.

"Global Harvest has yet to apply for permits, but they propose to build a large open-pit mine as well as an even larger underground mine. Both endeavors will require a great deal of water, which Global Harvest is proposing to acquire from creeks here, here, and here. All three feed into the headwaters of the Gruening River, which then flows through this gap into the Kanuyaq River. These creeks are flourishing habitats for five different species of salmon, a source of food for Alaskans native to the area going back ten thousand years."

Really, she was going to have to start keeping a scorecard. By using "Alaskans native to the area" he included everyone who wasn't Native, too. A feat of rhetorical gymnastics that many Alaska state legislators had yet to achieve.

"The mine site sits in a high, broad valley facing southwest, between spurs of the Quilak Mountains. Global Harvest proposes building the largest dam in the world to contain the acid mine drainage and metal leaching produced when rain and snow fall on tailings and when chemicals used to process the ore leak or spill."

Acid was a scary word right there. Acid rain, anyone?

"This proposed dam will be made of earth, not concrete."

Ah, a little selective omission, an essential ingredient in every compelling argument. The planned dam was going to be bigger than the Three Gorges Dam in China, and the plans called for two dams, not one.

"All five species of salmon who call these waters home—"

Anthropomorphizing fish, now, reminding her again of PETA's fish kittens. A hard sell, she'd have thought, but that was just her.

"—along with rainbow trout, lake trout, arctic char, arctic grayling, and Dolly Varden spawn, migrate in the waterways downstream of the Suulutaq Mine. It is one of the richest and most unspoiled fish habitats left in the world. Entire coastal towns rely on the commercial catch of salmon every summer in the flats off the mouth of the Kanuyaq River. Sports fishermen come from all over the world to fish the mountain streams. Alaska Natives have been subsisting on the salmon catch from these waters for generations."

Now the prospective mine was poisoning the playground of the rich, not to mention the food supply of an entire race.

"The valley where the open pit is to be dug is home to the Gruening River caribou herd. While a small herd by comparison to the Mulchatna and Western Arctic caribou herds, the Gruening River herd has been found to be biologically unique, a herd that may be a bellwether for all other North American caribou herds. As such it is targeted for extensive study by accredited global wildlife institutes. The Gruening River caribou herd has also been a traditional part of the subsistence lifestyle of the Natives in the area, a significant protein essential to their physical health and cultural well-being."

A little vague, there. What study had found the Gruening herd unique? Which institutes had done what targeting? Nice inclusive conspiratorial touch at the end, though. Most of us eat meat.

There was more about the grizzly bears (Kate could have offered up some eyewitness testimony to the health of the Park grizzlies but she refrained), the moose, the sheep, the goats, and the migratory birds, and the stated determination of the federal government to open up all eligible federal lands in the area to hard rock mining, a blatant "*Après moi, le deluge*" message if Kate had ever heard one.

McKenzie's presentation lasted fifteen minutes and not one minute more, and concluded with a list of sponsors, as he reeled off names that featured green heavy hitters like the Sierra Club, the Environmental Defense Fund, Ducks Unlimited, and Earthwatch. There were familiar corporate names as well, companies like Apple, Wal-Mart, General Electric, and, to Kate's secret amusement, RPetCo Alaska. The list ended with a lengthy catalog of do-gooder nonprofits, ranging from familiar names like Rockefeller and Carnegie to what must have been nonprofits new to the business of saving the planet, Clean and Green, Big Blue Marble, Alaskans for Sustainable Jobs, The Seventy-one Percent Society, Clean Air for All.

She had to admit she was impressed. It argued a breadth of support that crossed ideological lines. Of course, she reminded herself, they could all have bought in at the lowest level.

Throughout, McKenzie was confident, informed, and succinct, his passion leavened with humor and his fanaticism tempered with reality. He didn't impugn the morals of GHRI's executive body, he didn't refer to those managers of federal lands as rape, ruin, and run boys. He was gently, implacably, immovably rational. Kate decided it was probably the most dangerous thing about him.

He dropped his arm. "So?"

"Pretty effective," she said.

"And?"

"And what?" She shrugged. "It's not me you have to convince."

"Come on," he said. "You're the head of your Native Association, an association that is the only recognizable form of organized government within a hundred miles of the mine. What you say and do carries a lot of weight." He drew closer and touched her arm, turning her gently toward the map. "Look at it, Kate. Twenty million square acres of virtually untouched, unspoiled land."

"You come on," she said. "Oil in Katalla. Copper in Kanuyaq. Coal in Ahtna. Private and commercial gold mines in virtually uncountable numbers going back over a hundred and fifty years. The Park is no stranger to the mining industry, Kostas."

He looked disappointed.

"Besides, you're a little premature, aren't you? GHRI hasn't even completed their EIS yet. That and the permitting process is going to take at least two years. All they're doing at present is trying to define the limits of the mine, which isn't easy because it seems to double in size every time they take another core sample. And let's not forget that they have every legal right to do this. They bought their leases from the state in open auction, fair and square."

He listened to her with attention and without condemnation. Probably tucking everything away so he could come up with a way of refuting it the next time he gave his speech.

"And," she said, "there is the little matter of jobs, in an area that hasn't had them in large quantity since 1936, in an economy that is in the toilet."

"Say all that's true," he said. "Doesn't necessarily make it right."

She laughed and shook her head. "That's what I enjoy most about environmental groups, their propensity to reduce everything to abstract ideology. Forty billion ounces of gold at a thousand dollars an ounce isn't right or wrong or abstract, it's concrete. It's tangible, it's a commodity which is in demand, which means there's a market for it, which means someone is going to pay somebody else to get it out of the ground and get it to where somebody else can buy it. It's called capitalism. I'm sure you must have heard something about it in high school."

When he spoke, his voice was neutral. "So you're going to come out a hundred percent for the mine? There's no moving you to our point of view?"

"I'm here, aren't I? I'm always willing to listen. The only thing I really know is I don't know enough." She thought of the aunties, and Axenia. "But I represent almost three hundred shareholders and all their children and grandchildren to come." She thought of George Perry's air taxi, and of Johnny and Val. "I have to think about their future."

"This is their future," he said, indicating photographs of gigantic strip mines hung on the wall. Heavy equipment was crawling up and down their sides like tiny yellow and green ants. Some had raised their own dust storms. None of them were a pretty sight. They weren't meant to be.

"I appreciate your passion and I respect your cause. But I can't allow ideology alone to push me for or against." She pulled out her phone and looked at the display. "I appreciate the time you've taken to show me your operation." She nodded at the door. "I like your logo, too. Who was the artist?"

More civil than friendly now, he said, "I'll find out and get that name to you."

"Thanks."

"And please, take a brochure," he said, snagging one off a nearby table. "There's a form to fill out if you'd like to join. We're an IRS-certified nonprofit 501(c)(3), which means we're deductible. Would you like to write us a check? We're happy to accept any amount, and for three dollars you get a lifetime membership, a subscription to the Gaea newsletter, and a mug. With the logo you like on it."

He escorted her to the door, and to everyone's surprise when he opened it Holly Haynes walked in. She saw Kate and her eyes widened.

"Hi, there, Miss Haynes," McKenzie said with his attractive smile. "Did you come to volunteer?"

Kate laughed. McKenzie had a smart mouth.

Haynes looked from Kate to McKenzie and her expression hardened. "No, I came here to complain about that commercial you've been running that says we're dumping toxic mud into the groundwater that feeds into the Kanuyaq River."

Kate left without waiting to hear McKenzie's answer. She climbed in the Subaru, checked her phone for messages, and left the parking lot.

A beige, four-door sedan fell in behind her and followed her all the way home.

SEVENTEEN

SHE WAS UP AND dressed and on her second cup of coffee by seven o'clock the following morning, staring out the window at the beige four-door sedan idling next to Westchester Lagoon. It had been there when she woke up, and it was still there an hour later.

The phone rang. It was Kurt. "I got news. Come on down to the office."

She stopped at City Market for three canelas and more coffee and drove downtown. The sedan followed at a discreet distance. She parked in the Captain Cook parking garage because Kurt had told her that he validated parking.

Agrifina greeted her with a reserved smile. "Mr. Pletnikoff is expecting you, Ms. Shugak. Go right in."

Kate inclined her head in formal recognition of the power of the keeper of the keys. "Thank you." Mrs. Podhoretz had nothing on Agrifina Fancyboy.

She pulled Kurt's door closed behind her and said, "I swear, that girl out there thinks she's living in 1950."

"I told you, she's channeling Lauren Bacall, only shorter. And, you know, Yupik."

"I brought her coffee and a pastry but I'm scared to give them to her. She might think it's only something Thelma Ritter should do. And I'm not that funny."

Kurt rolled his eyes and delivered the goods himself. He

came back in, grinning. " 'Please tell Ms. Shugak it was very kind of her to think of me.' "

"Alaka," Kate said, "where's Emaa when we need her." Emaa could out-formal the Queen of England. She could have matched Agrifina politesse for politesse, whereas all Kate wanted to do was run very fast in the other direction.

They settled on the couch with coffee and pastries, a vast array of paperwork spread over the coffee table.

"First," he said, "an article in *The Wall Street Journal* about a venture capitalist firm called True North Investments. It was formed a few years ago to fund resource extraction projects above the Arctic Circle. Their spokesman will neither confirm nor deny that they are interested in acquiring a share of GHRI stock, possibly a controlling interest."

Kate digested this. "A takeover?"

He nodded. "I found the same story elsewhere, *Business Week*, *Forbes*, *Kiplinger*, a couple of others. They all said pretty much the same thing."

He blew on his coffee and took a big bite of the pastry. He was as big a ham as Brendan. She wondered if the characteristic was endemic to people who snooped for a living. Maybe because they worked so much out of the limelight, they had a tendency to go for the big reveal whenever they had a captive audience.

Kurt washed down his thorough mastication of the bit of pastry with a healthy swallow of coffee, patted his lips with a napkin, and smiled. "At least some of the blind deposits into Allen's account?"

"Yes?"

"Are from True North Investments."

"Really." Kate sat back. "Allen was accepting money from True North Investments? A possible competitor to Global? For whom he was working at the Suulutaq Mine? And accepting a paycheck, I might add."

He didn't miss her too-demure expression, and said smoothly, "I'm guessing you already know about RPetCo. It was just too easy to trace."

She nodded. "Brendan popped it in about two seconds." Lest he feel that she had not thought him capable of finding out this information himself, she said, "He said it was impossible to trace the source of the other payments."

He grinned. "Only the best butter. I know a guy who knows another guy in banking in New York who knows somebody else in Switzerland. They were able to follow the money trail for us."

Kate choked on her coffee. "Switzerland?"

He waved a hand. "Don't ask. It's a, you should pardon the expression, global world, Kate. The money had been run through a dozen banks and some of them were offshore. This is how this works. And my contacts made sure I knew that they don't find answers easily and never this quickly."

Kate wondered how big a fee Pletnikoff Investigations was paying the guy in Switzerland. She did not ask. There were advantages to being a silent partner. "Is there any way you can acquire True North's financial records?"

"No way," Kurt said. "They are very big hitters with serious internal security. They're a private concern so there's no published prospectus and no published annual report, either."

"Is there a president or a board of directors?"

He fished around and came up with a piece of paper, which he handed to her. "Came over the fax five minutes ago. Wasn't cheap, either."

She read down to the bottom, and smiled. "Worth it, though."

"What?"

"I'll tell you in a minute. What else have you got?"

"That's about it. Allen's working for Suulutaq and taking money from two of their competitors. Put it together and what have you got?"

"Other than kabbibity-bobbity-boo? My guess is corporate espionage."

"I knew that, I just gave it to you to be nice."

"I know. Here's something you don't know." She handed him the list of True North Investments' corporate officers. "The last name?"

He looked. "John King?" He looked at her. "So?"

"So the president and CEO of RPetCo Alaska is also named John King."

"Crap," he said after a minute, "I knew that, but it's such a common name I didn't make the connection. You're saying this is the same John King?"

"I'm betting on it." She gave him the gist of yesterday's interview with the president and CEO of RPetCo.

"He didn't tell you about sitting on the board of True North Investments."

"No, and I didn't know enough to ask him yesterday." She meditated for a moment. "I don't know that it has anything to do with the murder of Lyda Blue," she said at last. "If I had to guess, I'd say King learned about True North's plans to acquire Global when he was named to True North's board and decided to acquire some information on his own for a possible Global takeover by RPetCo."

"Yeah, but what are the odds King would hire the same guy True North is using?"

"Are you kidding me? True North probably hired Allen first. King's on the board, he hears about him. Why go to all

267

the bother of finding someone else when the perfect spy is already in place?"

"And he would know Allen would be open to such a proposal, how?"

Kate snorted. "Allen was a corporate spy. By definition that means for sale to the highest bidder. Why wouldn't he want to sell the same information twice?"

"Why'd King have to buy it? Wouldn't he have access to the same information through his seat on True North's board?"

"I doubt in the kind of detail he would require for his own bid." She thought about Phyllis Lestinkof, and the Grosdidier brothers' clinic, and what might or might not be going on there. "There is such a thing as plausible deniability."

Kurt followed this serpentine reasoning with a knit brow. "He that much of a twister?"

"He's that much of a survivor." Kate took a bite of pastry and washed it down with coffee. "We keep all this under our hats, for now at least."

"Okay by me, I'm just the delivery boy."

"I don't know what to do with any of this information, anyway," she said, speaking more to herself than to him. "I'm pretty sure that was Allen's skull Jim found, and if so he's dead. The guy I thought was dead is alive but he's checked out mentally."

"Permanently?"

"Nobody knows. He's got what the doc thinks might have been a bullet hole in him. Jim found a .22 pistol at the scene that may or may not have been used to fire the bullet, which we don't have, and have no way of recovering. The dead girl had what we think is the gun's holster in her desk drawer.

According to the baker at the mine, these two guys knew each other well enough to share a morbid fascination with death, and how to get there." She drained her cup. "Honest to god, Kurt, I don't know what the hell's going on here. The best that can be said is I'm doing it on the state's dime."

"Well, you know more now than you did when you came," he said, stacking the paperwork together and putting it into a file. He handed it to Kate as her phone rang. She listened, said, "Thanks, I owe you one."

She hung up. "That was the ME. Blood samples from the skull matched the records in Gammons's file, which is to say the skull belonged to Richard Henry Allen."

"What about the pistol?"

"It belongs to the holster found in my vic's room."

"And still no way to prove it fired the shot that wounded Gammons?"

"Circumstantial, sure, the gun was there, Gammons was there, Allen was there. Oh." She sat with her hand outstretched, the cup motionless about an inch from the tabletop.

"What?"

She shook her head. "I don't know, exactly. I think I just said something smart, but I don't know what." Her phone rang again.

It was Lempe at Providence Hospital. "Ms. Shugak? I'm calling to let you know that Mr. Gammons spoke this morning when he woke up."

"I'll be right there." She closed the phone and stood up. "Doc says Gammons woke up. Thanks, Kurt. Bill for your time included?"

"In there." He nodded at the folder.

"Good." She went over to stand at his window, looking

down at K Street. A beige four-door sedan was idling in one of the fifteen-minute meter spots. "One other thing."

"What?"

"I was followed here this morning."

"What!"

"Yeah, a beige four-door sedan. Actually, it followed me home last night from Gaea."

"Gaea?"

"Start-up environmental group. The director's pretty ballsy, he smuggled himself out to the mine a couple of days ago."

"Why?"

"Because Gaea has taken on the Suulutaq Mine as their primary cause. I think McKenzie—that's their executive director—wants to use it to make Gaea's name and get lots of donations. Anyway, the sedan was parked outside the townhouse when I woke up. I stopped at City Market to see if they'd stay with me, and they did."

He joined her at the window. "Well, you're flying home today. Be hard to follow you in that."

"Yeah, but I'm curious." Gammons wasn't going anywhere in the next hour. "I like to know who's following me. And why."

"Can't say as I blame you." He looked at her. "There's a back door out of the basement."

TEN MINUTES LATER KATE walked up the sidewalk and crossed behind the sedan to knock on the driver's-side door. The driver started, stared at her through the glass, thought it over, and rolled down the window.

Kate grinned. "Fred Gamble of the FBI, as I live and breathe."

The agent next to Gamble grabbed for the door handle,

found his own door held closed against him, and looked through the window to see Kurt's smiling face.

GAMBLE, KURT, AND KATE assembled back in Kurt's office. The second agent, embarrassed at being tagged so easily, didn't argue when told to wait in the car.

Gamble, short, balding, still wearing what looked like the same pilling polyester suit Kate had last seen him in how many years ago now, accepted a chair and asked for coffee. Agrifina provided some and he crossed his legs as much as his potbelly would allow and disposed himself to chat, if they made it worth his while.

"Last time I saw you, you were on your way to Iowa," Kate said.

"Omaha," he said, wincing.

"What happened?"

He gave an airy wave. "Other opportunities. Things happen. You know."

Kate knew. "Where did you pick me up?"

Gamble looked shifty, but then she remembered that shifty was his natural expression. "We, um, acquired information about you asking a local DA to run a certain name through the system."

Kate looked polite. "Did you?"

Gamble shifted and tried to cross his legs the other way. "Yes, well, this is someone we've been trying to track down for a few months, as large payments from an organization in which the FBI has been interested for some time have been rather flowing in his direction."

Kate's eyes met Kurt's. Maybe they should let Agrifina talk to Gamble. They seemed to have graduated from the same school of involved syntax.

She decided to throw the dice. "Why are you interested in True North Investments?"

She paused to enjoy the look of shock that spread across his face.

"Yeah," she said, "we know about their interest in Global. What do you know about them we don't?"

Gamble thought it over. "Quid pro quo?"

Kate rolled her eyes. "Sure. I'm just trying to find a murderer, that's all. What's up with True North?"

"Well." Gamble fussed with a lint ball attached to the knee of his trousers. It came free, along with a significant amount of thread. He made up his mind and looked up. There was an air of expectation about him that warned her he was about to drop a hell of a bomb and that he was expecting a big reaction.

"There is some suspicion that True North is a front for laundering money for the Carlomagno Coahuila drug cartel," Gamble said.

He needn't have worried about her reaction.

"Holy shit," Kate said.

EIGHTEEN

BY THE TIME SHE got to the hospital Gammons had relapsed into his waking coma. She swore at length, startling a passing nurse in pink scrubs and provoking the admiration of a group of interns, who paused in their rounds to hear her out, rapt expressions indicating they were taking mental notes for future reference.

When she ran out of breath Lempe said, "Yes, well, Ms. Shugak, as I told you before, there isn't a great deal to be done."

She suspected he was hiding his personal glee that Kate Shugak had been thwarted in her scorched-earth search for the truth. "What did he say?"

"I wasn't there, I—"

"Who was there? Who can tell me what he said?"

The nurse in pink had been there. She approached Kate with caution, keeping enough distance between them so that if need be she'd have a head start. Kate fixed her with a basilisk stare. "Nurse ... Pritchard, is it?" She was reading from the name tag fixed to the pink top.

Pritchard gave a timid nod.

At least it wasn't Ratched. Kate indicated Lempe with a jerk of her head. "The doc here tells me you were in the room when Mr. Gammons woke up."

Another timid nod.

"What did he say?"

Pritchard gave Lempe a nervous glance and Kate stepped between them, staring into Pritchard's eyes. Pritchard was six inches taller than Kate and outweighed her by seventy pounds but she took a step back. "What. Did. He. Say," Kate said again.

Pritchard's face might actually have lost a little color. Her voice came out in a rapid squeak, like somebody fast-forwarding a tape. "It was like he woke out of a nightmare he was screaming what are you doing Rick no no don't please don't."

It took Kate a moment to apply proper attribution and punctuation. "He said, 'What are you doing, Rick? No! No, don't! Please, don't!'"

Pritchard nodded, looking longingly at the door.

Kate was remorseless. "Those were his exact words?"

Another frightened nod.

"Okay, thanks."

Pritchard spun on her heel and scuttled down the corridor.

Kate turned to look at Gammons, back in his chair, staring out the window. "If he says anything more, it would be useful if accurate notes were kept."

Lempe gave her a curious look. "Does what he said help your case?"

"Part of it," she said.

KATE CALLED BRENDAN ON her cell phone as George was loading the Otter for the flight home. It was an all-freight flight this trip, which was good for her Costco purchases, but he had had to install a seat for her. He was still grumbling when Brendan picked up. "Brendan? It's Kate."

"Kate! My one, my own, my only true love."

"Any other news on those names?"

"As a matter of fact."

"Brendan, my plane is about to leave."

"Your friend Allen was an embezzler, a con man, and a big-time recidivist. He left a paper trail in various names from Minnesota to California, everything from identity theft to credit card scams. He must have been pretty good because he'd only been convicted once, for running a pyramid scheme out of a phony investment office in Tucson. He made the mistake of hanging around too long and a bunch of his investors showed up and beat him up bad enough that he couldn't run when they called the cops. Even then, he was out in three months with good behavior. You got all that?"

"I got it. Brendan, you've got a leak in your office."

His voice changed. "What?"

"The FBI knows you were running Allen. They've been following the money, too."

"Why?"

She told him.

"Holy shit."

"That's what I said." George caught her eye and tapped his watch. "Gotta go, babe. Thanks for the help."

She climbed in next to George and he had them in the air five minutes later. He was silent most of the way home, which suited her fine because she wanted to sort out everything she'd learned in Anchorage, to try to bring some sense of order to it.

Allen had been a ringer for both John King and True North, running a wholesale market in proprietary information out of the Suulutaq Mine, from whom he was drawing a third paycheck. You had to admire the efficiency of his opportunism. Even for a man of Allen's past, though, playing three sides against each other had to be wearing.

Lyda had noticed something, hence the file on her computer.

But Allen had predeceased her, so he hadn't killed her. Who had?

Who had shot Dewayne Gammons? It was Lyda's pistol, it fit the holster in her drawer. Who took it? Or had she given it to someone?

Allen's body was in the clearing with the gun.

Gammons was wandering around the woods with a bullet hole in him.

A circumstantial case could be made that Allen shot Gammons. Why? Why would one friend shoot another? They could have been brothers, they—

"Oh," she said out loud. "Oh!"

"What oh," George said over the headset. "What's with the ohs?" His eyes roved the sky. "We got traffic? Where?"

She looked around as if she'd just realized where they were. Beneath them the Kanuyaq spiraled out like a broad silver ribbon. Ahead of them the Quilaks loomed large and menacing. "Sorry, George," she said, contrite. Bad idea to make loud noises sitting next to a pilot in midair. "I think I just figured something out. Maybe. Possibly. There's a chance I might actually know at least part of what happened here."

"A part of what happened where?" George said.

"Just fly the plane," she said. "Can't we go any faster?"

A miffed George put them down on the Niniltna airstrip in good time. Kate abandoned her purchases and ran down the hill to the trooper post.

"He's not here," Maggie said, "there was a shooting over in Tebay Lakes, possible fatality. He said he wouldn't be back until tonight at the earliest."

Kate had been so preoccupied she hadn't even noticed that

Jim's plane was gone. "Damn it," she said, frustrated. She almost stamped her foot.

Maggie sniffed. Kate still wasn't forgiven for standing up for the mine, even if she hadn't. She hadn't, had she? After the conversation with Kostas McKenzie the evening before she wasn't so sure.

Mutt came to the door of Jim's office and looked out at Kate with a long, meaningful stare.

"Hey, girl," Kate said.

Mutt turned her back on her.

"Oh, come on, Mutt," Kate said.

The doorway to Jim's office remained empty.

Then the door behind her opened and Jim walked in, and Mutt bounced out right past Kate as if Kate wasn't even there. There followed a red carpet welcome for Jim Chopin that would have shamed the producers of an Oscar Award ceremony.

Jim, bending down to exchange salutations, quirked an eyebrow at Kate. "Told you she'd be pissed."

She grabbed his arm and hauled him into his office, almost shutting the door in Mutt's face. Mutt gave an admonitory yip and looked at Kate with reproachful eyes.

"Your eyes sparkle, your cheeks are flushed, words tremble upon your lips. Ace detective that I am, I deduce that you have news." Jim hung up his jacket and ball cap and removed his gun and holster and put them away in the bottom drawer. "Let me make some coffee. All they drink in Tebay Lakes is Folgers." He shuddered. Jim Chopin was a world-class coffee snob, a soul mate to Howard Schultz whether the Starbucks boss knew it or not.

"I think I know what happened," she said. She wasn't quite dancing in place, but close.

"You know who killed Lyda Blue?" he said, pausing in the act of filling the carafe.

She deflated a little. "No, dammit," she said. "At least not yet. But I think I've got it figured out about Gammons and Allen."

"Gammons wake up?"

"No, dammit, and would you just let me talk it out first?"

"Sure," he said, "fine, believe me, I've had enough drama for one day."

She allowed herself to be diverted, she told herself, only for a second. "Why, what was going on in Tebay Lakes?"

"Bob Ellis called in on the short band, all excited, and said there'd been a shooting and that someone was dead and there was a crazy guy with a gun shooting up the place. I get there and it's Boyd Beebe shooting at his house because Ellen locked him out again."

"Bob and Boyd getting into the home brew again?"

His expression hardened. "Yeah, they were both shit-faced. I told Ellen she has to stop making that stuff."

"Her root beer is pretty good," Kate said. Jim looked up from ladling a generous quantity of Tsunami Blend into the filter. She shrugged. "Their daughter ran off a couple of years back. I found her for them. Ellen always drops off a case of root beer for me when they come through town. I haven't shared any with you yet?"

"You have not." Jim switched on the coffeemaker and stood there willing it to brew faster. "Ellen was a little well to live herself when I got there. Tell me something. How many people you think move to the Bush so they can drink themselves to death?"

"What did you do?"

"Confiscated the rifle."

278

"What if a bear shows up?"

"We can only hope it eats them." The coffeemaker beeped. At last, at last, thank god almighty. He filled two mugs, handed her one, and went to sit behind his desk. He cradled the mug in both hands and let the aroma waft upward, through his nostrils, past his sinuses, to infuse his cerebral cortex and stimulate his synapses.

"So—"

"Just let me enjoy this one moment, okay?"

Kate flung herself into the chair opposite and tapped a bad-tempered foot.

He drank, drank again, and felt the caffeine flood into his bloodstream with a revivifying buzz. Dealing with drunks could sap your very will to live. He opened his eyes and sat back. "Okay. Talk to me."

"I want to talk through it out loud and you pick holes, okay?"

He saluted her with the mug and leaned back to prop his feet up. "One of the things I'm best at."

"First of all, let me just say this is the weirdest damn case you've ever had me work on."

"Thank you. We aim to please."

"Yeah, you can yuck it up all you want, Chopin, but just wait till all this lands back in your lap." She raised herself up by the arms of the chair, crossed her legs beneath her, and shook her bangs out of her eyes. She was so damn cute, and how much he would rather be throwing her down on the nearest horizontal surface and having his way with her. He was sure it would beat the hell out of whatever was coming next.

It would beat the hell out of pretty much anything, come to that.

"Okay. I'll try to tell this linearly." She frowned. "I'll try." She took a deep breath and began to speak in headings and subheadings.

"True North Investments is an international venture capital firm that backs natural resource exploration, discovery, and extraction."

Jim opened his mouth, caught her eye, and closed it again.

"John King, president and CEO of RPetCo Alaska, the majority producer in the Prudhoe Bay oil fields of Alaska, sits on the True North board of directors.

"Global Harvest Resources Inc. discovers the second-largest deposit of gold in the world in our backyard. It may in fact turn out to be the largest gold mine in the world if they ever manage to define its limits.

"Global Harvest is an international corporation but they're more oriented toward exploration and discovery than they are toward production. This time, the projected deposit being so large, they have decided it will be more profitable to run it themselves.

"True North looks at the Suulutaq Mine and looks at Global Harvest and scents the possibility of a buyout or a takeover. They start making investments in Global Harvest stock, but they need more information for a more informed decision. They look around and find a Minnesota con man named Richard Henry Allen and recruit him to go to work for Global Harvest at the Suulutaq Mine, with instructions to weasel his way into the good graces of the mine geologists so he can get the copies of the data that the core samples are producing.

"Meanwhile, sitting on True North's board, John King gets wind of this. He's been RPetCo's CEO for over six years and the price of North Slope crude is dropping and so are RPetCo dividends and the shareholders are getting restless, thinking they might like a change of corporate leadership. King thinks that to save his job, maybe RPetCo might need to branch out, expand its resource base. The acquisition of Global Harvest by RPetCo Alaska might be just the jewel to cement the CEO crown on his head in perpetuity.

"But he needs information, too, as he doesn't have access to the actual data that Allen is feeding True North. So King figures since Allen is already in place he might be willing to sell the information he is stealing twice, and he is right. Allen, by the way, had a bank balance in Minneapolis amounting to a little under three hundred thousand dollars."

Jim choked on his coffee. Kate watched the resulting mop-up with some satisfaction. "So Rick Allen was a corporate spy," he said.

"Yes."

"For not one but two masters." He thought. "Three, if you count the fact that he was also drawing a paycheck from Global Harvest."

"He wasn't spying for Global Harvest, for them he was doing a real job."

"Fine," Jim said. "That still doesn't explain why he and Gammons went tarryhooting out in the frickin' woods in May."

Kate leaned forward, her face lit with the excitement of the chase. "Dewayne Gammons and Rick Allen are in the batch of first hires for the Suulutaq Mine. Lyda told me Gammons drove here with some of the other guys looking for work. What do you want to bet Allen was one of the other guys?"

He made a come-on motion with his hand.

"Okay, so we know from hearsay they were at minimum acquaintances. They could have driven up the Alcan together in Gammons's truck. According to our friendly neighborhood bigamist, Randy Randolph, when they were working nights they snuck into the kitchen together for pastry fresh out of the oven, while, and this is important, engaged in a macabre conversation about death and ways to die."

"You'll remember I've met Randy Randolph," Jim said, "and I find it difficult to believe that he has ever used the word 'macabre.' And that if he has used it, he has never pronounced it correctly."

"Shut up."

"Okay." Jim drank coffee. "Tell me this much. Have we even got positive IDs on the goddamn bodies yet?"

"Brillo called me this morning just before we took off. The blood type on the skull is the same blood type in Gammons's file, which is to say Allen's. Preliminary finding is that prior to death occurring the skull received a serious blow to his forehead by a sharp object. It was gnawed on by a bunch of different critters after death."

"And the sharp object?"

"Brillo's best guess? The front hoof of a moose."

"So even in Allen's case we're not talking about a murder." Jim wondered how he was going to justify what was going to be an astronomical contract fee to his boss.

"Wait," she said, "just wait. Gammons's doc says he thinks one of Gammons's wounds was caused by a small bullet. He took photos and let me take 'em over to the crime lab."

"And Brillo says?"

"He won't swear to it, but he admitted it does bear a striking resemblance to a wound inflicted by a small-caliber bullet."

"Did you ask him if the .22 you gave him was small enough?"

"I did, and he said it was, although he said even after laying outside for what his gun guy guessed was, get this, at minimum a month, the pistol is an older weapon and he didn't think it was regularly used.

"Brillo says if we can send him Allen's belongings, he'll probably be able to find some skin or hair and run the DNA on the skull and nail it for sure. We should do that, but I already know. The body in the woods is Rick Allen, it was misidentified as Gammons because the physical report in Gammons's personnel file was actually Allen's physical report, and vice versa."

"Who switched them?"

"Allen." She patted the air. "Wait. I'm not making you guess, I'm going to tell you straight out. I think Rick Allen came to the Suulutaq Mine as a spy, first for True North Investments, who are rumored to be in the market for a hostile takeover of GHRI, and second for John King.

"He worked with Haynes, she said so. He was on and off the rigs, in and out of the office, he collated and filed reports. He had unlimited access to confidential data. It's why he was so valuable to True North and to John King, and why they paid him so very well.

"I think he milked True North and John King for every dime he could." She took a deep breath. "And I think he aided and abetted Dewayne Gammons in his attempted suicide. I think he meant to take advantage of their physical similarity. I think he meant to take advantage of Gammons's depressive state. I think he switched the physical reports in their files."

She sat back, with an air that invited, nay, expected applause. "You think Allen was setting Gammons up to take his place," Jim said.

"Yes."

"Why?" Although he had a pretty good idea.

"Either something happened to make him afraid he was about to get caught, or he'd saved enough money to, I don't know, go to Aruba."

"And that would be fine if it made any sense. If he meant Gammons's body to be identified as his own, why drive Gammons's truck out there, and leave it, leading us to the natural assumption that it was in fact Gammons?"

"Something went wrong. From what Lyda Blue and Randy Randolph and Gammons's boss say, Dewayne Gammons was naturally on the brink of offing himself five or six times before breakfast every morning. The doc at the hospital says chronic depression a lot of times only gets worse the older you get. So Allen conceives of his master plan and zeroes in on Gammons as a likely victim. Randy hears them talking about death. Allen's probably encouraging Gammons, egging him on. A good con man is first and foremost a good psychologist. One day Gammons decides he's ready and asks his good buddy Allen to see him off at the end of their next shift."

She paused and their eyes met. They both broke down in a guilty snicker over her unintentional double entendre. Kate pulled herself together. "One thing we haven't done yet is find out where Gammons parked his truck in town. Maybe somebody saw both men get in it and drive off. At any rate, they drive out there and head into the woods."

"So, Allen's got his master plan," Jim says, "but what if Gammons changes his mind at the last minute?"

"That's why the pistol!" Kate said.

"The pistol was Allen's backup plan?"

"Yes! And I think Gammons did change his mind, for whatever reason, could have been ordinary everyday cold feet, could have been his burgeoning relationship with Lyda. At the

284

last minute he changed his mind and I think that's why all the rounds in that pistol were fired, and why Gammons has a bullet hole in him. No wonder the guy's lost it, who wouldn't under those circumstances? You're depressed and suicidal to start with, and then you meet a girl you like and who seems to like you back and maybe life isn't so awful after all, but you've locked yourself into a course of action—and you're a young man with an overload of testosterone which by definition means you're susceptible to peer pressure—and then at the last minute you change your mind and then your best bud—and in this case your only bud—tries to shoot you. You get away, only to wander around in the woods for a month afterward where probably every living thing you run into is trying to eat you. Jesus," she said in sudden realization, and perhaps her first glimmer of sympathy. "I might opt out myself in those circumstances."

"So what happened to Allen?"

"He's banging away with the pistol, trying his damnedest to kill the son of a bitch that's supposed to be the dead him. If he's dead True North and John King won't come looking for him when the data flow stops, or, and what I think is more probable given Allen's past history, when they find out he's double billing. The shots startle a moose, maybe a cow, she barges out of the brush and stomps the bastard that's scaring the bejeezus out of her two twin calves born the day before. And the ravens and the bears clean up the mess, and if Father Smith hadn't stumbled across Gammons's pickup when he did we might never have found the remains."

He took a deep breath and let it out, thinking.

"What?" she said.

"While you were gone, I got a wild hair and fingerprinted Gammons's pickup. I lifted some prints from their belongings.

On my way back from Tebay Lakes I stopped off in Ahtna and had Kenny run them through the system for me. Gammons's prints are all over the truck." He waited a beat. "So are Allen's."

"See!"

"Wait a minute, Kate. How much of a coincidence is it that when Allen needs to find a substitute for himself, there's Dewayne Gammons right there ready to hand? Practically his twin on a hundred-man crew on a remote site in interior Alaska. I mean come on."

Kate leaned forward. "It's only a coincidence if you're looking at it from our point of view," she said. "If you look at it going forward, from Allen's point of view, a year or how-ever long ago it was that True North hired him, it's not a coincidence. It's a plan."

"You think he went looking for Gammons?" Jim said after a moment.

"I do. I think Allen knew from the get-go he wouldn't be able to get away with it forever—Brendan said he was a pretty good con man, only one conviction with three months served—and I think he was looking for a fall guy among his fellow employees from that day forward. Hell, he may have scouted Gammons in Washington, may have been the one to talk Gammons into coming to Alaska and applying at Suulutaq in the first place. True North was probably looking at keeping him in place for the long term, which he knew increased the chances he'll get caught. He looks at Gammons and thinks, Wouldn't it be convenient if I died? Nobody comes after a dead man."

She sat back. "Remember, Jim, we wouldn't even have known that the guy who stumbled out of the woods into my yard was Gammons if Lyda hadn't been at the airstrip that day. No, Gammons was right where Allen put him, a virtual twin with chronic depression. Allen only had to nurse it along, and according to Randy Randolph he did that right well."

"Randy, by the way, did not begin his career in multiple marrying in Alaska," Jim said. "I ran his record, too, and he's got wives strung out in a line from here to North Carolina."

Kate laughed. "Just don't tell Bonnie, or Suzy. Or that third one—what was her name?—who took you out in front of the grocery store."

"Mrs. Randy Randolph," Jim said, with dignity, "and I was not taken out, I tripped."

"You went ass over teakettle," Kate said.

"Getting back to the subject at hand," Jim said. "Allen switches the medical reports, cleans out Gammons's room of anything approaching a life just to be sure, and drives out to see his best buddy off into the next life.

"What he doesn't know is that Gammons has made friends with one Lyda Blue, and life is not quite as dark and hopeless as it once was. Gammons changes his mind, Allen pulls out the pistol and fires it to change Gammons's mind back or to kill him and maybe, I don't know, make it look like suicide. Only one of the bullets hits Gammons. One of the others hits or frightens a moose who, unfortunately, takes exception to this injury to his or her person, and stomps Allen to death on the strength of it." He sat back in his chair. "It's all very tidy."

"Except for Lyda Blue," Kate said.

"If she was murdered, Kate, she either saw something or she was a part of the scam. She had guilty knowledge she couldn't live with, or she was aiding and abetting and she was afraid she was going to get caught."

"You don't think she was taking a cut," she said, and it wasn't a question.

287

"Maybe she did it for love. It's been known to happen." He leaned back and rubbed his face. "I need more coffee." Getting up to refill his mug he said, "Speculating is fun and all but how much hard evidence do we really have?"

"The payments traceable back to True North and RPetCo Alaska. The switched files. Gammons's bullet wound. Lyda's pistol, the weapon that probably inflicted the wound. The truck. The fingerprints."

"How did Allen get hold of Lyda's pistol?"

"You said it yourself, it's a small camp. Allen was a con man, a swindler and an embezzler and a thief. A guy like him would make a regular habit out of inventorying the contents of every room in the camp."

He sat back down and frowned at his coffee, which didn't deserve it. "Con men don't usually upgrade to murder, Kate. It doesn't fit the profile."

"It doesn't mean he wouldn't, if he felt under enough threat."

"Under threat, from a venture capital firm and an Alaskan oil corporation? What was he afraid they'd do, string him up by their silk ties?"

"Ah," she said, and it was as near a cackle as he'd ever heard her make, "now we come to the best part. At the same time, independently of anything going on at Suulutaq, the FBI—"

The coffee mug landed on the table with a thud that should have cracked its bottom. "The FBI?"

"—in the person of Special Agent Fred Gamble, of whom you have heard me speak before—"

"I thought he'd been transferred to Oklahoma."

"Omaha," she said, with an airy wave. "Other opportunities. Things happen. You know. Special Agent Gamble is I believe still striving to find a headline case that will get him reassigned to somewhere that isn't Alaska. In pursuit of this goal—"

Oh yeah, he could see she was really enjoying herself now.

"In pursuit of this goal, it came to his attention that a venture capital firm called True North Investments was making many investments in Global Harvest stock and that John King, president and CEO of RPetCo, was on the board of directors."

"Where did Gamble pick up your trail?"

"At RPetCo, when I went to see John King." She looked demure. "He thought, given our prior dealings, that I might be able to shed some light on his investigation."

Jim closed his eyes and shook his head. "You know, Prohibition gave us two things, organized crime and the FBI. Honest to god, I wonder sometimes which was worse." He opened his eyes. "I shudder at the many prospective answers to this question, but why is the FBI investigating True North and John King?"

"Because True North is in receipt of large quantities of money with no provenance."

"Translation, please?"

It burst out of her with a velocity that made him realize how hard it had been for her to hold it in for the last fifteen minutes. "True North is suspected by the FBI, the DEA, and various other governmental agencies of laundering money for the—wait for it—Carlomagno Coahuila drug cartel."

"Holy shit," Jim said.

"That's what Brendan said." Kate raised her mug to her lips for the first time. It was cold. She got up to refill it, and settled back in her chair with the air of one who had brought the news from Marathon to Athens on time and under budget and had lived to tell the tale.

"I hope that True North business doesn't come back to bite us in the ass," Jim said. "Drug cartels are hell on leakers."

"According to Gamble they're going to have a lot worse things to worry about shortly."

"Yeah, well, I'm considering the source there." Jim looked at Kate. "So you think Allen found out about the drug money laundering and decided to vanish."

"Yes. He might have known from the beginning. A good con man is also a first-class researcher. He wouldn't have come into this without checking into True North's background."

"Say I'm prepared to accept this ridiculous story as something approaching the truth. How does the death of Lyda Blue figure into it?"

Some of the light went out of Kate's eyes, and he was sorry to see it go. She was awful cute when she got on the scent. "I haven't figured that out yet. It has to be connected to Allen and Gammons, it just has to. We know from the file on her computer that she found out Allen was stealing data. And we know Gammons was shot with her pistol. All three of them were connected. Her death has to be, too."

"I'll check with her family, see if they can identify it as belonging to her. But, Kate." Their eyes met. "He was dead a long time before she was. If she was murdered, he didn't kill her."

"I know," she said. "There has to be something else, something I haven't seen, or accounted for. We need to go back out to the mine and talk to a lot more people, especially the geologists. If Lyda noticed something, they might have, too. Oh." She sat up. "I just remembered. Truax was throwing a guy off the mine when I got there the day Lyda died."

"Oh yeah? Who?"

"His name is Kostas McKenzie. He's the executive director of a nonprofit environmental activist organization called Gaea. He snuck in on a plane that morning and was snooping around."

Jim perked up. "Any chance of popping him for Lyda Blue's death?"

"No," Kate said, with regret. "I checked with George and he was telling the truth about when he got to Suulutaq. Rigor was too far advanced for him to have done it."

"Damn."

"Yeah. Especially since I think there is going to be trouble from that direction before very long. I went down to their office last night. Gaea has targeted the Suulutaq Mine for their trophy wall."

"Yeah, well, I think Global Harvest can defend itself." He looked at the clock and stood up. "You know what? I've had a day, and I'm going to need some beer to get through the rest of it."

"Roadhouse?"

"God, no. The last time I went to the Roadhouse for a quiet beer I had to break up a fistfight between a Park rat and a Suulutaq Mine worker over Dulcey Kinneen. And then Bernie insisted I counsel Dulcey against renting herself out by the hour. Let's just go home."

The Suulutaq Mine had a lot to answer for and it wasn't even in production yet.

NINETEEN

THE NEXT COUPLE OF days were quiet and uneventful. Jim talked to Lyda Blue's people and discovered that the pistol had belonged to her mother and that so far as they knew Lyda had never shot it. "Probably never cleaned it, either," Jim told Kate. "Allen's lucky it didn't blow up in his hand." He added, "And if that damn bear had left enough of his hand we could have tested it for gunshot residue and proved at least part of your theory."

"Are you interviewing people at the mine?"

"Yeah."

"It going anywhere?"

"No."

With each passing day, and no new clues in the death of Lyda Blue, Kate knew a steadily increasing sense of failure.

And the summer had begun with such promise. Of course, her downturn in spirits could also be attributed in part to the approach of the dreaded NNA board of directors meeting. Kate and Annie had put together an agenda, and had discussed weapons and tactics. It was summer, after all. Maybe Demetri would be up at his lodge, and Old Sam down Alaganik way. Maybe someone would have burned Ulanie Anahonak at the stake. Her heart warmed at the thought.

Yes, maybe they'd have the minimum quorum allowed by

amended bylaw, so as to produce the maximum peace.

She could only hope.

HOW MANY DESIGNS FOR the new NNA logo now, Ms. Mike?" Kate said.

Annie Mike, sitting erect at the small table in the corner, tapped some keys on her computer. "One hundred and thirty-seven. Fifty-two of them are from the same three shareholders."

There was a rustle around the table, but everyone was too afraid that Dominatrix Kate would rule them out of order if they spoke and so they maintained a prudent silence. With the exception of Old Sam, who said, "Yeah, and how many are worth the board looking at 'em? Five? Wait, what am I saying. Any?"

"Out of order, Mr. Dementieff," Kate said, but her voice lacked the edge it did whenever anyone else spoke without being recognized. He grinned at her, unapologetic.

Besides, he was right. Kate had seen the submissions, and the art displayed therein was, well, amateurish at best. She looked down at the mug sitting at her right hand, which boasted the current logo, a Rorschach blot of barely distinguishable Alaskan icons in busy black. "I move that we commission a professional artist to come up with a design for a new logo," she said. "I have a name in mind, and I have a sample of his work." Annie got up and passed out Gaea brochures. McKenzie had made good on his promise to send her the artist's name, who by a miracle had turned out not only to be local but to be Alaska Native as well. She wasn't Aleut and she wasn't an NNA shareholder, but you couldn't have everything.

Demetri looked up from the brochure. "You turning into a

radical environmentalist on us, Kate? These folks can get pretty extreme, and they're saying a lot of not very nice things about the Suulutaq Mine."

"For the moment, let's focus on the logo. It's the kind of thing I was hoping we'd get from the contest, a single clean image that feels familiar and universal and is beautiful in its own right."

"Second," Auntie Joy said. She had loathed all the prospective logos they had received, a very un-Auntie Joy reaction.

This was the second meeting of the Niniltna Association board of directors following the January shareholders meeting and the successful vote to increase the board's size from five to nine. Alas for Kate's hopes, all members of the board were present, and when she looked around the circular table in the upstairs room at board HQ in Niniltna, she still didn't know what new kind of dynamic she had been the proximate cause of producing for this quarterly meeting, or for the future of the association. On the whole, she had to admit things were going a lot more smoothly than she had anticipated. Which only made her spider sense tingle in anticipation of disasters yet to unfold.

On her right sat Auntie Joy. One of the four aunties and the only one on the board, Joyce Shugak was in her eighties, a subsistence fisher on a creek that emptied into Alaganik Bay, where all the other Park rats fished commercial. Married young, widowed young, and childless, she regarded everyone in the Park as one of her own, be they Native or white, square-heads or roundeyes. Aided by a spiritual nearsightedness that allowed her to see only the good in them no matter how badly they behaved, she beamed out upon the world with an impartial benignity and a cheerfulness viewed by more crotchety beings as interminable. On one hand, she was every Park rat's grandma. On the other, it was sometimes hard to credit that she was actually of this world.

Next to Auntie Joy sat Marlene Colberg, one of the newly named board members. Marlene, midfifties, was a commercial fisherman, with a set net site on Alaganik Bay next to Mary Balashoff's that she had inherited from her father. Her siblings had wanted nothing to do with it, decamping from the Park and some of them from the state as soon as they were old enough, so she fished it alone. She was six feet tall, broad-shouldered, and weighed over two hundred pounds, none of it fat, a heritage from her Norwegian father, so she was certainly up to the physical challenge. There wasn't that much to be seen of her Aleut mother in her features. Her blond hair was cut shorter than Old Sam's, her eyes were deep blue, and her mouth a straight, firm line over a square and equally firm chin. Her hands, large-knuckled and scarred from a life spent picking fish and mending and hauling gear, were folded on the table in front of her. They looked unaccustomed to inaction. Her expression betrayed a little impatience, as if she had better things to do than waste five minutes talking about something as unimportant as a company logo. Kate remembered that Marlene had protested her nomination to the board, and had only acceded to it when overwhelmed by support from other shareholders. She was the least interested in governing of the new bunch, and probably the best of them.

Between Marlene and Harvey Meganack was Herbie Topkok. Herbie ran Park Sled and ATV out of his garage, which was the local parts store for Honda, Kawasaki, Arctic Cat, Yamaha, Polaris, Suzuki, and whoever else made a snow machine or a four-wheeler. Kate was pretty sure that Herbie had a backdoor arrangement with Howie Katelnikof in the matter of spare parts, and she thought he might also have been the source of the four-wheelers the Suulutaq Mine workers were using to get back and forth into town. He was maybe five four, also in his midfifties, and a relatively new Park rat, as his parents had met at Chemawa in Oregon and had settled there to raise their family after graduation. Herbie, the eldest and a mechanic for a Ford dealership in Portland, had been the only regular visitor to the Park of the four children, traveling to Alaska every summer and working one log at a time on a cabin on the Kanuyaq just north of Niniltna on his parents' ANCSA land allotment. When his third and last child graduated from high school, he made the move permanent. His wife had lasted one winter before heading back to Oregon. Herbie made enough out of the business to support himself in the Park and his wife Outside, and other than nonconjugal visits over the holidays, also Outside and with the children and the growing brood of grandchildren in attendance, they both seemed content with the status quo.

Herbie, skin the color of toast, eyes black and a little protruding, stocky and taciturn, looked less than enthralled by the subject of the logo, too. On his right, Harvey Meganack glowered at Kate, but she was used to being glowered at by Harvey and it didn't bother her. She even carried the battle forward into the enemy's camp. "Anything to add, Mr. Meganack?"

He ground his teeth, and it was obvious that it pained him when he had to agree with the board's chair. "No. Branding is important. We need a new logo."

Harvey was as usual clad in neatly pressed charcoal gray slacks and a white, long-sleeved, button-down Oxford shirt that looked lonely without the maroon silk tie that Harvey didn't quite dare wear with it, not in the Park. A commercial fisherman like many of the people seated at the table, a registered guide like Demetri, the proud holder of a two-year engineering degree from the University of Alaska, and the boon companion of State Senator Pete Heiman, Harvey was a boomer of the first water. He owed his mop of dark hair, his round cheeks, and his incipient second chin to his Aleut mother, and his medium height, his five o'clock shadow, and his middle-aged spread to an Italian great-grandfather. Like many shareholders, he owed his Park rattery to a stampeder ancestor.

"Good," Kate said briskly, and smiled at Demetri Totemoff, on Harvey's right. Without moving a muscle Demetri managed to look faintly amused. Born in the Park, married in the Park (his wife was Auntie Edna's daughter, Edna Jr.), raised his kids on the Park, hunter, trapper, and proprietor of an increasingly high-end hunting lodge in the southern foothills of the Quilak Mountains within sight of the Alaskan coast, he was pro-business only insofar as it didn't impact the wilderness experience of his clients. Of course, this particular wilderness experience included daily maid service and a four-star gourmet chef. His clients arrived in Anchorage on private jets and were whisked directly to Demetri's eyrie in a scrupulously clean and perfectly maintained Beaver, which landed on the lake the lodge was built on and which taxied right up to the lodge's dock so the clients never even got their feet wet.

Demetri, in fact, had clients who never left the lodge, and he was ambivalent about the prospect of an open-pit mine that had the potential to spoil the perfect view of mountains, glaciers, and wildlife they had hitherto enjoyed. The mine wasn't anywhere near within eyesight of his lodge, but he had wondered out loud if once completed it could be seen en route between the lodge and Niniltna.

Well, the jury was still out on that, and since Demetri was declining to comment on the logo issue, Kate's gaze moved to the woman sitting at Demetri's right, last seen at the Suulutaq Mine on the arm of Vern Truax. Thin, tense, she had thick eyebrows always pulled together in a frown over eyes that sat too close on either side of a long, bony nose, with a tip that flattened against her short, hairy upper lip in a way that bore an irresistible resemblance to the beak on a seagull. Her skin was sallow, too, which only heightened the resemblance.

For a woman who was mostly Athabascan, she was surprisingly unattractive. Kate thought how much it helped when someone she was destined to dislike anyway was physically unlovely to boot. She was still trying to work out how Ulanie Anahonak had been voted onto the NNA board. For one thing, Ulanie behaved like a dry drunk, impatient, rigid, intolerant, and pompous. Essentially as though Ulanie were the only person in the room, Kate thought. For another, she appeared to be a functioning illiterate. She never seemed to find time to read the minutes of the previous meeting that all board members received from Annie weeks before the next meeting, and she appeared incapable of sticking to the agenda, jumping some items and ignoring others. She'd been hostile to Kate from the beginning. In that respect she reminded Kate a little of Axenia.

Ulanie wasn't well liked within the Niniltna Native Association. It was a mystery where her votes had come from, one Kate thought it might be worth solving one day, when she had time.

On Ulanie's right sat Einar Carlson, another blond, blue-eyed Aleut by way of a Swedish immigrant who had worked at the Kanuyaq Copper Mine and married into the Park. Einar fished summers and worked construction in the winters.

In his forties, a confirmed bachelor, he was tall, spare, and mostly silent. He lived in a one-room cabin across the river from Niniltna, a cabin built by his grandparents when they were first moved from their village in the Aleutian Islands by the military after the Japanese invasion in World War II. Like many Aleuts dispossessed in that war, they had never moved back, choosing instead to make a home in the Park and to raise their children there and in the fullness of time to be absorbed into the Niniltna Native Association. There were fifteen years between Kate and Einar and she didn't know that much about him, but in the hothouse atmosphere of the NNA board there would be no avoiding getting to know each other very well indeed.

Between Einar and Kate sat Old Sam Dementieff. His grin was razor sharp, his bright eyes all-knowing. No point in trying to fool herself that he couldn't read her like a book. Kate wondered who had nominated him for the board and why he'd accepted. He wasn't exactly a political animal.

Old Sam was Eliza and Quinto Dementieff's son, although Kate had overheard the aunties speculating about that once when she was very small. Eliza had given birth too soon after marrying, One-Bucket McCullough had disappeared shortly thereafter, and Quinto had stared everyone down and raised Sam as his own. Old Sam and Abel Int-Hout, the homesteader next door who had raised Kate, had been good friends, and at least in her eyes they resembled each other a great deal. There wasn't a rock or a tree in this part of Alaska either man couldn't find again blindfolded. Abel had married and had three sons, Old Sam had remained single and childless so far as everyone knew, in his later years taking up with Mary Balashoff. They'd probably been together as long as they had because they were so often apart, Old Sam wintering in the

Park and Mary, with the exception of occasional booty calls to Niniltna, the lone year-rounder on Alaganik Bay.

Old Sam was an outlaw, that much Kate knew. The taste of illegal king still lingered pleasantly on her tongue. She smiled back at Old Sam, who let's face it put the rat into *Parkus rattus*.

The motion to contract the services of the Gaea logo artist for a new corporate logo was carried by a unanimous voice vote and Annie Mike was authorized to contact the artist and inquire as to price and delivery date. "All right, under old business, the board will recall the suggestion made at the last meeting to encourage shareholders living in Anchorage to have regular meetings in Anchorage, so as to foster tribal unity and to disseminate news from the board to the shareholders. I would like to report that I have spoken to my cousin, Axenia Shugak Mathisen, and she has agreed to organize the meetings, one a month for the next six months. I propose we revisit the situation at that time to estimate the program's success and to decide if it warrants extended funding."

She had a moment to marvel at her own pomposity before Old Sam said, "I still think it's a bad idea. Who knows what kind of trouble they'll get us into over there?"

"Any more old business?" Kate said. "No? Good, let's move on to new business."

As expected, Auntie Joy's hand shot into the air, and with no enjoyment at all Kate said, "The chair recognizes Ms. Shugak."

Auntie Joy rustled the stack of papers she had in front of her, but she forgot to pass them out around the table. Kate didn't remind her. She cleared her throat and looked around the table. She wasn't nervous, precisely, but she'd never set forth a proposal of her own before, and the only person on the board she'd talked to about it beforehand was Kate. Auntie Vi, of course, was another matter, and they all knew what was coming.

"I make a motion to charge for people berry picking on shareholder lands," she said.

Nobody said anything. Harvey was going to before Kate caught his eye and stared him down.

Auntie Joy took a deep breath, and continued. "Lots of people come into the Park nowadays. This mine tell people we are here. Tourist come. They pick our berries. That okay," she said quickly, glancing around the table, "so long as we charge them."

And so long as they didn't find Auntie Joy's secret nagoonberry patch, Kate thought. That would escalate the fee from dollars to a life.

"Lots of berries," Auntie Joy said. "Plenty for to make money from." She looked down at the papers clenched in her fists and frowned. She looked up at Kate. "That's all."

It was a traditional Native way to end a story, but it wasn't all, not by a long shot. "Is there a second?" Kate said.

"Second," Ulanie Anahonak said.

Kate wondered what Ulanie wanted from Auntie Joy, and had a presentiment that they were all going to find out very soon. "It is moved and seconded that the Association charge a fee for nonshareholders to pick berries on Association lands. The motion is on the floor and open for debate."

Harvey raised his hand. It still pissed him off that he had to wait for Kate to recognize him before he spoke, but she'd enforced it with enough brutality during the last two board meetings that they were all now cowed into obedience, for the moment. "The chair recognizes Mr. Meganack."

Harvey rose to his feet. "A lot depends on if it's affordable.

The picking fee will have to be high enough to pay for signs marking Association land so people can tell where they're supposed to pick, and for the labor to put them up and to maintain them."

They all thought about the hundred or so miles of hitherto unmarked roads and lanes and hiking trails and moose tracks connecting the Park to itself, the Roadhouse, and the outside world.

Harvey waited for it to sink in, and added, magnanimous in victory, "It's not a bad idea, Joy. Might have to tweak it a little, but sure, we can chew it over."

"It's not a good idea," Old Sam said.

"Out of order," Kate said.

Old Sam gave her his bad-boy grin and a shrug of what might have been apology. She kept looking at him, and after a moment he raised his hand. Kate waited just long enough to make the silence felt, and said, "The chair recognizes Mr. Dementieff."

He leaned forward to look at Auntie Joy. "I'm sorry, Joy, but it's a bad idea. Park rats been marrying each other and burying each other and going to school together and hunting and fishing and flying together for a long time now. There was that bump in the road after ANCSA, when Native rats got money and land and white rats didn't, but we got through it, and so far as I know nobody got killed over it and everybody who was friends before is still friends now."

He looked around the table, his dark, seamed face pulled into sardonic lines. "Only shareholders can pick berries on Association land, Joy? That means no white Park rats or black Park rats or Filipino Park rats can pick berries on Park land?"

It was clear that Auntie Joy hadn't thought of it that way. "Not what I mean," she said. "I talk about—"

"It's what would happen, though." Old Sam sat back and folded his arms. "I'm not saying we can't do it. I'm saying we shouldn't. It'll probably cost us more money than it'll make us, and how we gonna enforce it? We gonna hire rent-a-cops and dress them up in NNA uniforms with our ugly-ass logo all over 'em and turn 'em loose? Yeah, that'll work, especially if we hire our own and give them sidearms." He paused to let the rest of them imagine what would happen if they put somebody like Josep Shugak in a uniform so he could enforce tribal law on sworn enemy Sergei Sondergaard's ass. There would be blood, and not over who picked what berries where.

"But mostly," Old Sam said, "we shouldn't do it because it'll just piss people off. We got enough berries to share, I say let everybody pick 'em where they find 'em. It's the generous thing to do, and it'll keep the peace in the Park. For a while anyway."

He said the last words under his breath, and only Kate heard them.

There was a brief silence. "Is there any more debate?" Kate said.

Demetri raised his hand. Kate recognized him and he said, "No matter how low the fee is, people will resent it. It won't stop them picking. They'll just avoid the marked areas so they won't have to pay the fee, and look for unmarked areas to pick in. Some of those areas are private property, especially the areas you can drive to. I'm sorry, Joy, but something like this just seems like kick-starting a war."

Another silence. "Anything more to debate?" Kate said.

There wasn't.

"Very well," Kate said. "The question before the board is on the adoption of the motion to charge a fee for nonshare-holders to pick berries on Association lands. All in favor?"

Auntie Joy raised a defiant hand. Ulanie Anahonak raised hers, too.

"All opposed?"

Everyone else raised their hand.

"The nays have it, the motion is defeated." It was the longest Auntie Joy had gone without her usual radiant smile, and for a moment there Kate was afraid she might even burst into tears. "I have an item of new business, too," she said, leaping into the breach. "As you all know, what with the discovery of the ore deposits at the Suulutaq Mine and the influx of people and the increase in business in the Park, we've been getting a lot of pressure to bring in a cell phone service."

Demetri raised an eyebrow but refrained from comment.

"Two phone companies have already approached me and two other members of the board to inquire into the prospect of a partnership with the Niniltna Native Association in the construction and operation of a cell phone service. Mostly they need someone to run interference with Park rats for site selection for cell towers, for which they are willing to give the Association a percentage of the proceeds. I move that we create a subcommittee to conduct negotiations with these companies and any others that pop up in the meantime, with the caveat that the subcommittee's primary function is to look after shareholder interests and not the cell phone company's interests."

Old Sam grinned his vulpine grin and Kate realized that had come out a little more tart than she'd meant it. "Second," he said.

Harvey, Demetri, and Marlene volunteered for the subcommittee, and the motion was carried with little discussion.

Ulanie Anahonak raised her hand.

"The chair recognizes Ms. Anahonak."

Ulanie sat up very straight and pursed her lips. She looked like someone's maiden aunt, circa 1900, lacking only the corset and the leg-o'-mutton sleeves. Although Kate wouldn't put it past Ulanie to be wearing a hair shirt underneath her REPEAL ROE T-shirt. "I make a motion that we fund an external audit on the Grosdidier brothers' clinic."

Kate thought back to those few moments at the clinic, Phyllis Lestinkof in tears as Matt ushered her out, Ulanie leaving without treatment and without displaying any signs of needing any, either. This wasn't going to be good.

No one else thought so, either. The silence following Ulanie's motion was even more deafening than the silence that had followed Auntie Joy's. Annie Mike's fingers paused for a moment on her keyboard, and she looked up to meet Kate's eyes for a fleeting moment. "Second," Kate said, although the tone of her voice left no one in the room under the illusion that she was in favor of Ulanie's proposal.

Auntie Joy's hand was first in the air. "The motion before the board is to fund an external audit of the Grosdidier brothers' health clinic," Kate said. "The floor is open for debate. The chair recognizes Joyce Shugak."

"What for this audit?" Auntie Joy said straight across the table, glaring at Ulanie. It did not appear that Ulanie's support for Auntie Joy's berry-picking motion was going to automatically instill reciprocal support in Auntie Joy for Ulanie's motion. "Those boys good boys. They do good work. They keep us healthy, they save our lives. Not needed to look over their shoulders."

"What, Ulanie," Old Sam said, "you worried Matt and the gang are dealing prescription drugs out of their garage?"

Old Sam did have a way of cutting to the chase.

"I don't know anything about prescription drugs," Ulanie said, keeping a commendable hold on her temper, "but I do know they're giving advice about birth control."

Well, that did it. The table erupted. Kate sat back and let it. Riot didn't have to be an unproductive process.

"Horrors, Ulanie," Marlene said, her voice cutting, "is it possible that licensed health-care professionals are advising women how not to get pregnant? On our dime? In our Park? What is the world coming to?"

Demetri looked at Ulanie with obvious distaste. "We pay them to look after our health, Ulanie. That includes reproductive health. And the advice they give their patients is none of our damn business."

That was a long speech, coming from Demetri, the second in one day. Had to be a record.

"Besides," he said, "we run an outside audit of all Association books and activities once a year. The board reports the results to the shareholders every January. Why pay for another that targets only one of our programs? Especially one that's doing so much good?"

"You seen the numbers?" Old Sam said to Ulanie. "What am I saying, of course you ain't seen the numbers or you wouldn't be making such a goddamn fool proposal. Since the boys opened that clinic? Alcoholism in the Park, down. Clap, down. Rapes, down. Child abuse, spousal abuse, down. Okay, maybe only a couple percentage points for some of them, but we're sure as hell headed in the right direction. Pretty sure the boys have single-handedly stopped the spread of AIDS in the Park, too. If it ain't broke, don't fix it."

Through it all, Ulanie sat where she was, erect, her lips pursed in their regulation disapproving pucker, clearly not expecting this wholesale condemnation but not flinching away from it, either. One thing you could say for Ulanie, she wasn't a coward. She waited them out, looked at Kate, and raised her hand.

"The chair recognizes Ulanie Anahonak. Ms. Anahonak."

And Ulanie said sweetly, "I repeat my motion. I move that the board fund an outside audit on the Niniltna Health Clinic. Is there a second?"

There wasn't, immediately. Ulanie used the brief silence to say, just as sweetly, "I'm sure the Grosdidiers are doing a wonderful job down at their clinic. The audit will only prove that to be true, and reinforce how well we're being taken care of. Won't it?"

Kate opened her mouth, for the first time in one of these meetings without knowing what was going to come out of it. Into this dangerous breach Annie Mike said, without displaying any vulgar rush to fill the dangerous silence following Ulanie's words, "Forgive the interruption, madam chair and ladies and gentlemen of the board, point of order?"

Kate's mouth shut with a snap. "Yes, Ms. Mike?"

Unfazed, Annie said, "According to the bylaws, outside audits of nonprofit arms of the corporation will require a majority of the board as cosponsors."

"So what?" Ulanie said. "Einar?"

"Excuse me, Ms. Anahonak," Annie said, "but I believe the bylaws as written provided for a three-person majority of the original five-member board before a motion involving expenditure could even be proposed. This was, I believe, an attempt on the part of the Association's founders to expedite debate and promote constructive action."

For "Association's founders" read Ekaterina Shugak, Kate thought, and for "expedite debate" read "avoid bloodshed during board meetings." Clever Emaa.

Ulanie's face had reddened and her mouth wasn't pursed anymore, it was a tight, thin line.

"However, the language of the clause reads 'a simple majority.'" Annie looked at Kate. There was the faintest suggestion of a raised eyebrow.

"Thank you, Ms. Mike," Kate said, not a muscle moving on her face to reflect her inner rejoicing. She turned to Ulanie. "Ms. Anahonak, the board now numbers nine. A simple majority is five. As a matter affecting the debate, I would like to poll the board on those inclined to favor Ms. Anahonak's motion."

Ulanie's hand shot up. Einar raised his hand. Harvey looked like he would have if he'd been in the majority. Everyone else's hands stayed firmly at their sides. Kate said, "I move that we table Ms. Anahonak's motion until the next board meeting, so that she will have had time to consult with her colleagues as to the, uh, viability of said motion."

"Second," Marlene said.

"Moved and seconded," Kate said. "The motion is to table until the next board meeting Ms. Anahonak's motion to commission an outside audit on the Niniltna Health Clinic. All in favor?"

Everyone except Ulanie raised their hands.

"Opposed?" Ulanie raised her hand.

"The motion is carried," Kate said. "Any more new business? No? Then this board meeting is adjourned. Thank you, ladies and gentlemen. Ulanie, hold up for a moment, would you?"

There was an infinitesimal pause in the general decamping, but after a few curious looks the board filed out.

Kate watched them go, one by one. Nine people, representing three hundred more. Good people, for the most

308

part, reasonably intelligent, reasonably well informed on tribal matters and Alaska Native issues. At the same time, the weight of their need for leadership was crushing. Emaa had known this better than anyone else. Emaa had led them better than anyone else. Kate felt that at her best she was only an also-ran.

She thought of the investigation into Dewayne Gammons, which had evolved into an investigation into Rick Allen, which she was still convinced was somehow connected to the death of Lyda Blue. It was a finite puzzle and she had solved two-thirds of it by asking the right questions of the right people. Even if she never figured out what had happened to Lyda, she had found many of the right answers.

Life on the NNA board should be so simple.

She looked at Ulanie, who had remained in her seat, her mouth still in that sour purse.

"Ulanie," Kate said, "what were you doing at the Suulutaq Mine on July sixth?"

Whatever she had expected, it wasn't this, and Ulanie paled visibly.

"You were with the superintendent, Vern Truax. You looked pretty cozy. Want to tell me what that was about?"

Ulanie found her voice. "You were spying on me? Who do you think you are? Where do you get off, spying on me?"

Kate shook her head. "I wasn't spying on you, Ulanie. Believe me when I tell you I have better things to do than follow you around. I was at the Suulutaq on business. Which kind of underscores my point." She leaned forward and caught the other woman's gaze, holding it with her own. "Ulanie, hear me. This conversation has nothing to do with you and me or any disagreements we might have about running this organization. The Niniltna Native Association must speak with one voice. The Suulutaq Mine is changing the Park right now, while we're sitting here, and it will continue to change it in ways we don't expect and cannot anticipate. Our way of life is in the process of being fractured into a thousand pieces, and we're barely beginning to reassemble those pieces into something new, something the shape of which we can't even see from here."

Ulanie bridled. "I don't see what that has to do with my visiting the mine. Mr. Truax has made the board welcome there any time we care to visit." She gave Kate a defiant stare. "That's all I was doing. Visiting."

Kate nodded. "All right, Ulanie. I'll do you the courtesy of believing you. This time." She leaned forward and dropped her voice. "But Vernon Truax looked very happy to see you that day, very happy indeed. If I find that you have been passing privileged information about the activities of this Association to him or anyone else who works for Suulutaq or Global Harvest or the Slana Alliance for the Preservation of Black Cats, I will run you off this board so fast it will make your head swim." Kate sat back, her eyes cold. "And then I'll go to work on you."

Ulanie's face flushed an ugly red. She stood up, shoving her seat back so hard it banged off the wall. "I don't need you or anybody else telling me how to behave, Kate Shugak. You're just like your grandmother, thinking you know what's best for everybody. Well, I've got news for you, there are plenty of people who don't think so, and maybe we'll band together and run you off this board!"

"I can hardly wait," Kate said.

Ulanie didn't have an irony button and was missing a sense of humor anyway. She snatched up her papers and stormed toward the door.

"Ulanie," Kate said.

Ulanie wanted to keep going, but something in Kate's voice halted her. She turned and her glare should have melted Kate to slag and her chair along with it.

Not noticeably melted, Kate said, aware that she was throwing down the gauntlet and equally aware there was no way around it, "Lay off the Grosdidiers' clinic."

"Abstinence is the only—"

"I don't care."

"Millions of murdered babies—"

"I. Don't. Care." The quiet force of Kate's voice stopped Ulanie in mid-spate. "Abstinence, birth control, abortion, these are private, personal issues that have nothing to do with the board of directors of the Niniltna Native Association. I won't allow you to start a culture war among the Association shareholders, Ulanie. I know your reputation, and even if I didn't I'd have your behavior at this board meeting to instruct me. You're a backbiting little rabble-rouser with a talent for sowing division and none at all for governance."

Ulanie looked like her head was going to explode. Kate only wished it were physically possible. "The clinic is off limits. You're perfectly free to find something else to stir the shit about. Preferably a legitimate issue like education or jobs. But lay off the Grosdidier boys. They've been instrumental in a wholesale rise in good health stats across the Park, across race, age, and gender. The life of every Park rat, shareholder and nonshareholder alike, is better because of what those boys are doing. I won't have that fouled by anyone for political advantage." She paused. "Or for the sake of plain old meanness."

"It's a free country! I can say anything I want to anyone I want!"

"You sure can," Kate said. "So can I. I could, for example, ask you about your visits to Vern Truax at the Suulutaq Mine in front of the board."

Ulanie snarled.

"Better, in front of all the shareholders at the January meeting."

The slamming of the boardroom door shook the entire building.

Kate looked at Annie. "You think she heard anything I said?"

Annie smiled and shook her head. "Kate?"

"What?"

"Are the Grosdidier boys performing abortions in that clinic of theirs?"

Kate thought back to that morning. *If you'd come here right away*, Matt had said to Phyllis. "Not abortions, no, but if you made me guess, I say they have morning-after pills available."

Annie was silent, and Kate was forced to ask the question. "You got a problem with it if they are, Annie? Alaska's a pro-choice state. We legalized abortion a year before Roe."

"I'm hazy on the relevant law," Annie said. "Can EMT-2s do abortions?"

"Licensed MDs only, in a state-approved hospital or facility."

"Correct me if I'm wrong," Annie said, "but we got the clinic approved by HHS last year. The argument to do so was in the remote possibility that a surgical procedure was necessary, if for whatever reason we couldn't get the patient out of the Park to a hospital. Doc Oc signed off on it."

Doc Oc was Dr. Octavius Francesco Botticelli, an Italian-American transplant who had moved to Ahtna from

Philadelphia twenty-five years before. He'd married a Park rat, opened a clinic, and settled in for the duration. A recognized authority on Alaskan maladies from alcoholism to tuberculosis, he sat on the state medical board and had personally overseen the construction and staffing of the Ahtna General Hospital.

Kate smiled. "I remember. He said it was the best-equipped clinic he'd ever seen, and that he could perform anything in it with the possible exception of open-heart surgery, and he wouldn't even rule that out." She shrugged. "You know how he talks. He called the boys docs in a box. But he was pretty impressed. He signed off on it the first day and he rammed it through the state medical board in a week."

"Well," Annie said. "I guess it seemed like a good idea at the time."

"We should have expected this," Kate said. "Or something like it. There are always going to be people like Ulanie, thinking the world has to run on their clock."

"You can't think of everything, Kate."

"Emaa could," Kate said.

"You're not Ekaterina," Annie said, and smiled to take the sting out of her words.

Kate stacked the papers in front of her into a loose file. "What's next, do you think? She gonna go after those abnormal godless homos Keith Gette and Oscar Jimenez?"

"Now that," Annie said, very firm, "is seriously not allowed. Their basil makes the best pesto in the world, and I will not have that meddled with."

"Good point," Kate said. "I wonder if Ulanie's into pasta."

Annie saved the minutes, closed her laptop, and sat back to regard it with a thoughtful frown. "You were right to challenge her. I don't say you couldn't have done it with a little more tact, but it had to be done. You had to slap her down, hard."

"I'll probably have to do it again, too," Kate said. It was not something she was looking forward to.

"And again, and again," Annie said. "As a matter of curiosity, why didn't you call her out in front of the board?"

Kate sighed. "I would have if I'd thought the vote was going her way."

Annie raised an eyebrow. "There's more of your grandmother in you than you'll admit, Kate Shugak."

Annie unplugged her computer and the two women rose to their feet and made their way to the door.

"Annie?"

"What?"

"Tell me there is such a clause."

Annie was all elaborate surprise. "Of course there is, Kate. Paragraph C, subsection D, clause 1J, in the operations section of the bylaws. You can look it up in your own copy."

She gave a faint smile. "And you should."

"EMAA WAS A STEAMROLLER," Kate said, "and I'm a sledgehammer. It's about time the Association had a diplomat running things."

"You grooming Annie to take over?" Jim said, careful to keep his tone free of any opinion one way or the other. Unless and until it involved bloodshed, the trooper in him shied away from getting involved in anything to do with the Association.

He looked at Kate. Well. Anything to do with the Association other than sleeping with the chair of the board.

She was making bread to the sound of the hammered piano chords in John Hiatt's "Have a Little Faith in Me," good old-fashioned yeast bread for toast, his favorite, especially when they had some of Auntie Joy's nagoonberry jam in the pantry. They did, he knew because he'd investigated when he'd walked in the door and seen Kate up to her elbows in bread dough.

That wasn't why she was making this particular bread, though. She was making this particular bread because it required serious kneading, and kneading bread dough was as close to therapy as Kate would ever get. Whenever she came home pissed off, he got great toast the next morning, and sometimes the night before. "Did you know about the boys giving out birth control?"

She gave him a brief, irritated look. "They've been teaching classes in it at the school, Jim."

"But you're worried about this audit."

She slammed the dough down with unnecessary vigor.

"Is this one of those moments when the trooper is supposed to take a backseat, and the boyfriend step up?"

She looked at him.

" 'Cause you know I ain't never doing that again," he said.

"Yeah," she said. "I know. Never mind. What's the latest on Lyda?"

"We're two weeks out and nothing," he said. He eyed her with some caution. She had been so adamant that Lyda Blue had not committed suicide, but really, what else had this bizarre series of events been about but suicide, personal and professional? "My boss is making noises I should split the difference and call it accidental. He pointed out, not without reason, that however squeaky clean Jules keeps his kitchen, mistakes will happen. And her dad told me that she'd almost died of the same thing twice before, once when she was a kid and once when she was working at a mine Outside. She was a new hire for Global at one of their other sites."

"Somewhere in Montana."

"Yeah. Truax confirmed it."

Apropos of nothing she said, "I think Truax and Haynes got a thing."

The music switched to Dion's "If I Should Fall Behind." He always felt like he should be on a fifties street corner in New York City when he heard that song. "Truax and Haynes, huh?" He thought about it. "Their thing have any bearing on Lyda's death that you can see?"

"No." She kneaded. "Was Brillo able to do an analysis on the crumbs you found next to her bed?"

"Traces of peanut oil."

She sighed. "So. Accident, suicide, murder. Pick one."

"Afraid so."

"Hard on Jules."

"Yes."

She went back to kneading the dough, and he retired to the couch with the latest Codex Alera book, having won the three-way wrestle over the most recent Amazon box with absolutely no shame over his superior size and strength. Between the Canim, the Vord, and Invidia Aquitaine, Tavi's problems were way worse than his, thank god. Perspective, even if fictional, was a wonderful thing.

Later, when red salmon filet, fresh greens from the garden, and bread out of the oven was on the table, she smiled at him over their laden plates. "Good to have you home."

"Good to be home."

They ate in silence for a few moments, but he'd seen her expression. "What?"

She gave a half smile and shook her head.

He actually put down his fork. "What?"

"This is your first night home in a week."

He was taken aback. "It's the job."

316

She sat back, laughing. "It wasn't an accusation, just an observation."

Reassured by her laughter, he said, "What, then?"

She picked up his hand and brought it to her mouth. Her lips tickled the skin of his palm and he tried not to jerk free. Her tongue traced his lifeline, and then her teeth closed over the mound at the base of his thumb and bit down, hard.

The near pain shot straight to his groin. "Jesus, Kate." His heart rate doubled and he was having difficulty breathing.

She soothed the wound with her tongue and released his hand. "I missed you, is all." She went back to her food, all innocence and unconcern, although the corners of her wide, full mouth were perhaps a little more indented than before.

He blinked down at his plate, trying to focus. The bass on Queen's "We Will Rock You" beat up through the soles of his feet. He picked up his fork but that only made him more conscious of the throb in his hand, which only made him more conscious of the sudden and acutely uncomfortable fit of his pants.

"Fuck this," he said. He shoved his plate back, stood up, and reached for her, all in one smooth motion. It might have been harder if she'd fought him, but no, she came laughing into his arms. She laughed harder when he cleared the table with a sweep of one arm and threw her down on it.

One thing that could be said in favor of the Suulutaq Mine, this summer the kid wasn't around to cramp his style.

TWENTY

LABOR DAY

THE DAY WAS CLEAR, the air cool, and the leaves on the alders and the aspens had turned a brilliant yellow-gold. Old Sam had been waiting for most of the morning, and he was going to keep on waiting until that big, fat bull moose he had scouted in the area came ambling out of the woods and wandered in front of his sights.

There was some delicacy about this particular operation, as moose season in this section of Park didn't open for another two weeks, but Old Sam wasn't trophy hunting, he was hunting for meat. This of course made all the difference, and only tightasses like Chief Ranger Dan O'Brian would say otherwise.

The location was near the clearing where the bones of the lost guy, whoever the hell he had turned out to be, had been found last spring. He had stumbled across plenty of moose sign when he'd been tracking that griz, most likely the result of the come-hither effect of the Park's biggest stands of diamond willow, a good five acres of prime moose browse. It hadn't been an area that easy to get to, until the Smiths bladed in their trail, which meant that the area hadn't been hunted much, which meant the moose were that much more plentiful, less wary than moose in other areas of the Park, and fat.

318

It also meant less bushwhacking on the way in and a shorter distance to pack the meat out. Old Sam wouldn't have admitted it at gunpoint but his stamina was wearing a mite thin. A passable trail a convenient mile from ground zero was something that was growing more attractive every year.

His purpose was twofold. He was hunting for the cache as well as for his annual end-of-season barbecue, where tradition entailed roasting a whole moose quarter on a rotating spit of his own design over an open pit. Old Sam liked his meat crisp on the outside and bloody close to the bone, and this took time and care. Near the end of the process the word went forth, to Kate and Jim and Johnny, Bobby and Dinah and Katya, Ruthe Bauman, the four aunties if they hadn't pissed him off too much lately, some of the less annoying of his fellow board members, Bernie and his kids, and other select Park rats. Although Old Sam wouldn't have thought of it that way, it was one of the Park's premier social events of the year, to which an invitation was a coveted prize.

And woe betide the Park rat who showed up without one. The Kanuyaq River was an easy toss from the cabin.

Old Sam hated party crashers.

Now, maybe he could have waited until the season opened, but if he wanted to have the barbecue before the temperature dropped below freezing in the daytime he had to build in some time to let the meat hang. Hence the highly satisfactory illegality of the situation. Old Sam grinned to himself. There wasn't much he loved more than putting one over on the goddamn Parks Service. Unless it was running a scam on the Fish and Game. That this hunt would be a twofer only added to his enjoyment of the day.

It was Labor Day, and everyone was in town for the parade and the salmon bake at the gym and the farmer's market and craft fair at the school. Unless he'd managed to finagle a way out of it Chopper Jim would be leading the parade in his white Blazer, and the Grosdidier boys would be bringing up the rear in their fire-engine-yellow Silverado with the mobile pharmacy in the back. In between Miss Niniltna would be holding court on the back of a flatbed draped with the school colors of blue and gold, the Kanuyaq Kings varsity and junior varsity teams would be dribbling in formation behind her, and the Suulutaq Mine would be swaggering behind them and tossing candy like they worked for Hershey's. Every kid in Niniltna with a bike or a trike would be dressed in last year's Halloween costumes and part of the parade only when they weren't scrabbling for their share of the candy.

He was sorry to miss the fry bread and smoked fish at the gym, but he figured everyone felt that way, especially Chopper Jim and Dan O'Brian, which considerably improved his chances for a nice, quiet, successful hunt.

Yes, he had been there a few hours, and he expected to be there a few hours more, but he was in no hurry, and he was a man who enjoyed his own company. His thoughts ranged freely across the years and the Park and all of the people in it. He thought of people who had gone, like Emaa, and of people who should have been gone a lot sooner, like Louis Deem, and of people still around, like Kate.

He was a mite concerned about Kate. She had a habit of rescuing people, which was all right in moderation, but not so much when you went into it wholesale. It was particularly aggravating when it substituted a greenhorn for an experienced deckhand just about the time the first salmon hit fresh water.

Although he had to admit that Petey Jeppsen and Phyllis Lestinkof had not been completely worthless on the *Freya* this past summer. They were both clumsy and ignorant, of course, practically couldn't tell a humpy from a dog at the start of the season, but they'd shouldered in and worked hard. Neither one had taken their first paycheck to the bars uptown when they delivered in Cordova, and when they got seasick they remembered to puke to leeward. Further, when Kate had joined them for the silver season in August, neither Petey nor Phyllis had complained at being bumped down to second and third on deck. Petey'd had no problem taking orders from Kate, either. Sometimes the male of the species could get a little uppity when placed in an inferior position to the female, especially on the deck of a fishing boat in Prince William Sound.

He heard the brush rustling before he saw it moving. He pulled the Winchester tight into his shoulder, finger on the trigger.

He was rewarded when the biggest sumbitchin moose he'd seen in ten years strolled out like the king of the forest. Lordy, was he beautiful, a thick shining brown hide, a graceful, evenly balanced rack richly covered in velvet that was only now beginning to fray and peel, moving with a princely stride on haunches that would feed a family of four for six months.

Old Sam smiled, blew out a long quiet breath, and centered the front sight on one big brown eye.

It was an hour later, when he'd gutted the bull and pulled the skin halfway down the carcass, that he found the bullet hole.

Now, this wasn't necessarily unheard of. Plenty of clueless assholes wandering around the Park with too much gun and no idea how to use it. Not to mention a lack of backbone to go after one they'd wounded, as was right and proper, hell, in Old Sam's book a moral obligation.

Old Sam hated bad shots.

The hide had closed up over the hole the bullet had made going in, which was why he didn't see it until he pulled the skin down. The flesh had closed up after it, too, which told him the shot wasn't recent. It took a bit of finesse to extract the bullet without ruining the surrounding meat, and when he had it he sat back on his haunches and looked at the piece of metal he was holding between a bloodstained thumb and forefinger.

It was a little bullet. Damn little, a .22 if Old Sam was any judge, and he was. Who the hell went up against a moose with a .22?

He remembered the pistol Jim had found in the clearing, which wasn't more than half a mile from this very spot. It had tripped up Jim, and it had probably tripped him up a month before that.

He remembered Kate talking about the two guys tarryhooting off into the woods, one a suicide until he changed his mind and the other with a gun so he could change it back again. He remembered mention of a hoofprint in the skull that had been found. He examined the four hoofs on his moose. He didn't find anything except grass stains and pine needles.

He sat back and gave thought. Well, now, he was in something of a pickle, wasn't he. The moose was illegal, no doubt about that. If he took the bullet in and handed it over to the authorities, he'd have to say where he got it, and that illegality would become clear. There could be consequences, which could affect his barbecue.

But the bullet might be evidence of some kind in this crazy-ass case of Kate and Jim's, where there didn't seem to be any crime committed other than spying on a gold mine. It was difficult to get himself worked up over that.

Old Sam hated being a responsible citizen.

He cut the feet off at the first joint and put them in a game bag. The bullet he tucked into the pocket of his shirt and buttoned the flap after it just to be sure.

And then he went back to butchering out the moose.

Old Sam hated waste worst of all.

KATE LOOKED AT THE bullet, and at the package wrapped in white butcher paper labeled 5# ROST in black Marks-A-Lot. "I'm as susceptible to bribes as the next law enforcement professional, Uncle, but you know I'm going to have to tell him where I got it."

"Yeah, I know, but not before I get it all hung. Ain't nobody, even Dan O'Brian, going to take it then. Not if they want some of my barbecue."

Because despite the years-long war between Old Sam and the Parks Service, Dan O'Brian was one ranger who had a standing invitation to the barbecue.

Old Sam nodded at the roast. "That's the part the bullet come out of. Leave it sit out a day or two, it ought to be just about right." He left.

Mutt stuck her head over the counter and sniffed interestedly at the roast.

"Go catch your own," Kate told her. She put the roast on a shelf up high and then, because Mutt was sulking, said, "Want to go into town?"

"WELL, SHIT." JIM LOOKED at the bullet Kate had placed on the desk in front of him. "I thought we were done with that goddamn uncase."

It took until the following Saturday, the day of Old Sam's barbecue, before the report came back from ballistics. The bullet taken out of the moose had indeed been fired from the pistol Jim had found in the clearing with the body. Kate had driven in early, and the two of them sat in his office, digesting the news in silence.

At length, Jim stirred. "Okay. As crazy as I thought your theory was, I'm bound to say it's looking more like that's the way it went down. Allen had earned enough money from his various employers, it was time to leave, and he set up Gammons to take the fall so they wouldn't come looking for him if they found out he'd been double-crossing them both."

"All neat and tidy," she said, almost a growl.

"Boy, Kate, you really want to arrest someone out at the Suulutaq in the worst way, don't you?"

"Don't you?" she said.

"Not as bad as you do," he said. "I'm guessing it's because you hate the Suulutaq Mine so much."

She looked up, startled. "What are you talking about? I don't hate the mine."

Jim had been thinking about what Old Sam had told him back in July, thinking and watching Kate and listening to her, and thinking some more. "Yeah you do. You hate that goddamn mine worse than anyone else in the Park. Oh, I know, you haven't said so, and you've been the voice of reason and responsibility when you're in your board chair persona. But you hate it like poison. You see it changing the Park out of all recognition, and you see the dollar signs lighting up the eyes of your shareholders, Auntie Edna selling takeout, Auntie Balasha selling souvenirs, Auntie Vi plain selling out. You hate every bit of it. If you could you'd shut Suulutaq down and boot Global Harvest not just out of the Park but out of the whole goddamn state.

"And it's not because you really believe the mine will

destroy the land or the wildlife. You want jobs for Park rats, industry for a tax base so there can be schools and hospitals and libraries. But you'd rather do without all of that stuff than have the Park change on you. You'd rather do without than have your life changed as much as that mine is going to change it."

He leaned back in his chair and rubbed both hands over his face and linked them behind his head, looking at her with that impartial cop stare that could do a whole character dissection without ever touching a scalpel. "Failing that, you want there to have been a murder. You want me to haul Truax and Haynes in here and charge them with everything from murder to polluting your personal environment."

Kate's mouth opened and closed a couple of times. "That's just not true," she said. Was it? She rallied. "I liked that girl. I spent more time with her than you did, and I don't believe she would have killed herself."

"You're still not even comfortable with your new house, Kate. Face it. There isn't a nickel's worth of difference between your attitude to the mine and Gaea's."

"You're wrong," she said.

"Why is Howie Katelnikof still walking around on two good legs?"

"What?" Kate was really confused now.

"He shot at your truck. He put you and Johnny in the ditch and Mutt in the clinic. We both know it. Hell, every Park rat with an IQ over two digits knows it. We've all been holding our breaths for the last year, year and a half, to see what you're going to do about it. I myself have lived in daily expectation of scraping his remains up off some back road with a shovel, and I say a nightly prayer that you won't leave any evidence behind I'll have to act on."

325

"What the hell's this got to do with the mine and how I feel about it?"

"Howie's a Park rat, one of your own whether you like it or not, so he can take a shot at you and get away with it. A Suulutaq miner, that's a different story. You'll move mountains for a perp walk featuring one of them."

The silence this time was a little more fraught. Kate tried to think of something to say that wouldn't leave her wide open to more incoming. Too much of his ammunition was already finding its target. "Has her mother stopped calling?"

He nodded. "Yeah."

"Who gets Allen's money?"

"There's a sister. She said he was a better brother to her dead than he ever was alive."

"Ouch."

"Yeah. Not what I'd choose for my epitaph. But then I suppose the dumb bastard thought he'd never need one. He was going to live forever under a palm tree somewhere." He made some additional notes to the Allen file, saved it, copied it, and closed it. "So. You hanging around town until it's time to go to Old Sam's?"

"God no," Kate said, relieved that they seemed to be well and truly off the topic of her relationship to the Suulutaq Mine. Fucking mine was taking over every conversation she was in lately. "I'm heading back home. That is, if you're done psychoanalyzing me, doctor." She realized too late that there was maybe a little too much edge on the remark and rushed to fill the awkward silence following it. "I have to go back anyway, I'm supposed to make rhubarb sorbet for the barbecue."

That proved a useful distraction. "Got enough rhubarb left in the freezer?" he said, looking anxious. "I'm sure you could pick up extra from Annie or Auntie Vi if you need it. Or Dinah."

She was forced to smile. "I've got plenty."

"You're going to make a lot, right?"

She laughed and got to her feet. Mutt followed.

"Just don't start serving it up until I'm standing in front of you with a bowl and a spoon." He paused, a pile of pink call slips in one hand. "Oh, hey, I forgot to tell you. I finally took those numbers Lyda had on her computer over to the mine."

She looked over her shoulder, one hand on the door. "I thought you'd already done that."

"No. Didn't seem much point, with Lyda's death being ruled accidental and the corporate spy already accounted for. But I had to go out to the mine to talk to Randy Randolph yesterday—"

She groaned.

"Yeah, another one showed up from Outside, and she may be the one with the oldest date on the marriage certificate yet. Anyway, before I flew out I printed out the numbers in Lyda's file, and when I got there I showed them to Haynes. She checked them out against the core sample log."

"What'd she say?"

He shrugged. "She said that Lyda had gotten the numbers transposed but that otherwise they corresponded with core samples Allen had forwarded to his extracurricular employers."

Kate's brows came together. "Lyda got the numbers wrong?"

"Yeah, I think Haynes said she got the core sample data right. She just got the dates wrong."

Kate turned to come back in the room. Mutt stuck her head around the door frame. Her vigilance had been unrelenting ever since Kate had gone to Anchorage without her.

"Lyda got the dates wrong," Kate said.

"Yeah, I just said that. Didn't I just say that?"

"No, she didn't," Kate said.

"Kate—" Her name was a drawn-out exasperation.

"I'm telling you she didn't get the dates wrong," Kate said. "Truax wasn't pissed off she was dead, remember, he was pissed off that he'd lost the person who made his camp march along like Napoleon's army. Did you keep the dates?"

"Kate—"

She came around the desk to stand in front of his monitor. "Let me see them."

Like Brillo, Jim knew it was always going to be easier and less time-consuming if he just gave her what she wanted. He called up the file and displayed it.

"Still got the dates of the pay-ins to Allen's account?"

He displayed those, too. "We did this before," he said. "We noticed the dates were off when you first showed me Allen's bank records, and we compared the two. It didn't bother you then."

"One a month," she said, ignoring him. "April, May, June, and then July 1, five days before she died." She straightened, her face a mask, her eyes focused inward on the working out of some internal calculation. "April, Allen was still alive and spying. May, maybe, but by June he was dead, and by July he was even more dead." She looked at him. "She didn't screw up the numbers, Jim."

It took him a minute, and when he got there what she was intimating strained his credulity to the breaking point. "Kate. You think somebody else was selling Suulutaq data?" The significance of the last two dates hit him between the eyes. "And if you're right, if Lyda's dates are correct, that means somebody else continued to steal data after Allen disappeared."

"Lyda's desk was right there," Kate said, "in the room where they do all the work. This wasn't her first mine, she was familiar with the routine. She saw something and she started keeping track. It just wasn't Allen she was keeping track of."

He was skeptical, to say the least. "Setting aside the statistical improbability of one corporate spy in a hundred-man camp, who was the second?"

"It isn't a hundred-man camp, Jim, it's a four-billion-dollar camp," she said. "She said in her note at the bottom of the document, there may have been more incidents of data theft." She went around his desk and was out the door.

"Wait, where you going?"

"I'll be right back!"

Bingley's store was down the hill, past Auntie Vi's and around the corner. Kate took the steps two at a time. She found what she was looking for between the sugar and the spices.

She was back in Jim's office five minutes later, out of breath. "Got the keys to the Cessna?"

"Why, where we going?"

"To Suulutaq."

TWENTY-ONE

WHAT MAKES A COP? An observant eye and a good memory. At one time Kate had prided herself on having both. "She had two bags of groceries when she was in the café that day," Kate said, her voice grim over the headset, "so she knew the store was there and that it had what she needed."

There was no point in protesting after they were in the air so he shut up and listened.

"Lyda's allergy would be known in camp, especially to people who had worked with her before."

"Okay, means," he said. It was kicking up twelve to fourteen knots out of the southwest and the Cessna skipped over a few bumps. "Opportunity, obviously. What about motive?"

"It's all about the proprietary information, Jim."

"You think she was in it with Allen?"

"One possibility. He worked with her, she admitted as much to me, and Truax confirmed it."

He tried to reconcile this information with what he knew. "It was about the money for her, too?"

"Partly, probably, but I think there are a couple of other things. For one, principle."

He groaned. Sex and money were easy-to-recognize motives that were even easier to prove in court. Sex and money he knew he could handle. "Principle?" There was pain in the very articulation of the word.

"Principle. She came out to the house on the Fourth of July, remember? Before Gammons stumbled into the yard and all the hullabaloo started she told me she was pretty ambivalent about the Suulutaq. 'I just don't know if the world needs another gold mine,' she said, that's quoting her verbatim. I think she is really unhappy about this whole project."

"Ambivalence isn't usually a motive for murder, Kate."

"Agreed, but it might have been more than ambivalence. It just clicked in your office fifteen minutes ago who was sitting between her and Demetri. He had his back to us and I thought he was Demetri's friend."

"Who the hell was it?"

"Kostas McKenzie."

"The Gaea guy?"

"Yes."

"You're sure?"

She thought of the solid shoulders, the square set of the head, and compared them to the man she'd met on the Suulutaq airstrip and in his office in Anchorage. "Yes."

"Okay," he said, pretty much at his last tether of self-control, "you're saying she's been turned to the green side by an environmental group?"

"Yes. But there's more."

"What?"

She ignored his long-suffering tone for the moment. "She and Truax have a thing going on, I know I read the body language right on that."

"So? I would think selling out her lover would be the last thing she'd do."

"Yeah, but Mrs. Truax spent the Fourth of July at Auntie Vi's B and B with Mr. Truax, and Haynes wasn't happy about it. It's one of the reasons I think she came out to the homestead.

She was staying at Auntie Vi's, too, and she probably didn't want her nose rubbed in it." Kate thought back over the conversation, pulling and tugging at every word, and said, "Son of a bitch. You know what else?"

"What?"

"She felt me out about Allen's body, wanting to know if it had been positively identified. And then later, she tried to convince us that it wasn't Gammons who came stumbling out of the woods." She turned and looked at him, and then had to shove Mutt's head out of the way so she could see him. "Because if it was Gammons, she knew we'd have to identify who the body really was."

"Why didn't she want us to identify the body as Allen's?"

She faced forward again. "I don't know."

They flew in a tense silence for a few minutes. "She was right there while he was stealing the data," Jim said.

"She saw him," Kate said.

"Maybe that's what gave her the idea," Jim said.

"And Lyda saw her," Kate said. *There might be something else, another reason Wayne took off*, she heard Lyda's hesitant voice say. "There was something Lyda tried to tell me just before I left the mine that day, something about maybe Gammons didn't try to commit suicide."

"Why not?"

She shook her head. "I put my foot in it, said something smartassed, and she froze up on me."

He looked at her.

"Don't say it," she said. "I know. There is no excuse." *I could have gotten Lyda killed*, she thought, and knew he was thinking the same.

They were halfway to the mine, the two arms of the Quilaks enclosing the valley looming larger through the windscreen.

"Maybe Gammons caught Allen thieving," Jim said a few minutes later.

Kate readjusted her ideas. "And maybe Allen marched him into the woods at gunpoint?"

"Maybe. Maybe just speeding up the last part of the plan."

"But before Allen disposed of him, Gammons said something to Lyda, and then Lyda started keeping watch. Wait a minute." She turned to look at him and again had to shove Mutt's head out of the way. "She didn't know Lyda and Gammons had a relationship."

"She didn't?"

"Not until I told her so."

He looked over and saw the rigid set of her jaw. He concentrated on driving the plane.

They set down on the mine's airstrip a little after noon and they went directly to the mess hall. The tables were full and the hubbub was loud, but it tapered off when they saw Kate attended by a state trooper in blue and gold and a full-grown gray wolf. Kate spotted Van and Johnny and went to their table, although Mutt beat her to Johnny by thirty seconds. Kate bent over and said in a low voice, "You seen Holly Haynes?"

They exchanged glances. "I think she went out to eighteen-E," Van said.

"One of the rigs," Johnny said, his hands buried in Mutt's fur.

"How do we get out there?"

Johnny looked over at Jim. "Drive. There's not what you'd call a road, but it's navigable."

"Thanks."

"What's going on, Kate?"

"Tell you later."

Jim caught up with her outside. "Let's go find Truax."

"You go find Truax," she said, "I'm going to find Haynes."

"Hold it," he said.

She stopped. Mutt stopped, too, great head swiveling back and forth between the two of them.

"I want to find her and talk to her, too, but we don't really have any proof we can confront her with."

"Means, opportunity, and we got about three different kinds of motive. Goddammit, Jim, I'm not going to—"

As they stood arguing a pickup came around the corner of a building and bumped over the uneven surface to a spot in front of the bull rail in front of admin. Haynes got out, wearing coveralls covered in mud up to the collar. She pulled off a hard hat and ran her fingers through sweat-soaked hair.

She saw them and her hand froze.

"Haynes." Kate's voice was hard and uncompromising. "We need to have a conversation."

Haynes dropped her hard hat and ran.

She hit the double doors of the admin building. Kate hit the doors on the backswing, got through them and saw Haynes halfway up the stairs.

"Vern! Vern!" Haynes was screaming the mine superintendent's name loud enough to be heard in Fairbanks. "Vern!"

She vanished around the corner and Kate heard her feet pounding down the hall. Kate took the stairs three at a time and as she got to the top she heard Vern say, "I'm right here, for crissake, stop yelling! What the hell's the problem?"

Kate got to the door of his office to find Haynes standing with Truax on the other side of his desk. She was looking up at him, pleading, and he was looking down at her, displeased. Kate was reminded of the day Haynes had come running to Vern on the airstrip with news of Lyda's death. Just so now had she looked at him then, her last hope of heaven, of succor, of rescue. Ally ally oxen free.

Kate started forward. Truax saw movement from the corner of his eye and looked around to frown at her. "Kate? What the hell is going on?"

Kate looked at Haynes, who was teary and trembling. "Ask your staff geologist. Or should I call her your mine squeeze?"

"Kate," Jim said sharply.

Ignoring Jim, Kate said to Truax, "Your girlfriend there killed your favorite employee."

"I didn't mean to," Haynes said, still looking up at Truax. "It was an accident."

TWENTY-TWO

JIM HAD CUFFED AND stuffed Haynes into the back of the Cessna, where she rode next to a very attentive Mutt. In Niniltna, Jim transferred her to one of the cells. He read her her rights, and the last thing Truax had said to her was, "Sit tight and keep your mouth shut until the lawyer gets there." Of course Truax might change his mind about the lawyer when he learned that Holly had taken up data sales where Rick Allen had left off.

Regardless, Haynes was talking. Jim set up the video camera and reminded her once every couple of minutes that she had the right to remain silent, making sure the camera picked it up. She'd stopped trembling and her eyes were dry. She spoke directly to Kate, standing outside the bars of the cell.

"I didn't mean to kill her," she said for what was maybe the tenth time. "I just wanted her to be sick enough so we could medevac her to town. Get her out of the way so I could have a little breathing space and figure out what to do next." She fixed Kate with the same pleading stare that hadn't worked on Truax. "You understand, don't you? You'll help me make everyone else understand, won't you?"

Jim crooked his finger at Kate and let her take his seat opposite Haynes. In a low voice into the mike on the camera he said, "Kate Shugak, private investigator, contract employee, taking over the interrogation at"—he looked at his watch—

"two fifty-four P.M." He folded his arms and leaned against the bars.

Haynes didn't even notice the switch. Later, when her attorney pointed out that there had been nothing but circumstantial evidence against her and that all Jim had to swear out an arrest warrant was her detailed confession on videotape, she would be very sorry indeed that she had been so forthcoming. Kate was glad she didn't have to take notes, she never would have been able to keep up.

"You'll help me, won't you?" Haynes said.

"Sure, I'll help you," Kate said. The image of Lyda Blue standing next to Haynes was as clear as Haynes herself, unsmiling, intent, bearing witness. "Let's start at the beginning, shall we?"

It took two hours because Haynes rambled and backtracked, and because she was determined to justify every single one of her actions. Sleeping with a married man, selling core sample data, intercepting the cookies Jules made especially for Lyda, soaking them in the peanut oil she'd bought at Bingley's store, delivering them to Lyda's door, carrying them inside her room. Taking a seat and watching Lyda bite into the first one.

She had seen Allen go into the admin building late one night in March. "It was the first week we were on the job," she said in disbelief, like it should have taken longer, as if in decency Allen should have had to work up to outright theft. "Of course I figured out right away he was selling it."

"Why didn't you tell Truax at once?"

"I was gathering evidence," Haynes said. She liked the sound of that so much she said it again. "I was gathering evidence. I was going to show it to Vern when I got enough of it, when I was sure what he was doing."

Kate could feel Jim's eyes on the back of her head but she

didn't turn around. "What changed your mind? Why didn't you show it to him?"

Haynes didn't answer this time.

"Did he break off your affair?"

Haynes looked up, startled.

"Was that why you didn't tell him about Allen? Revenge? Stick it to him for going back to his wife?"

"He wouldn't divorce her," Haynes said.

"And you weren't that happy about the mine anyway," Kate said. "'I'm just not sure the world needs another gold mine,' you told me. So you decided to sabotage it by selling proprietary information to Gaea, an environmental organization with the Suulutaq on its hit list."

"I didn't sell it," Hayes said. "I never sold it."

"You gave it away?" How Kate kept the contempt from her face she would never know.

"I mailed it to Gaea anonymously. They never knew who it came from. I never would have sold it for money." Haynes looked shocked at the very suggestion. Evidently murder was an acceptable vice compared to corporate espionage.

"You continued to, uh, steal it and give it away for free after Allen disappeared, is that correct? When did you send off your first data sample?"

"I don't know, I can't remember."

"Was it April?" Kate said, thinking of the first date on Lyda's document. "Before?"

"I don't know. I can't remember exactly."

It was before, Kate thought. You were probably copying Allen's actions from the first night you saw him. That's why the dates were different, you were doing your thing a day or a week behind Allen, at least until he disappeared. "When did you find out Lyda Blue knew what you were doing?"

Haynes's eyes wandered around the cell, pausing briefly on the camera. "Something she said made me wonder. She started to come into the office earlier every morning. She watched me send in the rig reports. But then she didn't do anything, and I figured … And then you told me she was Dewayne Gammons's girlfriend. I knew he and Allen were friends. I panicked, I guess." She looked at Kate, again with the big cow eyes. "I never meant to kill her, I just wanted to get her out of the way for a little while so I could think."

And clean up any evidence you might have left in case Lyda told Truax, Kate thought. "And so you doctored the cookies and delivered them to her door."

They'd found no empty peanut oil bottles in Haynes's room or in her office upstairs in the admin building. They'd found no hard evidence of any kind, in fact, other than the dates and numbers in Lyda Blue's hidden file. Again, Haynes was determined to explain, clarify, give painstaking details of her anxiety, her agony of mind. "I told her I wanted to talk to her about some stuff in the office, stick picker rotation, you know, busy work. It was just an excuse. I told her the cookies were from Jules. She didn't suspect anything."

She looked at Kate, begging for understanding, for sympathy. "I couldn't sleep at all that night. And then when Vern told me to check on her, and I found her like that …" She shuddered. "It was so awful. You saw how upset I was that day, didn't you? When I came running up to the airstrip to tell Vern what had happened?"

"Yes," Kate said. "I saw. When did you buy the peanut oil, Holly?"

Haynes looked confused.

"The day we met, Memorial Day in Niniltna, remember? I saw you with grocery bags from Bingley Mercantile. You said that camp food no matter how good it was palled after a while, that everybody squirreled away snacks in their room. Did I see some peanut oil in one of those bags? A whole month before you used it?" She'd seen nothing of the kind, but it was worth a shot.

"I—," Haynes stuttered, and the expression on her face told them she was only now beginning to comprehend their lack of sympathy. And what it meant.

"I'm going to check, Holly, but I'm betting you were on the same job with Lyda Blue the last time she had an anaphylaxis. She almost died, her father told us. You had to know how violent her reaction to the peanut oil would be."

"Kate." Jim's deep voice held a warning note.

Kate mastered her fury and stood up. "You saw the body. Lyda Blue died hard, Holly, and I promise you, I'm going to make it my personal crusade to see that you go down for it just as hard."

IN HIS OFFICE, JIM backed up the taped confession to his computer and saved it, and then he made a couple of copies just to be sure. He looked at Kate, sitting in silence across from him. Mutt was leaning up against her, offering her the comfort of her body weight and warmth, a sure sign of Kate's mood. "You okay?"

She took a minute to answer. "Yeah," she said at last. She rocked her head from side to side, stretching the tension out of her neck, and knotted a hand in Mutt's conveniently placed fur. The texture of the gray hairs, so familiar, so necessary, steadied her. She looked across at Jim, who watched her with a steady gaze without sympathy, but with all the understanding she could wish for.

"You couldn't have known."

"No," she said. "No, I couldn't. But it doesn't change the fact that Lyda Blue is dead, and I couldn't save her."

He thought of Old Sam and the conversation in the woods. "You can't save everybody, Kate."

She didn't argue with him, she just changed the subject. "You going to run her into town?"

"Hell no," Jim said. "She can sit in the cell overnight. I'm not missing Old Sam's barbecue." He looked at the clock on the wall. "Time to go or it'll all be et."

The last thing Kate wanted to do was go to a party, but she knew it would be the best thing for her. "Can't have that," she said.

His smile approved her attempt at humor. It was a start. "Your truck or mine?"

THE FLOWERS ON OLD Sam's roof had long gone to seed, but the cabin was surrounded by a field of topped-out fireweed, their stalks a deep red bank of color. Old Sam got out the weed-whacker so that the area around the barbecue was clear. The moose haunch was revolving slowly over a bed of red-hot coals. There was a trestle table laden with bowls of potato salad and coleslaw and a platter of deviled eggs, the latter Auntie Joy's annual offering and Old Sam's particular weakness. Another trestle table served as the bar, over which Old Sam dispensed beer from a keg, wine from a box, and single-malt to the select few who could be counted on to appreciate it with the reverence it deserved. He pulled Jim a beer with a fine head of foam and broke out one of a lone six-pack of Diet 7UP for Kate, rolling his eyes as he did so. "Where my rhubarb sorbet, girl?"

Kate gaped at him. In the press of other business she'd forgotten all about it.

That was good for a five-minute peroration on the shiftless ways of the younger generation, too lazy to wipe the oil off a dipstick, no respect for the wishes of their elders, too ignorant to know how to mash up a couple of sticks of rhubarb and dump in some sugar and probably too dumb to stick it in the freezer afterward anyway. Jim sidled off in what he imagined to be surreptitious fashion, and she was left to stand against the flood as best she could. She bent her head and hoped she looked meek enough to inspire pity. Mercy would have been too much to ask for.

It made her feel a little better to be yelled at so comprehensively.

It was a real Indian summer kind of evening, warm, windless, no mosquitoes, and in the affectionate presence of family and friends Kate began at last to relax. By mutual unspoken agreement she and Jim said nothing of what had happened out at the mine that day or of the prisoner incarcerated in the cell at the post. No way this evening, a stellar event in the Park year, should be eclipsed by anything so mundane as murder.

Johnny and Van were already there, playing red rover with Katya. Kate was glad to see it because Katya was very proprietary of Johnny, and it had taken her some time to learn to share him with Van.

Katya's father was holding forth to the circle surrounding his wheelchair on the comparative merits of Creedence Clearwater Revival and Paul Revere & the Raiders, with some commentary on the side about the Smothers Brothers. A few steps away Bernie Koslowski, showing more life than he had in a while, was refighting the Vietnam War with Demetri Totemoff and George Perry, although Bernie had been a campus commando and Demetri and George had run through

342

the jungle. Dinah was taping the conversation for that documentary on Vietnam War vets she'd been working on ever since her first experience of Bobby's annual Tet Vet celebration.

The four aunties were lined up on the bench in front of the cabin with Annie Mike, the five of them sipping paper cups full of bad box chardonnay and chattering away like four round plump brown wrens and one hot pink cockatoo. "Hi, Aunties," Kate said, and was surprised at her own relief when all four faces lit up at the sight of her.

Dan O'Brian was turning the spit and Kate clicked her tongue. "And you a Park ranger," she said.

"A hungry one," he said, and grinned.

When the moose was done Old Sam did the honors with a butcher knife the size of a samurai sword, producing thick, tender slices running with juice that tasted of forest and stream and home. There was sticky rice and soy sauce for those who wanted it, and boiled potatoes and butter for those who didn't, and enough fry bread for all.

There was plenty for seconds, and some went back for thirds, and the talk got louder and the laughter more frequent. All the old stories were trotted out and retold to advantage as the sun sank in the sky, and the surface of the river turned to molten gold as it progressed downstream in a manner infinitely more stately than any holiday parade.

And for one evening at least, nobody talked about the elephant in the room, the gold mine fifty miles away that would change the very fabric of their lives forever.

It was getting on toward dusk when Old Sam said, "You know, I think I'm going to sit down," and went down the dock on unsteady legs to subside onto the bench there.

Kate grinned, watching him.

"Old man can't hold his liquor like he used to," Bernie said, next to her.

"He can still drink you under the table." Kate raised her voice. "Come on, everybody, it's getting cold. Time to clean up and head home."

It broke up reluctantly, as all good parties do, and everyone pitched in to cut and wrap the remains of the moose, bag the leftovers, wash the dishes, and burn the paper plates and cups. People left in twos and threes, their vehicle lights showing for brief moments before receding into the encroaching darkness. The air grew chilly and Kate shrugged into her jacket.

"Get your goddamn butts over to the house the next couple of days, before the kid forgets what the fuck you look like!"

"Okay, Bobby."

"And you, you ancient old fucker, thanks for the best hunk a moose I ever sank a tooth into!"

"I think Old Sam's passed out, Bobby."

"He's probably awake now."

"Hey, Kate, Willard was up on the Step yesterday."

"How'd he get there?"

"Damn if I know. He didn't have his truck and when I asked him all he would say is him and Anakin hitched a ride."

"Where the hell is Howie?"

"Come on, Kate. Is that a question any of us really want the answer to?"

"Who's running the Roadhouse?"

"I closed it for the night."

"I'm sorry, I must have heard you wrong. You closed the Roadhouse?"

"Yep. Locked the door, turned out the lights, put a sign out saying 'Closed due to barbecue.' "

"I'm trying to think. Has that happened in the memory of man?"

"I'm making enough money from those miner boys, I can afford a night off now and then."

"Well, there's something good to be said for it, then."

"My new pilot finally showed up yesterday."

"Would this be Sabine?"

"It would indeed."

"Does that whistle mean what I think it means?"

"It does."

"We may have a logo, Kate."

"Don't toy with me, Annie."

"I'm not, I promise."

"Did that artist come through?"

"No. Believe it or not, we got a really nice design from one of Demetri's nieces. We will need a professional to adapt it into a logo, and the artist who did the Gaea logo says she can do that, but I think everyone will like it."

"You know people will say it's favoritism, that her design won because her uncle's on the board."

"Let them."

Jim was the last to leave, walking back up to the post with a plate of leftovers for Holly Haynes, there to pick up the Blazer and drive home. Kate would soon follow in the Ranger.

Kate took a last look around. The little cabin had a view that wouldn't quit. The sun was a burnt orange memory on the horizon. Venus shone brightly in a clear night sky, preening at its reflection in the river below. Kate was unsurprised to see her breath when she exhaled. Winter would soon be upon them.

She went to stand at the end of the dock. "Come on, Uncle, let's get you to bed before you roll into the river."

Mutt was sitting on the dock in front of the bench, looking up into his face.

"Old Sam?" Kate said.

The old man didn't move.

Kate started down the dock. "Uncle?" Unconsciously her step began to quicken, until she was running. "Uncle!"

She skidded to a halt next to Mutt, who looked up at her with wise yellow eyes.

Kate didn't know her legs had given out until she felt her knees hit the wooden planks of the dock.

His eyes were closed and his head had fallen a little to one side. He looked like he was asleep.

His hand was already cool. She clasped it in both of hers and cradled it to her breast, and bent her head, and wept.

Mutt took a deep breath and raised her head.

The plaintive, mournful howl ululated into the still air, echoing down the river, and beyond.

TWENTY-THREE

GAEA IS THE FACE of the organization behind the brochures, the press releases, the radio and online ads, the television commercials and the ballot proposition. We're a registered 501(c)(3) nonprofit organization, we file our paperwork annually, and our reputation is squeaky clean. We are known for activism but not for fanaticism. We are respected but not feared."

"Fear isn't necessarily a bad thing."

"No," McKenzie said, "but the appearance of propriety is ninety percent of the battle. It behooves us to maintain—" He paused.

"The shine on our halos?"

"Exactly." McKenzie's smile was approving without being patronizing. "We must be seen to be on the side of the angels. By contrast, Global Harvest and the Suulutaq Mine must be seen to be on the side of the devil. That's about as subtle as the collective public mind can handle. Ask anyone who ever ran a bank."

He looked around the table at the four other men sitting there. Three were heads of their own new-made nonprofits, Eric Sackman of Green Energy, Rudy Villegas of Alaskans for Sustainable Jobs, and Chad Isaak of the Seventy-one Percent Society. Sackman was a former political consultant and a member of the board of Villegas's group. Isaak was a local attorney who had sat on the Anchorage Assembly and served in Juneau as a legislator. Sackman and Villegas had been major contributors to his campaigns.

The fourth man was a close friend and associate of the other three. He wrote checks. Big checks. "What are our chances of knocking out this mine?" he said.

"Fair," McKenzie said.

The four men exchanged glances. "Only fair?" the fourth man said.

McKenzie showed his palms. "Global Harvest has got a head start. They've done a good job with publicity and community outreach. We can't outspend them, I'll tell you that right now."

"What can we do?"

McKenzie leaned forward. "We can out-shout them. We can plaster the airways with pictorial evidence of their industry's violations of the land, the water, and the air. We can fly up people from out of state who live near open-pit mines and put them in front of every social organization in Alaska. We can attack the executives of the Suulutaq and Global Harvest on a personal level."

"A personal level?"

McKenzie met the moneyman's eyes without flinching. "They're human, they screw up. I've had a private investigator gathering information on the top tier of Global Harvest management for the last year. There is plenty there to exploit."

"What does that do, besides embarrass them?"

"The trick is not to let up. You hit them with something, and then you barely let them get their feet under them before you hit them with something else. You don't feel sorry for them, you don't lose your nerve, and you don't let up. You remember that you're in this for the long haul, and you believe absolutely that failure is not an option."

"And then what happens?"

McKenzie shrugged. "Some of them will be fired. Some of them will be forced to resign. Some will resign regardless because they know a sinking ship when their feet get wet."

"And?"

"And the incredible disappearing power structure will disrupt management, which will put operations in flux. There will be pressure from shareholders and from the public to investigate, to clean house. I've got a couple of tame reporters who will print anything I give them, and we're starting a couple of blogs, one under our own name and at least two that will be anonymous." He smiled. "The Gaea blog will take the high road. The anonymous ones will throw the mud."

"And then?"

"And then we turn the lawyers loose on them. Every application they file, every permit they apply for, the lawyers scrutinize every line and challenge every discrepancy in court. I did have access to most of the discovery data coming from the mine, but that person has now, ah, left their employ. I'm working on developing a new source even as we speak, and I'm confident we will regain that access before very long. That information will only better inform any future legal actions by our attorneys."

"Sounds expensive."

"It will be. But the mine has a high national profile. We have one commercial, running only in Alaska, and every time it runs it brings in an average of ten grand. Once we achieve some success, once our name is a solid brand, and once we begin running commercials nationally, we'll get even more."

The man leaned forward, his eyes intent. "It cannot become known that I am supporting this organization. They'll kick me off the board the moment they learn of it, and your source of inside information on the Niniltna Native Association will dry up."

"I understand."

He gestured around the table. "I know these guys. I don't know you. If there's a leak, I'm going to figure it came from you. I won't be happy about that."

McKenzie met his eyes without flinching. "There won't be any leaks."

"All right." Demetri Totemoff opened his checkbook. "Fifty thousand to start sound okay?"

GOLD.

Number 79 on the periodic table. "Au," from the Latin *aurum*.

There are only an estimated 42 metric tons left to be mined from the earth's crust. With annual world production of gold ore at nearly 2,500 metric tons, only seventeen years of gold mining remain.

Hurry, hurry, grab up the last of it before someone else gets to it first.

Quick, carve away the surface, lay on the chemicals, separate the ore from the slag.

Drill your holes, build your dams, force the hard earth to yield up the soft gold it holds so close and so dear.

Mine it, refine it, sell it.

Gold to airy thinness beat.

Gold.

ACKNOWLEDGMENTS

Grateful thanks to Quinsey Jorgenson,
who knows far better than I do
what Vanessa's wearing these days.

Even more grateful thanks to her brother,
Cale Jorgenson,
who went to college so
I could have his room on overnights.

Thanks again to Gary and Jeanne Porter,
who I swear keep doing stuff
just so I can use it for my books.

And thanks to Mayhem in the Midlands
for making me Zoe Sharp's crash test dummy
so Kate could knock that little weasel on his butt.

DANA STABENOW

'…NIQUE IN THE CROWDED FIELD OF CRIME FICTION' MICHAEL CONNELLY

THOUGH NOT DEAD

…te Shugak's uncle Sam dies, leaving her
…etter instructing her to 'find his father'.
…e only problem is, Sam's father has been
…ssing for nearly 90 years…

A KATE SHUGAK INVESTIGATION

18

1918

Niniltna

THE BLACK DEATH DIDN'T get to Alaska until November. When it did, it cut down almost everyone in its path.

The territorial governor imposed a quarantine and restricted travel into the Interior, stationing U.S. Marshals at all ports, trailheads, and river mouths to interdict travel between communities. He issued a special directive urging Alaska Natives to stay at home and avoid public gatherings. Theaters closed, churches canceled services, schools were let out, but because of the inescapably communal nature of traditional life, Natives were infected and died disproportionately. In Brevig Mission, only eight of eighty people survived. In some villages there were no survivors at all. When the influenza pandemic passed late the following spring, those left alive were too weak to hunt for food, and even more died of starvation.

In Niniltna in March 1919, Chief Lev Kookesh and his wife, Alexandra, froze to death because they were too sick to get up and feed the fire in their woodstove. Four miles up the road at the Kanuyaq Mine, mine manager Josiah Greenwood lost his wife and both sons, and one out of four of his workforce.

Some of the uninfected turned to predation and thievery.

Harold Halvorsen was beaten to death in a fight over his last bag of flour. Bertha Anelon was assaulted in her own bedroom and died of her injuries two days later, alone in the bed in which she had been attacked. The offices of the Kanuyaq Mine were broken into half a dozen times, the cash box stolen, the glass case housing the Cross of Gold nugget shattered and the nugget gone, the company files rifled and set on fire. Toilets and refrigerators were ripped out of mine workers' homes as residents lay on their beds with no strength to resist. Food, clothes, photographs, personal papers, and jewelry vanished, most never to be recovered by their owners.

Empty homes where entire families had died were stripped and abandoned. Cemeteries overran their boundaries. After seeing their last living family member into the ground, many survivors left for Fairbanks or Anchorage or even Outside. Village populations halved by the epidemic were halved again by emigration.

Eventually, inevitably, people rallied. In Niniltna, the memorial potlatch for Chief Lev and his wife was seen by many as a start down the road of recovery from an eight-month-long nightmare of disease and death, a time to mourn the dead, a time for the living to nourish their souls and rebuild their homes and towns. Moving forward was necessary for survival, even if they also understood that life would never be the same for any of them ever again.

Organizing the potlatch fell to Chief Lev's only child, Elizaveta, age seventeen. Her life had nearly been forfeit, too, except that someone had come to their house, a man, a young placer miner, miraculously uninfected, who told her he had been checking house to house for anyone left alive. He found her in her bed, suspecting her parents were dead in the next room but too weak to get up and find out. Now on her feet and like the rest of the survivors, thin and pale and grieving, she was determined to do her best by her tribe, by her parents, and by her chief. The girls from down at the Northern Light still living helped her wash and dress the bodies in their finest clothes. The young placer miner, named Herbert Elmer "Mac" McCullough, kindled a coal fire in the cemetery and used the heat to dig their graves in the still frozen ground.

Some remaining survivors weren't too sick to grumble, starting with the scandal of women no better than they should be helping to lay out tribal elders. Elizaveta had always been a wild child, they told each other, although much of that could be laid at Lev's door. He was the one who'd taught her to hunt and fish and trap in the first place, over the objections of his mother and her sisters and the rest of the elders. Theirs was a conservative and traditional tribe who thought a woman's place was in the home, sewing skins and making babies. Lev had even allowed Elizaveta to spend the previous summer working his gold claim in the Quilak foothills, and with Quinto Dementieff there, too. Chaperoned by her father, it was true, but still.

That summer before the black death had been profitable for everyone. Lev had even opened a bank account in Elizaveta's name. Alexandra was horrified, but Lev was adamant. "She earned it," he told Alexandra, and handed the passbook to his daughter.

Elizaveta was thrilled. She felt a little taller with the passbook in her possession, more substantial somehow. When she went to Kanuyaq to clean house for Angie Greenwood, she looked at the flush toilet she scrubbed out every week in a different way. Suddenly no luxury was unattainable with your own money jingling in your pocket.

All that was changed now, of course. She had used all of her savings to buy gifts for the traditional gift giving at her parents' potlatch, tools, blankets, kitchenware, jewelry, canned food, all of it ordered in bulk from the Sears, Roebuck catalogue. Then there was the cost of shipping it all to Cordova, from where by special dispensation of Mr. Greenwood it was brought in on the Kanuyaq River & Northwestern Railroad free of charge. Mr. Greenwood, a kind man, had always been punctilious about maintaining good relations with the people in Kanuyaq, white and Native, amateur and professional, and his own grief did not deter him now. When the day came, her parents' spirits had no cause for shame at what was given to family and friends in their name. No shame either in the hall of the Alaska Native Brotherhood, which she had decorated with pine boughs tied up with green and red ribbons. It gave the long, rectangular room a celebratory, albeit somewhat Christmassy air. Mac had helped her put them up the night before, which was when it had happened, a delicious, delightful interlude of much mutual pleasure. It had been so long since Elizaveta had felt happiness of any kind.

The jewel in the crown of the hall's decorations came when she placed the tribe's icon at the head of the room, on a tall table with a round top, next to the sepia photograph of her parents. She had had the photograph blown up to a large grainy simulacrum of itself by a photographer in Seattle for a fee that had used up the last of her savings. Her father was seated and serious in his regalia, her mother standing behind him in beaded deerskin, one hand resting on Lev's shoulder, an equally serious expression on her face. They looked stiff and very stern, not at all the way Elizaveta remembered them. The frame was made of pine carved with rosettes and trailing vines and gilded with gold paint, a suitable testament to the importance of the people in the photograph.

The icon was a Russian Orthodox triptych, known to the Park as the Sainted Mary. There were three panels, depicting from left to right Mary holding the infant Jesus in a barn, Mary holding the dead Jesus at the foot of the cross, and a resurrected Jesus revealing himself to Mary before a rolled stone. The Sainted Mary was eight inches high, and all three panels together eighteen inches wide. It was made of wood that had been gilded by the original artist's hand. The gilt was now tarnished and flaking. The illustrations were made of pierced and enameled metal with bas-relief figures. The frame was studded with dull colored stones, two missing from their bezels.

It was old, very old, no one could say how old. They knew it had come with the gussuks in their tall ships from across the sea, but no one knew how it had come into the hands of the tribe, although those who counted Tlingits among their ancestors could make a pretty good guess.

It was understood that it was not a personal possession, that the chief only held it in trust for the tribe. The icon had miraculous powers, among them the ability to heal. Most recently Albert Shugak had prayed to the Sainted Mary and had recovered the use of his legs, it was believed until then lost forever in the battle of Verdun. He had married Angelique Halvorsen six months later, and she was now pregnant with their first child, their family one of the few only lightly touched by the black death. The Sainted Mary also held the power to grant wishes. Almira Mike prayed for a son and within the year the Sainted Mary had answered with the birth of William, a happy, moon-faced child. Myron Hansen prayed to the Sainted Mary for a new boat, and his great-uncle in Seattle died and left him a fortune.

Since Chief Lev had had no sons, in whose custody the icon

ould next be placed was a matter of vital importance to the
ibe.

For this and many other reasons, not least that after
during the horrors of the past year the tribe was in sore need
something to show them that they were in fact still a tribe,
ith pride and traditions and a history going back ten thousand
ars, it was imperative that they elect a new chief as soon as
ossible.

It was in this spirit that they gathered, family from Ket-
ikan, friends from Sitka, tribal members from Juneau, close
n from Fairbanks and kissing cousins from Circle, and shirt-
il relatives from Ahtna. They came from all the villages on the
ver from Tikani to Chulyin, all the villages on the road
tween Ahtna and Valdez, an astonishing assembly given the
cimation of their ranks. Mac McCullough helped Elizaveta
stribute the gifts, although many of the guests would not
eet his eyes, deeply resenting the intrusion of this round-eyed
ussuk into this most important, almost sacred, tribal rite.
stead, they looked at Elizaveta, with reproach. Elizaveta, who
spite her parent's death had something of a glow about her.

Well. They all knew what that meant. They accepted their
fts in a spirit of one part entitlement to three parts righteous
dignation, gorged themselves on the thin stew made from
st year's moose and hunks of bread fresh made from the last
the village's flour, and returned to their tents having taken
ly the most formal leave of their hostess.

The next morning the Sainted Mary was gone.

So was Mac McCullough.

"I don't have it," Elizaveta said, her face white and set, the
ow erased from her features. They didn't believe her, and
ey were not respectful when they searched her house. They
rew everything out of the cache and unwrapped the pitifully

few packets of moose meat left there to make sure that it was moose meat, they dumped out the nearly empty sacks of rice and beans and sugar and flour, and there was even talk of exhuming the bodies of her parents until some mercifully sane person pointed out that the Sainted Mary had been on display well after Lev and Alexandra were put into their graves.

When at last they were satisfied that Elizaveta truly did not have the icon, suspicion then naturally fell on the missing miner. He was gone. So was the icon. He must have stolen it in the night and made off with it. There could be no other explanation. What else could you expect from someone the other gussuks had nicknamed One-Bucket, allegedly for his ability to pull three hundred dollars' worth of gold out of a creek in one bucket? *Gatcha*, that Elizaveta would shame herself and her tribe so by taking up with such a one.

The tribe fed runners on the last of the potlatch stew and dispatched them to Ahtna, to Cordova, to Fairbanks, and even farther afield with descriptions of the missing man and their missing treasure, seeking news, offering a reward for his apprehension and for the return of the Sainted Mary to her rightful place. Alas for their plans, a spring storm blew in off the Gulf of Alaska the second night after the potlatch and dumped twelve feet of snow from Katalla to Kanuyaq, rendering the roads and trails impassable and any efforts at tracking impossible. Neither One-Bucket nor the icon did they find, and as the days and weeks passed, Elizaveta, shunned by family and neighbors alike, grew even more thin and more pale.

A month after the potlatch came a knock at her door. She was afraid at first to open it. The knock came again, with more force and this time accompanied by a voice she knew. "It's me, Elizaveta. Open up."

It was Quinto Dementieff, a fellow student—and fellow sufferer—at the BIA school in Cordova. They had been friends since childhood, their friendship strengthened by the summer spent together on Lev's gold claim.

She made him coffee, offered him toast from the batch of bread made from the very last bit of flour. There was no butter or jam for the bread, and no sugar or canned milk for his coffee.

He ate and drank without comment, and when he was finished he pushed the mug away and said, "Marry me."

She had been sitting with her head bent over knotted fingers. She looked up at his words, astonished.

"Marry me," he said again. "At least I'll know you'll be eating."

Her eyes filled with tears and she dropped her head again. "I can't."

"Yes, you can."

One hand slid over her belly. "You don't understand, Quinto. I'm—"

"I do understand," he said. He returned her wondering look with a level gaze. "Marry me."

Her hand still on her belly, she looked around the room. "It's not only that, Quinto. I can't stay here. We couldn't stay here. Everyone is so angry, so—"

"We won't stay here," he said. "We'll move to Cordova. Mr. Greenwood says he'll give me a job on the docks."

"You talked to Mr. Greenwood about this?"

"I told him I was going to get married and I needed a job to support my wife and family. He's a good man."

Quinto Dementieff was the son of an Aleut father and a Filipino mother whose parents had been part of the wave of Filipinos who immigrated to Alaska to take all the good jobs in the salmon canneries for a paycheck half the size of what the born-in-the-territory locals would accept. Elizaveta had been an outcast from the morning after the potlatch. Quinto had been an outcast from birth.

He had also been in love with Elizaveta since they were both ten years old. He reached out to take the hand resting protectively on her belly between his own and kissed it. "Marry me, Eliza. There will be many children. What's one more?"

They were married by the justice of the peace in Ahtna just two days later. The resulting scandal almost eclipsed the loss of the Sainted Mary and kept the tribe's gossips busy for a decade. Of all the people a chief's daughter could have married, and she chose a Filipino! When there were so many good Native boys to choose from! That Eliza girl, so headstrong, so foolish; there was never anything to do with her. First she takes up with a gussuk who robbed the tribe of its most precious possession and then she elopes to Cordova with a Filipino. (Quinto's half-Aleut side was easily ignored.) But it was only to be expected. Look at her father, a good man in most ways, and not a bad chief, but so lacking in wisdom in the raising of his daughter. Alexandra had tried to warn him, oh yes, but had he listened? Stubborn, pigheaded man, no, he had not, and see how it had turned out, Elizaveta married outside the tribe and the Sainted Mary lost to the tribe forever, looted by yet another white man who pretended to be their friend so he could steal everything that wasn't nailed down and sell it Outside to make his fortune.

Elizaveta and Quinto settled in Cordova, two hundred miles away, at that time far enough not to hear all the whispers or endure the glares and the pointed fingers. "Easy to be shunned from a distance," Quinto said cheerfully, and for the first time in months, Elizaveta smiled.

Her pregnancy was not an easy one, and their first and only child, a son, was born the following January.

They named him Samuel Leviticus Dementieff.

ONE

"HE WAS EIGHTY-NINE," KATE said, looking up from a file box.

"Well, we all knew he was older than God," Jim said.

They were at Old Sam's cabin, where Kate was sorting through the old man's belongings. Kate and the aunties had decided that the potlatch would be on the fifteenth of January, which gave them a little over three months to label Old Sam's possessions for the gift giving, and to allow everyone from Alaska and Outside who wanted to attend to make travel arrangements and contact friends and relatives in the Park for a place to unroll their sleeping bags.

It was also the day of the annual shareholder meeting of the Niniltna Native Association. The price of gas being what it was, travel to and from Niniltna was not cheap, no matter if you did it by plane, boat, pickup, four-wheeler, or snowgo. Plus, it cost the same to rent the high school gym for an event that lasted four hours as it did for an event that lasted all day. Kate Shugak was a frugal and practical woman.

There was a file marked "Will" in the back of the box. Kate pulled it out and opened it.

Jim looked at her bent head, and at Mutt, who was leaning up against Kate's side. Whenever Kate was hurting, Mutt was always as close to her as she could get without actually climbing into her lap. Since Mutt, the half gray wolf-half husky who allowed Kate to live with her outweighed Kate by twenty pounds, leaning seemed the better option all around.

Old Sam's cabin was built on a floor plan common to the Park anytime between twenty-five and a hundred years before, a ground floor twenty-five feet square with a sleeping loft reached by a ladder made from two-by-fours. The rungs on the ladder were worn smooth from decades of use. Jim hoped that when he was eighty-nine his knees would be in good enough shape to climb eight feet up a vertical ladder to get to bed.

He looked back at Kate.

If she were waiting for him in that bed, he'd find a way.

The one room downstairs had a counter with an old chipped porcelain farm sink set into it, with shelves built into the wall above and below. The sink came with an old-fashioned swan-necked spout and two spoked faucets. Old Sam had tapped into public water when it had come into Niniltna twenty years before, but the outhouse was still outside. When asked why no indoor toilet, a growled "You don't shit in your own nest" was his invariable reply.

There was an oil stove for cooking and a woodstove for heat and an old Frigidaire refrigerator that must have been added when they ran the power line out from Ahtna back in the sixties. More built-in shelves covered every inch of the back wall from floor to ceiling beneath the floor of the loft, one section for weapons and ammunition and the rest for books ranging from Zane Grey to a leather-bound, three-volume edition of the log of Captain Cook that made Jim's mouth water just to look at it. A brown vinyl recliner with a dent in the seat the size of Old Sam's skinny ass occupied one corner, next to a pole lamp and a Blazo box standing on one end. The box was covered with mug rings and was filled with a stack of magazines, *National Geographic, Alaska* magazine, *Playboy*. There was a workbench next to the door where Old Sam cleaned his guns and did the fine woodworking on projects he'd allowed Park rats to talk him into, wall shelves and cupboards, mostly, with an occasional bed frame or dining table thrown in.

"He revised his will only last month."

Kate was sitting at the chrome-legged dining table in the center of the room, on one of three mismatched chairs. The table had a lazy Susan in the middle of it, filled with salt and pepper shakers, a sugar bowl, a Darigold one-pound butter can with a plastic lid, a bottle of soy sauce. Old Sam liked his sticky rice, a legacy of his half-Filipino father.

Had liked. It was still difficult to accept the fact that the old man was dead. It was especially difficult to imagine life in the Park going on without his acid, perspicacious, and occasionally uncomfortably prophetic commentary. Old Sam had been an entire Greek chorus all by himself.

"He had a lot of stuff," Jim said. "Do you want help?" It was Monday morning, and he was past due at work.

She looked up. "Less than two weeks ago."

"What?"

"He revised his will less than two weeks ago."

"Maybe he had a premonition."

She snorted. "There was never anything the least bit fey about Old Sam."

Jim thought of the old man built of bone and sinew, quick, smart, smart-assed. Indomitable, indestructible, and until the day before yesterday, immortal. Kate was right. If anyone had ever lived in the real world, it had been Old Sam Dementieff. Jim was going to miss the hell out of him. "Do you need help here?" he asked again. "I can take a day."

"Thanks, but I got this." She tucked a strand of short dark hair behind an ear, exposing the high, flat cheekbone and the strong throat bisected by the long scar that had faded over the last eight years to a thin white line. With hazel eyes set in skin darkened to bronze by the summer just past and a full seductive mouth set over an obstinate chin, she was a five-foot, one-hundred-and-twenty-pound package of dynamite clad in black sweatshirt, blue jeans, and tennis shoes.

His dynamite. The pronoun came to him without warning, and under its influence he stepped forward to pull the file from her hands. "Come here." He picked her up and sat down again on the chair, setting her on his lap.

She didn't protest. Her head found a place on his shoulder instead, and a moment later he felt the warmth of her tears soak through his shirt.

"Hey," he said, tipping her head up.

She took a shaky breath and tried to smile. "He'd make fun of me if he could see me now."

"Bullshit," Jim said. "He'd be proud you cared enough. Listen, Kate. He went out the way we all wish we could go. He hunted his own moose, packed it home, butchered it out, and threw a feed for everyone he loved. Damn fine feed, too."

Her smile was wobbly. "Yeah, it was."

"And then he turned off the engine and left the shop." Jim's shoulders rose and fell in a slight shrug. "What do you Injuns say? It was a good day to die."

She sniffed and gulped back a laugh that was half sob.

He leaned in, his lips moving across her skin, sipping at the salt tears. Her breath caught, warm on his cheek, and her head turned so her mouth was close to his. He accepted the invitation and their lips met in a long and gentle caress, his hands warm and strong at the back of her neck and on her hip.

It was becoming less frightening to him, this need he found to comfort, to console, to demonstrate an affection that had nothing to do with sex. Although if the nearest bed hadn't belonged to a man not dead forty-eight hours … He raised his head and hazel eyes met blue in a long look. "Better?"

She was a little flushed, and the full lips quirked at the corners. "An effective laying on of healing hands."

He grinned and kissed her again, quick and hard. "I'll lay more than that later."

She laughed.

Old Sam would have, too.

* * *

THE LOSS OF OLD Sam Dementieff notwithstanding, Jim drove to the trooper post with a lighter heart. Probably part of that was due to Kate's being as willing to accept his comfort as he was unafraid to give it. They'd been circling each other for so long, wary, suspicious, and let's face it, just plain scared of all the baggage loaded on that slow-moving barge called relationship. You couldn't move a barge on its own, you had to hire a tug. Up until Kate, the women with whom he'd kept company had lasted the length of a ride in a cigarette boat between Miami and Havana. Sometimes it felt like he'd served more time for Kate than Jacob had for Rachel.

He knew she was still working out the trust issues. Jack Morgan, a government-certified Grade A one-woman man, was a hard act to follow in that respect. It didn't help that despite a visible lack of offspring, Chopper Jim Chopin's *nom d'amour* had once been Father of the Park. Come to think of it, Old Sam had been the one to hang that on him. Right after

Misty Lambert had burned the clothes he'd left behind, during the monthly meeting of her book club with all eight members in attendance and more invited over to celebrate the event. At least half of whom he'd slept with at one time or another.

They'd all got a big laugh out of it at the time, both the ritual immolation and Old Sam's nicknaming, but the truth was, Jim Chopin was probably quicker with a condom than he was with his sidearm. Living with Johnny Morgan was as close as he ever wanted to come to being a father. As the only Alaska state trooper in twenty million acres of national Park, he already had eight thousand children requiring primary care.

He pulled up in front of the post, making a mental note to stop in at the high school to suggest to Johnny, man-to-man, that he spend the night in town. Johnny was old enough to recognize the justice of the appeal, and besides, given the way things appeared to be heating up between Johnny and Van, the kid would expect some reciprocity in the not too distant future. Jim had a vivid memory of what sixteen was like. If he couldn't keep his hands off Kate now, at sixteen he would have kept her horizontal for days at a time.

He laughed at himself and got out of the truck. His dispatcher met him at the door, a pink message slip in hand and an expression on her face that wiped his mind free of blithe spirit. "What?" he said, mind racing, sorting through the usual suspects. Howie Katelnikof, Martin Shugak, Wade Roche and what might or might not be going on out at his place, Dulcey Kineen's latest escapade, which he hoped this time did not involve the road grader. "Cindy threatening to shoot Willard again?"

"No, Jim," she said, and right away he knew from the gentleness of her reply that it was going to be bad. "I just got off the satellite phone with Nick."

Nick Luther was head of the Alaska state trooper detachment in Tok, which had been Jim's old post until two years before, when volume of business caused Juneau to open a new trooper post in the Park. He wondered now why he had never wondered before if someone in the state capital had known about the discovery of the world's second largest gold mine in Suulutaq before making that decision.

His mind tended to head off on tangents whenever he wanted to avoid what was coming at him like a steamroller. He took a deep breath. "Go ahead," he said. "Serve it up." When she still hesitated, he said, "Whatever it is, letting it sit won't make it smell any better."

"There's no easy way to say this, Jim," she said. "Your mother called."

His spine stiffened. "Yeah?"

"I'm so sorry. Your father died."

* * *

KATE SAT ON THE bed and watched him pack, putting clothes she had never seen him wear into an actual suitcase she'd never seen him use. Out of uniform he wore T-shirts and jeans. Traveling within Alaska he used a pack. The charcoal gray suit looked like something the new and improved Kurt Pletnikof would wear to meet his better-heeled clients in Anchorage. The silver, hard-sided suitcase looked like it had been bought out of the SkyMall catalogue, with which Kate was familiar only because it was in every seat pocket on every Alaska Airlines 737, offering everything from basketballs autographed by Magic Johnson to $900 wine fridges, none of which was much use to anyone about to make a connecting flight to Igiugig. "Gee," she said, "looks just like downtown."

He shot her a quick look, and she wondered if that had come out more intimidated than she had meant it to. "California, here I come," he said.

Try as she might she could not detect any joy in his tone.

They were in his room at Auntie Vi's B and B, or what had been Auntie Vi's B and B before she sold it to the owners of the Suulutaq Mine to be a bunkhouse for mine employees in transit. Auntie Vi was now running it for them. A condition of sale had been that Jim got to keep his room there, which he had had since first moving to the Park to open the post. Mine manager Vern Truax had been more than happy to accommodate a law enforcement presence fifty miles from his mine.

"Right back where you started from," Kate said.

This time he stood up and looked her straight in the eye. "I won't be staying long."

"You don't have any brothers or sisters," she said.

"No."

"And your mother is how old?"

"Seventy-nine."

"Ten years younger than Old Sam."

"Yes."

She thought of how healthy Old Sam had been, right up until he sat down on his dock and died. "Your mom in good shape?"

"Depends on what you mean by 'in good shape.' I'd bet a whole paycheck she looks pretty damn good. She'd sure as hell spend it getting that way." He zipped the suit into a garment bag, something else Kate recognized only from catalogues, and snapped it into the lid of the aluminum suitcase.

"You're, what, forty-two now?"

"Yeah."

"She was thirty-seven when you were born."

He added a couple of white, button-down shirts, neatly folded, to the suitcase. T-shirts, shorts, and socks followed. "I showed up late, when they'd pretty much given up on having kids. Dad was forty-five."

"You never talk about them."

He shrugged. "Not much to say. They were hard of hearing before I was in high school. It was like growing up with grandparents."

Wow, she thought. Didn't that sound affectionate.

When she thought about it later, she wondered if that lack of affection might have been part of what had driven Jim north in the first place.

He pulled a shoebox from beneath the bed and added it to the suitcase. The ditty bag full of toiletries went into a daypack with Craig Johnson's latest Walt Longmire novel and Naomi Novik's *Victory of Eagles*. The books had been waiting for him in the post office when he had cleaned out his mailbox that morning. He hoped two books were enough to get him from Anchorage to San Jose, because the rest of his to-read pile was back at Kate's house. He was six four, and there was nothing worse than being shoehorned into last class with nothing to take his mind off the discomfort of having his knees jammed up against the seat in front of him. He'd once been stuck on a flight from Phoenix to Seattle with a Steve Martini book whose perp he'd guessed before they reached cruising altitude. Never again. "Where the hell's my— Oh, here it is," he said, producing a clip-on reading light and tossing it into the daypack with the books. "They've got the seats so close together on the new jets that I can never get the overhead light to shine on anything but the top of the head of the guy sitting in front of me. Especially when he leans his chair back into my lap."

"Jim?"

"What?"

"Why did you come to Alaska?"

He zipped up the daypack. "I read *Coming into the Country* when I was too young to resist."

Always with the smart remark. Fine. "Is anyone coming in to the country to cover for you while you're gone?"

He snapped the suitcase closed and set it on the floor. "Nick will check in with Maggie every morning. Otherwise, I'm relying on you, babe. Oh." He paused to look at her. "Kenny says there's been a rash of break-ins and burglaries in Ahtna over the last month. He says he thinks it's partly due to the economy, people looking for anything they can sell to raise cash. Just FYI, in case it spreads down the river."

"Got it," she said. He felt distant from her somehow, as if he were already in Los Angeles. Land of surf and sand and sun. When he looked at her again she realized she'd said the words out loud.

"I'm not staying there, Kate," he said again. "I work in Alaska. I live in Alaska."

You're in Alaska, he could have said, but didn't.

Instead, he put the daypack on the floor next to the suitcase and took her down to the bed with a soft tackle. Caught off guard, she looked up at him with a startled expression. "Let me just mark my spot," he said, and reached for the buttons on her jeans.

* * *

HE MADE GEORGE'S LAST flight into Anchorage with sixty seconds to spare. She stood flushed and rumpled at the end of the forty-eight-hundred-foot dirt airstrip, watching the de

Havilland single Otter turbo rise into the air, bank right, and head west, its signature whine receding over the horizon.

Mutt gave a soft, plaintive whimper. Kate looked down and said in a stern voice, "We are strong and beautiful women. We can do anything."

And Mutt proved it on the walk back to the red Chevy super cab by catching the hem of Kate's jeans in her teeth and dumping Kate on her ass.

ABOUT
KATE SHUGAK

KATE SHUGAK is a native Aleut working as a private investigator in Alaska. She's 5 foot 1 inch tall, carries a scar that runs from ear to ear across her throat and owns a half-wolf, half-husky dog named Mutt. Resourceful, strong-willed, defiant, Kate is tougher than your average heroine – and she needs to be to survive the worst the Alaskan wilds can throw at her.

To discover more – and some tempting special offers – why not visit our website: www.headofzeus.com

MEET THE AUTHOR

In 1991 Dana Stabenow, born in Alaska and raised on a 75-foot fishing trawler, was offered a three-book deal for the first of her Kate Shugak mysteries. In 1992, the first in the series, *A Cold Day for Murder*, received an Edgar Award from the Crime Writers of America.

You can contact Dana Stabenow via her website: www.stabenow.com

 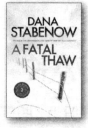  

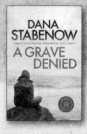